THIN AIR

Bette Nordberg

THIN
AIR

BETHANY HOUSE PUBLISHERS

Minneapolis, Minnesota

Published by Bethany House Publishers
A Ministry of Bethany Fellowship International
11400 Hampshire Avenue South
Bloomington, Minnesota 55438
www.bethanyhouse.com

Printed in the United States of America by
Bethany Press International, Bloomington, Minnesota 55438

Library of Congress Cataloging-in-Publication Data

Nordberg, Bette.
    Thin air / by Bette Nordberg.
        p.   cm.
    ISBN 0-7642-2398-4 (pbk.)
    1. Survival after airplane accidents, shipwrecks, etc.—Fiction.
2. Women—Washington (State)—Fiction. 3. Rainier, Mount (Wash.)—
Fiction. 4. Recluses—Fiction. I. Title.
    PS3564.0553 T48 2002
    813'.6—dc21   2002008681

In Memory of My Brother

Donald J. Roberts

1948–2001

And for all the other veterans

Who gave their lives

So that we could live ours.

No thanks could adequately express our gratitude.

BETTE NORDBERG graduated from the University of Washington as a physical therapist in 1977. In 1990 she turned from rehabilitation medicine to writing and is now the author of *Serenity Bay*, *Pacific Hope*, and numerous dramas, articles, and devotions. She and her husband, Kim, helped plant Lighthouse Christian Center, a church in the South Hills area of Puyallup, Washington. For the first twelve years, Bette wrote for and directed the drama team at Lighthouse. Today, she teaches Christian growth classes and plays worship keyboard. She also teaches at writing workshops around the Northwest. Bette and Kim have four children, two in college and two at home.

The author may be contacted at her Web site: *www.myfables.com*.

One

Bellevue, Washington
Tuesday, October 23, 2001

IN EVERY WOMAN'S MIND, she hides a photograph album of sorts. Deep in some secret place, she stores the indelible memories of ordinary moments—which by some unexpected turn of events become extraordinary.

On this particular morning, without knowing quite why, Beth Cheng took a mental photograph of her husband, Allen, as he reached for the ringing wall phone with his left hand and shifted their wiggling baby higher onto his right hip.

"Chengs'," he said. Tucking the phone under his chin, he used the baby's bib to catch a rivulet of drool rolling down Noah's face and threatening his own dress shirt. "Oh, yeah, John," Beth heard the subtle change in Allen's voice. "Yeah, she's here." Allen pressed the receiver against his chest. "It's John." His eyebrows drew together, and a frown flitted across his features. "Again."

Beth put down her butter knife, wiped her hands on a towel, and moved toward the phone.

"Don't forget I have a board meeting this afternoon," Allen whispered as he held the phone out for her. "I can't cover for you today."

As she accepted the handset, Beth paused to run the palm of her hand along her husband's cheek. Mouthing a tiny kiss, she brought the receiver to her ear. She took a deep breath before speaking, taking in the familiar scent of Polo cologne lingering on the receiver. "Morning, John," she said with a tone of resignation.

Allen turned away, depositing the youngest of the three Cheng children into a high chair. Bending over, Allen spoke to the squirming child as he pushed the tray toward him. "Now," he said, handing Noah a spoon, "Please be patient while Daddy finds the cereal." Before Allen even reached the cupboard, the pounding of handle against tray rivaled the sound of a performing drum band during the Seafair parade.

"Today?" Beth asked, using one hand to cover her free ear. "John, you said we wouldn't be able to fly again for another couple of weeks. I have so many things to do here today." Frustrated by the banging spoon, she turned to face the corner between the kitchen wall and the upper cabinets in a vain attempt to create her own office. At any time of the day, noise characterized the busy Cheng household, but today the thumping spoon, the nearby television, and the sound of her husband digging through cupboards made telephone conversation even more difficult. "Oh, all right. If it's our last chance, I guess I'll have to be there," she sighed. "Right. I'll meet Bill there. Noon at Thun Field." Then with unmistakable sarcasm she added, "Thanks a lot, John."

"What was that about?" Allen placed a bowl of Cheerios in front of Noah and sat down facing the high chair. Just as Noah threw the first handful of cereal, Allen snatched the bowl away and placed it on the kitchen table, safely out of reach. Wrapping the legs of the high chair with his own, he brought a sippy cup to the child's mouth, offering juice. The baby accepted readily, dropping the spoon to grasp the cup with eager dimpled hands. He drank, though a steady stream of orange fluid dripped off his chin, down his bib, and onto the tray before him.

"John has a plane and a pilot for us this afternoon," Beth said as she returned to spread mayonnaise on slices of white bread. Then, thinking of the time, she faced the door to the living room and raised her voice. "Bekka! Abbey! Turn off that TV. If you don't finish getting dressed, you'll be late for first bell." She stood listening intently, her head tipped and her hands on her hips. Satisfied, she returned to the lunches. "Anyway," she continued, "there's a small weather window today, before storm systems move in tomorrow. I have to finish the fall section of my report by next week. Bill, our hydrologist, is going up for more photographs, and since they've already contracted the plane and pilot, John thought we could save some money by sending me along. If I can get one last count of mountain goats, that part of my field report will be finished."

"But you do the goat counts so late in the day."

She nodded. "Twilight is the best, actually, but we'll probably start earlier today. Bill will take his hydrology photos first."

"Who will watch the kids?"

"I'll call my mom." Expertly, Beth slapped ham slices on the three sandwiches. She picked up a stack of sliced cheese and capped each piece of ham. "She can start dinner, and I should be home by the time you get the dishes done. After all, I can't count anything after dark."

"I hate that you have to work." Allen shook his head as he offered cereal to the baby. Ignoring his father, Noah slapped his hand in the puddle of juice and giggled.

Beth sighed. "We've been through this before," she said without looking up. "I have a degree. I can help. Why shouldn't I? Besides, we agreed that if you accepted this pastorate, I would have to work. We're supposed to be here," Beth explained in an even, logical tone. "So, I work."

"Just because we agreed on it doesn't mean I have to like it." Allen picked up a yellow washcloth. Shaking his head, he continued, "But things at church are turning around. We're growing. And the board promised to reconsider the salary after our second year."

"I know, honey. But I like it," she said as she snapped open a paper lunch bag. "Working, I mean. I only take the jobs I want. I work from home . . ."

"Except when you're up flying around that stupid mountain."

"Yes, except when I'm doing aerial photography or species surveys," she agreed, nodding. Turning toward him, she leaned against the counter, crossing her arms. "Sweetheart, doing environmental consulting has helped us financially. You know that. And with Mom so close and you able to work at home some days, the kids are always with family. I mean, how many other jobs are there for a wildlife biologist in the middle of the city?"

"I can think of one really important one," he said, tugging at the sticky fingers of his son's hand with the washcloth. The baby pursed his lips and pulled his hand away, clearly resisting Allen's efforts.

"What?"

"Feeding Noah. I'm late for my Bible study group." Allen removed the hand towel tucked into his belt and threw it onto the table as he stood. At the sink, he rinsed a clean rag in hot water. "I think we ought to talk about your work again, honey. I just don't like it. Maybe we can think of some other way." He dabbed a rag across the front of his shirt. "Speaking of environmental impact," he continued, "if the city of Bellevue had any clue as to how much damage one eleven-month-old boy can cause just by eating breakfast, we'd have to get a permit to feed him."

Allen gave up, throwing the rag in the sink. He picked up the soap and began washing his hands. From behind, Beth reached around his waist to give him a warm hug. "I'll feed the baby," she said, leaning her cheek against his back. "But it'll cost you. Big time."

He dried his hands on a paper towel and turned to pull her into his arms. "Whatever it takes," he smiled. "I guess it's the cost of doing business."

Mount Rainier
Ten miles NE of the unincorporated town of Clearwater
Tuesday, October 23, 2001

From his position on a tree stump at the edge of deep woods, Dennis Doyle saw blue smoke rise in a transparent tower from the chimney of the small home. From a distance of fifty yards, Doyle saw the house in clear detail. Brown siding, white trim, long narrow driveway, neat lawn. Though completely isolated, surrounded only by rugged mountains, and miles from Clearwater, the house reflected simple country living at its best.

Doyle noticed lights glowing toward the back of the home, the area he guessed to be the kitchen. And as he watched, the door to the back porch opened and a man exited, crossing the yard to open the driver's door of a car parked in the driveway. Doyle saw the exhaust rising behind the car as the man started the engine. Doyle saw him climb out and begin scraping heavy frost from the car windows with a long-handled scraper.

Doyle shivered as he watched, aware that winter pressed eagerly upon the heels of fall. He turned up his collar and deliberately moved his gaze away. His half-shepherd, half-mutt dog had managed to invite himself into a nearby pasture, evidently hoping to torment a horse grazing peacefully on the last bits of a hay bale. So far the horse paid no attention to the dog.

Still, Doyle worried that barking might draw the attention of the man scraping his car windows in the distance. Doyle felt the familiar squeeze of fear in his chest, and he wondered for a desperate moment how he might call the dog without distracting the man.

Dennis Doyle had chosen this stump carefully, confident that he could watch from here without being observed. But one bark would change all that. Doyle's breath came faster, and little puffs of a warm cloud seemed to hang in the air around his face.

He had no desire to be seen.

Just then the door of the house opened again, and a blond woman clad in a pale blue bathrobe stepped out the back door. Holding the robe closed with one hand, she descended the steps to the yard. With bare feet, she danced across the cold ground toward the car. In her other hand she carried a mug full of steaming liquid. Doyle saw the morning sun glint off the sides of the container and watched intently as she crossed the driveway and handed the cup to the man, who wrapped one arm around her shoulder and squeezed lightly. Then she turned her face to him and they kissed—a gentle kiss that seemed to hang for a long time in the silent, cold air. Doyle turned away.

Where had that stupid dog gone now?

He spotted him lying peacefully beneath the grazing horse, his soft brown snout resting on his front paws—as if every dog in the world preferred to nap beneath a quarter horse. Doyle stifled an urge to whistle.

Grunting, he turned his attention to the edge of the pavement. Only fifty feet from this stump, civilization began.

Asphalt. Roads. People. He let his gaze trace the edge of the road where blacktop met gravel. How long had it been since he had allowed his own feet to touch pavement? He did not know. Could not guess. Long years ago, Doyle had stopped keeping track of time. Why would he care about time? He wanted only to live out his own life.

Lately, Doyle's allotment of years felt like they were lasting far too long.

Movement in the driveway caught Doyle's attention. The small car crept backward, pulled into the street, changed direction, and started down the road. As the woman waved, the white Import accelerated. She would be alone now, he knew.

Doyle watched her return to the house and waited until she closed the back door. Then he whistled. Immediately, the dog's ears pricked up and his head rose. Without hesitation, the dog trotted away from the horse, back under the fence, and across the edge of the pavement to Doyle's side. Sitting attentively beside him, the dog slid his snout onto Doyle's leg, and with clear determination, eased his nose under the palm of Doyle's hand. Content, the dog waited, watching his master with a longing expression and attentive, deep brown eyes.

Doyle's hand did not move. He did not pet the dog, nor did he caress the soft black fur dotted with blotches of tan. Instead, keeping his eyes on the roadway, he allowed himself only the fleeting pleasure of motionless touch.

The sound of an approaching vehicle caught Doyle's attention, and he stiffened involuntarily. He did not move until the vehicle came into view, and he recognized the gray-green Jeep Cherokee. Without slowing, the Jeep turned a tight circle along the edge of the pavement and stopped, facing away from Doyle. In reverse, the vehicle backed up until the rear cargo door hung just over the edge of the road. The driver's door opened, and a lean gray-haired man climbed out. He walked deliberately toward the edge of the road and stood waiting, his hands on his hips.

Doyle sighed, took a deep breath, and rose from the stump.

"You here?" the visitor called, gazing directly at Doyle yet not seeing him.

"I'm here." Doyle moved out from under the cover of a giant cedar. His right knee ached from sitting so long in the cold morning air. As always, it took a few steps before the painful limping subsided.

The man smiled and walked through the grass toward him. "Got anything?"

"Just one."

He stepped closer. "A box?"

"Yep." Doyle dropped his green canvas rucksack onto the grass-covered ground and opened it. Without taking his eyes from the man before him, he bent down and brought out the box. Before it had fully emerged, the tall man had both hands out, eager to receive the treasure.

"It's beautiful," he said, running his index finger along one corner.

Tiny dovetails, no larger than the smallest fingernail on a woman's hand, lined up perfectly along the smooth edge. The man held the box up, examining the lower surface. Four matching feet had been carved in one piece with the bottom. He brought it down and removed the fitted top. The inside of the box, like the outside, displayed the same attention to detail. "You've outdone yourself, Doyle," he said, his voice awestruck. "It's one of your best."

Doyle shrugged. "How much?"

"Forty?"

Doyle nodded his agreement. Suddenly uncomfortable, he glanced once around the edge of the woods, then across the pasture to the couple's house. He had been down too long. He needed to get away. Back into the mountains. Alone.

Reading his glance, the lean man asked, "Supplies?"

Doyle nodded and reached into his pants pocket. Removing a battered sheet of paper, he handed it to the driver. Tiny frayed holes ran along the edge where he had torn it from his spiral notebook.

"I've got the other stuff." The man pointed to the Jeep with his thumb.

"Good."

The two men walked together toward the vehicle, Doyle stopping several steps away from the door. The tall man held the box against his side as he unlocked the rear cargo door. Carefully, he wrapped the box in newspaper and tucked it into a side compartment. "I think I brought everything you asked for. All the usual supplies. I put the extra money in an envelope on top." He picked up a cardboard liquor box and held it out to Doyle. "I cashed your check and put that inside too."

Doyle snatched the envelope and placed it on the rear bumper of the SUV. "You keep the money. I got no use for money," he said, nodding toward the mountain. He took the box with both arms. "Thanks."

"I shouldn't keep your money," the man began. He bent down

to pick up the envelope and turned around with his hand extended, "You might . . ."

But both Doyle and the dog had disappeared.

———————

Just as Beth packed the last of her working tools in the car, the chime of the front doorbell announced that her mother had arrived. She stepped into the kitchen from the attached garage, calling, "Come on in, Mom."

Standing at the counter, Beth opened the back of her camera and slid a new roll of film into place. "I'm in the kitchen," she said. "Just a few things to finish." As she pulled out the loose film end, Beth heard her mother's scuffed footsteps and smiled to herself. Though born and raised in the United States, her mother's Japanese heritage still showed itself in hundreds of little ways. Nearly sixty years old, Harumi Harding always removed her outside shoes and slipped into ostrich feather scuffs whenever she entered Beth's home. Sometimes Beth wondered what her mother's life might have been like if she hadn't married outside of her Japanese traditions.

"Hey, Lizzie," Harumi cooed, dropping her purse on the counter and reaching for her daughter. Beth felt her mother's arms surround her, giving her a warm hug.

"Thanks for coming, Mom," Beth answered, returning the embrace. "I'm sorry about the short notice. I didn't think I'd have to work this week, but John has a plane chartered, so off we go."

"Anything special for the kids this afternoon?"

"Yes, unfortunately," Beth said as she zipped the camera back into its case. "Piano lessons today."

"Don't you do those on Mondays?"

"The teacher had to reschedule. I'm sorry; is that too much to ask?"

"No problem. What about dinner?" With the refrigerator door open, Harumi scanned the shelves. "Should I cook?"

"No, Mom," Beth smiled. "I have dinner thawing on the counter." She pointed at an aluminum pan of frozen lasagna and slung the strap of her camera case over her shoulder. Feeling in her pants pockets for the car keys, she pulled out her key ring.

"Lizzie, I taught you to cook . . ." her mother began.

"Don't start, Mom," Beth cautioned, holding up one hand. "I can't do everything. Today, frozen will do." She shook her head. "It's fine. Really." She bent down to kiss her mother's cheek. "I'm going to be late. Thanks again, Mom." She started toward the door to the garage, and before she took three full steps, she stopped. "Oh, no," she said, slapping her palm to her forehead. "I meant to stop by the drugstore. Oh well, I'll do it after I get home tonight." She opened the back door. "Allen will be a little late. He has a meeting. Noah went down for his nap about half an hour ago, and the girls will be home around three."

"We'll manage. Don't worry."

"I never do." Glancing at her watch, Beth realized that she needed to hurry in order to catch the plane. She blew her mother a kiss and, slipping over the threshold, punched the button that opened the garage door.

Forty minutes later, Beth pulled into the parking lot at the county airport south of Puyallup. Though she'd been here dozens of times over the course of her work with the agency, she always loved the breathtaking view of the mountain from the airport. Mount Rainier seemed so enormous from here, so close. Though she had taken dozens of pictures from the runway, none ever seemed to convey the impact of the real thing. She gazed at the snow-covered peak again, completely enchanted. "It's beautiful, Lord," she said, smiling. "You've outdone yourself today."

From the parking lot, she couldn't see anyone from Davis and Graham. She checked her watch, opened the car door, and slid out. Stepping to the passenger side, she pulled her working tub off the backseat. Taking a quick inventory, she checked to be certain she had everything she needed—clipboard, notebooks, camera bag, binoculars, and her topographical map.

She reached into the middle of the seat and grabbed the wallet-on-a-string that she'd started carrying after having children. Dropping it into the tub, a question came to mind. What would she do while the hydrologist worked? They would not start the goat count until late afternoon. How would she use her time until then? She glanced around the car and spied the travel Bible Allen had bought for her diaper bag. She'd left it in the car after Bekka's soccer practice last week. Snatching it off the seat, she dropped it into the tub with the rest of her supplies.

She could catch up on her devotions—in this morning's craziness, she'd managed to forget her quiet time. It wouldn't be the same in the plane, but it had to be better than nothing. But something felt wrong—missing. She looked down at the tub. Suddenly it occurred to her that she'd managed to leave home without a jacket.

"Phooey," she said aloud. How could she keep warm in that drafty old plane without a coat? She stepped back into the car. Nothing on the backseat. Nothing under the seats. "I'll freeze to death in that plane without something warm," she muttered. Perhaps Allen had stashed a coat in the back.

In the cargo compartment of the Outback, Beth had to dig through the accumulated possessions normal to all families with young children. Nothing under the emergency kit. She reached down and lifted the stroller. There. A yellow down jacket that her husband kept for changing tires. Though the coat was too big to wear, she could drape it over her knees to keep her legs warm. She rolled it into a ball and dropped it on top of her other supplies. At least she'd chosen a wool sweater, polar fleece vest, and heavy jeans. And she'd remembered to wear wool socks under her hiking boots. With any luck at all, she might keep from getting hypothermia. *Why can't little planes have heaters that work,* she wondered. After locking the car, she headed for the terminal where John had instructed her to meet the pilot.

Two

DOYLE FASTENED THE SUPPLY BOX onto the back of his sled, picked up the lead line, and began dragging the shabby contraption up the needle-covered trail. He didn't bother to whistle for the dog. Gilligan, he knew, would follow unbidden. Doyle could always count on his dog. After all, dogs don't ask questions; they never complain or make unreasonable demands. A dog had no expectations of a relationship—at least, nothing more than food and shelter. *Not like people*, Doyle thought. No wonder a man's best friend is his dog.

In truth, Doyle considered Gilligan, his nine-year-old half-mutt, his only real friend. Doyle chuckled as he remembered the puppy he'd found tied in a sack at the edge of the lower clearing. The last surviving member of a litter left to die, the little ball of fur had not gotten completely out of the burlap feed sack before he was bestowing puppy kisses over both of Doyle's hands.

Though Doyle had freed the dog—after all, no animal should be forced to remain with the dead—he had no intention of keeping him. Doyle ignored the puppy, refusing to pay him any attention at all. But the pup did not understand the arrangement and dutifully shadowed Doyle through the rest of the day, never letting the man out of his sight. Eventually, after the dog followed him all the way back up the mountain to his cabin, Doyle relented. He gave the puppy water, and the puppy gave Doyle his undying loyalty.

Both survivors, they deserved one another—Doyle and the dog. Two days after finding him, Doyle dubbed the dog Gilligan. What better name for a castaway?

As the toe of his boot got caught in an exposed root, Doyle stumbled. He shook himself from his memories and picked up his pace. He'd been down the mountain too long. His need to go back, to be alone, drove him up the slope at an amazing speed for a man whose knee barely functioned. He chastened himself for letting his mind wander. To stay alive, Doyle must stay alert. Staying alert seemed harder these days; staying alive felt useless.

At the crest of the next hill, where the trail switched back in the opposite direction, Doyle pulled the sled to one side, dropped the line, and strode deliberately into the woods. Breaking through heavy underbrush, he pushed through the forest to the edge of a steep slope and gently drew down the draping branch of a small Douglas fir. From here Doyle had a clear view of the narrow roadway leading down the mountain, though as yet, he saw nothing. Letting go of the branch, he chose a broad, flat boulder and sat down. Carefully, Doyle checked the angle of the sun. He pulled his bag from his shoulder, pawed through it, found his binoculars, and brought them to his face, scanning the roadway far below.

Doyle held his breath. By now, he expected to see the Jeep. Yes. There it was, far below, traveling swiftly down the mountain away from Doyle.

He did not move. Instead, he watched, his gaze trained on the progress of the Jeep, until at last it passed around a curve and disappeared below the trees. Satisfied that his visitor had not followed him, Doyle tucked the binoculars back into the canvas bag and stood. He needed to hurry. To go back. To be alone.

There. He felt it again. That same heavy feeling of pressure climbing into his chest. This nagging ache had overshadowed his entire morning. Though he could not understand it or identify it, a deep heaviness had dogged him lately. On and off through the past summer, he had felt it. Like living at the bottom of the ocean, Doyle's life felt pressed down, foggy and difficult. He moved back to the trail and started up toward the cabin. This same leaden sensation so filled his days, so clouded his vision, that it felt as though everything on the entire mountain had begun to ask the same question: "Why bother?"

For most of the last thirty years Doyle had managed to avoid this very question by using all his energy in the simple exercise of meeting his physical needs. Busy days and exhausting work effectively forced all contemplation from his conscious mind. But lately, though he continued to chop his own wood, kill his own food, boil his own water, and keep a continual watch over his perimeters, something had changed. The question kept coming back to haunt him.

Why bother, indeed?

Hearing the sound of a branch breaking behind him, Doyle dove sideways like a runner tagging base. Taking cover below a thick canopy of Oregon grape, his heart pounded as he crawled stealthily away from the path. He moved silently until he could clearly see the trail behind him. Doyle pulled a small handgun from behind his waist and aimed it toward the trail from which he'd come. Watching. Waiting. Gently, he removed the safety and cocked the trigger.

Suddenly Gilligan came bounding into sight, crashing through the underbrush, barking fiercely, as though he were in hot pursuit of an unsuspecting squirrel. Placing both paws on a nearby tree trunk, he looked up and whined pitifully. Doyle shook his head and cursed as he climbed out of his hiding place, brushed himself off, and stepped back to the trail. Clapping his thigh with one hand, he slid the gun back in his pants with the other. "You miserable mutt. Come!"

Once again, he picked up the sled line and started off. His knee ached, and his pride felt equally bruised. *Diving into the brush because of a stupid dog,* Doyle rebuffed himself. At least no one had seen his action. Not this time. Though his paced slowed, Doyle continued steadily on up the steep trail.

In the past three months, his arms and legs seemed to have gained twenty pounds each. These days, work took more energy than he could muster. Even the mountain air, which had for so long invigorated and refreshed him, seemed thicker somehow. Heavier. Harder to pull in and out of his lungs.

Just yesterday afternoon, Doyle had gone up to the meadow to split alder for his winter supply. Through his gray flannel shirt, bright sunshine warmed his back. Above him, a light breeze rattled the few remaining alder leaves, creating the music of castanets. He lifted his ax once, perhaps twice. But the effort seemed overwhelming, and he chose instead to sit below a bare tree staring at nothing, fighting with his memories.

Yesterday, the memories had won.

Now, the faintest discomfort began again in the region below Doyle's collarbone, forcing him to stop moving. He paused, panting from the steep climb, waiting for the pain to go away. Gilligan had run off again to chase some invisible enemy. Doyle whistled, and the dog ran immediately to his side. Sitting patiently, the dog fixed his gaze attentively on Doyle. After some moments, the discomfort in his chest subsided. *I'll feel better in the cabin,* he thought, starting off again. *If I can just get home, everything will feel better.*

Beth carried her plastic tub into the terminal building. "Afternoon, Diane," she said, dropping the box onto the reception counter. "Bill here yet?"

"Hey, Beth." Diane looked up smiling. "I didn't think I'd see you again so soon. Can't Davis and Graham ever let you have a couple of days at home?"

"Not that lucky. Have to count mountain goats today." Beth leaned over the counter on her elbows, smiling back at Diane. "If I can finish today, it will be the last count for my report." Even from this distance, Beth could smell the vanilla body lotion Diane loved. Though Diane had to be about the same age as Beth's mother, it was obvious that they had taken two very different approaches to living. Today, Diane wore giant hoop earrings below stylishly cut auburn hair. Above her closely fitted black T-shirt, she had tied a leopard-print scarf. Diane's ruddy complexion hinted that her hair color had once been genuine—a long time ago.

"How's the Elk Ridge expansion coming along?" Diane asked.

"Are you kidding? We have so many experts—all kinds of experts—who still have reports to file. The Elk Ridge Ski Resort can't expand without Forest Service approval. And the Forest Service won't make any decision until all the environmental consultants turn in their work. My company is just one of the firms they hired."

Beth cupped her chin with one hand. "You want my guess? I don't think they'll build another building upon that mountain for the rest of this century."

"I don't understand the way things go these days. Elk Ridge Resort has been up there in the same place for fifty years."

Beth nodded. "It's the way the law reads. I didn't write it."

"I know," Diane nodded. "But the area is zoned for public recreation. How much impact can a couple of new buildings have?"

"You know better than to ask me that. I'm an environmentalist—remember?" Beth laughed and dropped her voice to mimic a politician. "I have no official comment at this time."

"All right. Point taken. Still, I feel for the guys up there. They have to expand. I mean, have you tried to park up there lately?"

Beth caught her breath. "Actually, I don't ski."

Diane seemed genuinely surprised. "I didn't know that. I thought everyone in the Northwest knew how to ski."

In spite of herself, Beth shuddered. "I guess I've just never liked the snow." She brightened, "Still, I don't have to ski to like the project. Writing reports keeps the company busy, and when they're busy, I have a job. Now," she said, picking up her tub, "where can I find Bill?"

With the index finger of one hand, Diane marked her place in her logbook. With her other hand, she pointed to the side of the building. "He's out at the hangar talking to the pilot." Diane managed the records of the flight school operating out of the county airport, and it looked to Beth as though she were in the process of recording this month's pilot training hours. "The pilot?" Beth smiled. "You mean Jack isn't flying for us today?"

"Nope. Out with another group."

"Oh." Beth tried not to let her disappointment show. "Jack always has a running commentary about the sights. I hate to fly without him."

"Everybody feels that way." Diane looked up, smiling. "Actually, I think Jack Anderson missed his calling. Should have been a tour bus driver."

Beth picked up her tub. "Jack wouldn't have survived in the city."

"Maybe in Alaska." She picked up a red pencil and began making notes, already concentrating on her task. "You'd better get out to the plane though. They've filed the flight plan. I think they're in a hurry."

"Heard anything about the weather?"

"Looks good."

"Okay. Well, then, I guess I'm off." Beth sighed and turned

away just as the phone on Diane's desk rang. As she backed out the glass door of the terminal, she smiled. "Wish us goats."

"Goats," Diane called, giving Beth a little wave as she reached for the telephone.

Walking around the building, Beth tried to block the unwanted memories rushing into her mind. It didn't seem to matter how many years went by, they always returned whenever she got to thinking about snow. It wasn't that she was afraid, really. She just had no desire to ski or sled or have anything to do with snow. Unbidden, she saw again the flashing lights and frosty air, exactly as they had been the night of the accident.

"Bummer," she said, shaking herself. "Just when you least expect it, it comes back. And I've already worked through it." She stopped walking and shook her head. "I'm done with it, Lord," she repeated, this time with emphasis.

She expected to find Bill, the agency's hydrologist, waiting for her behind the terminal near the fuel pumps. Usually by the time Beth arrived, their pilot had fueled the plane and begun his preflight ritual.

But today she didn't see the plane in its usual place. She glanced down the runway toward the hangars south of the field. In the building closest to the road, she spotted Bill Peterson loading equipment into the tail of a white six-seater.

In his concentration, Bill did not see Beth. Sighing again, she shifted the weight of the tub onto her hip and started toward the plane. As she came nearer, she waved with her free hand, calling out, "Hey, Bill!"

"Beth. Good to see you," he returned her greeting. "You ready to go?" He stepped away from the storage door and ducked under the wing as he moved toward her. "Here, let me carry that." Bill Peterson, lean and fit, wore an open flannel shirt, quilted and lined for warmth. Underneath, he had chosen a close-fitting turtleneck. She gladly handed him her tub.

"Thanks. Gets heavy after a while."

"This all you're bringing today? My, my. Traveling light, are you?"

"Not enough warning to bring much. I didn't even get time to pack a lunch."

"You can't afford that. You'll waste away to nothing."

She laughed. "Not much chance. Nice haircut, Bill. Who's our pilot today?" Bill Peterson's hairline had receded into near extinction. Rather than try to hide it, Bill kept his gray hair cut in the shortest of military styles. His perfectly shaped head handled the cut well. Wearing prescription aviator-style lenses, Bill had a kind of solemn dignity combined with mature good looks that reminded Beth of her own father.

"Thanks. Glad you like it." Raising his eyebrows, he held one finger over his lips and then pointed to the open hangar door behind them. Lowering his voice, he continued, "The pilot is a guy named Bohannan. Ken Bohannan. He's in there."

"Know him?"

"Only met him today. Seems efficient enough. Why?"

"Nothing really, I just enjoy flying with Jack." Beth went around to the other side of the plane, wondering where to have Bill stash her things.

Bill followed, carrying the tub. "You mean I'm not enough for you?"

Beth laughed. Bill had to be nearly sixty. "You're always a delight," she said with genuine warmth. "But you can't fly a plane. Who gets to ride shotgun?"

"I do," he answered. "When John called this morning, he said you'd be counting goats. If you sit in front, you'd never count anything over the dash. From a fixed wing, you'll have to count fast— even from the backseat."

"True." She smiled. Beth didn't explain to Bill that she usually sat on a pillow when she rode in the copilot's seat. Embarrassed about being so short, she refused to draw attention to her stature intentionally. When she first began flying with Jack, he had noticed her stretching to look out over the front windshield. Without a word, on their very next trip, Jack placed a padded box over the copilot seat. "Sounds good to me," she agreed. "I like the back. Are you taking photos today?"

"Yep. I've already done most of the groundwork. I've got reams of maps. Every waterfall, stream, puddle, and runoff. I've drawn every bridge or road or log that falls across every water flow within fifty miles of the ski area. I only need photos for low season documents today."

"Can't get much lower than now," Beth agreed. This year, the summer rainfall hadn't added much to the state's yearly total. As a result, autumn water levels continued to drop. Bill's job was to document the mountain's water runoff for one entire year. Having started early last fall, he'd almost completed his report. "Must feel good to see the finish line."

"I guess," Bill said, laughing. "But you know as well as I do—there's always another race."

She nodded. Bill held a bachelor's degree in forestry from the University of Washington. Though he graduated almost thirty years before Beth, he had gone on to become a hydrologist, studying water management—long before Puget Sound population growth made water management an urgent priority. Bill's love for the Cascade Mountain Range was obvious. He knew every inch of it by heart—every stream, every river, every lake. His work was an expression of his devotion to the resource itself.

Beth opened the back door of the plane. "Well, then, if you're in front, I'll just stick my stuff in back." She turned to take the tub from him and slid it onto the floor in front of the rear seats. "What have you got back there?" she asked, noticing the boxes stacked in the cargo hold.

"Oh, that. We have orders to drop off some equipment at the Rocky Creek Ranger Station up near Clearwater. I was just loading it." He stood behind the wing as she turned to face him.

"What kind of stuff?" Beth asked.

"They're working on a black bear survey for district six. We're flying in supplies for the wildlife team."

Before she could ask another question, he answered, "It's that island theory again. Ever since the research folks decided to promote large islands of natural habitat connected by corridors, the bear problem has gotten completely out of hand." His thin lips formed a grim line, and his eyebrows furrowed in disapproval.

Beth nodded her agreement. "I know. The worst one is that corridor between Lake Sammamish and Lake Washington."

He shuddered. "Imagine having a bear in your front yard. Right in the middle of Bellevue."

"No joke," she scowled. "It's happened. I may be a wildlife biologist, but I'm also a mother. No mom—not even a biologist—wants some disoriented black bear lumbering down the street looking for salmon berries." She started toward the stack of boxes at the rear of the plane. "It's enough to make you feel like you have multiple personality disorder."

"Not you, Beth. You're too scientific and level-headed to give in to multiple personalities."

"I don't know," she said, shaking her head as she handed him the top crate. "You try motherhood. It's enough to drive anyone crazy."

Three

DOYLE'S TREK TO THE CABIN took the rest of the morning. It frustrated him that the hike from the lower meadow back to the cabin had grown longer and longer over the years. Though the distance had not changed, Doyle had. It had never occurred to him when he'd first moved to the mountains that he would grow old here. He never expected to stay this long.

Doyle always believed that eventually he would go back. Someday, he believed he would win the war raging inside him. Yes, Doyle would return to civilization triumphant, his enemy vanquished for all time. Lately, though, he'd come to wonder if he would die here, alone in an isolated mountainside cabin. Even as he considered this option, he felt a wave of emptiness wash over his soul. No one would ever know of his passing. No one would care that he died. When Dennis Doyle left his past behind, he had burned every bridge. And the thought suddenly made him very tired.

No matter how much he resisted it, his body had grown old. He was only fifty-three, but he felt much older. He probably looked older too, with his hair turning gray and his skin growing leathery from too much time in the sun. For years, Doyle prided himself on being fit, and it frustrated him to realize that he could no longer perform to meet his own rigorous standards. With no change in his diet, he'd still managed to gain weight. His knee continued to deteriorate, until lately it collapsed without warning—often at the most inconvenient moments. But while Doyle's body aged, the demons inside stayed young and vigorous and as treacherous as ever.

Doyle pulled the sled up to the cabin porch just as the sun began to descend from its daytime peak. Doyle looked up, spotted the sun in the clear blue sky, and guessed the hour to be just past noon. He was hot and sweaty, and a pain in his left shoulder felt like a twisting knife. Doyle wanted more than anything to rest. The thought of a long, uninterrupted nap teased him like a mirage to a desert traveler. Dropping the sled line, Doyle sat down on the stoop, panting. When at last his breathing returned to normal, he stepped onto the porch, leading as he always did with his stronger leg.

As he scanned the porch, he pulled a single key from his pants pocket. Everything appeared as he had left it. Nothing disturbed. Nothing moved. His ax leaned against the wall near the door. In the porch corner, the beginning of his next project rested on the seat of the homemade chair. His carving tools remained in a partially opened cigar box below the chair, exactly as he'd left them.

Before opening the door, Doyle turned to search the ground around the porch. No other footprints marred the dusty ground around the cabin. He chided himself. In all the years he'd lived in this remote location, no one had ever come to his cabin. Why the elaborate rituals to protect himself? Why the constant sense of fear? Though his mind knew better, he could not stop the habits so firmly ingrained into his daily life.

He glanced back at the chair, tempted to sit for a while, to rest outside in the fresh air and sunshine. Quickly, he rejected the thought. Though he might sit down, Doyle knew he would never really rest. There could be no real rest for Doyle. Never again.

On the day Doyle discovered the cabin more than twenty years before, the same wooden chair sat in precisely the same place. He'd never moved it from the sheltered cover of the porch. In the midst of a snowstorm, after camping out on the mountain for several years, Doyle had stumbled onto the cabin, finding it abandoned and suffering from serious neglect—just as he had been at the time. Though it appeared to belong to some old hunter, Doyle moved in without hesitation and spent the next five years cleaning and repairing the damaged cabin, making it his own.

Doyle turned back to the door, sighing heavily. Gilligan trotted out of the woods and up onto the front porch, plopping himself down across the single step. He dropped his muzzle onto his front paws, dark eyes watching his master.

Doyle grunted a greeting before turning his attention to the lock on the front door. The dog lifted his head and thumped his tail appreciatively. The old padlock opened with a squeak, and Doyle twisted it off the hasp. Carefully, he opened the door, checking inside like a police officer on a bust. Out of habit, he drew his pistol and entered, as though he expected to discover an entire battalion hidden inside. He scanned the perimeter of the single room. Satisfied at last, he laid his gun on the square table leaning against the back cabin wall and turned his attention to a small kerosene lamp. Using a wooden match, he lit the wick and adjusted the flame. Even at noon on a sunny day, darkness threatened to overtake the little cabin. Suddenly chilled, Doyle longed for a fire.

It had greatly amused Doyle to discover a cabin complete with a potbelly stove. Someone had gone to great lengths to haul the thing up the mountainside. Clearly, the original owner had died or moved on. Now, by squatter's rights, the tiny one-room dwelling belonged to Doyle. After all, he reminded himself aloud, "Possession is nine-tenths of the law."

Doyle began laying a fire in the old stove. Only days before, he'd cleaned out the firebox. Without the old bits of wood, he found his fire more difficult to get going. Leaning over a neatly stacked collection of paper, Doyle selected several pieces and wadded them up, forming a pyramid on the bottom of the stove. Other than this fire-starting ritual, Doyle had no use for paper.

He did not enjoy reading. He didn't write or keep a journal. Doyle collected paper like modern men collect aluminum cans. As he came across paper in his territory, Doyle folded it carefully and slid it into his pants pockets—saving it for the stove.

Carefully, with small bits of bark and tinder, Doyle built the shape of a log cabin over the paper. Satisfied with his design, he turned to strike a match. Touching the flame to his fire, he began blowing gently through pursed lips, ruffling the hair of his long mustache as he blew. As the flame spread, Doyle added larger pieces of wood, until he felt certain the fire would burn on its own.

He closed the stove door, adjusted the air intake, and pulled up a chair. Holding his hands out to catch the first wave of warmth from the metal, Doyle no longer felt hungry. The sadness had caught up with him again. He opened the stove and added two larger pieces of wood.

Instead of food, he considered having a good stiff drink. In the supply box he'd received that morning, Doyle had spotted a brand-new bottle of scotch. Perhaps after a drink, he might be able to sleep. After a good nap, he wouldn't be so tired. In fact, he might even be able to tackle chopping wood this afternoon.

Doyle went outside to retrieve the bottle. Nothing like the bite of scotch to take the chill out of a fall afternoon. As he pulled the bottle from the paper bag, he reached for a tin cup. Setting his chair by the fire, he changed his mind, dropped the cup, and opened the bottle. No need for manners here. After all, Doyle had no one around to impress. He drank his scotch straight from the mouth of the bottle.

———

Beth had never met Ken Bohannan before. When Bill Peterson introduced him, she extended her hand and smiled. His light brown hair had begun receding, leaving him with shining blue eyes below a high forehead. His mustache revealed hints of gray, and his smile seemed warm and genuine. He seemed friendly enough—though clearly anxious to get them into the air.

"Everything weighed and loaded?" he asked.

"All inside," Bill answered.

"Do you have the list?"

"Right here." Bill pulled an aluminum clipboard from under his elbow and handed it to Ken. "I tried to balance the weight in back," he said. "You may want to check it."

"I'll do that," Ken smiled. "But first I'm going to taxi over to the gas pump. You can walk or ride," he said, gesturing to the plane with his thumb.

"We'll meet you over there," Bill said, stepping back.

Ken climbed into the cockpit via the strut and dropped into the pilot seat. Moments later, the propeller of the single engine plane came to life. After warming up, the plane taxied toward the pumps. Beth watched Ken pull up next to the hose and shut down the engine.

"So," Bill said to Beth, "since we have a minute, let me go into the coffee shop and buy you something to carry along for lunch."

"You don't have to. I can buy something later," Beth said, her arms crossed over her chest.

"We could be up a long time today. With these shorter fall days, the restaurant closes earlier. Besides, I'd like a treat from the bakery. Come help me pick out something sinful."

Bill chose the three gooiest cinnamon rolls in the display case and had them packed in a box. "We can eat them when we land at the ranger station," he said while waiting for his receipt.

Carrying a bag full of lunch goodies, Beth climbed into the back of the little six-seater. She had never flown in this particular plane, so Beth listened carefully to Ken's instructions as he handed her a set of headphones and showed her where to plug them in. She dropped the headset over her ears and adjusted the microphone just in time to hear Bill ask about the plane.

"We haven't had her very long," Ken answered.

"New?"

"Is to us. Jack felt we needed a larger plane to carry more passengers. He looked for this one for a long time. Found it late last summer."

"How does she fly?" Bill asked, turning toward the pilot.

"Like a garbage can," Ken answered, smiling. "I prefer the little 182."

His preflight check procedures had been laminated and attached to a small ring with other lists of the same exact size. Beth knew from flying with Jack that the other cards held lists of various flight procedures. After many of these trips, Beth knew that every action had a procedure list. Pre-start. Pre-takeoff. Pre-landing. Thinking about these lists, Beth smiled. She lived by her own lists. Obeyed them without question. She liked her days carefully planned out. *Maybe I would have made a good pilot,* she thought as she buckled her seat belt.

Ken began checking off the procedures aloud. She listened half-heartedly to the long oration. As he flipped switches or touched controls, he responded with "Check" and moved to the next item. At long last, Ken Bohannan started the engine, and they taxied toward the end of the runway.

Beth checked her seat belt again, as she always did before take-off. Then she reached down and grabbed her notes from the last goat survey. She intended to review them before she began her count today. Having her last results firmly in mind would keep her focused as she looked for her bands of goats. As she flipped to the second page, Ken turned the plane into the wind and started down the runway. Beth never felt the plane leave the ground.

———

Doyle's neck screamed as his weary muscles tried desperately to protect him from the destruction happening everywhere around him. His body seemed to have turned into a turtle, as if by drawing his head inside his body, the enemy could not hurt him. The aching extended from his neck down into his shoulders and into his upper back. How he longed to stretch out his arms and roll his head around on his shoulders. But Doyle knew better. It might be his last move.

The smell of gunpowder burned his nostrils and coated his tongue. Though he kept his head down, his eyes stung. Prolific tears, stimulated by smoke and dirt, rolled down his cheeks. He recognized the wet palms of raw fear. Heavy thumping continued in the trees surrounding the clearing, the pounding synchronized with the desperate beating of his own frightened heart. Rounds exploded nearby—making a noise like speeding cars crashing head-on into one another. With every explosion, his body took cover, flinching, ducking. Trying desperately to survive.

Doyle continued to crawl toward the landing zone. He knew that enemy snipers waited everywhere in hopes that he would raise himself enough to become a target. Doyle refused to give them the satisfaction. Instead, he inched forward, clutching his weapon. His men needed him to make it. Through the hail of bullets and dust and explosions, inch by inch, he led the way. He would not give in to fear. Would not stop. The injured, being dragged toward the clearing behind him, needed Doyle's weapon to provide cover during the evacuation. He had to make it.

Spotting his goal just inches away, Doyle rolled and dropped into an abandoned trench. From there, he signaled for his men to follow. One by one, Doyle watched as his men dove into the shelter. Doyle's group had only one M–60 and a grenade launcher among their many M–16 rifles. Still, they hoped to fend off well-hidden and fully armed VC until the choppers arrived. It seemed to Doyle that they had radioed for dustoff hours ago. Getting the injured to the evacuation site had been the hardest part of the job. Now all they had to do was hang out and stay alive until the choppers arrived.

But in Vietnam waiting was never simple.

Since midnight, Doyle and his men had fought for their lives, living through the fiercest firefight in the entire three weeks they had been stationed in the mountain camp. Hours of heavy attack left nearly half of the

Montagnard troops stationed with them dead. Doyle's closest friend was back there somewhere, being dragged, inch by agonizing inch, toward the landing zone. Doyle intended for Gary to make it. If he survived to the clearing, Doyle knew he would make it home in one piece. Doyle heard the heavy whumpa-whumpa of the Hueys as they approached and breathed a sigh of relief. Ducking his face into the ground, he protected his eyes from the stinging dust blown up by the descending chopper.

Moments later, with silent gestures, Doyle stationed his men around the landing zone, directing their weapons toward the enemy waiting just out of sight. He directed the loading of the injured onto the first chopper himself. Carefully, deliberately, Doyle made certain Gary was aboard this aircraft.

The Viet Cong would allow at least one chopper to land and take off before shooting down the rest. Doyle counted on their predictability; he gambled Gary's life on it. When the side door closed, Doyle signaled the all-clear to the pilot and ran to the edge of the clearing as the chopper rose above him. He'd done it. Soon, Gary would be safe in a hospital bed somewhere away from all this terror.

Just as the helicopter cleared the trees, the sound of an incoming screamed overhead. Instinctively Doyle dove for the ground, burying his face and clutching his helmet. With grass and dirt pressed into his flesh, he heard himself swear as he hugged his weapon with his right hand. For long moments, Doyle lay frozen, unwilling to move or breathe. No explosion had ever been louder, but he did not raise his head to look. Doyle knew without seeing that the helicopter had been hit, blown into tiny fragments that even now dropped onto the rocks and grass around him. He tucked his face into the wet earth as pieces of burning metal rained down around him. Bits of the helicopter slammed into his back as Doyle begged to be spared from death. His mouth formed wordless prayers as his breath blew puffs of dirt up into his face.

The attack mocked Doyle. What did he know? What made him think he understood anything at all about this faceless enemy? The chopper. The crew. The injured. Gary. All of them—dead. And it was his fault. The realization nailed him like a direct hit, and he screamed out in utter agony.

Doyle sat up.

His heart thudded against his chest wall. *A dream,* he told himself, panting. *Another stinkin', stupid dream.* Just like all the rest. He wiped damp palms on his pant legs and pushed wet hair off of his face. His head ached and his muscles burned from the effort of the dream. He took deep breaths, trying in vain to calm himself. Why had he even tried to sleep? *A fool*, he thought. *After all these years, still a fool.*

Four

DOYLE BROUGHT HIS FEET over the edge of the cot. The afternoon had turned cold, though weak daylight still filtered through the dirty window behind him. He stood for a moment, waiting for the pain in his knee to ease. Flexing and straightening, he waited until the joint began to move more freely—all the while feeling like the tin man in that old Oz movie. Hoping to ward off the chill, Doyle hobbled to the stove, planning to add wood.

Instead, Doyle reached for his rucksack. He never should have gone down the mountain today. Being around people always brought back the nightmares; he'd learned that long ago. The effect took weeks to wear off. No wonder he avoided going down.

Now, Doyle reasoned, he needed to move, to check his perimeters, to become part of the mountain again. He would camp out tonight and stay away from the cabin for an extended mission. Yes. He would feel better being outside. Alone.

He looked forward to hunting fresh game. Something about sleeping outside before an open fire always managed to calm the demons fighting inside Doyle's head. He needed to become part of the forest. To reunite with nature.

He packed quickly. Matches, bedroll, ammunition, collapsible shovel, canteens, and a single small pot without handles. In an effort to kill the fire, Doyle opened the stove and spread out the wood. He gathered his carving tools and the last project from the porch and put them in the only cupboard in the cabin. Taking his canteens back outside, he walked behind the cabin, where a steep bare hill protected his position from intruders. There, against the hill, water from an underground spring followed a hardwood sluice out of the ground and dripped freely into an ancient oak barrel. Doyle held one tin container after another under the dripping water, listening until the rising pitch indicated full canteens. Draping each strap across his shoulder, he piled all four of them around his waist. Whistling for Gilligan, Doyle picked up his pack and started up the narrow trail away from his cabin.

───────

Not long after takeoff, Bill Peterson had Ken flying through the rough terrain surrounding the expansion zone for Elk Ridge Ski Resort. Beth watched for a while as Bill snapped pictures and jotted notes. Even she could see that the water volume coming off the mountain had diminished as a result of the long dry summer. The heavy cascading waterfalls of last spring had dwindled to trickles. Many of the smaller streams had dried up completely. This water cycle, Beth knew, was part of the yearly majesty and mystery of Mount Rainier.

Extending more than fourteen thousand feet in the air, the mountain top remained snow-capped all year long. The only perceptible difference in the seasons was the dangerous glacial crevasses exposed by warm summer sunshine. During those months, far below the peak, warm-weather hikers flock to alpine meadows, hoping to catch a glimpse of the dazzling beauty of wildflowers in full bloom. Some years, after a winter of heavy precipitation, the subalpine snow might not disappear until late August. Once, Beth had gone to see the wildflowers in September. That year, the flowers barely bloomed before surrendering to autumn's first snowfall.

As the racket of the plane's engine settled into a steady rumble, Beth read her notes and checked them against the map she had made of her last trip into the mountain. The mountain goats Beth counted were not considered endangered or even threatened. In fact, the four bands she surveyed seemed to thrive in the wilderness above the ski area. Still, in order to prove that the expansion had no effect on local wildlife, the ski area had to present accurate year-round population figures of animals in the area. Davis and Graham had been hired to provide those numbers.

Only a year ago, Beth had begun working on the ski area assignment with a group of biologists, counting the elk population in Region IV. For that project, they'd used a helicopter to chase elk herds into the low river valleys from the air. With a gun, they'd tranquilized several elk, landed the helicopter, and taken blood samples. After administering vitamins and fitting them with a radio collar, they'd let the elk go. A single scientist had been assigned to track the animals, hoping to gather enough data to discover the reasons behind diminishing elk populations.

In the spring, her boss at Davis and Graham had assigned Beth to the goats. She'd done her first goat survey then, counting adult goats and newborn kids from the front seat of a slow-moving fixed-wing aircraft. Finding the goats hadn't been hard. From the air, she spotted huge clumps of shedding fur caught in branches of trees and bushes. These fur balls led them directly to the goat bands. First she counted bands of kids and nannies. Then Beth looked for lone billies. Her records included some of the first counts ever made of the bands in that area.

Today, Beth felt anxious to see how many of last year's babies had survived. In most parts of their habitat, goats remained above the tree line all year long. But in western Washington, because of deep snow layers west of the Cascades, the goats sometimes came down well below the tree line. This exposed the newborns to avalanche danger and falls from precipitous cliffs. How many had made it through the summer?

The ground cover at lower altitudes also made her goats harder to find. Beth could not look for clumps of fur to mark their autumn positions. This time of the year they would be adding fur—not losing it. Looking at her notes, she wondered if she would be able to tell which bands were which. Would the goats have moved between bands so much as to render her research numbers invalid? What if she had missed a band last spring?

Beth glanced through the pictures she had taken last spring, smiling again at the kids she'd caught with her telephoto lens. Though very young, they scrambled up rocky terrain with a confidence that surprised her. She had one picture of a lone billy, high on a peak, looking up at the plane. Slightly perturbed by their presence, his expression seemed to say, "Don't bother my wives. We don't want you here."

"There," Peterson said, pointing out his side window. Beth looked up.

"I see it," Ken said, nodding.

"What's up?" Beth said, leaning forward to catch a glimpse of the view from Bill's window. Her stomach growled.

"We're done with the water work," Bill said triumphantly. He tucked his camera back into the bag and zipped the cover closed.

"Great. I'm starved."

"Me too," Bill agreed, glancing at his watch. "We can picnic as soon as we get on the ground." He gave her the thumbs-up sign.

Beth looked down just in time to see the Rocky Creek Ranger Station pass below her window.

———

From his home at the fifty-seven-hundred-foot level of the mountain, Doyle regularly maintained a vigil over the roughly seventeen square miles of land he considered his personal territory. Doyle had not purchased the land. In fact, it belonged to the Federal Forest Service, as part of the Wright's Peak Wilderness. Officially, no one lived on Forest Service land, but his illegal squatting on federal property did not bother Doyle in the least. Still, he had no wish to draw attention to his presence. Doyle did not intend to be discovered—ever. From time to time over the years, he had spotted officials inside his perimeter, but not one of them had ever seen Doyle.

None of them even knew they had been watched—not the rangers, the forest resource managers, or the fire specialists. Doyle made it his business to be aware of everyone and everything within his perimeter. This he did by routine reconnaissance missions, exactly like the one he was starting on today.

Nothing made Doyle feel more at home than the long treks he made around the boundary of his personal territory. Today, walking along in the late afternoon, Doyle allowed himself to enjoy the cool mountain air. He noticed the changing color of the vine maples and the effect of frost on wild blackberry vines. He saw that the grass in open places had not yet greened from fall rains. Instead, faded and yellow, it had the beginning of dieback, typical of early winter. He walked steadily, though slowly, almost due north, along the ridge. Staying at the same elevation, Doyle chose a pace he could continue indefinitely without fatigue or knee pain.

In his mind, Doyle had already chosen a camping spot for his first night away from the cabin. High on a ridge, hidden in a natural alcove, this campsite featured rocky protection from the wind. There, in a mountain crease, morning fog hugged the hillside long after sunrise. Doyle knew that smoke from his campfire would mingle with the heavy mist hanging between the trees, rendering him completely undetectable. He could rest there—eat and sleep—protected from the weather, without fear of observation.

At his present pace, he would reach the campsite before sundown. The afternoon sun had already begun its game of hide-and-seek along the ridgeline to his left. He glanced toward it, seeing the brilliant flashing edge of the sun as it dipped behind the higher peaks. Though darkness would come soon enough, Doyle resisted the urge to hurry.

In spite of the increasing chill, he worked up a sweat, and his thirst drove him to look for a place to sit down and enjoy a cold drink. He stepped off the trail and moved into the dark shadows below old growth trees. Dropping his knapsack on the ground, he pulled one of the canteens off of his shoulder and took a long swig. He sat down on the soft ground, cushioned by old needles, and leaned against the rough bark of a spruce, wiping the dampness from his forehead with his sleeve. The dog flopped onto the ground, settling against Doyle's thigh.

After drinking his fill, Doyle filled his hand with water and offered it to the dog. Gilligan's head came up quickly, and he brought his mouth to Doyle's cupped palm. After licking the small reservoir dry, the dog stood up and turned away, whining.

For a moment, Doyle wondered what had distracted Gilligan. Then a noise caught Doyle's attention. He looked up, identifying a low and distant rumble as the sound of an approaching airplane. Still far off, he guessed.

Taking his time, Doyle limped farther off the trail to hide in a more secure location under the shelter of low cedar branches. As he waited, the sound grew louder, closer. Only then did Doyle realize that the plane would pass directly overhead. Glancing at the position of the sun, he made certain that he would not reflect light upward as he trained his binoculars up through openings in the tree branches to observe the plane.

A single-engine plane flew directly over him, low enough for Doyle to clearly read the numbers on the fuselage. This one was bigger than most planes he had seen above his forest; he could clearly identify a man in the pilot's seat just before it disappeared over the ridge.

———————

Through her earphones, Beth heard Ken begin the pre-landing checklist. The little plane banked fiercely and dropped into the valley below them. Though Beth had landed at the Rocky Creek Ranger Station many times before, she still hated the tight turns and nearly vertical drop demanded by steep canyon walls.

She forced herself to breathe, focusing on the back of the seat in front of her. Worse than any carnival ride, the descent to the runway always left Beth feeling shaky and slightly nauseous. The sensations began again, and in spite of her experience, she closed her eyes, squeezing her hands shut, waiting for the first bump of wheels on grass. Though she tried not to, her imagination pictured the thick branches of fir trees whizzing by—just inches from the small plane's wing.

She tried not to think about the damage a tree might do to the wing. Instead, she anticipated getting out, breathing fresh mountain air, and stretching her legs. Within minutes, she would be standing on good old terra firma.

The wheels bounced once before the plane settled onto the runway. A little rougher than usual, but the dangerous approach considered, Beth appreciated being on the ground any way she could get there. The plane turned and taxied, bumping along toward the small windowless building standing at the side of the runway.

Beth looked out the window, trying to spot the Explorer driven by Tom Freeman, the ranger who always met them here. No car occupied the space behind the cabin, and she noticed that the pullout beside the runway was also empty. A lone gas pump stood at one end of the covered porch.

"Hmm," Bill said, still speaking into the headphones, "I don't see anyone."

"Well, maybe he's just not here yet," Ken answered, shutting down the engine.

"Not like Tom," Beth ventured.

"Maybe he got hung up," Bill said, pulling off his headset and hanging it over the controls. "Could be along any minute now. I'm starved. Let's climb out and have our lunch in the sunshine while we wait."

"Maybe we should radio Tom," Beth said.

"We could try," Ken said, "but I don't think we'd get him. With these steep canyon walls, no one would hear us. Not unless they were right on top of us."

"So let's eat," Bill said, smiling as he popped off his seat belt.

———

As the plane passed in front of the sun, Doyle dropped the binoculars. He did not want to call attention to himself. More effective than a signal mirror, Doyle knew a passing plane could spot the sun reflecting off his lenses from more than two miles away. As the drone receded, Gilligan stuck his nose into Doyle's hand and whined.

"More water?" Doyle smiled. "What a hog you are. If you weren't such a good-fer-nothin' dog, I'd let you fend for yourself." He lifted his canteen and offered the dog another handful of water, repeating the procedure until the dog seemed satisfied.

As Doyle put the cap on the canteen, Gilligan stood, put his paws on Doyle's lap, and began licking the old man's face. *Thank you,* his vigorous bath seemed to say.

Doyle pushed the dog away and wiped his face with the bottom edge of his jacket. "A simple thanks would be enough," Doyle objected. "I don't need a bath."

He stood, slowly and deliberately. He stretched his leg and began working the knee joint. If he wanted to make camp by dark, Doyle needed to keep moving.

Back on the trail, Doyle focused on the ground in front of him and the vegetation nearby. Working his perimeters required a kind of concentration and focus that kept his mind from going off on mental rabbit trails. He'd taken too many rabbit trails this fall, and he longed to avoid them whenever possible.

Doyle knew his mountain—every bush and tree, every creek, stream, and rock. Nothing escaped his notice. When humans invaded his borders, whether he saw them or not, Doyle's personal alarm system went off. Unlike other hunters, Doyle did not need tracks to sense invaders nearby, though he did sometimes use them. For Doyle, any disturbance in the environment caught his attention—things as insignificant as newly broken branches, disturbed grass, or underbrush that had been bent or damaged.

Doyle could not risk having anyone nearby without his knowing. And he went to great effort to guarantee his isolation. After all, he'd had the best in covert training. With his carefully laid system of traps and snares, Doyle felt confident that no one could get inside his territory without his knowledge.

Occasionally, when his perimeter had been invaded, Doyle had been known to track the invader—sometimes for days. Always watching, yet never seen, Doyle would keep his vigil until at last the visitor managed to permeate the boundary on the other side and safely escape. Doyle could not afford to have someone stumble upon his cabin.

Last year, in the deep snows and short days of coldest winter, Doyle had followed a hunter tracking a wounded elk. On one of his perimeter checks, Doyle found blood-stained snow around tracks made by the stumbling elk. He followed the tracks for most of the afternoon, at last finding the dying elk and putting him out of his misery.

Carefully, Doyle sectioned the body and carried it back to his cabin. Then meticulously, he covered the blood with fresh snow and dropped branches from nearby trees over the site. After that he turned his attention on the hunter, who had long since lost track of his prey.

Doyle found the hunter huddled around a meager fire, fighting hypothermia nearly two miles from where the animal had died. From there, while remaining unseen, Doyle trailed him all the way to the western boundary of his territory. Slogging through heavy snow, it took the hunter two days to reach the logging road that took him back to civilization. Doyle did not feel safe until he was certain the hunter was gone.

As Doyle walked along, he found the brush along the eastern edge of the ridge undisturbed. He let himself relax a little in his isolation. So far, he'd never had to defend his territory. Even the poor lost hunter had made it out on his own. Still, Doyle could not, would not, allow anyone to discover his poaching presence on federal land. He had no doubt that he would do whatever was necessary to continue living undetected in the mountains.

They owed him that much. After what he'd been through, it was the least they could do—let him die in peace.

Five

OUT ON THE GRASS, relaxing in the late afternoon sun, Beth ate lunch with Bill and Ken. They chatted about inconsequential things—Bill's latest fishing trip, Ken's recent career move to Sound Flight. Bill wanted to know how Beth's girls were doing and asked about their progress in school.

Though light conversation continued through the meal, all three of them, it seemed to Beth, kept one eye on the gravel road winding down the canyon to the ranger station. They could not afford to waste what little sunlight remained on a picnic.

Ken asked the obvious question, "Where is this Forest Service guy driving from, anyway?"

"All the rangers have been moved to the park entrance," Bill said. "They hardly use this station at all anymore."

"So they'll do the bear survey from here?" Beth asked, shuddering. It seemed too far from civilization.

"Yeah. This station is right in the bear corridor. The wildlife guys shouldn't have any trouble collaring them here." Bill brought his box of cinnamon rolls out with a flourish. Handing Beth and Ken napkins, he announced, "Enough about rangers. Now for dessert!" He scooped the first roll out with his fingers. He served Beth first and then Ken, careful not to drop the precious pastry on the grass.

The bakery made portions large enough to satisfy the appetite of a hungry logger, each roll larger than Beth's hand and covered with a thick coat of heavy icing. While Beth accepted the roll smiling, she secretly wondered how she would ever finish it. Still, Bill had bought them to share, and she would not hurt his feelings by refusing his gift. Beth would make a valiant effort

The rolls tasted every bit as good as they looked, and all three adults found themselves licking the last drops of sweet icing from their fingertips. Pulling a water bottle from underneath his jacket, Ken poured clean water on his hands and began rubbing them together, struggling to clean off the sticky icing. When he finished, he offered the bottle to Bill and Beth. After they'd all had a turn, they all stretched out on the grass and enjoyed the sunshine. Beth noticed that the temperature had begun to drop, as it always did on sunny fall days. She caught Ken checking his watch.

"We can't stay here forever waiting for this Forest Service guy to show up."

"I know," Bill said. "We're wasting company time."

"And money," Ken agreed.

"What do we do with the supplies?" Beth asked. "Should we leave them here?"

"I don't think so," Ken said. "Even in the middle of nowhere, expensive equipment like that would disappear instantly."

"Here?" Beth laughed. "There isn't anyone within a million miles of this canyon."

"You'd be surprised," Ken answered. "There are all kinds of folks holed up in these woods."

"On federal land?" Bill shook his head. "I wouldn't think that's possible."

"Not legally," Ken said. "But they're here." He sat up and picked at the pieces of pale yellow grass that stuck to his skin. "I think we should get our work done. If they still need this stuff we can always fly it in another day." He stood up and glanced at the sun. "It's about time for Beth to do her counting, anyway."

"Sounds good," Bill agreed. "We'll take the equipment out with us."

"Okay," Beth shrugged, trying to sound agreeable. "If you guys can let me use the ladies' room, I'll be ready to take off in a minute."

The men grinned as Beth started across the field to the outhouse behind the cabin. "No hurry," Bill said, waving. "Take your time."

Spinning on one foot, Beth turned to laugh at him. "Right. Like I want to take my time in there." She threw her thumb over her shoulder, pinching her nose with the other. She turned back and jogged a couple of steps. "I'll hurry," she yelled, waving them off.

Moments later the little plane took off, heading down the valley where lower elevations gave more room to climb to altitude. As Ken banked right, his voice came over Beth's earphones. "Okay, ladies and gentlemen, let's go find those goats."

———

Doyle sat smoking a cigarette, staring into the glowing embers of his campfire, his bad knee stuck straight out in front of him. Occasionally, he turned the rabbit he'd secured to a makeshift spit. Dripping juices sizzled as they hit the coals, sending the tempting aroma of roasted meat into the chilly air. Doyle had not eaten since dawn, and intense hunger had driven him to hunt with a savage determination. Fortunately, he'd come upon the rabbit soon after making camp.

Gilligan lay on his side, his back resting against Doyle's thigh, eyes closed, dreaming doggie dreams. Once in a while he whined and jerked in his sleep, though he did not wake. In these moments, Doyle touched the dog's thick fur, easing the nightmare. *If only someone'd do the same for mine,* he thought.

A clear sky hung like a dome over the camp. As he roasted his early dinner, Doyle worked to keep his mind free, avoiding all introspection. He had learned from long experience that unless he kept careful control of his thoughts, his pain lay in ambush—like a patient sniper—ready at any time to reclaim its victim. Only in a carefully maintained state, void of self-examination and human interaction, did Dennis Doyle remain pain free.

In the old days, years ago, Doyle tried to achieve this mental state with street drugs. Though the drugs helped for a while, Doyle swore off them for good when he left civilization. The cost of vacating his conscience had been too high.

Doyle pulled his blanket up around his shoulders and turned the rabbit.

In a drug-induced rage, Doyle had nearly killed a stranger. A man in a bar—an innocent loner whose only mistake had been an off-color political comment. After spending time in jail, Doyle went home to find his apartment empty, his wife and only son gone.

In spite of his determination to avoid thinking about the past, Doyle remembered the note she had left him—word for word. She'd classified Doyle as a "dangerous monster." His anger would kill someone eventually, she'd said, and she didn't want to be his next victim.

Here in the mountains, sitting before a hot fire, Doyle didn't feel like a dangerous monster. And no man deserved to have his son taken away. Before he could stop himself, he imagined the soft blue eyes and wispy blond hair of the toddler she took from him. She might as well have taken all his vital organs. He closed his eyes against the memories, and in spite of the fire, he shivered.

Now, so many years later, Doyle relied only on the wilderness for mental freedom—fortified by an occasional affair with a bottle of scotch. On this particular trip, he'd left the bottle behind. But at this moment, thinking about his wife and the words of her note made him wish he'd brought it along. He could use the safe oblivion of an alcoholic fog.

He studied the carcass of the animal hanging from the skewer before him, feeling not an ounce of regret for having killed. After all, Doyle reasoned, the animal died so that he could eat. It was the way things were in the woods. Survival. Kill or be killed. It had been the first lesson Doyle learned in the bizarre life he began at the ripe old age of nineteen. That lesson, that first crucial lesson, Dennis Doyle had learned very, very well.

Doyle felt a moment of triumph in his role of victor. Being alone and self-reliant in the forest made Doyle feel the most alive. Sitting on the cold moist earth, the ground solid below him and the sky expansive above him, he felt almost complete. Almost.

Here Doyle knew exactly how to manage. At least they'd given him that much, though they'd given him little else. Dennis Doyle could survive in any jungle in the world, and the thought of it tipped the edges of his stern mouth into the slightest hint of a smile. Triumphant. Capable. At least he had that. He gave the rabbit a final turn.

The temperature had dropped, Doyle realized, in the single hour since he'd made camp. He stood and walked back to the tarp he'd hung between stakes directly against the hill. The dog, instantly awake, followed him. Sitting on his haunches in front of the posts, Gilligan cocked his head as if to say, "What now?"

Walking around the front of the shelter, Doyle gauged the difficulty of moving the covering closer to the fire. The tarp would trap the heat, holding it close to him during the night. However, moving the lean-to would leave space behind him—between his back and the hill—an unwise choice. No. It would be safer to expose only one side, he reasoned. He would not move the shelter. Better to be safe and cold—but alive.

His hips often ached at night, especially when the temperature dropped near freezing. He thought about his bones being smashed painfully into the hard ground later this evening when he tried to sleep. Why had he built his fire so far from the shelter? *A foolish mistake,* he thought. *Or maybe the mistake of an old fool.* For a moment, before he could stop himself, Doyle wondered what it would be like to sleep in a real bed, between clean sheets, on a soft and comfortable mattress.

Turning abruptly, Doyle went back to the fire and sat down, mentally flogging himself for allowing such a ridiculous idea to enter his mind. He didn't want a bed. He wanted the mountain, the fresh air, and the isolation his world here offered. Holding up the palms of his hands, he toasted them near the fire. The rabbit would be finished soon, and he relished the taste of fresh meat. From the supplies he had picked up this morning, Doyle had chosen one red apple and placed it in his pack. The apple and the rabbit would make a fine meal, he told himself sternly.

Few in the world would eat better tonight.

After combing the mountain highlands carefully, Ken Bohannan managed to find only two of the four bands Beth needed to include in her records. The summer had been long and dry, and she wondered if the lack of vegetation had driven the goats to lower altitudes than normal. Using her map and the reports of last spring, Beth continued to suggest places to search.

Ken seemed happy to oblige. Skillfully, he buzzed one meadow after another. But they could not find the animals.

"What do you think has happened?" she asked Bill.

"I don't know goats," he answered, smiling at her over his shoulder. "I only know water. This is your call."

"Let's keep looking," she answered. Together, they plotted a circular route around the mountain, staying at nearly the same altitude where she had last seen the animals.

"Look," Bill said, pointing out the side window. "I think we've found papa."

"Wonderful," Beth said, sliding across the seat and aiming her Nikon F–5 camera at the billy. She balanced the weight of the camera carefully and focused the zoom lens. "Can you circle him?" she asked.

"Will do. Give me a minute," Ken said.

"Think he's one of the ones you've already shot?" Bill asked.

"I don't know. I'll have to get the pictures together." Beth tried to calm the wave of excitement she felt as they flew closer to the magnificent animal. She needed a steady hand in order to get a good photo from the plane. How she loved them. She loved their shaggy winter coat and their amazing ability to climb rock walls as though they were paved sidewalks. She loved their gentle, curious faces. As the plane came back around, the billy looked up, and Beth snapped several shots.

"The band has to be around somewhere," she said.

"We can look," Ken said. He glanced over at Bill.

"I'm just along for the ride at this point. You two decide what's next."

"Only two things to consider," Ken said. "We have another hour's worth of fuel. And, the sun is going to set in about forty minutes. That gives us a little twilight to fly. Then I'd like to be heading back."

"Okay," Beth agreed. "Let's keep looking as long as we can."

"Right."

"And, one other thing," Ken added, banking the plane to continue the search for goats. "As the sun goes down, fog banks sort of grow out of the hills here. I need you both to help me keep an eye out." He glanced over his shoulder, and she nodded her agreement. Bill had already begun spotting out the side window.

They moved east and searched two more mountain meadows for the bands that so far had successfully eluded them. Just as they rose again to climb over the canyon wall, Bill pointed toward the nose of the plane. "There," he said, "at one o'clock. See that white patch?"

Beth leaned forward, craning her neck. "Yes. I think you've found one!" In the distance, the band of goats looked like spots of leftover snow. But as Beth watched, the spots moved.

Ken turned again toward the band, and a shudder went through the plane. "Evening winds," he said, leveling the plane and adjusting his controls. "A little change in the wind around the mountain." He grinned at Bill. "This mountain sometimes makes her own weather."

They approached the band and circled twice, allowing Beth to count and take pictures. "Aren't they beautiful?" she asked, focusing on the animals through the lens of her camera. "Now, can we make another pass to count the babies?"

She looked up in time to see Bill Peterson roll his eyes.

"I'm supposed to document the survival rates of the kids."

He shrugged.

Much to her surprise, after two more passes, Beth found this particular band full of nannies but with very few kids. She could not explain the absence of babies, and it plagued her. Perhaps the band had gotten separated? What had gone wrong? All of the bands she'd counted last spring had highly successful breeders. Where had the babies gone?

"Can we look just a moment longer? I wonder if this band has been separated from the kids."

"We can try," Ken agreed. He started the plane up another canyon. Beth noticed how slowly the plane flew and realized that he was trying to give her as much time as possible to scan the ground for her missing kids. Beth kept her forehead glued to the window, her camera in her lap, searching the green area below for any sign of the goats.

Suddenly the little plane banked. Startled, Beth looked forward to see a swirl of clouds pass in front of the windshield. Then the plane banked again, turning a circle more suddenly, more tightly, than any she had ever experienced. It seemed to Beth that the left wing stood still while the plane circled around it.

The whole thing happened so quickly that she felt no fear. The sudden move simply startled her. Holding on to the door handle, Beth tried to avoid sliding across the seat and slamming into the downhill passenger door. Suddenly an alarm went off inside the cabin. Bill Peterson said something, and though she didn't understand all the words, she could not mistake the sound of fear in his voice.

And then through her earphones, Beth heard Ken Bohannan swear.

It was the last sound she heard.

Six

THOUGH THE DISTANCE FROM Allen Cheng's church office to the front door of the old brick parsonage could not be more than two hundred feet, today Allen felt grateful that the house lay not a single step farther. The late afternoon meeting had left him discouraged and bone weary, longing for a quiet evening and the gentle encouragement of his wife. Beth would know just the right words to lift his sunken spirit.

Maple Hills Baptist, now more than sixty years old, faced the same struggle as many other inner city churches that were being abandoned by families heading for the suburbs. But unlike other churches, Maple Hills refused to give up. Determined not to wither and die without a fight, the board hired Allen to fill the vacancy left by their retiring pastor. In spite of limited enthusiasm and a budget stretched by a dwindling congregation, the board believed Allen Cheng could infuse new direction and growth to the congregation. His energy would draw younger families—the same ones buying older fixer-upper homes in less desirable parts of the city.

When Allen accepted the job in the old Baptist church, he hoped to forge a strong alliance between the longtime members and the more recent attendees. He wanted a unified ministry, one characterized by love and acceptance and enthusiasm. But after meetings like today's, Allen wondered if he had the leadership skills to pull it off.

Lately, he found his congregation struggling with hot emotions and divergent opinions. No matter how hard he tried, Allen couldn't bring unity to a group where each member had his own agenda, and each one was determined to have his own way.

Tonight, the Service Planning Committee struggled with the music format for the Sunday morning worship. Some wanted upbeat contemporary worship. Others hardcore rock. And, of course, there were those on the committee who could not worship without singing the same hymns they'd sung growing up.

Allen shared their concerns, though he wanted more than anything to create a home for the young families who visited Maple Hills. Clearly the music chosen for the service could never make everyone completely happy. Tonight, his goal had been to get his members to hear one another, to express their love and commitment toward each other in spite of divergent opinions.

From his point of view, the meeting had been an utter failure.

As he opened the front door of the parsonage, Allen spotted Beth's mother behind the ironing board. Wearing ostrich feather scuffs and her shoulders barely clearing the height of the board, Harumi diligently ironed his work shirts. Only then did he remember that Beth would not be home for several hours. As the sinking realization hit him, Allen bit back his disappointment and forced a smile for his family.

Noah, standing inside his playpen, happily tossed a puzzle ball out onto the floor of the living room. Bending again, he picked up a stuffed lion and sent it sailing onto his sister's shoulders. Clearly, Noah wanted attention. As Allen bent over the rail to give a hello kiss, the baby raised his pudgy arms.

This evening ritual warmed Allen, drowning out the feelings of inadequacy he'd brought home from the meeting. Allen gave Noah his usual spot, draped over his daddy's shoulders. Happily Noah slapped his daddy on the head and giggled with delight.

"Hello, girls!" Allen said, nudging them with the tip of his shoe.

Bekka, the oldest, rolled over onto one elbow. "Hey, Dad," she said, giving a little wave. He smiled as she turned back to the television.

Until now, Abbey had been fully engrossed in an *I Love Lucy* rerun. Suddenly seeing her father, she came alive. "Daddy!" she said, jumping up off the floor. "You're home!" She threw both arms around her father's hips, hugging him tightly.

"Hey, kiddo," Allen answered, patting her back with one hand. "I'm glad to see you too."

"Now we can eat dinner," she said, without trying to hide her relief. Dropping back down on the floor, Abbey tucked her chin in her hands and focused on *I Love Lucy* again.

Allen rolled his eyes at Harumi and smiled in spite of the obvious slight. "Evening, Mom," he said, leaning down to hug his tiny mother-in-law with one arm.

"Hello, Allen," she said, returning his greeting. "There are already a dozen messages for you on the pad by the telephone."

"Great," he answered with sarcasm in his voice. "I haven't been out of the office for five whole minutes. Dinner started?"

"There's a prepackaged lasagna in the fridge," she said with the same enthusiasm she might use to announce a casserole of dog food. Pulling his freshly ironed shirt from the board, she wrapped it over a wire hanger and hung it over a doorknob. "But I made miso katsudon instead. The girls set the table. Beth has a salad in the fridge. It's all ready to serve."

"Eclectic, huh? What would we do without you?" Allen asked. Noah leaned over, arms stretching toward his grandma until he threatened to fall from Allen's shoulders.

She reached for the baby with gentle arthritic hands. "I don't know," she answered, giving Noah a kiss followed by a loving pat on his diapered behind. "But I'm glad to be needed. Right now, though, I should go home and feed Grandpa," she said, more to the baby boy in her arms than to her son-in-law. She handed Noah to Allen and opened the tiny closet beside the front entry. Stepping out of her scuffs, she pulled out dark blue rubber boots and put them on. As she slipped on her wool coat and moved through the front door, she said, "Tell Lizzie to call me tomorrow, will you?"

"I'll do that," Allen said, holding the doorknob with one hand and Noah with the other. "And thanks again, Mom. I really do appreciate all the things you do."

"Bye, girls," Harumi called from the doorway.

Though their gaze never left the television screen, they answered, almost in unison. "Bye, Grams." Allen waved again and closed the door behind her.

———

Beth became vaguely aware of something poking into her right shoulder and squirmed in an ineffective effort to move away from the discomfort. Suddenly pain ripped through her chest, and she could not breathe from the intensity of it. She lay very still, on her right side, taking shallow, cautious breaths. With the softest panting, she blinked back tears. The pain eased some, and she opened her eyes.

What happened? Where am I?

Slices of green divided her visual field, and she blinked again, wondering and confused. The smell of earth came to her, the strong scent of bacteria in wet ground. It reminded her of a freshly watered houseplant. She opened her eyes again to see a deep blue background behind blades of green. Twilight.

Sky. Earth. Grass.

Gently, cautiously, she eased her head from side to side, grateful to discover that she felt no pain in her neck.

Something had happened, though Beth had no idea what it was or how she had become so badly injured. While her body screamed for attention, she continued her careful, nearly motionless assessment of her body with the objective skill of a lab technician taking notes on a vital experiment.

Careful not to move her chest, she opened and closed her fists. First her left. Good. It obeyed. Next her right. Though her fingers moved, they accomplished only a tiny arc before intense pain squelched the motion. She knew something serious, something terrible, had happened to her right arm. She would leave that for later. She wiggled her toes. As they moved inside her boots, a new pain made her wince. Something in the skin above her right knee screamed. Another injury. A bad one.

Breathing cautiously, without moving her head or trunk, she stretched out her left hand to touch her right thigh. Her fingers found a tear in the denim above her knee, and for an instant she mourned her favorite jeans. They'd been expensive—too expensive for a pastor's salary. She'd bought them only for flying, because of the warm flannel lining inside. Now they were ruined. How could she explain this to Allen?

Flying? A ripple of recognition fluttered to the surface of her memory. Flying.

Her fingers continued their exploration along the torn edge of fabric. A big rip. And wetness. More pain, though not like the pain in her chest. She bent her left elbow, bringing her fingers to rest in front of her eyes, and tried to focus.

Blood. Dark and partially clotted, her own blood covered the tips of her fingers. The scientific part of her brain realized that she had been injured long enough for her blood to begin clotting. Was it wet because of the severity of the wound? Or had she begun the assessment immediately after the injury? If only she could remember what had happened. She closed her eyes, trying to bring it back. But no matter how hard she tried, no memory would return.

She began a methodical evaluation of her skeletal structure. From her toes, she moved on to assess the condition of her ankles, her knees. Gently, she tried to straighten her hips. More pain, but not so intense this time.

Her lower back felt as though she'd been thrown against a wall by a very strong enemy. Sore. Stiff. But nothing permanent. A sense of gratitude filled her. "Thank you, Lord," she breathed. Whatever she had lived through had been traumatic. A terrible accident of some kind, though she could not remember anything about it. She knew only one thing. She had survived.

So far, her legs, with the exception of the wound in her thigh, seemed relatively healthy. As though she had become a doctor, Beth thought deliberately, carefully, using all of her energy. It seemed to her that she had broken some of her ribs. That would explain the intense chest pain. Her left wrist, elbow, and shoulder seemed fine. But something intensely painful had happened to her right arm. Between that injury and her ribs, getting up would be a challenge.

But she could not stay here, curled up on her side, in the middle of heaven only knew where. She needed to move, to assess her situation. Beth had to get up. In the middle of this thought, she remembered the plane. She had been riding in an airplane.

So much reasoning seemed overwhelming. Exhausted, Beth gave herself permission to rest. Closing her eyes, she willed the muscles in her body to relax. She could rest for a few minutes and then figure out what to do next.

She must have gone to sleep, for when she opened her eyes, she realized that the sky above her had changed. The deep blue hue had darkened to an endless black punctuated with hundreds of stars and a brilliant nearly full moon. Of course, it got dark so early in late October that it could've been seven o'clock or midnight. Without a watch, she had no idea. So far, no one had come to help her. Why not?

She had grown cold. Very cold. Already Beth had begun to shiver.

As the moments passed, the shaking became more intense. *I can't lie here forever,* she thought. *I have to get up. I have to get warm.* Forgetting her injuries, she tried to push herself up onto her right elbow. The arm refused to cooperate. Fierce pain stopped her breathing, and for an instant, she thought she might faint. Involuntary tears came to her eyes, and Beth blinked them away. Taking slow calming breaths, she rolled over onto her back. Holding very still, she waited for the wave of agony to subside.

All right, she thought. *That won't do.*

Looking into the sky, she remembered. She had been in a plane, with Bill and a pilot. Someone new. She tried to think of his name, but nothing would come. A crash. They had been in a crash. Her mind brought up images of the moments before impact. Images so real, she closed her eyes in objection.

Still, she saw them. Trees growing larger and moving closer and closer. The shadow of the plane passing over the dark forest below them. She saw Bill cross his forearms over his face and lean forward in his seat. She remembered a scream. Who had screamed?

She remembered the first jarring force of the tiny plane as it sliced through the treetops. Trees tearing away parts of the wings. Wings ripping through bits of trees. Someone had yelled, "Hold on." Had the voice belonged to Bill? The pilot?

She tried to remember more, but nothing came. She felt a dull throbbing in her head, along with the sound of an intense ringing, as though someone had filled a stadium with people playing tiny high-pitched sleigh bells. She closed her eyes against the noise, but it would not stop. From inside her skull, the ringing pelted her ears, growing even louder as she tried to block it out.

Bill. I need to find Bill, she thought. She rolled from her back onto her left side, struggling to sit up as she did so. Her body moved in slow motion as she shifted, and the world around her swam—like an air mattress in a swimming pool. She swayed, overcome by the most intense dizziness she had ever felt. She reached out with her left hand and clutched at the grass, hoping the dizziness would pass.

As she held on, the wild rocking eased slightly, and she tried to relax. Fingering her face tenderly, she explored the skin.

Beth's forehead itched, and she reached up to scratch. Her hair had stuck to her skin in a solid crusty mess. Along her forehead, near the right temple, she discovered a gash. The tissue below it had swollen, leaving a gaping fleshy wound.

Perhaps this explained her dizziness. More than anything, Beth wanted to lie down again. To curl up and go to sleep. This simple temptation seemed stronger than any she had ever experienced. But Beth knew better. Somehow, she knew that if she curled up to sleep, she would die.

Seven

BY THE TIME THE CHENG FAMILY ate dinner, Allen had managed to turn the rice into a crusted solid mass, the bottom layer firmly attached to the pan. The lettuce in the salad had wilted, and tiny portions of scalded miso sauce floated over the breaded pork. He knew his mother-in-law would be horrified at the mess he'd made of her impeccable Japanese cooking. Allen laughed at himself, glad that she would never know.

More than culture separated his Chinese heritage from Beth's Japanese roots. Raised in the hills north of San Francisco, Allen's second-generation Chinese mother had been as American as drive-through hamburgers and french fries. To Allen's mother, cooking Chinese meant ordering Mongolian beef from the takeout up the street. Harumi, on the other hand, loved to cook all of the dishes from her Japanese past.

Beth had never picked up her mother's penchant for Japanese cooking.

So, as Allen expected, the girls complained through every bite. He kept quiet until he felt he must put an end to their misery and then astounded himself by saying, "There are children in Africa who would love to have your dinner tonight."

Bekka laughed out loud. "Oh, please. Not that, Dad."

"I guess it was lame."

"Duh." Abbey giggled. "Can we have some dessert?"

"Ice cream," Allen agreed. "If you rinse your plates and put them in the dishwasher."

"What about Noah?"

"I'll rinse his plate," Allen answered. *And then I'll hose down the walls and the floor and the high chair.* He tried to remember when the girls were babies. *When is it,* he wondered, *that kids finally decide to eat more than they throw?*

After cookie dough ice cream, Allen put Noah to bed. Then Allen and the girls sat on the couch and read out loud from *Hatchet.* Though Abbey did not yet join in reading, Bekka took her turn. Of all his parental duties, Allen treasured the quiet moments they spent together just before the girls went to bed. Normally the four Chengs occupied the couch together, Allen with his feet on the coffee table, Beth with her legs thrown over his knees, her feet wiggling constantly, and the two girls draped over and around their parents.

As they sat reading in the lamplight, Allen couldn't help but miss Beth. He glanced at his watch. *She should be home soon,* he thought, looking forward to her return. Then he could tell her about his day and let her calm his nerves. When Bekka finished the last page of the chapter, Allen closed the book.

"One more, Dad," she begged.

"Nope," he said, patting her knee. "That's enough for tonight. Time for bed."

Abbey had grown very drowsy, leaning against his shoulder. To his surprise, she did not object. He stood and guided the girls toward their bedrooms. While Bekka changed, he brushed Abbey's teeth and washed her face. At last, he knelt between their twin beds and prayed with them.

In the living room, as Allen reached to close the door to the hall, he found his dress shirts hanging over the knob, waiting to be put away. Leaving that for Beth to take care of, Allen sat down with the cordless phone and began returning his phone calls. Estelle told him that Joseph Leider had been hospitalized. Scott had called to let him know that the speaker they had booked for outreach night had cancelled. His pianist apologized for her rudeness at the meeting. Before he realized it, another hour had passed.

And still no sign of Beth.

He did not know when uneasiness began to gnaw away at his subconscious. But when he placed the phone on its charger and glanced at the clock over the fireplace, Allen felt full-blown anxiety hit him squarely in the gut. Ten o'clock.

Allen went to the kitchen and dialed Beth's cell phone. No answer. He left a voice message asking her to call as soon as possible and headed for the door to the garage. They kept a Washington State map in the glove box of the family car. With the map, Allen could figure out exactly how far it was from Bellevue to Thun Field. He made it all the way into the garage before he remembered. Beth had taken the car, and with it, the map of Washington.

All right, he would use her computer to get the information.

Within minutes, Allen pulled Thun Field up on his screen and had directions from their house to the airport. Using the mileage, he calculated the time needed for Beth to drive home. Forty minutes. The sun had set four hours ago. What could be keeping her?

Perhaps she had stopped at the store on the way home. For a moment, he considered calling her mother. Maybe Beth had said something about her plans to Harumi. Checking his watch again, he dismissed the idea. Calling would only alarm Beth's mother. Beth would never forgive him if he caused Harumi undue fear. No. She deserved protection; she had already been through too much to frighten her unnecessarily.

Allen tried to recall the name of the company hired to fly Beth's team around Mount Rainier. He'd heard it, maybe even seen it. He tried to jar his memory. But the name would not surface. He looked through Beth's desk. Finding no reference to the flight company, Allen called the downtown office of Davis and Graham. He got nothing more than an answering machine.

Allen looked up the number for Thun Field and dialed. No answer. The moments ticked by, and Allen struggled with his memory, trying to think of someone—anyone—he could call. *Where could Beth be? Why hasn't she telephoned?*

He dialed her cell phone again, hanging up before the end of the recorded message.

Though Allen tried to stay calm, by ten-thirty he fought an increasing certainty that something horrible had happened. He called the State Patrol and asked about their car. No accidents involving a maroon Outback had been reported on the highway between the airport and the house. The officer took the license number and promised to call immediately if something came up.

Desperate, Allen decided to call John Graham, the CEO of Davis and Graham. He rifled through Beth's desk until he found her address book. Filled with Beth's precise architectural printing, it held only personal numbers—no business contacts at all. *Where does she keep them?* He walked through the house, desperate to find a phone number for anyone who might know something.

In the kitchen, he discovered her Rolodex sitting by the telephone. Why hadn't he seen it there before? He rattled through the cards, grateful to find it full of her business contacts. Allen dialed the home telephone number for John Graham.

A woman's sleepy voice answered.

"Is this John Graham's home? Of Davis and Graham?"

"It's a little late for a business call, isn't it?"

"I'm Allen Cheng, Beth's husband. May I speak to John? It's urgent."

Within minutes, Allen explained his concerns and had John's promise to call Bill Peterson. "If Peterson is home, then they're down and safe," he assured Allen. "Sound Flight is the best in the business. I'm sure everything is fine. Maybe she stopped somewhere for a bite to eat. Give me your number, and I'll get right back to you."

Hanging up, Allen had the frightening certainty that he needed to call the church prayer chain. Beth would never be this late without contacting him. Not unless something had gone terribly wrong. But what? He could not call the prayer chain without tying up the phone line. He would not do that now. Not yet.

———

Sitting perfectly still, Beth closed her eyes against the swirling stars and took a long faltering breath. She needed to think clearly, to consider all her options. She blew the air out slowly and opened her eyes. Taking in her surroundings, she realized that she sat in the bottom of a small hollow near the edge of a mountain meadow. Trees formed a wall surrounding the clearing, though she could see few details in the moonlight.

Looking down, she turned her attention to the gash in her upper thigh. Blood had soaked through her jeans on both sides of the long tear stretching from just above her knee to her upper thigh. For a moment, she fought rising panic. She recognized the danger so much blood represented. She could look forward to shock, perhaps even death, due to extensive blood loss. She felt hysteria rising in her chest as she took tiny gasps of breath, accompanied by an exponentially growing fear and tears.

No. No! She would not let herself think of these things, not allow her frightened thoughts to run down this road. She had to remain calm, clearheaded. Forcing herself to look more closely at the tear in her jeans, she ran the fingers of her left hand along the edge of the tear. Clearly the fabric had been damaged more than her skin.

Carefully, she pulled the denim apart and examined her thigh. The wound was shorter in length than the damage to her jeans, and it continued to bleed—even this long after the accident—however long that might be. The tear seemed clean, as though cut by a piece of glass or very sharp metal. The resulting injury looked like a surgical flap. Fortunately, the wound did not expose muscle or bone.

No nerves seemed to have been severed; it could have been much worse. "Thank you, Jesus," she breathed, brushing the tears from her cheeks with her left hand. At this point, her thigh didn't even seem to hurt—at least not compared to the pain in her chest and right arm.

Though the cut had not produced serious damage, it had caused extensive loss of blood. Suddenly Beth remembered the comment of an old college biology professor. *"When it comes to blood, a little always looks like a lot—especially when it's yours."* Somehow his humor didn't seem funny here—on top of this mountain all by herself.

Before moving around, Beth knew she should stem the flow of blood. But what could she use to put additional pressure against the bleeding wound—a shirt, a belt? She must find something. Once she had the bleeding under control, she could figure out what had happened to the airplane and the men inside.

Surely Bill had survived. *Bill will know what to do next,* she thought. A tiny glimmer of hope sparked inside her. *I'll find Bill, and everything will be all right.*

Tucking her feet underneath herself, she bent her knees and turned over onto her one strong hand. The pain in her chest, even from this small movement, made the horizon swirl again. She held still, taking shallow, painful breaths. Bending her arm, she lowered her head, trying to control the dizziness. *Patience,* she told herself. *It will pass.*

When the pain subsided, she moved again. Bringing first one knee up under her chest and then the other, Beth did not let go of the ground until she managed a squatting position. Carefully, she stood, feeling the ground reel underneath her. For a moment it felt as though she were standing inside a Ferris wheel—the horizon moving in a giant circle around her. Her head pounded in protest as her heart made a heroic effort to keep up with the change in her position. Again, the pain in her ribs returned. This time though, her arm won the contest in an excruciating objection to her getting up. She screamed out in protest, holding her injured arm protectively in front of her face.

"Oh, Jesus," she said, letting go of her tears. "Oh, Lord, this hurts. Please help me." She held still until the pounding in her elbow subsided. *If only I could immobilize my arm, it might feel better.* Holding it very still, she considered her options. Glancing down, she took inventory of her clothes. She wore a polar fleece vest and a wool ski sweater. Perhaps if she could sling the arm . . .

With her left hand, she gently unzipped the vest. Slipping her left hand inside along her chest, she brought it out again through the right armhole. Using the pressure from her good hand, she pulled the armhole down, enlarging it, while holding the vest away from her chest. Then she slipped her injured right hand inside the larger hole. The motion brought a knifing pain in her elbow, hitting her like a bullet as it shattered glass. A wordless, agonizing scream dropped Beth to her knees, still holding the injured hand inside her vest. She rocked back on her heels, letting herself cry out in long anguished sobs.

Frozen in this position, Beth sat, unwilling to move again. Eventually the pain subsided, and she let go of the injured arm. Still crying, Beth brought the zipper back up the vest and locked it in a partially closed position. Reaching inside, she pulled her right hand farther into the vest until it rested on the top of the partially closed and locked zipper.

Long moments passed with no relief. Beth wondered how long she could endure such insufferable pain. The throbbing in her elbow refused to ease. Still she did not move. Eventually, though she did not know how much time passed, the writhing pain softened from a throbbing agony to a constant ache. Slowly, her tears ebbed, and she found she could take regular, though shallow, breaths. The arm felt bearable for the first time since she'd tried to stand up. Then Beth groaned aloud as she remembered. *I still have to go through the whole process of getting up again.*

How quickly her world had been reduced to the simple elements of endurance and pain. Beth brought one knee up, placing her left foot solidly on the ground before her. She took a few moments to breathe as she steadied herself. *Even if someone knew our plane went down,* she thought, *it will be morning before anyone will come to look for us.* For the first time since the accident, she wondered if she had what it took to survive until help came.

Then she imagined the faces of her family. She saw the girls sitting across the kitchen table, trading color crayons. She thought of Noah giggling as he splashed puddles of orange juice on the high chair. She pictured Allen reading his Bible at the desk in his tiny office. With a stab, Beth realized that she hadn't told Allen how much she loved him before he left for work this morning. She needed to tell him. Needed to say it to all of her family.

Beth knew she had no choice. For the sake of her children and for Allen, Beth had to survive. She took a deep pain-filled breath and stood.

Eight

ALLEN SAT ON THE END of the couch, his hands tightly
folded between his knees, staring at the base for the cordless telephone resting on the end table beside him. He wondered how long it would take John Graham to contact Bill
Peterson. *Even if he finds Peterson at home, we still won't know where
Beth is.*

Only the ticking of the oak wall clock interrupted the quiet of
the old parsonage. While Allen's prayers ascended silently, he
watched the telephone, willing it to ring.

It did not.

Desperate, Allen slid off the couch and onto his knees. Burying
his face in his hands, he prayed. "You know where she is, Lord," he
pleaded. "Help me to figure out what has happened." The sudden
ringing of the phone made Allen jump. Before the ring died in the
air, Allen picked it up. "Yes?"

"Allen, this is John." The voice on the line sounded concerned,
heavy. "I've called Bill. He's not home yet either."

"What did his wife say?"

"Bill isn't married. No one answered." Allen heard John take a
long slow breath. "I called his cell phone and didn't get him there
either. So we really don't know anything yet."

Allen stood and paced back and forth in front of the old couch,
running one hand through his hair. "What do we do now?"

"I've tried to call Sound Flight, but all I have is a business number. I've paged the emergency number on the recorder. So far no

one has returned the page. As soon as I get a call back, I'll be in touch."

John Graham seemed about to hang up. "Wait," Allen said. "I have a really bad feeling about this. Please, let me know as soon as you hear anything."

"I understand," he said. "I promise I'll get right back to you."

As soon as he could get a dial tone, Allen called the church prayer chain.

————————

Determined to survive until the rescuers arrived, Beth found new strength. She made a slow turn as she took in her moonlit surroundings. She recognized mountainous terrain and saw small alpine trees nearby. Then she started walking up the hill out of the depression. It didn't take her long to find the plane. Even before she got to the top of the hill, she spotted the crushed fuselage lying at the very edge of the gully. The rear passenger door hung partially open directly above her. Beth looked at it in surprise, unable to remember if she had climbed out or been thrown from the plane when it crashed. The fact that she had no memory seemed eerie to her, frightening enough in itself.

She approached the plane in wonder. The crash had so badly damaged the plane that Beth had trouble determining what she saw. The windshield, still intact though shattered, hugged the ground. Somehow in the crash, the plane had rolled, landing upside down, tipped slightly with one wing touching the ground.

She glanced back over the fuselage. In their descent through the trees, the wheels and landing gear had been stripped from the plane. Still, the right wing had managed to come to rest without any significant damage.

Beth approached the side closest to her and stepped onto the underside of the wing, which sloped slightly uphill. Dew covered the cold metal wing, and on the slippery surface, Beth lost her footing. Trying to maintain her balance, her arms jerked away from her body, and she cried out in agony. Grabbing the wing strut with her left hand, she held tight, panting, until her pain eased. She would not make that mistake again. Beth bent over and peered into the cockpit.

In spite of her care, the motion and new position made her ribs scream. She suddenly felt dizzy. A wave of nausea passed through her stomach, making her knees tremble violently. Her stomach heaved, and Beth bent forward, unable to resist the motion of her stomach. She wiped her lips and took a moment to breathe, remaining bent over the wing, closing her eyes until the nausea passed. Part of her wanted to kneel and rest. Another part refused permission.

She did not want to have to stand up again.

Opening her eyes, Beth turned toward the cockpit and stared into the darkness beyond the door window. As her eyes adjusted to the dim light, she tried to assess the damage. In spite of her own pain, what she saw made her gasp.

Bill, still buckled into the seat of the plane, hung upside down in his safety harness, his face white. Both arms hung limply from his shoulders, his hands resting motionless on what had been the ceiling of the small plane. He seemed dazed. Then with a deep breath, he turned his face away from the door.

Beth reached for the handle and tugged at the latch. Though the latch released, the door refused to open. Beth pulled harder, ignoring the knifing pain she felt in her arm. The door remained firmly stuck. Frustrated, she stood up. Suddenly angry, she slammed her fist on the door and gave the window a quick kick with her boot. How could she get Bill out of the plane if she couldn't even open the door?

In the heavy dew, Beth's foot slid off the wing, throwing her off balance again. Once more searing pain knifed through her elbow, and she froze, hugging herself and breathing shallow, calming breaths. Glancing around, she noticed the rear door, hanging partially open on a single hinge.

At least she could get in that door. From there, she could crawl along the ceiling to the cockpit and help Bill.

Beth stepped to the rear door and looked inside. It was darker back here and more difficult to see. Though she had carefully stowed all of her equipment before the flight, the crash had thrown everything onto the ceiling of the small plane. Her little crate and all of her notes and supplies littered the ceiling. Her camera bag had been caught between the front seat and the window.

In order to crawl through the fuselage, she had to clear space. Using only her left hand, Beth began pulling things out of her way, dumping them out onto the grass beside her. Though every movement, every lift and reach, brought new pain in her ribs, Beth forced herself to continue. Everything, including her purse and Bible, her papers and notes, had been scattered all over the wreckage. Just as she brought out her plastic crate, she realized how important all of these supplies had suddenly become. Her survival might depend on these things she had tossed on the ground. Changing her mind, she put the crate on the ground and began dropping items inside.

When the ceiling was clear, she knelt down on the grass and crawled inside. Inch by painful inch, she struggled forward through the center of the fuselage, squeezing herself into the space between the seat backs and the ceiling. Beth's tiny stature scarcely fit into the crushed space. Her ribs screamed as she moved, pulling herself forward with only the help of her left hand. She blinked back tears as beads of sweat gathered on her face. Resting a moment, she closed her eyes and took slow, shallow breaths. Then brushing the sweat from her forehead, she tried to press on.

Beth tried to balance on her left side, protecting her injured right arm. But in this position she could barely use her stronger side. She settled onto her stomach. Using her boots against the windows and pulling with her left hand, she shoved herself toward Bill, stopping frequently to rest and wait while her pain subsided enough to continue.

"Bill," she whispered. "Hold on, Bill. I'm coming." She stopped again to rest. "Bill, can you hear me?" She rested her cheek on the back of her hand, waiting for a wave of nausea to pass. "I'm almost there, Bill."

At the front of the plane, she fought the strange uphill position of the copilot's seat. "Bill, it's me. Beth." She took his face in her hand, looking directly into his eyes. His glasses had come off, and she noticed that the tiny creases around his eyes had squeezed into deep furrows. His lips pursed together in a clear expression of pain. The muscles of his jaw were tight, and his eyebrows were drawn together. Though he stared directly back at Beth, she saw no sign of recognition in his eyes. Seeing him gaze at her, his expression blank and his face upside down, brought another wave of nausea. She fought it back, trying to remember what she knew about head injuries. "You okay, Bill? Tell me where you hurt." Gently she patted his cheek. "Focus, Bill. You have to help me."

He gave a barely perceptible nod.

"Should I try to get you out?"

He closed his eyes. Again a small nod. "Pilot," he whispered.

Beth realized that she had not yet examined Ken, who was still strapped into the seat next to Bill's. Embarrassed, she agreed. "I'll check." Examining the pilot would force Beth to roll onto her left side.

Even the thought seemed overwhelming.

After an agonizing shuffle, Beth managed to roll over enough to face the pilot's seat. She was shocked to discover that Ken Bohannan must have died in the crash. Stunned, Beth tried to remember the last minutes before the impact, but could not. Something about finding a meadow. He had tried to control the plane on the way down, she remembered that much.

The wing on the pilot's side of the plane had been folded like a fan, digging a deep hole into the ground beside the plane. The cockpit itself had torn open, leaving a maze of electrical wires hanging like braids around Ken's face. Torn metal from the cockpit wall had pierced Ken's body, taking his life. His expressionless face rested against the broken window, dried blood completely covering the collar of his shirt, vacant eyes seeing nothing.

His death brought fresh tears, and Beth put her head down against the vinyl ceiling and let them run down her face. For a moment, intense hopelessness engulfed her. How could they survive, alone and injured? What did she know about plane crashes or rescues or the wilderness? Why had God allowed this man to die now, when she needed him so much?

With a pang, she saw the selfish trail of her own thoughts.

Beth reached out and gently closed Ken Bohannan's eyes. "Oh, Lord, I'm so sorry," she whispered.

Allen decided to stay busy while he waited for John Graham to call back. For a few moments, he made a valiant effort to prepare the lesson for his Senior Sentries Sunday school class. He brought out his Bible, laid out his reference book, and began to take notes. After reading the same passage nearly three times without absorbing anything, Allen closed his Bible and gave up. Too distracted to read, he sought other activity.

In the kitchen, Allen made a plate of food for Beth. She would be hungry when she finally got home. He covered her mother's food with plastic wrap and placed it in the fridge. He put leftover salad into a cereal bowl and slid it on top of her dinner plate.

For a few moments, Allen stood staring at the photographs attached by magnets to the refrigerator door. Moving next to the sink, he rolled up the sleeves of his cotton shirt and began washing the pots Harumi had used to make dinner. Remembering Beth's preference for a sparkling kitchen, he scrubbed the sink clean and emptied the strainer.

Still no phone call.

Allen wiped down the kitchen counters, moving canisters and knick-knacks out of the way in his effort to be thorough. In their tiny dining nook, he picked up the placemats and shook them out over the kitchen sink before stuffing them into a drawer. He wiped down the kitchen table and scrubbed Noah's high chair with a vigor he barely recognized. Beth hated it when the high chair felt sticky. Allen knew she'd be happy to see it shining clean.

He took the kitchen rag and dish towels out to the washing machine in the garage, where he discovered a load of towels waiting. Just as Allen started the washer and closed the lid, the ringing of the kitchen phone beckoned him, and he ran back to the kitchen from the garage. "Chengs'," he said breathlessly.

"Allen, this is John," his voice low and ominous.

Allen felt an involuntary tremble run through his body—like electricity. Something had gone wrong. "Have you heard from Sound Flight?"

"The regular pilot just called from the airport. He had to drive back to Thun Field to check on Beth's plane."

"Okay, so what's going on? Where are they?" Allen tried not to sound impatient, but he did not want details; he wanted answers.

He heard John take a deep breath before he spoke. "They aren't back," he began. "The hangar is empty."

Allen fell onto a wooden kitchen chair, leaning both elbows on the table. "What happened?"

"We don't know. That's the next question."

"How do we figure it out?"

"Right now, Sound Flight will call for an investigation. They do that by contacting the Air Force Rescue Coordination Center in Langley, Virginia."

"Virginia?" Allen interrupted. "Why Virginia? This is Washington."

"That's the way they do it. Langley supervises every air search. They call the Department of Transportation here in Washington State—and the DOT decides if there should be a full scale search."

"What do you mean, *if*?" Allen heard fear in his voice and fought to control it. He needed to stay calm. "Of course they should search. When do they start looking for the plane?"

"Sound Flight tells me that the first thing they have to do is establish that the plane is really missing. I mean, it may have landed somewhere else. You know, weather or mechanical trouble or something. Maybe they haven't had time yet to let us know."

"Not very likely."

"True—especially with a rented plane. But it happens. Sometimes people change their plans without letting anyone know. The transportation people have to check first and search later."

"Then what?"

"Then they have to figure out where to start looking. The state is just too big to cover without some idea of where to start."

"How long will all this take?"

"The DOT rep should be calling me any minute now. Once he's certain the plane is really missing, things should kick into gear immediately."

Nine

BETH RESTED AGAIN, her head lying on the cockpit ceiling, trying to control her emotions before beginning the agonizing roll back toward Bill.

"Bill," she said, nudging his shoulder.

"How is Ken?" He breathed the voiceless question.

"He's gone, Bill," Beth whispered.

Again he nodded. He did not seem surprised.

"Can you move? Can I get you out of there?" Beth reached up, searching for his seat belt buckle. It had to be near Bill's lap; but with everything in this upside-down position, she could not find it. Beth began again, tracing the harness webbing up from his shoulder.

"I can't feel my legs," he said. "Numb."

Beth's hand stopped moving, shocked by the horrible realization of his words. It couldn't be possible. "How about your back?"

He answered a different, more pressing question. "I can see them, but I can't feel them. And my back hurts—an ache. I think I've broken my back, Beth."

Beth thought quickly, trying desperately to overcome the panic that rose up in her stomach. *Think! Reason!* She pinched the skin above Bill's knee, hard. "Did you feel that?"

He shook his head. "Nothing."

"How about this?" She grabbed a pinch of flesh up near his ankles. Staring into his eyes, she gave a vicious twist of his flesh. He never even flinched.

His diagnosis seemed accurate. The crash must have severed Bill's spinal cord, leaving him paralyzed. The realization washed over Beth, leaving her trembling with fear. She'd studied human anatomy in college, but she'd never taken a course in first aid. She had nothing to offer her friend—not now, when he needed her most.

"Get me down." Bill's hoarse whisper shook her from her thoughts.

Though Beth knew it was not usually wise to move someone with a spinal injury, she couldn't leave him hanging upside down.

Beth traced the path of the harness again, found the buckle, and using all her strength, managed to unlatch the harness and lower Bill onto the ceiling of the plane. Once he had dropped from his seat belt, he lay helpless, unable to rearrange his own body. Beth managed to turn him onto his stomach and drag and pull his legs out behind him, until his shoulders and head faced the rear of the plane. In spite of useless legs, Bill used his own strong arms to drag his body toward the rear door, bumping his head more than once on the rear seats hanging above him. Beth waited for him to pass, and then crawled behind him. Before he reached the door, he paused, breathing hard. "I can't go any farther."

"It's okay, Bill," Beth said from behind him. "We can rest here for a while."

"No. I can't move another inch," his breathy voice floated back through the plane. The sound of it frightened her.

"What can I do? Do you need something?"

"No." A long silence filled the black interior.

She listened to Bill breathe, worried that at any moment the sound might stop.

"Beth," he said. "Pull off Ken's jacket."

"What?"

"We need to stay warm." Bill spoke in short, tight words. "Do it."

The thought of removing the dead man's coat made Beth shiver. "Okay," she agreed. She began the slow turn toward the front of the plane. With one arm, she managed to unfasten the pilot's safety harness and slip his arms—one at a time—from the webbing. His lap belt held him firmly upside down. Button by button, she opened the front of the denim jacket, lined with plush faux fleece. Then she grabbed the sleeve cuff and tugged until she managed to pull the jacket from one limp arm. The act of removing the jacket felt like a horrible violation to Beth. Though she knew better, it felt as though she left Ken exposed. Unbidden, tears flowed down her cheeks.

"And take his shirt too."

"Bill, I can't do that."

"You have to. You're bleeding. It's all over the ceiling."

Though Bill knew, Beth tried to minimize her injury. "Just a cut on my thigh."

A pitiful cough punctuated what seemed to have begun as a chuckle. She stopped moving as she listened for Bill to catch his breath.

"Get his shirt," he continued. "You can tear it up and use it to stop the bleeding."

"I can't tear up the fabric. I only have one good arm."

"My arms work. I'll tear up the shirt." He sounded irritated, and Beth wished she hadn't refused him. He paused, and she sensed that he needed to gather strength. Again his voice came back to her, still weak. "Don't argue. Get the shirt."

Beth managed to free Ken's other arm from the jacket. She pulled it off over his head and threw it toward Bill. Kicking it with her knee and boot, she inched it back toward him. Then, staring into the pilot's unmoving face and feeling like a vulture, she whispered, "I'm sorry, Ken," as she began unbuttoning his collar.

Beth focused on the small white buttons holding the pale shirt closed. Her cold and frightened fingers fought to undo them. One by one, she managed to open the shirt. Once again she tugged at the sleeve, realizing with frustration that she faced two additional buttons on both cuffs. Sighing, she pulled Ken's wrist toward her and held the fabric with her teeth, his limp hand brushing her cheeks. In this position, she managed the sleeve buttons quickly.

Eventually triumphant, Beth pulled the shirt from the pilot's body. His T-shirt, once white, had dark splotches of partially clotted blood. Beth turned her face away. "I got it!" she said. Bill did not answer.

Surprised, Beth realized that she hadn't heard a single word from Bill throughout the entire procedure. She stuffed the shirt yoke into her mouth and began dragging herself toward the rear door of the plane. "Bill," she called through the fabric. "Bill, you still with me?"

Dropping the shirt, she squeezed through the space under the hanging seats and came up beside her friend, reaching out to touch his back. With a sigh of gratitude, she felt it rise and fall rhythmically. He was breathing. "Bill, you okay?" she whispered.

"Yeah, just tired," he answered. "Get my knife."

"Your knife? Where?" With her feet to the windshield, very little moonlight reached the inner reaches of the fuselage. In the darkness, Beth could not imagine where to look.

"Shirt pocket. Right," he coughed and sputtered. Clearing his throat, he said again, "Right pocket."

In order to reach the pocket, Beth had to slide over Bill's back to the other side of the plane. As she moved over him, embarrassment warmed her face, and she felt grateful for the darkness. Beth dropped off of his back, landing on her right shoulder. A long moan escaped from her throat, and Beth rolled onto her front. She lay still until the throbbing quit, grateful to relieve the aching shoulder.

"You okay?"

"Yeah." She took a deep breath, blinked back tears, and willed the pain to recede. "Just need a minute to regroup." She put her hand on Bill's back, then moved it to his side, feeling for the pocket. She discovered a zipper near the side seam, and after finding the tab, struggled to open the pocket. "Got it," she said triumphantly as she pulled out his key chain.

Like a blind woman, Beth ran her fingers over the heavy ring covered with keys until she felt the familiar shape of a multitool. She scooted forward again, opened the tool, and put the knife in Bill's right hand. "Here you go."

"Give me the shirt," he answered, his voice breathless. He grunted as he pushed himself up onto his elbows. She handed him the fabric and listened as he tore the fabric into strips. "They're too short to go around. Tie several together. Then make X shapes over your thigh, and tie the cut closed."

One by one, Bill handed the strips to her, and Beth used her teeth and her good hand to make knots. When she had tied together four lengths of fabric, she brought her knee up and began the arduous task of wrapping her thigh, starting at the knee and working toward her hip. The work took all her concentration and sapped energy like running a marathon. In spite of the chilled air, Beth felt herself sweating and then recognized the first wave of hunger as it twisted her stomach.

Beth did not understand why she had so much trouble finishing this small task. It had taken so much time, and she felt drained. At last she made a small knot by tying the fabric to itself. She collapsed beside Bill. "Done."

He did not respond.

"Bill?" Her voice betrayed fear.

"Just tired," he answered. A long pause. "So sleepy."

Cool mountain air continued to seep into the back of the plane, both via the hole in the cockpit and the partially open rear door. As moments passed, Beth grew cold, the perspiration on her skin cooling quickly. She needed to close that door.

Beth crawled over Bill one more time, though this time more slowly than the last, and scooted past the rear door, pushing her feet out the opening. As she exited the plane, she rolled and dropped onto her seat in the damp grass. She took a moment to rest, leaning against the fuselage.

Beth closed her eyelids and prayed for help. It didn't take a rocket scientist to figure out that they were in big trouble.

After a few moments, she grabbed the door and struggled to pull it toward the plane. As her one strong arm fought with the damaged hinge, the door began to swing reluctantly closed. Now certain that she could close it from inside, Beth rolled over and crawled back into the plane, pulling her way into the blackness with her good hand.

At that moment Beth remembered the down coat she had brought from the back of her car. Could she find it in the dark? She crawled toward the back of the plane, scooting along on her back, feeling in the dark for the coat. After several passes she felt the nylon fabric caught behind the rear seat.

She gave a yank, and as the coat came free, Beth let out a triumphant whoop. She slid back over the ceiling toward her friend. Again she touched his back, anxious to feel the reassuring rise and fall.

She reached over his body, feeling for the heavy jacket she had taken from the pilot. Grabbing it, she pulled it over Bill, tucking it between his body and the plane. Then, rolling slightly, she cuddled into Allen's coat. Using her feet, she scooted as close to Bill as she could.

Already cold, Beth knew that the mountain night would bring even lower temperatures. If they were to survive, she and Bill needed to pool their heat. As her body warmed, she relaxed, and exhaustion quickly overtook her. Beth wanted nothing more than sleep.

She snuggled down, pressing her back into Bill's arm, and allowed the sweet darkness of sleep to overtake her.

Ten

ALLEN SURVIVED A LONG LONELY NIGHT using the only tools he trusted. Opening his Bible, he read his favorite promises of protection over and over again. Though he tried to cling to them, on this night they felt frighteningly empty. He paced, read, and watched the minute hand creep around the face of the living room clock. Between fleeting moments of sleep, he spent long periods in intense, pleading prayer.

Allen stood peering out the window of the kitchen door, dressed in Dockers and a sweater, a mug of coffee in his hand. "Lord, you know where Beth is right now," he whispered into the pre-dawn dark. "Keep her."

So far his phone had not rung. For this Allen felt grateful. In his anguish, he did not want to have to handle people—even the people he loved.

Allen decided that he would call his parents, who lived in California, at seven. They would never forgive him if he didn't keep them informed. After that, he would let Beth's parents in on the terrible news. Sipping coffee, Allen prayed for Harumi. How could he tell her that Beth's plane was missing? How could he add even one ounce of grief to her already overloaded heart?

Though Beth's older sister died long before Allen and Beth married, Harumi still grieved. Now that Allen had children of his own, he understood. Though a parent might come to accept the loss of a child, Allen believed that a remnant of pain must remain forever. Sometimes, when Allen watched Harumi, he saw the pain flit across his mother-in-law's expression. He'd seen it the first time Harumi held Rebekka, and once again when they'd all posed for an extended-family portrait. He'd caught Harumi dabbing secretively at tears and guessed what she had been feeling. *It wasn't the whole family. . . .*

Allen knew Harumi would want to help him in this crisis. She would want to care for her grandchildren. He wanted to believe it would be good for her to stay with the kids, to be able to do something helpful. Still, his stomach churned with anguish. How he wished he could spare her from more grief.

Allen also knew that his father-in-law, Richard Harding, would want to go with him to Thun Field. Not a bad idea, considering the shape of Allen's mind this morning. He should not try to drive. With no sleep, he'd barely managed the coffee maker. Allen realized he was in no condition for commuter traffic.

With any luck at all, Allen and Richard would be able to arrive at Thun Field about the same time the search and rescue operation began. Allen needed to be there—to watch and wait—to be the first to hear any word about Beth.

Though he would never admit it, Allen also hoped to be out of the house before too many of their small congregation heard the news. He shook his head and took a sip of coffee, slipping one hand into his pants pocket. Though he loved his parishioners, he didn't want to be with them now. *They'll descend like vultures,* he thought. No—like hens, bringing food for his body and advice for his soul.

Something inside Allen felt their unwritten expectations for his behavior. Now, in his overwhelming concern for Beth, Allen didn't want to have to perform, didn't want to have to care for other people in the midst of his own personal trauma.

Beth's parents would have no expectations. They'd known Allen since his college days, when he'd first started to date their daughter. Over the years, they had always allowed Allen to be himself, to say what he needed to say, even to cry when his emotions overcame him.

Privacy. Yes, that was it. *Terror is a private emotion,* Allen thought. *I'd like to be terrified alone—not on a stage in front of all those people.* He shivered, though he was not chilled, thinking about what this day might bring. At a time like this, the freedom to honestly express his emotions seemed like a precious gift.

Allen drained the last of his coffee and set the mug in the sink. Then, with resignation, he checked the clock and picked up the telephone.

―――――――

When the light of dawn woke Doyle, his hip hurt, like a giant toothache starting near his lower back and continuing all the way into his groin. He rolled onto his back, trying to ease the pain. *Ah, better.* As usual, his injured knee refused to flex. Patiently he lay on the hard ground, alternately stretching and flexing the stiff joint, sliding his heel along the ground as he did. After gaining more motion with every attempt, Doyle rolled over to stand.

The night had been colder than he'd expected. In the still air, his breath came in puffs of condensation, forming small clouds around his head. Bending, Doyle snatched his blanket from the ground and wrapped it around his shoulders, holding it securely with one hand.

Doyle found the water in his canteens partially frozen. He shook one container vigorously, hoping to loosen the ice enough to drink. Greedily, he pulled frigid liquid into his mouth before offering some to the dog.

Sitting on a rocky outcropping, Doyle ate his breakfast of salmon jerky and a biscuit as he watched the sun rise through heavy morning fog. Tufts of low-lying clouds clung tenaciously to the furrows in the hills around him. Soon, facing due south, Doyle saw the summit of Mount Rainier reflect a brilliant yellow white as the rising sun ricocheted off the glaciers. Doyle turned away from the blinding light.

As the sun climbed into the morning sky, the mist hung on around him. The temperature rose as well—but not enough to ease the unrelenting ache in his hip and knee. Doyle drank the contents of one canteen before breaking camp. He smoothed the ground with a leafy branch and hid the logs from his fire. By the time he set off up the trail, the ground held no trace of his stay there. No one covered his tracks more effectively than Dennis Doyle. As he moved away from camp, Gilligan trotted behind without question.

Doyle's territory included subalpine meadows, some old growth forest, and large areas of clear-cut and replanted land. Ever worried about the possibility of intruders stumbling onto his cabin, it was

Doyle's habit to keep careful watch over his land. He wanted more than anything to be left alone, to live unnoticed and undisturbed in the hills around Mount Rainier.

Staying at the five-thousand-foot level, Doyle frequently surveyed his own perimeter, keeping careful watch for intruders approaching from the lower hills. As he walked he kept his gaze sharp, his ears tuned, watching for any sign of disturbance in the foliage and for obvious footprints.

Doyle had ways of watching for strangers. In the mountains, only geography determined access to the land at higher elevations. Few hunters climbed the bare face of rocky cliffs. Instead, they came up through the natural draws, unconstrained pathways leading from the riverbed below to subalpine meadows. These pathways were also often chosen by larger animals—deer, elk, and occasionally, bear.

One of the ways Doyle watched for intruders and gauged the level of activity along his perimeter involved nothing more complicated than string. Along these trails or openings, Doyle had strung lengths of string to a signal object low and out of sight. If the signal object had moved or changed position, Doyle knew with certainty that someone or something had crossed the line.

His favorite device—though he had other, more dangerous ones—was a simple tin can. When connected at its mouth to a trip string and hidden in a nearby bush, the can simply turned over. Normally, this happened without the invader ever realizing his mistake. Then, when Doyle discovered his can had been tipped, he examined the ground for tracks or animal droppings. Doyle knew every animal that lived in the mountains. He could track a subject for miles, even days, if safety or privacy required it. From the string and the signals left at the perimeter invasion, Doyle knew exactly what species he hunted.

About a half mile from camp, Doyle planned to check the third of his boundary traps. He'd found the other two undisturbed—exactly as he had left them. The next one would be the last signal on this side of his perimeter check. If this one remained untouched, Doyle would change direction and head west through the deepest part of his forest kingdom.

By the time Doyle reached his next trip wire, he had grown thirsty and tired. Unwilling to rest before checking security, he carefully explored his trap. No sign of anyone having come this way. Doyle took out his binoculars and scanned the valley below. Nothing. A long sigh escaped his chest. No one.

Alone. This knowledge brought Doyle a measure of relief. But the relief did not last. Moments later, quietly and softly, the familiar heaviness settled back into his soul like ash from a forest fire.

———————

Beth's father took the news of the missing plane with stoic strength, promising Allen that he would drive him to Thun Field as soon as he could get dressed and out the door. "We really don't know anything yet, Allen," he said with confidence. "Don't go working yourself up over this."

"What about Harumi?" Allen asked. "What will you tell her?"

"I'll tell her what we know—which really isn't much. She's a strong woman, Allen," Richard Harding said. "Her faith is unshakable. She'll get through this no matter what happens."

As the shuffle of slippered feet came into the kitchen, Allen turned to see who had gotten up. "Okay, then," he spoke into the telephone with false cheerfulness. "We'll see you when you get here."

Bekka wrapped her arms around her daddy's waist and greeted him with a sleepy hug. "Morning, Dad," she said. "Where's Mom? I need my Brownie shirt ironed."

Allen stooped to return the embrace. "Good morning, sweetie," he said. "Let's sit down at the breakfast table. I want to talk a minute." He took her hand and led her over to the nook. Bekka sat in her usual place, both elbows on the Formica surface, her face resting on one fisted hand.

"Dad, I'm hungry. Can I have some cereal?"

"In a minute, honey." Allen settled himself into the chair at the end of the table and glanced out the window at the growing dawn. Taking a deep breath, he plunged forward. "Bekka, your mom didn't come home last night," he said. "We don't know where she is right now." He put both palms down on the table. Spreading his fingers apart and then drawing them together, he noticed sweaty prints from where his fingers touched the table. He glanced at Bekka's round face and deep brown eyes. Her expression remained calm, unchanged.

Allen chose his words carefully. "We don't think Mommy's plane landed at the airport. But we don't know where it is yet."

"You mean she crashed?" Her eyebrows rose with the question.

He blinked and took a long breath. In her usual childlike way, Bekka had uttered the unspeakable, and Allen fought the emotions rising inside his chest. "We don't know what happened, exactly. But we're going to find out. Grams is going to come stay with you again today while Grandpa and I go to the airport to help them search for Mommy's plane."

Bekka seemed to consider this explanation for a moment. "Can we have lasagna tonight?" she asked. "I really don't like Grams's cooking."

At seven forty-five Beth's father merged his little white Toyota onto the Valley Freeway. From the passenger seat, Allen stared out the window, seeing but not recognizing the sprawling commercial growth on the north end of the Kent Valley. As warehouse after warehouse flashed by the window, Allen saw only Beth. In his memory, he replayed his last moments with her, envisioning her face and the sparkle in her dark eyes when she laughed. He thought of the good-bye kiss he'd given her, hurried and careless, as he darted out the front door on the way to his office. Would those minutes be his last memory of her?

A fresh stab of sorrow hit him as he thought of their last conversation together over breakfast. He'd told her he didn't like her working. Though Beth had made huge sacrifices so that he could take the pastorate at this dying church, Allen had been unkind enough to sound ungrateful. Guilt threatened to engulf him. He hadn't even told her he loved her yesterday.

He could not imagine life without her.

"Should be there in a half hour," Richard said, glancing at his watch.

Allen looked out the window, scanning the mostly clear sky. "Weather looks good," he said with a dull voice.

"Um-hmm," Richard agreed as he observed the sky through the front windshield. He reached for the car radio and pushed the button for a smooth jazz station. Lowering the volume, he continued, "They'll find her, Allen. I know they will."

Allen heard the husky tone in his father-in-law's voice. He recognized the tears couched inside. "I hope so."

The parking lot at Thun Field had nearly filled with cars by the time they arrived. Allen noticed clusters of men and women dressed in the soft gray-green of Air Force uniforms. Most wore one-piece flight suits with a United States flag on one shoulder and a Civil Air Patrol patch on their chest. Some had shiny green jackets over their uniforms. Others wore bomber-style jackets of worn dark leather. Even before Allen opened the car door, seeing these men and women gathering to help sent a wave of gratitude through him. He unfastened his seat belt and took a deep breath.

Richard came around the car, opening the door for him. "Let's go find the DOT guy. What did you say his name was?"

"Armstrong." As Allen got out of the car, he spotted their Outback parked near the restaurant entrance. The sight of it hit him hard, and he had to blink to avoid tears. "The car," he said, pointing. "Let's go check the car."

They approached the car from the driver's side. Allen cupped his hands against the window and gazed inside. On the right front passenger seat, he spotted her cell phone. "Well, that's why she isn't answering the phone," he said, pointing inside. "The phone is still in the car."

"Can you tell what she took with her?" Richard asked.

Allen walked slowly around the car, trying to gaze inside. "Her work crate is gone," he said. "And she dug through the back—looking for something, I guess. The emergency box is open." He paused at the cargo door and looked in. "I don't know what she would have taken."

"Let's go through the car."

Allen looked up and sighed. "I didn't think to bring the keys."

They started toward the main office door just as a light wind sent alder leaves skittering across the parking lot in front of them. Allen noticed the bite in the morning air. Though he had not noticed it at home, there was frost on the ground here. For a moment, Allen allowed himself to wonder how cold it might be up on the mountain.

Eleven

JUST INSIDE THE DOOR of the Thun Field office, a plump auburn-haired receptionist met Allen and Richard with a sympathetic smile. "You must be family," she said, introducing herself. "I'm Diane Mills, the receptionist here."

Shaking hands, Allen introduced himself. "And this is Beth's father, Richard Harding."

"Coffee?" she asked. "I just made a fresh pot."

Allen waved off the suggestion. "I don't think I should drink any more," he said.

She poured a steaming cup of the brew for Richard. "Do you take anything with that?" She pointed at the cup.

"Just black," Richard answered.

"I've known Beth for a long time," she said with genuine concern. "Davis and Graham have flown out of Thun Field for years." She shook her head. "As many searches as we organize out of here, I never thought we'd be looking for her plane."

Allen nodded and glanced away, his hands on his hips. In the face of this stranger's sympathy, Allen's tears felt too near the surface to speak.

Richard touched his son-in-law's shoulder gently. "We're supposed to meet Harold Armstrong here," he said to Diane. "Can you tell us where to find him?"

"Oh yes. I'm sorry. The search operates out of our training hangar." She turned abruptly and started down a long hall lined on both sides by office doors. "I'll walk you out," she said over her shoulder. They followed her to a rear exit, where she paused to snatch a parka from a hook. Sliding her arm inside, she said, "As you'll see, this operation takes up a lot of space. The pilots need facilities and food. The planes need fuel and communications capabilities. At Thun, we have only one building that will hold that much activity."

Zipping her jacket closed, she led them out the door. Not twenty feet away stood another large building, with a metal roof, concrete block walls, and four metal garage doors. *This must be the training hangar,* Allen thought.

Inside, they found a flurry of activity. One group of men moved folding tables across a nearly empty room. In a separate corner, another group unstacked chairs and placed them along the wall. A petite woman, wearing a down parka and wool cap, set up an easel and dropped a large whiteboard onto it. Unfazed by the noise around her, she began writing across the top of the board. In the farthest corner of the building, a group of teenagers in camouflage uniforms sat on the cold concrete floor listening to instructions being delivered by an instructor of some type.

Along a separate wall, Allen noticed a folding table covered with pink bakery boxes. A commercial-size stainless steel coffee urn chugged away, and the aroma of percolating coffee filled the cold air. Diane led Allen and Richard through the busy crowd, stopping at the double table nearest the windows. "Harry," she called, waving one arm. The noisy screech of chairs against the floor nearly covered her voice.

An older man with a perfectly trimmed white beard turned to smile at her. He held out his hand, first to Richard and then to Allen. "I'm Harold Armstrong, air search and rescue coordinator," he said. "Folks here call me Harry. I know this is rough for you both. I'll try to make it as easy as I can. I'm glad you could come in."

With introductions complete, Diane excused herself. "I'll be keeping my fingers crossed," she said to Allen. "If you need anything, I'll be at my desk."

"Let me show you around," Harry said, turning toward the other team members. As he moved, Harry tapped his co-workers, drawing their attention to Allen and Richard. One by one, he introduced some of his team members and explained their functions.

"This is Cliff Simpson," he said, stopping at the middle of the longest folding table. "Cliff will be the mission coordinator for this search. We call him 'the big MC,' " Harry said, laughing. Allen plastered a weak smile on his face as he reached out to shake hands. These people would provide his only link to Beth. He wanted to be gracious.

They moved on. "This is Evelyn," he said, gesturing to the woman at the whiteboard. "She manages the sortie board for us. With that board, we can tell at any moment who is where, how many planes are up, and when they're due back."

Of another crewman Harry explained, "He'll sit at the COM phone." Pointing at a bulky portable telephone sitting at one end of the table, Harry continued, "We keep a truck outside. From inside the truck, they monitor radio communications with our High Bird. Then, as the COM truck hears information, he relays it to the operations desk inside via this phone." He patted the phone as one would an obedient dog.

Richard stopped moving. "The COM truck?"

"The communications truck. You can see it right outside the hangar door." Harry pointed out the window. The three men stepped over to the window and looked outside. On the other side of the glass, they saw an extended cab pickup truck parked very close to the building. Several antennae sprouted from the side of the truck, one of which Allen guessed to be nearly twenty feet high. Inside the cab, Allen saw an older man sitting behind the steering wheel and a teenage boy in the passenger seat beside him.

"Amazing," Richard said, shaking his head.

"Yes, but have you found anything yet?" Allen asked, turning back to Harry.

Harry smiled. "So far, we don't have any planes in the air."

"Why not?"

"First, we'll fly a route search. We try to trace the exact path of the plane."

"But as I understand it, they didn't take a set path," Richard said.

"True, and that makes this search more difficult." Harry crossed his arms across his chest and stroked his beard between his thumb and index finger. "Still, not impossible. We've been in touch with Davis and Graham, and we're recreating the itinerary they had.

For instance, they were supposed to meet a Forest Service ranger and deliver supplies to the station at Rocky Creek. We have to figure out if their plane ever landed there. Once we have those details, we'll be able to plan the search logistics."

As he spoke, Allen felt a fog of hopelessness close in around him. Beth was out on that mountain somewhere, and these people hadn't even put a plane in the air yet. *How can they find her by talking about it?* he wondered.

Harry droned on, "...We'll establish the grids we need to search. We'll brief our crews and send them up to listen for the ELT."

"ELT?" Allen asked.

"An emergency location transmitter."

As Harry explained, Allen realized for the first time what a long and painful wait lay ahead of him. These men and their strange world of acronyms and carefully scripted searches made him feel completely lost. Allen wanted only one thing—to find Beth. This search bureaucracy would try anyone's patience. Allen took a deep breath and closed his eyes. "Help me, Lord," he prayed, feeling his frustration bubble over, "because I can't wait through all of this. I'm gonna lose my temper with someone."

The whining dog caught Doyle's attention, and he stopped walking. Panting and sweating, he searched for the dog. Had Gilligan spotted something? Could this whine be a warning?

More than once, Gilligan had caught the scent of an oncoming black bear. Because of those experiences, Doyle had learned to listen closely to his canine companion. Only last summer, the dog's warning had given Doyle time to avoid getting caught between a mother bear and her two meandering cubs, all heading out for a swim in a high meadow lake.

Spotting Gilligan just ahead of him, Doyle crept off the trail into nearby brush and waited. Drawing the handgun he kept in the small of his back, he watched the dog. Gilligan did not continue on up the trail. Nor did he run off after some elusive game. Instead, the dog kept his attention completely focused in the direction of the upper meadow. Taking one or two steps forward, Gilligan stopped and glanced back toward his master. Cocking his head, ears up, nose in the air, Gilligan sat whining softly, as though trying to catch the scent of something he could not fully comprehend.

Though Doyle did not understand the dog's actions, he did not discount them. Still, he would not allow a spooked dog to keep him from making his rendezvous with the meadow. After several minutes of waiting, Doyle heard nothing, caught no sign of anything out of place. He decided to move on.

Tucking the gun into place, he shifted his pack higher onto his shoulders. He took a moment to adjust one of the straps, making certain he had the weight balanced evenly, and moved back onto the trail.

Doyle looked forward to his rest in the clearing. He had always liked the peculiar look of the small stunted trees surrounding the thickly grown meadow. He liked the view of the summit from there and the wild lupine that proliferated there in the summer. Doyle knew this might be his last chance to visit the meadow before winter snow covered it completely. Judging by last night's temperature, winter was only a breath away.

In order to avoid a steep ascent on loose rock, Doyle chose to access the meadow by a more solid and gradual ledge coming around from the north and east. He moved slowly now, exhausted by his long walk and the constant pain in his knee. His chest ached too, but he excused it, knowing that age and high elevation had begun to have an effect on his lungs. At the top of the rim, Doyle sat again, waiting for the pain below his collarbone to subside. Long minutes later, he began winding his way through the trees encircling the meadow.

Suddenly Gilligan growled.

Doyle stopped walking and moved behind a tree. Quietly, gesturing with one hand, he called the dog. "Psst!" Gilligan trotted up beside him and sat. Doyle covered his lips with the index finger of one hand. "Quiet, ya miserable mutt," he whispered. The dog cocked his head at Doyle and then, without changing position, turned his head back to the clearing and softly whined again.

The meadow. The dog had spotted something in the meadow. Over the years, Doyle had never observed fear in his dog. Greeting both cougars and horses with the same carefree attention, Gilligan seemed to believe in the benevolence of every creature. So why this

response? Doyle waited, still and silent, absolutely certain that the
dog knew something he did not.

———————

In the hangar at Thun Field, Harry's continuing explanation
interrupted Allen's frustrated prayer. "The FAA requires every airplane to have an emergency transmitter. It begins sending an emergency signal on impact. That's how we'll find your daughter."

Allen saw Richard wince.

Harry gave Richard an understanding smile. "Unfortunately,
the ELT sends a signal only when something goes wrong." Harry
paused, striking a thoughtful posture. He stood casually, his hands
behind his back, feet spread apart. "When things go well, we pick
up the signal right away," Harry continued. "The higher we fly, the
easier the signal is to hear."

"So you should locate the plane immediately?" Richard asked.

"We hope so."

Allen waited for an explanation, but Harry offered none.

"Now, if you'll come with me, I'd like you to meet Paula Douglas. She's our public information officer, and it's her job to take
care of you during our search operation."

Harry guided them across the room to where a group of men
stood chatting. In the middle of the group, a medium-framed
woman dressed in camouflage fatigues laughed. "Paula," Harry
said, "I'd like to introduce you to some of the family who'll be with
us." Allen watched the group take on a somber, serious air.

As he shook her hand, Allen made a quick assessment of the
woman who would help him through this nightmare. Her dark hair
rolled up behind her head, along with a touch of makeup added a
soft femininity to her military clothes and combat boots. High
cheekbones and almost black eyes suggested a Hispanic heritage.

"I'm so glad to meet you," she began. "Tell me about your relationship with the people on the missing airplane." Her tone suggested they were speaking about a mutual friend.

Allen told Paula about Beth's job with Davis and Graham. The
woman listened attentively, nodding as he spoke.

"During the search, it will be my job to keep you informed,"
she said. "Once any new information is confirmed, I'll relay it to
you and to the press."

Harry Armstrong excused himself gently. "I have a search to oversee," he said, backing away. "I'll certainly let you know anything as soon as I can."

Allen nodded and turned his attention back to Paula. "The press?" he asked, surprised. Allen hadn't anticipated that the press would care about Beth's plane. The presence of reporters seemed cold and frightening. Like vultures hovering over roadkill.

"Oh yes. We keep the press informed because frequently someone in their audience has seen our plane. After hearing a news story, the public realizes how important the sighting is, and they call in. More than once, a news report has led us directly to a missing airplane."

Allen nodded, feeling a lump form in his stomach. Though his mind knew that Beth's plane was missing, his heart sank with every mention of the words these people used so freely. ELT. Impact. Missing planes. He wished he could be somewhere—anywhere— else. His fear was much more intense than the anxiety he'd felt during the birth of their first child.

"As the search progresses, I'll let you know anything I can, as soon as I have confirmed information," she continued. "I wouldn't want you to get your hopes up and then be disappointed."

Richard joined in. "How many of these searches have you helped with?"

"This will be my fifth. Luckily, we don't lose many airplanes in Washington."

"Tell me honestly," Richard continued. "How many crashes have survivors?"

Paula nodded, anticipating his concerns. "Why don't we sit down," she suggested, glancing toward the doughnut tables. Choosing chairs near the coffeepot, they sat and she began again. "Yours is a good question," she answered, getting straight to the point. "I mean about survivors. But by itself, the answer would be misleading. You see, even if no one had ever survived a plane crash before, we'd want to believe that Beth made it through whatever happened to the plane." Lightly, she touched his wrist. "We search for every plane as if everyone on board is alive and waiting for us to come pick them up."

Without answering Richard's question directly, she had managed to give Allen the information he least wanted to hear. "When will they go up?" he asked, using his thumb to gesture toward the pilots clumped together near the operations desk.

"We have seven Civil Air Patrol planes here already. The Washington Air Search and Rescue group has five more. That's a good start."

"Wait," Allen said. "Two different groups?"

She smiled. "I guess it does seem a little confusing. Actually, every pilot here is a volunteer. They've all completed training to search for downed planes." She pointed to one man in a green flight suit. "He flies with the Civil Air Patrol. Around here they're called CAP flights. Their organization is affiliated with the U.S. Air Force." She dropped her index finger and scanned the room. "That woman there," she pointed to a tall blonde wearing a Nike running jacket, "flies with Washington Air Search and Rescue. We call it WASAR. Both groups work together under one search director. It's an amazing system once you understand it."

"But when will all those amazing people start looking for Beth?"

She ignored the sarcasm in Allen's voice. "As soon as our logistics officer has a plan, they'll start with a missions briefing. Then we'll fly the route search. Would you like me to let you know when the route search begins?"

Unable to speak, Allen nodded.

Twelve

WHEN THE FIRST RAYS of daylight glowed pink above the tree line, Beth sent her gratitude to heaven. Her tongue stuck to the roof of her mouth, resulting in an irresistible yearning for a tall glass of ice-cold water. She had not had anything to eat or drink since the crash. Trying to ignore her thirst, Beth reached over to touch Bill's back and was reassured by the regular rise and fall of his breath. He'd made it through the night.

The riveting, unrelenting torment of pain coming from her right side had managed to drag her from slumber over and over again throughout the night. She was chilled and exhausted, her left side aching from long hours of lying on it. Through the seemingly endless night, both discomfort and cold had interrupted what little sleep Beth had managed to get. She had gotten up once and made her way outside the plane. After a good deal of time and energy spent struggling with her zipper and her jeans, she felt somewhat more comfortable. *It will warm up now,* she thought, snuggling closer to Bill's side.

Beth's degree in biology had required classes in both anatomy and physiology. She understood the skeletal structure of the animals she studied and had even treated injured animals in her job with the Forest Service. Beth had already diagnosed her injuries. Her aching chest and difficulty breathing indicated broken ribs. Lying next to Bill in the morning light, she imagined her own X rays—showing tiny black spaces marking the separation of bones in her chest.

Even her family doctor would prescribe nothing more than pain meds and rest for these fractures. It was her right arm that caused the greatest concern. That pain had not relented through the night. Instead, it seemed to have grown steadily worse, until now it loomed like a fiery monster inside her skin. From below her right ear all the way to her fingertips, it felt like burning liquid pulsed through her veins.

In spite of the pain, Beth tried again to open the fingers of her right hand. They refused to move. She suspected either a fracture near her right elbow or a dislocation of the elbow. Perhaps both.

As the inside of the airplane grew lighter, Beth rolled onto her back. Slowly, with great agony, she used her strong hand to draw her right arm closer to her face. The excruciating motion made her eyes fill with tears, and she moaned with pain. Blinking hard, she tried to focus so that she could examine her hand more carefully. What she saw frightened her even more.

Swollen beyond recognition, her fingers now resembled link sausages bent into a useless claw and frozen in place. The wrinkles of skin around her knuckles had completely disappeared, filled with an edema so severe that her skin resembled the surface of an over-sized water balloon—tight and transparent.

No wonder they no longer flexed.

During the night, her entire hand had changed color. And more than the swelling, the color confirmed the damage she already suspected. Beth's hand had turned a frighteningly dark black; the bruising extended from the tips of her fingers to the place where her arm disappeared inside her sleeve. How much more bruising lay beneath her wool sweater, she didn't want to know.

Beth began to worry. She could not risk losing her right hand, her dominant hand. What if help didn't come soon? What about nerve damage? How long could the fracture go without being set? "Lord, I need help," Beth whispered. Using her left hand, she tried to straighten the injured fingers. Unable to ignore the pain, she cried out in agony. Her fingers remained stiff and motionless. She felt her worry grow into horror.

She turned her face toward Bill. "Bill," she whispered urgently. "Bill! You awake?"

She watched him turn his head, moving slowly, his forehead

always in contact with the plane's ceiling. As he opened his eyes, she noticed that his eyebrows furrowed in pain. "I have to move, Beth," he said. "Something screaming in my gut. I have to move."

"But should you? What about your back?"

"Please. Help me roll over."

"All right," she gave in. "I'll help." She took a deep breath, wondering how to begin. Instantly she regretted it. Her chest objected loudly, and Beth held perfectly still, waiting for the pounding to stop.

In the narrow space between the ceiling and the seats, Beth had only one way to help Bill. Once more, she began to crawl over his back, reaching for his right arm and shoulder. As she did, he moaned and she apologized. Only when she reached his shoulder did she realize that she could not turn him over using her right hand. She tried to tuck his elbow into her left hand and pulled hard. Though they both groaned with the effort, Bill remained on his stomach.

"Here. Let me try again," Beth said. She crawled toward the back of the plane, kicked the side door open, and dropped outside. Taking a moment to rest, she swiveled around to face the front of the plane. In this position, her uninjured side faced Bill. "Okay," she said, pulling herself over him. "Here we go," she said. Once again, she tucked her arm through his elbow. "Bill, I'm telling you, you'd better really like it on your back," she joked. "This isn't something we can do very often."

With her heaving and Bill pushing, they managed to turn his trunk over, though his feet did not follow. Too late, Beth realized that it would have been better to start the turn by leading with his ankles. "My legs," he said, his voice hoarse.

She shimmied herself back toward his ankles and pulled his right foot off of his left. Once again, she scooted back toward his head and dropped down beside him. The effort left her panting with exhaustion, her arm and hand throbbing.

As the morning sun shone brighter through the trees around the plane, Beth took a moment to rest. When she looked again at Bill, relief filled his features, though beads of sweat covered his face and rolled down into his hair. "Thank you," he said. "I couldn't breathe the other way."

She used the collar of the pilot's jacket to wipe his face. "Rough night?"

"Just long," he answered, a weak smile tipping up the corners of his mouth.

"What now, Bill?" she asked, trying hard not to let him know how frightened she felt. "What do we do now?"

"We wait."

"When will they find us?"

"Sooner or later."

An image of the plane resting in a snow-covered field came unbidden to her mind. Would she still be here in this plane, waiting for rescue, when winter came to the mountain? She fought a sudden wave of terror, swallowing it down inside her. "What do we do until then? There must be something we can do."

"A fire," he said. "That'd help."

Beth nodded. "I can try." The thought of a warm fire seemed inviting, reassuring. "Do we have matches?"

"Safety kit. Back of the plane."

She didn't like the sound of Bill's tight voice, his clipped words. She didn't like his shallow breathing. The sound of it worried her. She did not want to think that Bill might be in more pain, more trouble, than any human—even a strong one—could survive.

Beth needed Bill to make it. The thought of losing him and being left alone had begun to play along the edges of her thoughts, like a wolf trotting along the edges of a campfire in an old Jack London novel. "Okay. Anything else?"

"Water," he said. "Find water."

Even the word sounded wonderful. Water. Beth leaned over Bill's pale face and smiled. "I'll get you some as soon as I find it."

"The pilot," he said, "the pilot carried a water bottle." His face grimaced in a sudden wave of pain. When it passed, Bill smiled weakly. "And he smoked. Find some matches."

————————

An hour later, two planes left Thun Field to begin the search of what Davis and Graham and Sound Flight believed to be the route of the downed airplane. By then the rescue command center had settled into what Allen assumed to be purposeful chaos. He noticed that the whiteboard, carefully guarded by the down-jacket-clad woman, now had two lines of information. He assumed these represented the two search planes now in the air, though he felt frustrated by the long line of abbreviations across the top, which he could not understand.

Richard sat beside Allen with his eyes closed, both hands resting quietly in his lap. He seemed to be praying. When Allen could wait no longer, he asked quietly, "Dad, do you know what those letters mean?" He pointed to the whiteboard.

"I think so," Richard answered, nodding. "The first stands for sortie number. The next column seems to be the plane identification number. Then the next couple of numbers represent times. The woman is recording the actual takeoff and landing time and the ETA—the estimated time of arrival."

"What is a sortie?" Allen tapped his foot on the floor as he spoke.

"Usually it means a mission number. It represents everything about the plane—where it's going, its assignment, everything. It represents the whole job that individual plane must complete."

Allen had been thrown into an organization unlike anything he'd ever experienced. How he wished he were not experiencing it now. By this time, Allen could sit no longer. He'd already given in to another cup of coffee, and the jitters had taken over. Since they'd arrived, he'd found the bathroom, called home, and paced the perimeter of the operations area twice.

He found himself staring at every small group of activity, as if by osmosis he could determine the job assigned to every person in the room. He wanted to ask, to understand, but he knew that he could not—should not—get in their way. His eyes kept returning to the large black-and-white clock over the operations desk. The second hand crawled around the face in what seemed to be extraordinarily slow motion. Though he knew the search had only just begun, Allen was already having trouble waiting.

"Dad, can I borrow your cell phone?" Allen asked. "I promised my folks I'd call as soon as the search got underway."

Richard smiled. "I understand." He pulled the telephone from his jacket pocket and handed it to Allen.

Thirty minutes later, a loud, jangling ring echoed rudely against the empty walls of the metal building, startling both Allen and Richard. Allen found his attention riveted to the phone at the end of the operations desk. He watched as the man at the end of the table answered, took notes, and replaced the receiver. Quietly the officer passed the message on to the two men sitting beside him. Allen watched their expressions carefully, anxious for some indication of the content. From all he observed, someone had just phoned in the half-time score of a Husky football game.

Allen wanted to run over to the operations table. He wanted to scream, "What do you know? What did they say?" Instead, he sat perfectly still and scanned the room, looking for Paula Douglas. She would tell him what had happened.

He spotted her sitting with a group of Civil Air Patrol crewmen, playing cribbage. Dropping her hand, she laughed and pegged herself around the board. She had not even noticed the ringing phone.

————

With Bill's instructions firmly set in her mind, Beth decided to recover anything she could from inside the plane. From the one survival seminar she'd attended in college, Beth remembered one cardinal rule, "Know your assets."

She began by crawling into the space between the two rear seats. With daylight beginning to filter into the plane's interior, Beth could clearly see the objects tossed wildly about the fuselage. Much of the debris had ended up thrown onto the downhill side of the ceiling.

She found her binoculars under the papers recording the results of her mountain goat survey. These she dropped into her work crate. As she did so, she spotted her purse lying in the bottom of the crate. Suddenly hungry, she rifled through the black leather, hoping to find some candy. Eagerly, she went through the contents—her driver's license, a checkbook, some credit cards, a picture or two. Then, with a delighted giggle, she spotted a tin of breath mints hiding below her wallet. She snatched them up, holding them at eye level for a long moment. She felt her mouth water. At least mints contained sugar, she reasoned.

No. She would save these for later. Beth would not eat anything before she absolutely had to. She tucked them into the pocket of her jeans.

Beth crawled forward, toward the pilot's seat. If Ken Bohannan kept a water bottle in the cockpit, then it, too, would have been tossed around during the crash. She decided to look first near the pilot's seat.

Deliberately, Beth diverted her eyes from Ken's face as she plucked her way through the rubble around the cockpit. Cold air, seeping in through the broken walls, chilled her as she searched. All of Bill's papers and camera equipment had flown unchecked through the area, landing against the rumpled fuselage near the pilot's head.

Beth sorted through the debris, careful to keep anything that might eventually be of use. She found Bill's digital camera and slipped it into her crate. Then she spotted his binoculars and added them to her stockpile. Carefully avoiding the sharp edges of debris, Beth reached out to lift another group of papers from the ceiling. Though she did not expect to find anything of value, she refused to leave their reports behind. Underneath, her fingers discovered a neatly folded pack of heavy paper. She pulled it toward her and held it up to the light. With a gasp of surprise, she recognized her prize.

Without thinking, Beth brought the paper to her lips and kissed it. "Thank you, Lord," she said as she tucked the USGS topographical map carefully into the bottom of the crate among her other treasures.

At that moment, it occurred to Beth that she might be able to use the radio on the dash of the cockpit. Though she did not know how exactly, she followed the cord dangling from the microphone to the radio. Turning on the power switch, she picked up the microphone and depressed the side button. "SOS," she said, feeling foolish even as she spoke. "Mayday, this is a downed airplane from Sound Flight, come in," she said. She lifted her thumb from the microphone button and waited. No sound. No static. Nothing at all came back from the little radio. It, too, seemed to have died in the crash.

Beth felt a sinking feeling in the pit of her stomach. A wave of defeat threatened to wash over her. She swallowed hard and turned her attention back to the search for water.

She crawled toward the pilot's door, where the wing lay crumpled and wedged into the soft dark earth. The damage on this side of the plane frightened her even more in the morning light. The dash had caved in around Ken, and pieces of broken windshield littered the ceiling around him. Sharp edges of creased metal had diminished the pilot's space with the same effect as a collapsible dryer vent. Between torn sections of the plane, frayed lengths of wires dangled freely around the cockpit. Once again, Beth marveled that she had survived a disaster of such intensity.

Reaching up, she pushed Ken's hanging body away from the window. Holding him with her good arm, she scanned the space between the door and the lower seat. There! She spotted the water bottle jammed between his hip and the door. It seemed to have fallen from the storage slot in the pilot's side door.

Without thinking, Beth used her left hand to yank the bottle out. But it would not move. Suddenly angry, she jerked the bottle, determined to wrench it free. With a crackling noise, the plastic collapsed, and the bottle jumped toward her.

Her bullish approach had damaged the bottle, leaving a permanent crease in the sides. What a dumb thing to do! Her own temper might have destroyed her most valuable asset—a water container. She could not afford to act so impetuously.

Beth ran the outside of the bottle along her cheek. So far, none of the precious liquid had escaped the plastic. She removed the lid and examined the water inside. At least two-thirds full. Beth realized that she now had a small but convenient water supply. She rejoiced with her discovery, silently praising the Lord. Water!

Never had a bottle of Crystal Geyser looked more inviting. Beth resisted the urge to drink it all herself. A conservationist by training and compassionate by nature, she decided to offer the liquid first to Bill. She slid the bottle into her box, careful to tuck it in upright, holding it in place with Bill's camera and the binoculars.

Now for matches. With great care, she sorted through the remainder of the rubble. No matches. Beth tried to remember if she had seen Ken smoking at some point during their trip.

Beth had removed the pilot's jacket and shirt last night. She knew that the shirt held no cigarettes. But she had not gone through the pockets of Ken's jacket. Perhaps he had matches stored in a jacket pocket.

She continued to gather what she could from the debris in the cockpit. This morning, as she picked up the strewn pages of her goat survey, her findings seemed unimportant. *Funny,* she thought, *how your priorities change on the morning after an airplane crash.* A single accident had transformed her crucial paper work into nothing more than trash.

Thirteen

FROM THE COCKPIT, BETH CRAWLED back to Bill. "I found water!" she said. But he did not respond. "Bill?" She scooted closer. "Bill, I have water. Would you like some?"

Anxious to gauge his condition, Beth observed Bill's face carefully. As he opened his eyes, it seemed to Beth that the furrows in his forehead had deepened into permanent creases. He continued to sweat, in spite of the cool temperature inside the plane.

"Water's good," he whispered.

She moved toward him, dragging her crate behind her. "Okay," she said. "Just a second. I've got it." She held the bottle with one hand while she opened the lid with her teeth. She put it in his right hand, waiting patiently for his fingers to close around the bottle. Unwilling to lose a single drop, Beth cupped her good hand under Bill's head and helped him lift it. "Here, you drink. I'll help."

He brought the bottle to his lips and took a long swig. Beth watched as Bill couched the water in his cheeks. After a long moment, he swallowed.

"Good?"

"Very." He seemed relieved. "Now you."

"I'm not thirsty," she lied.

"You've lost blood," he said, as though he could not afford the energy to argue. "Drink." He pushed the bottle toward her. "We're in the mountains. Plenty of water here."

She let herself drink, enjoying the taste of cold liquid inside her mouth. She treasured it, letting it seep into her dry gums and roll around on her tongue. How good it felt. She swallowed, instantly regretting that she could not allow herself to finish the bottle. Having a little water seemed like greater torture than having none at all. She desperately wanted more!

"Do you know where Ken stored his cigarettes?" she asked. Bill gave an almost imperceptible shake of his head. "Okay," she said. "I'll find them somewhere."

Beth pulled Ken's jacket away from Bill and held the collar with her teeth. Pocket by pocket, she searched the coat. She came up with a set of car keys and a credit card. Inside the lining pocket, she found a small spiral notebook. She opened it and saw only a record of his flight hours and destinations. "Nothing here," she said, disappointed.

Beth smoothed the jacket over Bill, tucking it in under his shoulders. "Better?"

"Okay."

"I'm going to get into the baggage section from outside. Maybe there's something in back to help us. Who knows, maybe I'll find an emergency kit." She patted his shoulder, asking, "Do you mind if I pray for you?"

"Please."

"Father, my friend is hurting. Would you touch his body? Take away his pain. And, Lord, you know how much we need help. Please send help. Send it soon, Lord."

"Amen," Bill said. His gentle smile barely covered the pain she saw etched into his features. She patted his shoulder again and promised to return shortly. Sliding back out the door, Beth dropped onto the ground beside the plane. Once again, she took a moment to gather her strength and let the pain subside.

During the night, dried blood had plastered the fabric strips to her jeans. Gingerly, she ran her finger along the slice itself, pressing the wound and watching for fresh blood. She saw none. It seemed the makeshift bandage had stopped the bleeding.

Sighing, Beth stood. Her body's stiff muscles complained loudly as she moved. Ignoring the pain in her ribs, she bent from side to side, stretching her trunk and rubbing her back with one hand. Carefully, she bent her knees and tried to ease the stiffness in her legs. Her whole body felt cramped and sore.

Now able to see clearly, Beth examined her hand and found that it looked every bit as bad as it had in the early morning light. At least the pain had begun to settle into an unrelenting background noise in her consciousness. It surprised Beth to think that in less than twenty-four hours pain had begun to feel normal to her.

In the sunlight Beth could get a good look at the meadow where the plane had landed. Looking behind the plane, she spotted long gouges carved into the soft earth by the plane's wings. Bits and pieces of airplane lay scattered along the brush-filled clearing. Beth wondered how they had managed to miss the occasional clumps of trees scattered through the meadow. From this side of the plane she recognized the hollow where she had first come to consciousness. Thankfully, she had landed in soft grass, rather than some rocky riverbed. She might have had much more serious injuries.

She shook herself, pushing that train of thought from her mind. She had other more important things to worry about.

She waded through the brush surrounding what remained of the tail section. Coming around the other side, she found the baggage door and grabbed the handle with her left hand. The latch worked freely, and though the door moved, it opened only a couple of inches away from the fuselage. Stuck. Anger hit before Beth could stop it, and she kicked the plane's tail, letting go of a word she rarely used.

What had happened to her temper? Why did she get frustrated so quickly? Leaning back against the plane, she slid down the fuselage onto the ground. She propped her good elbow on her knee, put her forehead into her hands, and let herself have a good long cry.

When her tears finally subsided, Beth listened quietly to the sounds of nature around her. She heard birds and the soft rattling of wind in the crisp leaves of fall. She noticed the light covering of clouds drifting across the meadow. As she listened, Beth decided to put away her despair. After all, anger would not open the cargo door. All the frustration in the world would not save Bill. Beth made the logical determination that she would find some way to get into the back of the plane.

Grabbing the latch again, she pulled harder, yanking until she nearly fell over backward with her effort. As she stood back to think about the stubborn door, she heard her father's words pop into her memory. He'd said them years ago, when she'd been having trouble with an English class. After a long evening of homework, her father, a civil engineer, had taught her a new phrase. "Work smarter, Beth," he'd said. "Not harder." That night, he'd taken the time to teach her a technique he called active studying. His wisdom had paid off in better grades. Of course when he taught her the lesson, he'd meant for her to work smarter in her English class. But Beth recognized that his words applied here as well.

Kneeling beside the door, she examined the opening more carefully, realizing as she did that the top of the door had been buried in the ground by the rolling plane. The ground kept the cargo door from swinging freely! If she could clear away enough dirt, the door would open.

With one hand, Beth began pulling clumps of grass from the soil, throwing rocks out of the way. Still the door did not open. She stood, digging in the ground with the toe of her boot, kicking and breaking loose as much of the soil as she could. Kneeling again, she dug with her bare hand, throwing dirt across her lap as she worked. Slowly and deliberately she dug at the earth, rolling large rocks out of the way and pulling out clumps of brush. Beth found a stubby stick and used it—jabbing at the ground—to break up the earth before continuing to scoop it away, handful by handful.

When she had a small furrow below the door, she tried the latch again. Only the berm created by her digging stopped the door. She could do it. Even with one hand and badly injured ribs, Beth felt certain she would eventually crawl into the fuselage through the cargo door. The very thought seemed empowering, and Beth began to dig again with renewed vigor.

———

Silently, Doyle slipped off his backpack and tucked it under a nearby bush. With care, he dropped to the ground, where Gilligan began to lick his face mercilessly. Doyle pushed the dog away and pulled the gun from the small of his back. With the scent of pine needles and pitch making his nose itch, Doyle crept forward through the bush on his elbows. Inch by inch, holding the gun with both hands, he crawled toward the clearing.

Doyle did not want to startle a herd of elk or anger a bear. But this late in the morning, these animals were not likely to be the cause of Gilligan's distress. Only one species came out into the open at this hour of the day.

The species Doyle feared most.

Doyle felt his heart beat faster and recognized the familiar "high" of combat reconnaissance. He felt beads of sweat form on his forehead, and he paused to sop up the moisture with his sleeve. His mind cleared, and at that moment Doyle felt the intense focus that he loved. It seemed to Doyle that in the thirty or so feet he had crawled to the edge of the meadow, he had dropped twenty years and fifty pounds.

He felt young again, his body agile, strong, invincible.

As he approached the clearing, his pace slowed, and he began to search for a spot from which to observe the entire meadow without being seen. To his right, about fifteen feet up a small hill, a silver fir leaned into a gigantic boulder. Perfect.

Careful not to make any noise, Doyle crawled toward his destination. Once behind the rock, he brought his knees up to his stomach and unfolded himself into a crouch. With utmost care, he raised his head. The north end of the meadow was empty. Carefully, Doyle began to scan the meadow, using the trees along the far side as an indicator of his visual accuracy. His gaze moved from right to left, down the meadow.

Then at last he saw it, and the sight of it, lying helpless in the meadow, made his breath catch in his throat.

An overturned airplane.

———

Suddenly tired and very thirsty, Beth decided she needed a break from her work. Her arm ached from leaning over as she dug. The pounding of engorged blood vessels—from her neck all the way to her fingers—thundered in her ears. Hunger made her knees tremble, leaving her dizzy and weak. Beth backed up to the side of the plane and slid down the smooth cool metal of the fuselage, grateful to take the strain off her trembling muscles.

She needed food and water. So far, their only water supply consisted of the partially full bottle Ken had brought along. Perhaps the Forest Service had packed food in one of the boxes she had helped Bill load. In response to these thoughts, her mouth began to water, and her stomach cramped with hunger. *Stop it,* Beth told herself. *You must last as long as you can with what you have. Don't waste energy daydreaming. Rescuers will come soon.*

Part of her wanted to find a way to rest her right arm, to elevate it and reduce the swelling. *If only we had ice,* she thought. To elevate her hand, she would have to remove it from her vest. But she dreaded the thought of so much motion, and even more, the thought of immobilizing it again. She made a vain attempt to wiggle her fingers, hoping against hope that her arm might feel better. It did not. She groaned as her eyes watered with a new stab of pain.

She leaned her head back and stretched out her legs. Closing her eyes, she allowed herself to think of the children and of Allen. The missing plane would leave them frantic, she knew, and terrified for her well-being. How she wished she could let them know that she had survived. She imagined for a moment wrapping her arms around the girls, hugging and reassuring them. The joy of their reunion would surely overshadow the pain of her disappearance.

She glanced up at the sky, trying to guess the hour from the position of the sun. Still early, she thought. Why hadn't she remembered to wear a watch? Such a silly oversight—made much worse by the anxiety and restlessness she felt. How long had they been here? When would they be found?

About now, she guessed, Allen would be making certain the girls made it to school. She pictured them getting their lunches together, fretting over their clothes and books. It comforted her to know that Allen could handle anything. He would ease them through the uncertainty of the accident. He would help them to pray through their fear.

And he would be sensitive, aware of their need to talk about what had happened. In fact, Allen handled their emotional needs better than she ever had. His intuitive side had caused her more than one moment of envy over the years. When people came to Allen with their problems, he seemed to know exactly what to say and how to help. On the other hand, she often bumbled over other people's feelings. In fact, whenever possible, she tried to stay away from the emotional side of people's problems.

Allen is so different than I am, Beth thought. He always sensed the girls' fears and addressed them, sometimes before she even recognized a problem. He asked the right questions and gave them the right information. Yes, Allen would keep the girls calm and confi-dent until the rescue occurred.

If it occurred.

Beth rebuked herself for this train of thought. Daydreaming about her family brought her no closer to home. She forcibly shook the images from her mind, opened her eyes, and glanced again at the sun. No matter how badly she wished for it, she could not read the sun like a watch face. She knew very little about making fires or about finding food and water in the mountains. She knew even less about staying alive for a rescue. Beth wished she'd paid more atten-tion during that survival seminar in college. *If I could take the class now*, she thought, *I might actually listen to the lectures.*

Beth reached up to push hair off her sweaty forehead. As she glanced down, she noticed a new, bright red line of color along the crusty bandage covering her thigh. Her digging had caused the wound to begin bleeding again, though less severely than the night before. She ran her fingers along the bright redness. Tender. Of course, that should be expected of a filleted wound. *It should be tender,* she reassured herself.

Pushing all thoughts of infection out of her mind, Beth resumed her work at the cargo door, kneeling in an effort to con-serve energy. At last, sweaty and completely exhausted, Beth lay against the fuselage and used her feet to shove open the door. With a groan the door gave way, and Beth crawled into the tail section of the plane.

As she expected, all of the containers inside had been tossed around as recklessly as the cargo in the forward part of the plane. The boxes they'd so carefully loaded lay helter-skelter along the ceiling. Some had come open, spilling their contents and packaging all through the interior of the cargo area. Among these things, she recognized telemetry collars, broken vitamin and tranquilizer ampoules—all the supplies they'd planned to deliver to the ranger station only yesterday. She found other containers too, plastic stor-age boxes—like the ones found in office supply stores—and a brief-case she did not recognize.

Crawling along the ceiling, Beth dragged and shoved and kicked these supplies to the cargo door and pushed them out onto the ground. Outside, she would have more room to open them and inspect their contents. In her feverish search of the tail section,

Beth hoped for one thing above all others. Beth hoped to find an emergency kit.

Surprisingly, the back of the plane did not hold as much as she remembered. She slid out of the cargo area and dropped to the ground, taking a moment to rest before attacking the boxes. Certainly they held something she could use.

In the first box, foam frames held telemetry tracking units—receivers used to follow the collar signals of target animals. *If only I had a collar on,* she mused. *They'd have no trouble finding us.*

Disappointed, Beth went on to the next box. In this she found sealed vacuum tubes—used to take animal blood samples to the lab for analysis. Below the carton of tubes, she found carefully packed syringes. *Great,* she thought, *I can open an animal hospital, but I can't find any matches to start a fire.*

She went on to the next box—one larger than the others, though not heavy—and dragged it, tumbling the box over and over until the taped lid faced up.

Using one hand, she managed to open the lid. What she found inside brought out a delighted squeal—four rolled sleeping bags, wrapped and still bearing tags from the dry cleaners. "Praise you, Jesus!" she cried, pulling a bag from its cardboard nest.

She ripped open the plastic and, hugging the bag to her chest, buried her nose in the soft clean flannel lining. "Oh, thank you, Jesus," she whispered. Visions of herself sleeping warm and comfortably wrapped in a sleeping bag danced through her imagination. She resisted the urge to run around the plane and tell Bill.

On the other hand, if things went well, she might not need to spend another night at the crash site. Beth hoped with all her heart that tonight she'd be lying next to Allen, listening to the creaks and groans of their old brick parsonage.

Fourteen

FROM BEHIND THE ROCK, hidden by the trees, Doyle took his binoculars out of his pack. Lifting them to his face, he scanned the crash site, instantly recognizing this plane as the one that had buzzed his position the previous afternoon.

Whose plane was it? Why had they come?

He repressed a shiver of fear as he thought about who might be aboard this plane. Had someone spotted him living on federal land? Had they come to find his cabin? To take him away? To force him to live in some hospital somewhere? Small aircraft seldom flew over his territory, and he'd never had anything crash inside his perimeter.

Unbidden, memories of Doyle's past came rushing back. *He saw the American pilot draped over the wing of his fighter, his burned skin covered with mud. Doyle felt the water run over the top of his boots, filling his socks. He smelled fuel. Still, he crept closer, unwilling to let a fellow soldier's body go unrecovered in that hellish country. He felt arms around his shoulders pushing him down as a sudden burst of machine gun fire splattered across the surface of the muddy water. Doyle landed face first in the water, the other man's hands holding his head down.*

A trap. The enemy had used the body and the plane as a trap!

Was this plane a trap?

Focusing the binoculars carefully, he clearly recognized the body of a man—presumably the pilot—hanging upside down against the front side window. From the extensive damage to the nose of the plane and the absence of motion, Doyle guessed the pilot to be dead. He wondered about the rest of the passengers. Were there others? Though overturned, the plane seemed to have come down predominantly in one piece. From this position, both wings appeared to still be attached, though the crash had torn the landing gear from the fuselage.

Doyle glanced up and focused his lenses on the treetops lining the canyon, where some trees reached heights of fifty feet. Doyle examined them carefully for signs of damage along the tops and upper branches. Had the plane taken off parts of trees on its way down? He moved his gaze from one tree to the next, looking for obvious signs of scarring.

From the ground, Doyle could not see any damage. This discovery relieved him. A search party would look for these same clues. Tree damage would certainly guide rescuers to the crash site—rescuers Doyle could not afford to have tramping through his territory. Without damage, they might have trouble finding the plane. *If I had my way,* Doyle thought, *I'd make the plane disappear without a trace.*

He smiled a vaguely pleased smile and began a slow creep along the edge of the meadow, stopping every few feet to gaze at the plane. Perhaps he could do just that—make the plane disappear. He could bury the pilot, cover the plane with brush, and stop worrying about a search party discovering his presence in the woods. After all, soon snow would cover the mountain, and Doyle would have the winter to himself.

As long as there were no other survivors.

An hour later, Doyle had crept nearly halfway around the meadow, observing the plane from every angle. Feeling more confident that no one else had been inside the plane, a new sense of anticipation came over him. With no people nearby, the crash site had become a scavenger's haven. Doyle could pick through the spoils, replenishing his own supplies and picking up equipment otherwise unavailable to him. The prospect pleased him immensely.

Moving on, Doyle came at last to a position from which he could scan the opposite side of the fuselage. He crouched behind a fallen tree and rested his binoculars on the broken stump. Gazing at the wreck, he saw something that hit him like a round of bullets in the chest.

A woman.

Doyle lifted his face from the binoculars and stared. *What in the world?*

Even from this distance, he could tell that she had been injured. Though she'd managed to stuff one arm inside her vest, he saw her hand, blue and swollen, hanging over the zipper. One of her legs, stretched out in front of her, had been crudely wrapped with some kind of yellow bandage. A serious injury, he concluded. She seemed small, leaning against the plane, eyes closed. *Is she alive?* he wondered. *More important, is she alone?*

As he watched, she did not move. Her presence threw a wrench into Doyle's plans. He remembered the enemy traps of his past. And though he knew that things had changed, he had never managed to shake his constant sense of apprehension, his mistrust of all people and things. Yes, Doyle lived in a different country now. A different age. But some things—like the things men did to men— never really changed.

Staring again through the binoculars, he watched as she opened her eyes and bent forward, absorbed in an examination of her leg. She probed her thigh with her fingers, then leaned back against the plane. As Doyle observed her straight, glossy black hair, round face, and slanted eyes, he found himself seeing another woman. A woman he had not thought about in years. Unbidden, the memory came in a rush.

Before he could stop himself, the ground below the helicopter came toward him at high speed, splashes of green and yellow coming closer and closer. He heard the puncture of detonations and the unbalanced roar of the damaged engine. He flinched with each explosion as the muscles screamed in his neck. As their helicopter approached the clearing, Doyle and his men discovered their landing zone had been completely surrounded by enemy artillery. The surprise attack damaged the big bird, forcing them to land, ready or not. Doyle saw the door gunner take a fatal round. He threw the gunner aside, taking his position at the M-60. Then Doyle heard his commanding officer shout, "Shoot anything that moves!"

Doyle obeyed. Somehow, in spite of severe damage, the pilot managed to bring the chopper down. Without explanation, the enemy suddenly retreated. Silence filled the clearing. Shaking with terror, Doyle ran from the Hilo, diving into the thick vegetation for cover.

Moments later Doyle and his unit moved out to examine those they had killed. As he ran, crouched and tight, Doyle hugged his weapon, approach-

ing the last soldier he'd shot, the one who'd nearly gotten away.

Holding his gun to the soldier's head, Doyle roughly kicked the body over. Expecting to find a man, he found instead a beautiful young woman clothed in the black pajamas of the enemy. In death, her glossy straight hair, lovely face, and tiny body did not appear to be a threat. Still, as she rolled, an American M–16 dropped from her limp hands. Doyle searched the body.

In one pocket, she carried two pictures, both creased and worn. The first, of a black-suited soldier, smiling proudly. The second showed the woman squatting before a tiny hut with two young children. Doyle had killed a woman—not just an armed female soldier, but a mother and wife. Her face, peaceful in the repose of death, burned itself into Doyle's memory. He saw it clearly.

"No," he said, forcing himself back to the present. He felt the ground beneath his hands and smelled the forest around him.

Doyle knew that the woman's face would forever beckon him back down into the black hole of his past. He had to get away, had to leave that face.

His despair threatened to take hold again. Doyle felt it coming—the pain of a thousand horrible memories. Anguish so real that it seemed determined to swallow him whole. It did not matter that nearly thirty years had passed.

Doyle felt his breath coming faster, and the familiar dampness began forming on the palms of his hands. He dropped onto his hands and knees, lowering his forehead to the dirt. "No," he whispered. "Not again." The clamping in his chest began, accompanied by the familiar ache that rose into his neck and left arm. He rolled onto his side and closed his eyes.

Gilligan lowered his muzzle to Doyle's face and licked his nose.

Carefully, Beth set the sleeping bags aside, forming a neat pile of the things she knew they needed. She moved on to the next box that had been sealed with cellophane tape. This container seemed exceptionally heavy, and she wrestled it out into the open, where she held it down with one foot while she pulled at the lid with her single strong hand. The tape held firm.

She needed something stronger to break the seal. Looking around, Beth picked up the stick she had used to dig around the cargo door. On one end, a stub marked the place where a stem once clung to the branch. It seemed sharp enough. She dragged the stub across the clear cellophane tape, partially puncturing the seal.

She pulled and tugged. With a wrenching tear the box opened, and inside Beth found two full cases of bottled water. This time, she did not pause to give thanks. Trembling, she tore at the plastic seal holding the bottles to their cardboard base. Her mouth watered, thinking of the refreshing liquid almost within her reach. Giving up, she bent over and tore the plastic away with her teeth. Beth snatched a bottle and pulled open the snap top with her teeth. Still squatting over the box, Beth turned the bottle upside down, squeezing the water into her mouth. Gulping and swallowing, while at the same time half-choking with delight, Beth drank until she had emptied the sixteen-ounce bottle.

Satisfied at last, she dropped onto the grass and wiped her face with her sleeve. "Oh, thank you," she breathed with a reverent gratitude that seemed more sincere than any prayer she had ever uttered. "Thank you, Father."

Beth took another bottle and opened it. She walked around the plane, calling Bill as she did. "Bill, you'll never guess what I've found," she said. "Water. Lots and lots of water." She squatted by the rear door and crawled inside. "Bill, here. Look, water!" Beth held the bottle over his face.

He opened his eyes and smiled. "A lifesaver."

Beth said, "Can I help you drink? You can have the whole bottle if you want. I found two cases."

"Please." He nodded, lifting his head from the ceiling of the plane.

Once again she put the bottle in his hand and held his head to help him drink. "I found sleeping bags too," she said as he drank his fill. "Four of them. You and I can each use one, and I'll try to plug up the holes in the plane with the others. We can keep some of that cold air out." He lifted the bottle from his mouth, and she took it from him, watching as he panted. He caught his breath and wiped his lips with his fingers. Beth went on, "The Forest Service must have had a whole group of guys coming up to do the bear study. We have all their supplies."

"Good. Have you found matches?"

"Not yet. I'm still working my way through the boxes."

He closed his eyes, his eyebrows furrowed in pain. "We need a signal fire."

"I know," she agreed. "But shouldn't there be an emergency signal coming from the plane?"

"Yeah," he said. "Our job is to make it as easy as possible for them to find us." He brought the bottle to his lips, drinking eagerly again.

Lowering his head after he'd had his fill, Beth spoke. "Bill, how are you really doing?" She touched his forehead, brushing away the perspiration she felt.

"Hanging in there."

"Any change?"

"Nope."

"All right. I have work to do if I'm going to build a fire. Call me if you need anything."

"I'll wait here, if you don't mind." The edges of his mouth turned up in a wry smile.

"Right." She nudged his shoulder playfully. "Just like always—trying to get out of work." Scooting backward, she struggled back out of the passenger compartment and around the plane to the cargo area, where she opened the other boxes.

Beth could not believe their good fortune. In one of the boxes, she found two smaller cartons of freeze-dried camping foods. In another she found pens and pencils and forms, used by the Department of Wildlife to record samples taken in population surveys. She set these aside—unwilling to discard anything that might come in handy.

Beth found one medium-sized white plastic crate with a self-folding blue lid. She pried it open. With great delight, she discovered the emergency supplies she so desperately needed. The container held a medical kit, a small ax, a knife, and what appeared to be a fishing kit. Along with these, several small film cans had been stashed inside. Full of hope, Beth shook one. The rattle sounded promising. She tore off the lid and discovered a full container of wooden matches. "Yes! Yes!" she cried, bouncing the bottom of the tin on her thigh. "A fire! We can have a fire." She tucked the can into her pants pocket, determined never to misplace the matches. "Certainly the smoke of a fire will help them find us!"

She picked up the fishing kit and opened it. It contained a

couple of hooks, flies, and sinkers, and some nylon line. Though Beth had been trained in wildlife biology, she had never been an angler. Beth didn't like killing animals—even for food. And in the Pacific Northwest, where salmon fishing was as common as breathing, Beth could not make herself catch and eat a threatened species. She did not even order salmon at restaurants unless it was farm bred. Frustrated, she tossed the kit on the grass. "Great. Like they think I'll be out here long enough to go fishing?"

As she said it, a horrible dread hit her like a slap in the face. Questions ran rapid fire through her mind, each more frightening than the last. How long *would* she be here? What would happen if they couldn't find the airplane? How long could Bill survive in his present condition?

———

In the search center, the gigantic military telephone continued to ring. The sound bounced against the walls. Still Paula Douglas made no move. Instead, she picked up the deck of cards and began shuffling. Allen glanced at his father-in-law, wondering what to do. Surely she would be over to explain soon. He looked at the clock: 10:17 A.M. This was going to be the longest day of his life.

When Allen could no longer stand it, he walked over to where Paula Douglas played cards. "Excuse me," he said, leaning in over the card game.

She glanced up, smiling. "Oh yes, Allen," she said, handing her cards to an older man sitting beside her. "Play for me, John? And watch Charlie. He cheats when he pegs." The group laughed as Paula stood and stepped around the folding chairs toward Allen. "What can I do?" she asked.

"I heard the phone." Allen said quietly, gesturing with his thumb. "I wondered what that meant."

She nodded and glanced over at the operations table. "Probably nothing this soon. It will ring hundreds of times during a search. That phone is our direct line from the communications truck outside. The COM director will relay every question from the pilots, every takeoff and landing time, every request for a change of location, every weather report—every detail of the search will come in over that telephone." As she spoke, the phone rang again. "Most of the calls won't be important to anyone but the operations team."

This time they stood watching silently as another line of text went up on the whiteboard. The woman wrote in each of the columns using careful, precise letters. In the last space, she printed, "High Bird."

As though anticipating Allen's question, Paula gestured to the board. "High Bird is our name for the communications plane. We keep one airplane up at a very high altitude—say ten thousand feet—all the time. That's the plane we call High Bird." She held one hand up over her head, palm down. "You see, our radios are VHF. Very high frequency. They work only in a direct line of sight. When anyone flies behind an obstruction, like a mountain or down into a valley, we lose radio contact. High Bird is our communications relay. By circling up high, they stay in direct line of communication with everyone—the ground crew, the searchers, even the cadets."

"Cadets?"

"The pilots will locate the crash site by finding the ELT—the emergency location transmitter. But they can't do any more than that. Once they find the plane, we have to send in a ground team. Highly trained officers lead the cadets in the field. We drive them in as close as we can get. Then they actually hike the rest of the way in to the site itself."

Allen felt himself get a little dizzy. With no sleep and all this stress, his body had begun to retaliate.

"Allen, you should sit down," Paula said, concern on her face.

"Maybe I should. I didn't sleep very well last night."

"That's pretty normal. You sit, and the operations desk will let me know if anything important happens. They won't forget about us. I promise." She walked Allen back to his chair.

"How long will this whole thing take?"

"I wish I knew. In our last search, near Spokane, we found the plane in about six hours. So things could move very quickly. At this point, we just don't know."

They reached the chairs at about the same time Richard returned from a trip to the bathroom. Paula nodded at him and spoke. "We have our route searchers up now," she said. "If they pick up an ELT, we'll let you know immediately."

Richard nodded and put an arm around Allen. "How you doin', son?" he asked.

"I need to sit down," Allen admitted. "I don't know if I can do this."

"We have to," Richard said. "We expect Beth to make it for us. We need to be strong for her."

Fifteen

BETWEEN DAVIS AND GRAHAM and the records at Sound
Flight, the search crew had detailed a fairly reasonable esti-
mate of the path Beth's plane had taken. Ninety minutes
later, the search team had flown the route but was unable to
pick up a signal from the missing plane's ELT. The operations
manager began a more extensive search, sending up several planes
at a time, each assigned to predetermined search grids. During one
of his walks around the room, Allen glimpsed the FAA map spread
across the operations desk. Tiny transparent Post-it Notes marked
the search locations of the various planes. How he wished he understood what was happening, who was where, and what they had seen.
But thus far, Allen had been clearly excluded from the search
details. He stuck his hands in his pants pockets and tried to keep
moving.

Around noon, John Graham dropped by to check on the progress of the search and to check on Allen. He introduced himself
to Harry Armstrong and then sat quietly speaking with Allen and
Richard. After another hour, the owner and manager of Sound
Flight came by. "I think we should try not to worry," he explained.
"Ken Bohannan is one of the best pilots in the business. If anyone
could bring them down safely, it would be Ken."

Allen found himself speechless. Until now, he had avoided
believing that Beth's plane had actually gone down anywhere. Allen
envisioned her still flying out there, misplaced, perhaps, but safe.
Up in the air, where all little planes belonged.

While they waited, Bill Peterson's daughter and sons also came to the airfield. His ex-wife, Allen learned, no longer lived in Washington. The three congregated in another corner, forming a separate anxious, whispering, coffee-drinking group. Though the families acknowledged one another, they seemed to stay separate. Allen understood. This anxiety—this horrible waiting—left him feeling naked and raw. The last thing he wanted was to make small talk with people he didn't know. It was enough to nod across a cold concrete room.

As the day progressed, the search center got busier. More people joined the families to wait. Others came to help or to report on the missing airplane. Gradually, members of Allen's small congregation joined them at the search center. They offered hugs and condolences, but for the most part, they waited silently, leaving Allen lost in his own worry.

One by one, planes and crews came and went without a single report of anyone hearing the emergency signal from Beth's plane.

Paula approached Allen and Richard. "How're you two doing?"

Allen tried to smile but his face felt stiff. He shrugged instead. "We're here."

"Any news?" Richard stood, folding his arms across his chest.

"Actually, not yet. But not everyone in the first phase is back. We have additional flight crews coming in later this afternoon."

The sound of voices caught Allen's attention, and he looked up to see the door of the hangar close behind a small group of teenagers. Once inside, the seriousness of the scene seemed to sap conversation from them. Silent, they scanned the room.

"There he is," one of the kids said, pointing to Allen. The group crossed over to Allen and Richard.

Allen's father-in-law glanced down at him; an exchange of understanding passed between them. "Afternoon, kids," Richard said with kindness. "Shouldn't you be in school?"

"Not with Beth missing," a tall freckled girl answered with exaggerated concern. She stepped forward and enfolded Allen in a clinging embrace. He patted her shoulder, tears filling his eyes as he did. Bashful at this open display of affection, the boys glanced away. The tallest among them slid his hands into the enormous pockets of his green cargo pants.

"Paula, these kids go to our church," Allen said, pointing at each as he spoke. "Elyse, Josh, Ryan, Curtis, and Jessica." As they were introduced, each teenager gave a small smile and nodded. "This is Paula, ah . . ." he paused, "I'm sorry."

"Douglas," she said, finishing for him. "Nice to meet you, kids." Paula directed her next question to Allen. "And you're a pastor?"

Allen nodded, "Only a small church, really," he said. "Up in old Bellevue."

An awkward pause ballooned between them. "Well, kids," she said, "you're welcome to wait here with us. Help yourself to anything you need. And if you have any questions, I'd be glad to help." She touched Richard's elbow gently. "Now, if you'll excuse me."

The kids chose chairs nearby and sat down, falling into quiet conversation. Allen turned to Richard. "I'm not sure what to do with those kids," he whispered.

"I'll keep an eye on them," he said. "Don't let them worry you."

As Allen turned to sit, a slim, white-haired man approached. "You must be Allen," he said, smiling and extending his hand. "I've heard plenty about you. I'm Jack Anderson—the other pilot for Sound Flight."

"Oh yes! Beth has talked about you." Somehow this man's presence felt enormously reassuring to Allen. "She really respects you. What are you doing here?"

"Officially, I'm with the Washington Air Search and Rescue. I have a little plane out there waiting to go up."

"Ah yes, waiting," Allen said. Then, after remembering to introduce Beth's father, he continued, "Waiting seems to be what this thing is all about."

Jack Anderson nodded his agreement. He appeared to be about the same age as Beth's father. His hair, which had turned completely white, served as a startling accent to his clear blue eyes. Somehow his fair skin remained almost wrinkle free, though his chin and cheeks had the soft fullness of maturity. This man obviously worked to keep in shape; his trim body revealed the chiseled shape of muscles honed by deliberate exercise.

"So do you think you'll be going soon?" Allen asked.

"I'm waiting my turn, like everyone around here." Jack glanced around the room, nodding at his compatriots. "You understand."

"That's sort of our problem," Richard said, crossing his arms across his chest and shifting his weight to one foot. "We don't understand anything. And getting information—well, let's just say it would be easier to be a spy. It's like being thrown into the deep end of the pool."

"Actually, it doesn't look like anything is happening," Allen added.

"I know it seems that way at first. It takes time to get the whole thing moving. Once we hear the ELT, things really spring into action."

"So why haven't they heard it yet?" Allen asked. "They said it should be easy to pick up."

"If everything goes well, they do. Pick it up, I mean," Jack said. "But sometimes . . ." he paused, glanced around the room and seemed to check himself. He took a deep breath. "Well, lots of things could explain why we haven't heard it yet. Like a dead battery or a damaged antenna on the sending unit."

"You were going to say something else," Richard said, his voice intense, his eyes keen. "What was it?"

"Well, the other thing—the scary thing—is that the transmitter can be damaged by the impact of the crash itself," Jack said, brushing the edge of his mouth with his thumb. "If that happens, we might not ever pick up a signal. The only way we'd spot the plane is to find it visually."

"I want to go up," Allen said suddenly. "I need to do something. I've been sitting here completely helpless for hours, and no one has heard or seen anything. I have to go up. I can't just sit here any longer."

"Well, normally the mission coordinator doesn't allow that. I mean, let a family member go up with the search team." Jack looked skeptical.

"Why not?" Allen felt his stubborn streak coming out.

Jack Anderson looked from one man to the other and seemed to sense that an explanation, even a reasonable one, would not satisfy these two men. "I'll tell you what," he said, pausing with both hands on his narrow hips. "I'll find the search director and ask about it. You might even spot something you've heard Beth talk about. Maybe he'd be willing to bend the rules a bit."

As he turned to walk away, Jack nearly ran into Paula Douglas. She stepped around him and took a deep breath. "We have a problem," she said quietly. "It seems that the weather forecast predicts a storm front to come in late this afternoon. They say we could have low clouds and snow by tonight."

"What does that mean?" Allen asked.

"If the weather changes as much as they say it will," she answered, looking directly at him, "it means we may have to suspend the search."

Beth took another swig of water and went back around the plane to let Bill know of their recent fortune. "Bill," she said as she crawled close. "I found matches." When he turned his head to face her, the gray pallor of his complexion startled her. "Bill, are you all right?" she demanded.

His eyes seemed vacant, and his perspiration had increased. She reached out to take his wrist, feeling for his pulse. "Bill, stay with me," she said. "Don't you dare leave me." In the vessels of his wrist, Beth felt his heart beat a weak, thready rhythm.

He blinked and nodded, his chin barely moving. "Start a fire," he said, closing his eyes.

"Can I get you anything?"

"Fire," he repeated. "A signal fire."

For a long moment, Beth lay completely still, watching him breathe. Panic threatened to rise up in her throat, and she stifled a shout. She needed Bill to live. Beth could not wait for a rescue alone, even if it came before sundown. She could not bear to lose him now. They had come too far, been through too much. They had to make it. "Stay with me," she said. Then, as though a threat held more power, she dropped her voice and repeated the words, "You stay with me, Bill."

With a new focus, Beth crawled out of the plane. She sat for a moment, wondering how to build a fire in the middle of nowhere. First she needed to choose a location, someplace far away from airplane fuel, yet close enough to tend. As Beth glanced around the meadow, she searched for a place protected from the wind, and still clearly visible from the sky. She recognized the end of the canyon where the stall alarm had first gone off and saw the rocky bluffs rising abruptly up from the meadow. From this vantage point, she saw again the miracle of their survival.

She spotted the small depression where she first became conscious after the crash. Lying far enough away from the airplane, it provided an ideal location for a fire. She walked down the hill and began clearing the ground in preparation.

Fuel. She would need to gather both kindling and larger pieces of wood in order to start and keep a fire going. But how could she gather wood with one hand? She climbed back up the hill to the cargo area, ignoring the pain in her thigh, and picked up the plastic container in which the emergency supplies had been packed. Turning it upside down, she emptied the contents onto the grass and set another cardboard box over the supplies to protect them. Then, dropping the ax in the bottom of the crate, she tucked it under her left elbow and slowly headed off for the nearby woods.

Just off the meadow, scraggly small trees, buffeted by the inhospitable high altitude and severe winter conditions, provided many dead branches for her fire. She began by gathering tinder, chopping off twigs and branches that had long since been dead and dry, feeling the sting in her ribs with every movement. She added lichen to her container and dry needles from the ground underneath the stunted silver fir trees. The work was slow and tiring and her body hurt, but Beth thought of Bill every time she felt tempted to rest. *Why haven't I heard any planes yet?* Surely rescuers had started looking for them by now.

They needed a signal fire, and they needed it soon.

Doyle shivered, cursing the potency of his memories. He cursed the woman for bringing them all back. How long would he remain a prisoner of his past? For more than thirty years now, Doyle had been held hostage by the memories of a single year of his life. How could thirteen months hold so much power? Why couldn't he overcome them? How did others manage? Why couldn't he?

In the intervening years, Doyle had vacillated between trying to bury his memories and surrendering to the hopeless certainty that only his death would set him free. Sometimes he wished he had the courage to hasten his own end. At other moments, he vowed to overcome the demons left from that year of his life. Today, he realized, the demons might live longer than he did.

He rolled over onto his back, looking up to the sky. High clouds had begun to cover the sunshine as the afternoon approached. Lying there, Doyle realized he had no choice but to keep going. He knew he did not have the courage to take his own life. Doyle felt as much shame over his cowardice as he did over his other, more serious faults. Shame and cowardice conspired to weigh him down, keeping Doyle forever tied to his past.

Doyle heard movement nearby. The dog? He opened his eyes and scanned the forest. Gilligan, lying next to him, lifted his head and whined a soft, almost whispered warning. No. Something else.

Silently, Doyle rolled over and slunk away from the noise. Taking cover behind a man-sized huckleberry bush, he peered out to look for the source of the sound. From there, he recognized the woman, the survivor, carrying a plastic container through the woods. She made no effort to hide her noise—crashing through the underbrush like a bull moose.

As he watched, he realized that he had correctly guessed her injury. Pausing to lower the container to the ground, she used only one hand to lift an ax from inside the box. She leaned over and chopped off the broken lower branch of a scrawny tree, groaning aloud as she did so. She dropped the ax on the ground, broke the tinder in half with her foot, and placed it in the box. She did not use the hand tucked inside her red vest.

It looked to Doyle as though she hoped to build a fire. He frowned. A fire meant smoke, and smoke would help a search team find her. The same team would undoubtedly find him. For a moment he wondered how he might discourage this act of independence on her part.

Doyle lowered one hand to Gilligan's muzzle and held it closed. If the dog moved or made noise, the woman would surely spot them. Gilligan knew this game well. Obediently, the dog sat quietly, watching his master, unaffected by the hand on his muzzle. Like a statue, Doyle froze, one hand over his lips, the other still holding the dog.

Eventually, the woman lifted her box of wood and walked back toward the plane. Still Doyle did not move. From behind the bush, he watched while she disappeared behind the fuselage. Then, with great stealth, Doyle crept farther away.

———

With only one arm, filling the box took time. Eventually, Beth returned to the depression and turned over the box, emptying her wood. She set out again to the thicket, this time looking for larger pieces of wood. She filled the box with as much as she could carry and returned to the campsite. She checked on Bill and gave him water. Then she grabbed another water bottle and sat down beside the stash of supplies.

Looking up, she realized that hours had passed since she had gotten into the back of the plane. High clouds now completely obscured the sun. Still, judging by the position of the brightness in the sky, she guessed the hour to be early afternoon. Where were her rescuers? Why hadn't they found the little plane?

How she wished she could work more quickly. For a moment, she considered starting the fire now, but dismissed the idea. She didn't have enough fuel to keep the fire going while she searched for larger pieces of wood.

Her mind argued with the decision to put the fire off. *What if a rescue plane flew over now? What if they missed finding us because I don't have a fire started?*

It can't be helped, she decided. Sighing, she started off again for more wood, this time without the box. Forced to travel farther and farther from the plane, and working with only one arm, Beth walked out with her ax, cut off large pieces of wood, and dragged them back to the campsite, one piece at a time. By the time she felt certain that she had enough wood to maintain her fire, the afternoon light had begun to ebb. Beth sat down beside her fire pit, exhausted and hungry, and too tired to move another inch.

Beth allowed herself to rest, lying back in the grass, staring up at the sky. It seemed to her that the cloud cover had thickened even more, and the temperature had begun to drop. She looked around again at the trees, trying to see an indication of wind. *No,* she thought, *I always get cool after I exercise. That's all it is. I'll make one more trip,* she thought, and she started back for the woods.

Sixteen

WHEN SHE FINALLY HAD ENOUGH WOOD to build a fire,
Beth rested again. Then she wet her finger and held it up,
trying to account for any moving air in the meadow. She felt
a slight breeze coming up from the canyon below the meadow.
Using the flat edge of her ax, Beth pounded a long green stick
into the ground at a low angle, facing the wind. After the pain in
her ribs had settled once more into a dull reminder of her condition, she went up to the cargo area and brought back the paper
forms from the Forest Service along with the cardboard frames of
the telemetry supplies. These she tore into tiny pieces and piled at
the base of her stick. Along the stick, she leaned the dry branches
of tinder she had collected in the woods.

With any luck, the tinder would burn easily after she ignited
the paper and cardboard. Then, if things went well, the breeze her
finger detected would serve as a bellows, encouraging her fire to
spread. It worked like that in the movies anyway.

"Father," she prayed, "we need this fire. Help it to burn." She
struck one of the wooden matches on a nearby rock and then
brought the match toward the pile. Before she could touch the
paper with the match, the breeze blew out the flame. Exasperated,
she lit another and shielded it with her chest as she brought it to
the paper. Though the paper darkened, the match died before the
flame caught.

"Please, Lord," she prayed with a new sense of urgency. This
time, she piled the dry lichen around the paper and touched the

flame to the hairlike material. The tiny flame caught and flared. The paper flamed, and the cardboard began to glow, the edges blackening into ash. She almost giggled as her fire began to burn.

Still kneeling, Beth leaned back, watching as the tiny flames grew. They rose and licked at the tinder she had leaned against the green stick. With great care, she began to lay larger pieces of kindling until she had at last created a real fire—one strong enough to grow on its own. Beth wished that Bill could see this small triumph. *He would be proud,* she thought, smiling.

She never realized how much more difficult it was to build a fire in the wild than it was in a campground or a fireplace. After nearly an hour, the fire had grown enough to add real wood. A small bed of coals grew hot below the flames, and Beth finally felt confident enough to leave the fire unattended.

She wanted to check on Bill again and climbed the hill up to the plane. Dropping down on her knees, Beth crawled inside. "Bill," she said, "I have a fire going. Isn't that great?" She scooted closer.

He did not answer.

"Bill," she touched his shoulder. "Bill, you awake?"

He did not move.

At that moment, her heart began to pound as a new fear rose in her throat, making it hard to breathe. She leaned down, placing her ear over his mouth, listening for the sound of his breath. "Bill!" she shouted. "Bill, wake up!"

She reached down to grab his hand only to drop it in a frantic attempt to find his pulse. Though her fingers searched desperately, she felt nothing. But Beth refused to believe her fingers.

She shook his shoulder vigorously. Still he did not respond. She shouted again. He did not open his eyes. Only then did Beth finally accept the inescapable truth. While she had worked to make a fire, her friend Bill Peterson had died.

———

"Suspend the search?" Even as Allen repeated Paula's words, his mind refused to believe her message.

The public information officer nodded, her dark eyes intense, her expression unchanging. "If the clouds continue to drop and snow begins to fall, we can't continue. We'd be risking the search crews." She touched his arm. "Don't worry. It isn't as though we're quitting. We'll be here—waiting on the ground until the weather cooperates."

Allen felt as though someone had knocked the air from his lungs. He sat again, unaware of anything but a crushing feeling of helplessness that left him trembling.

"What's the long-term forecast?" Richard asked, leaning forward. His voice carried the same emotional edge that Allen heard in his own.

"Low clouds, snow in the higher elevations," she answered. "The people watching this incoming system say we still have some time before it arrives. And we'll stay in the air until we have to quit." She turned back to Allen. "If we do suspend the search, Harry says we'll all stay put. When the weather breaks—I guess I should say, if the weather breaks—we'll already be on site. We can be back in the air at a moment's notice."

"So maybe the weather issue won't interfere at all," Jack said from his position at Paula's elbow. "Maybe we'll be able to stay up long enough to locate the signal. That could happen any minute now, right? That's really all we need, anyway. The ground crew can go in under almost any weather condition."

Paula nodded again, agreeing with Jack's assessment. "We won't quit until the weather throws us out," she said with what seemed like forced cheer in her voice. "I just wanted you to know so you wouldn't worry if we have to stay down for a while."

This news was more than Allen could handle. He dropped his face into his hands and let silent tears flow. While he gave in to his grief, he felt the strong arms of Beth's father wrap around his shoulders. With Richard's gentle squeeze, Allen heard his father-in-law's whispered prayer in his right ear. Allen wiped the moisture from his face and looked up in time to see Jack Anderson stride across the room to the operations desk.

"We can't leave her out there," Allen said quietly to his father-in-law. "She's already spent one night up on the mountain. We know the temperature dropped below freezing last night." His voice broke. "She's not prepared for survival."

"Maybe not," Richard answered. "But she is a fighter, Allen. She won't give up. She has too much to live for."

"I don't know what I'd do without her," Allen said. "When she left, I was irritated about her job, frustrated with her flying. But really, she's done it all so that I could take this pastorate. I wanted it so badly, and she believed in me. She has to make it."

"She'll make it."

"But the snow. She's afraid of snow. It's the reason we bought the Outback."

"She'll make it, Allen." Allen felt Richard lean away and stand suddenly, his attention diverted. When Allen looked up, Jack and Cliff Simpson, the mission coordinator, stood before him.

"I've been to the operations desk," Jack announced. "We've been assigned a search sector."

Allen stood, wiping his face with the palm of his hands. He felt both elated and confused. Cliff spoke up. "Jack tells me you want to go up."

"I do."

"Normally, I don't do it," he said. "But in this case, I'm considering it only because Jack has enough seats to hold both you and two trained search observers. Before I agree, however, I want you to understand the risks involved. You need to understand that just by being there, you might distract the plane's crew; you could divert them from the one moment of attention they need to find the crash site. Do you understand these risks?"

Allen nodded, the grave responsibility sinking in.

"Now, the Civil Air Patrol has regulations preventing family members from flying on board search-and-rescue crafts. But the Pilots Association can allow it. Especially if one of our trained and certified pilots is willing to take you up. You must not interfere with the captain or crew in any way. You may watch but not interfere. Are you willing to submit to this requirement?"

Allen glanced at his father-in-law. "Yes," he said. "I don't want to interfere. I just want them to find Beth. I can't sit here anymore. I just can't."

Cliff, a heavyset man with dark-framed glasses, nodded, understanding in his eyes and responsibility in his features. "Okay. Though this is clearly not recommended, I trust you. You may fly the sortie with Jack. And remember, I can suspend the whole search based on your lack of cooperation. I will not endanger other lives because of you. Don't make me do it."

Allen smiled and shook his hand. "Not a problem. I promise."

"Fine." Cliff nodded again at Allen and Richard and turned back to his desk.

Richard's broad smile seemed to light up the room. "Thanks, Jack," he said. "It means a lot—to both of us."

"So when do we take off?" Allen was anxious to get up in the air as soon as possible.

"We're fueling the plane now," Jack said. "I'll do a mission briefing right over there," he pointed to a corner table, "with the rest of the crew in ten minutes. Get something to eat if you need it. And I'd recommend something to drink. We'll be gone a couple of hours. It's easy to get dehydrated up there."

Under Richard's supervision, Allen choked down a doughnut, followed by a bottle of room temperature water. It was as appealing to him as eating a clump of grass. With minutes to spare, still wiping his chin with a napkin, Allen sat down in the designated area.

Jack had already begun his work. Sitting at the end of the narrow table, he spoke quietly into a cell phone. Allen tried to catch his words but could not make them out. With one hand, Jack made notes on a piece of folded paper. When the call ended, he hung up and dropped the phone into his chest pocket.

"Now, have you been in a small plane before?"

Allen nodded. "Once. With a friend."

"Good, then this will be familiar to you." Allen heard the slightest drawl in Jack's voice. "I'd like to start by briefing you on the plane," he said. "You'll be sitting in the right rear seat. I'll have a trained observer in both the right front and left rear seats. My only job is to fly. I'll be responsible for navigation, for communication with the ground, and for keeping us in the air.

"Since our first objective is to locate the ELT, that will take precedence over observation. The right front observer will be listening to the receiver signal and managing receiver controls. Once we find a signal, we can begin the visual search.

"I'll start by briefing you with the safety equipment. There is a fire extinguisher in a holder below the middle of the rear seat." He mimed reaching for the extinguisher as he spoke. "You may use it on any open flame within the plane. In the cargo area, we carry white paper sleeping bags. They can be used to keep warm. They're also great for signaling from the ground. The white can be seen from a long way away." He ran his pen along the mission objective form as he continued.

"I'll give you air sickness bags when we strap in. Scanning the ground from the side window can be real hard on your equilibrium. Lots of people get sick doing it. Don't be embarrassed if that happens to you." A man came up to the table, pulling out the chair at Allen's right elbow. "This is Bruce," Jack pointed at him with his pencil. "He'll be flying right front seat." Allen and Bruce shook hands as Jack continued, "Allen is family." An understanding expression passed over Bruce's face. "Now, when Kevin gets here, we can finish the brief." Jack looked at his watch. "I have 1517 and 34 seconds. Confirm?"

Bruce raised his elbow and gazed at the heavy round watch on his right wrist. "I've got 1519 and 40 seconds."

"Okay, we'll go with your watch," Jack said, smiling at Allen. "It only works perfectly in the movies." A younger man approached the table, his step light, his face wearing a comfortable smile. "Kevin, about time!"

"A line at the bathroom," he said, jerking his thumb over one shoulder. "Why don't they put search missions in a place with more than one bathroom?"

After smiles were exchanged among them, Jack began explaining their mission. "We'll search in grid 239 Charlie," he said, tapping his finger on a topographical map laid out over the table in front of him. "From takeoff, we should be about fifteen minutes to the search area. Expecting light winds, ten to twelve knots and possible rain at altitude. The forecast calls for increasing clouds, dropping down into the search area. If things get soupy enough, we'll suspend our search and ask for another grid. We're looking for an ELT coming from a single engine Cessna, six-seater, overdue last night from Thun Field. The plane carried environmental equipment and specialists working for the ski area expansion. Persons missing: three." Jack paused and checked his notes. "So far, we have not picked up an ELT from the plane. I don't need to remind you how important it is for you to keep your eyes peeled. We fly assuming everyone on the plane is alive and waiting to be picked up. Anything you miss might make a difference to the survival of the crew."

"Now, any questions while the plane is being fueled?" He

paused briefly, glancing at the faces before him. "Then let's head out." As Jack stood up, his folding chair made a harsh scraping sound over the cement floor. He reached down and picked up a navy blue drawstring bag, handing it to Allen. "You can use this headset," he said. "Let's get out to the plane."

When he felt certain he had put enough distance between himself and the woman, Doyle paused to rest, taking a long drink from his canteen. The presence of a woman in his territory completely unnerved him. He felt his fingers trembling as he replaced the lid. He had never had this kind of problem up on the mountain before. Without a doubt, a rescue team would be on the way soon. The very idea frightened him. Would a search team discover his cabin? Could he manage to remain undetected while they rescued the woman?

But something else bothered Doyle as well. What if the woman was not what she appeared to be? What if the airplane was a trap? Would forest authorities down a plane and wait for him to come out of hiding? Could this woman be part of such a trap?

He did not know the answers to these questions. But Doyle knew he needed to keep an eye on her. He had to know what she was up to. He certainly did not want her to stumble onto his cabin—though the idea seemed unlikely. He did not want her rescue to lead anyone to suspect his presence on federal land. This high country was Doyle's only home, and he had broken a host of laws in order to stay on it. He could not afford to be discovered.

He looked up to find the cloud cover increasing. The sky looked like snow, and there was a palpable chill in the air. Doyle decided to return to his campsite for the rest of the afternoon and spend the night there. From there, under the cover of darkness, Doyle could return to the meadow and evaluate the situation. With certain adjustments, like building a smokeless fire, Doyle would not be detected by any air traffic over the mountain. An expert at concealing himself and completely self-dependent, Doyle could outsurvive anyone on his mountain. Even this strange woman.

Allen sat behind Bruce in the right rear seat of the little plane, while Jack went through what seemed to be an endless preflight checklist. Speaking into his headset, Jack rattled through the various controls and positions. The words grated on Allen. *Just fly the plane,* he thought. *Get on with it.*

Several minutes later, Allen felt the wheels of the little airplane leave the pavement as the craft rose up into the air. He looked along the ground for the plane's shadow but saw nothing. The overcast sky had thickened and lowered until the afternoon sun no longer cast shadows. A voice came over his headphones, "This is WASAR flight 847 Bravo, off the ground at 1536."

"Roger that, WASAR flight 847 Bravo. Off the ground at 1536."

"Heading directly to the search area," Jack Anderson said. "Can you hear okay, Allen?" He turned his head over his right shoulder and smiled at him.

"Yeah, fine," Allen said.

Jack gestured to the microphone. "Get the mike right up to your lips. I can't hear you."

Allen took the tiny foam-covered microphone and bent the flexible wire until it rested against his lower lip. "Better?" he asked.

"Great," Jack said, giving the okay signal with his thumb and index finger. "We'll be turning east soon, and as we climb to altitude we'll pass over the Orting Valley. From there, we'll fly over the hill toward Bonney Lake and Enumclaw."

This high up, Allen thought, the tiny plane seemed even smaller. Though he tried not to, he kept thinking about how it might feel to slam into the ground from this height. The thought made him shiver, and Kevin, who occupied the seat next to him, noticed. "Cold?" He reached in front of Allen and twisted the end of a pipe—closing outside air vents.

Allen merely nodded his appreciation. The plane continued to climb, and soon he had difficulty identifying the animals grazing in fields below. He could no longer differentiate the cows from the horses. He kept his eyes focused on the ground below, not because he expected to spot Beth's plane, but because he wanted to adjust his vision to the difference in perspective from this height.

He tried to identify the make and model of each car rolling down country roads below him. He tried to guess the length of the objects the cars passed. *How long was that barn?* he asked himself. *How wide would that driveway be?* Though he'd been told that Beth's plane had a wingspan of about thirty-two feet, Allen had no clue what thirty-two feet might look like from this distance.

"We're approaching the foothills," Jack said over the intercom. "Another five minutes to the grid."

"See that motor home there?" Bruce's voice interrupted his thoughts. Allen looked forward and saw Bruce pointing out the side window. He tried to follow Bruce's finger, looking down to see the vehicle. "It's parked just off that logging road down there."

Allen spotted it. "Yes. I've got it."

"You can try to fix that length in your mind. If the plane is in one piece, that's about the size of the wingspan we'll be looking for."

If the plane is in one piece. Bruce's words chilled Allen.

Seventeen

EVEN AS HE TRIED TO PUSH the words from his mind, Allen could not restrain the pictures that leapt uninvited into his imagination. *If the plane is in one piece.* Closing his eyes, he forcibly shook himself, determined not to let his thoughts travel down that road. *The motor home,* he thought. *I'm supposed to look at the motor home.*

Allen looked out the window and spotted a large beige vehicle parked just off a logging road. His eyes scanned the top as he struggled to find some way of memorizing its size. "It's bigger than I thought."

"When we get to the search area," Bruce continued, "you'll want to try to keep your eyes moving. Just let them track out on a single line, like this." Allen looked up at Bruce, who was pointing out the right window of the plane. "I use the landing gear and the wing tip, moving my eyes back and forth—slow and smooth. That way, I know I've covered every bit of the land we fly over."

"It can be pretty hard on your stomach if the weather is rough," Jack said, glancing back over his shoulder. "In fact, that's why I fly instead of observing. If I had to spot, I'd be filling one of those white bags every ten minutes." Allen heard Jack's deep voice chuckle over the headphones.

Allen smiled in spite of his anxiety. He had to give it to these people. They had a level of dedication and commitment he'd never even considered before today. He said a silent prayer, thanking God for the men and women who served in the search-and-rescue organization. What would he do without them? What hope would he have of finding Beth on his own?

"This is WASAR flight 847 Bravo entering search grid 239 Charlie." Jack's voice took on a flat, official tone.

"Roger. This is High Bird. I have you entering search grid 239 Charlie at 1558."

"All right, gentlemen," Jack said, pulling a portable GPS off the dash of the plane and balancing it on his knee. No larger than a child's pencil box, the steel gray plotter would be their only opportunity to return to the exact location of the downed plane. "We have both receivers tuned to the emergency frequency. If we pick up the ELT . . ." The plane hit a bump and the little Cessna dropped suddenly. Allen reached for the seat back in front of him. "Sorry, folks. The wind's pretty fierce here. It comes in from the west and gets caught in all these hills and valleys around the mountain."

Allen watched Jack make adjustments to his controls and fiddle with his plotter. He pulled a small aviation map from his right knee and moved it to his left. "Okay. As I was saying, when we pick up the signal, we'll want to locate it as closely as possible and send coordinates back to ground control. I'm going to fly a large pattern at high altitude, and we'll just listen. Maybe we'll get lucky."

While Allen watched the pilot work, he noticed tiny drops of rain forming little rivers that ran down the front windshield in thin parallel pathways. Another gust buffeted the fuselage, jarring the plane. Everything he saw reminded him of the predicted weather change. The ride had gotten rough, and Allen hoped he wouldn't be the first crew member to use the little white bag he held against his lap. He glanced out the window and focused again on the ground passing below. Bumping and dropping, swerving and righting itself, the little plane fought its way through the strong mountain winds. Allen had difficulty keeping his eyes fixed on anything below him. The rain came harder, and Allen saw it blowing sideways through the air outside the plane. *It's not really moving that way,* he rationalized. *It only looks that way because the plane is moving so fast.*

He glanced forward, over Jack's shoulder, trying to read the altimeter. But what caught his attention were the little balls of hail that had begun to pelt the windshield and bounce off the nose of the plane. Jack glanced back, his expression discouraged. "The weather," he said, pointing forward. Allen nodded, feeling even more anxious to find the signal.

"I'm going to change plans and start a visual search pattern," Jack announced. "Bruce, I want you on the receivers. Keep trying to pick up the signal. It might be bouncing around in one of those canyons below us. You guys in back, try to spot anything you can."

Allen looked down again, scanning the ground as it passed below. The terrain had changed from farmland to foothills. Fingers of steep gray canyons pointed up toward the white-capped mountain summit. He saw the warm color of granite peeking out from under evergreen trees perched over the face of high canyon walls. In the midst of this frighteningly naked geography, rivers snaked along the foot of the slopes.

"Rocky Creek," Bruce said, pointing down below them.

Allen nodded, watching the water snake away from the mountain through vast plains of smooth white river rocks. *Easy to guess where that name came from,* he thought. Then he remembered when Beth had collared the elk. Had she flown in these canyons to work this creek?

As they flew, Allen spotted speckles of dark green among the rugged hillsides, some of which were punctuated by tiny black lakes. Lush vegetation filled the high meadows, which had been lined with spots of deciduous trees. Autumn hovered fully formed over the mountain. Leaves of brilliant colors hung from partially clothed trees. Unlike the city, most of the mountain trees had already lost their leaves.

In all the land below him, Allen saw not a single sign of human life. He shivered again, thinking of the vast expanse of wild uninhabited land below. *How could Beth survive in all of this?* She was a fighter, yes. But she was still a woman. A city girl, with no real survival experience. She had already been down so long. As he watched, Allen prayed for Beth.

With the wind roaring around the plane and the engine fighting to keep them aloft, Allen nearly missed it. The first blaring tone of the ELT signal. He had expected a clear piercing sound. Instead, he heard the familiar whining of an ambulance trying to attract the attention of drivers in a busy intersection. If he had been driving, this same sound would have made him look into his rearview mirror, trying to locate the emergency vehicle.

But Allen was not on the ground, and this was not an ambulance. Allen caught the unmistakable look of triumph as it passed over Jack's features. The single ambulance whine was followed by another just like it.

Another gust of wind hit the plane, and Allen felt the plane lurch. At the same moment, his stomach lurched in sympathy.

The two men in the front seat started talking at once. But before they finished their first sentences, the signal disappeared. The two men fell instantly silent, concentrating only on the radio. Bruce fiddled with the receiver in front of him, while Jack banked a turn so hard that Allen found himself hanging suspended by his safety harness. Without it, he would have slid across the rear seat into Kevin's lap. In the high turn, Allen saw only a dark and angry sky as black clouds and falling hail sped by his window.

In this new direction, the weather bounced the little plane like a kite high over an ocean beach. Allen felt his stomach turn over again, and his doughnut and coffee threatened to reappear. He swallowed, focusing on the trees below. They heard it again. The signal. Two piercing beeps, and again it disappeared.

Jack began another turn, seeming determined to find the place where he believed the signal hovered. Allen looked out and glimpsed a small alpine meadow at the high end of a narrow canyon. As they flew away, down the canyon, the signal disappeared again.

"WASAR flight 847 Bravo, this is High Bird." Allen jumped at the unexpected sound. "Ground control has ordered the return of all aircraft to the base. Mission coordinator has suspended the search due to deteriorating weather. Over."

"High Bird. This is 847 Bravo. We have located a signal," Jack said.

"Are you certain of the source?"

"We are not," he answered. "The signal comes and goes. It seems to be bouncing some."

"Have you identified the coordinates?"

"Negative, High Bird. We have a weak signal."

"Any visual?"

Jack glanced over at Bruce, his observer, who without ever glancing away from the ground below shook his head. "High Bird, we have no visual at this time. We request permission to identify the coordinates of our ELT."

"Roger that. I'll relay your request. Stand by."

They waited. Allen felt his hands grow damp in spite of the cold dry air in the small plane. The plane bounced and rolled, and his stomach churned. *Father, let us stay,* he prayed quietly. *For just another minute. Let us find the signal just one more time.*

"This is High Bird. You have permission to stay for the coordinates of the signal. Five minutes max. The weather at Thun has deteriorated. Wind from the southwest at eighteen knots. Your orders are five minutes and no more."

Jack banked the plane again, and as the slope passed by Allen's windows, he could clearly see that the clouds had already dropped. Low hanging fog-like clouds covered more and more of the canyon.

They ascended once more up toward the high end of the canyon. Moments passed. Allen checked his watch. Five minutes seemed like an instant.

A gust of wind rolled the plane sideways, and Allen lost his breakfast into the white bag. Jack glanced over his shoulder at the sound of Allen heaving. He smiled sympathetically just as the signal beeped again. "I've got it," Jack called, turning in his seat. He reached for the GPS, accidentally knocking it to the floor below his foot. Jack swore, and Bruce unbuckled his seat belt as he bent to retrieve the small gray box.

Again Jack banked the plane. "I'm going to find it," he said, his lips set in an expression of fierce, stubborn determination.

Flying down the canyon, Jack listened for the tone. It did not come. He marked the coordinates anyway.

"High Bird, we have marked approximate coordinates."

"Roger that," High Bird responded. "Now get back to the base!"

"Wait," Allen said. "We know where it is. Let's look for it."

"Allen, we'll be back. When conditions clear up, we'll be back."

"But we're here," he objected.

"Not really," Jack said. "We're close. We know that. But up here, in this desolate country, we have to be exact. It will take hours to get a crew in here. And a helicopter. The ground crew could wander around for days looking for the plane. We'll be back, Allen. I promise."

Jack made one more breathtaking turn as he headed west toward the search base. On the way home, Jack flew at lower altitudes. Allen did not see the snow on the windshield change to rain. He did not feel the plane bounce along in the increasingly stiff winds. His stomach settled, but his heart turned over anxiously.

All he could see was Beth. All he could think of was how close they had come. He could no longer keep the tears from his eyes.

———————

Lying beside Bill on the ceiling of the little airplane, a deep sense of loss and sorrow washed over Beth. Though she and Bill had not been close friends, they'd worked together on several projects over the years. And now all of that was over. She would miss his wisdom, his kindness, and his humor. She would miss his reliable advice about the business of environmental protection.

He taught me to survive at work, Beth thought, *and I couldn't do anything to help him survive out here.* Though she'd tried to make him comfortable and keep him hydrated, she hadn't been able to save him. *There must have been something I could have done. Something more than stuffing the stupid sleeping bags into the damaged sections of the airplane. Something more than covering him up and giving him water. After all he's done for me, I couldn't even save his life.*

Her grief, now mixed with guilt, brought fresh tears as old memories surfaced. Bill had loved nature every bit as much as Beth. He loved his family too, and frequently reported the latest escapades of his grandchildren.

Beth ached for his family. Though Bill had divorced his wife years before Beth met him, he managed to enjoy a close relationship with three grown children. Beth pictured the large grouping of eclectically framed photographs he kept on his office desk. Bill frequently spent his weekends with the oldest grandchildren fishing. She thought of the pictures he'd shown her after the birth of his latest grandchild—the son of his only daughter.

Beth had met Bill's daughter only once, when she had come in to pick up her father at work. At a time when Bill's daughter should be enjoying life with a new baby, she now faced unbearable grief. Beth cried for Bill's daughter. How hard to lose your father.

Beth thought about how much her own father meant to her. How she would hate to lose him this way—in a senseless plane crash. She felt more tears well up in her eyes. Along with sorrow, Beth knew a measure of self-pity as well. This whole episode should not have happened. The pilot should have delivered them safely to Thun Field. Today, Beth should be at home with her family, thinking of nothing more important than the accuracy of her weekly grocery list. She choked down a moment of anger. After all, it hadn't been the pilot's fault. The crash had been an accident, not some huge conspiracy to keep her from her family.

Thinking of the girls and Noah caused a shiver to come over her, and she found herself again fighting tears. She took a deep breath and scorned her emotions. She had no time for tears—she had to keep going. Her family needed her. And surviving until help came would take all the strength she had.

As she brushed the moisture off her lashes, a new and more horrible feeling washed over Beth. From out of nowhere, guilt began to creep in with her sorrow and loss. Though she and Bill had worked together for the past several years, Beth had never felt comfortable talking with him about spiritual things. She'd tried once or twice, but he'd always dodged her questions, always changed the subject.

She remembered him once mentioning that he attended church with his family—when the children were young—somewhere near his Fall City home. But he never told her where or gave her any details about his church life. Over the past year, Bill had refused all of Beth's invitations to special church events. It struck her now that he'd grown quite skillful at redirecting any conversation he sensed going in *that* direction.

"Don't worry about me, Beth," he'd told her once. "I'm fine."

She never asked the hard questions, never asked Bill *why* he believed things were fine. Beth had always intended for the two of them to get around to those questions some other day. Now, for Bill, there would be no other days.

"I'm sorry, Lord," she whispered. "I didn't do anything the way I should have. And now it's too late." Over this irrefutable loss, Beth finally let her tears flow freely.

Eighteen

UNABLE TO COMPOSE HERSELF, Beth's grief over Bill's death seemed to wax and wane like the coughing spells of a bad cold. When at last her tears eased, she realized that it had been quite a while since she last checked her fire. Now, more than ever, she needed to be responsible. Only a bright blazing fire could help rescuers find her. *I have to keep the fire going,* she told herself as she dropped onto the ground outside the plane.

Beth felt chilled even before she stood up, and she wondered for a moment why the temperature continued to drop. As she rolled over and pushed off the ground, she glanced down at her left hand. To her amazement, a single snowflake landed on the back of her wedding band.

The sight of the melting snowflake so startled Beth that she looked up. Low thick clouds now covered the sky. Flakes of snow fell lightly onto her face, hanging on her eyelashes and leaving her skin wet and cold. She scanned the horizon, looking for a sliver of lighter sky—wondering if perhaps the snowflakes signaled the passing of a small weather system.

Beth held out one hand, watching as the large soft flakes landed and melted instantly. She knew snow well enough to know that these flakes had formed at a high altitude. The air temperature in the meadow had to be at least five degrees above freezing. If it stayed this warm, the snow would be nothing more than an inconvenience to her. But to rescue workers, it meant serious trouble.

Why hasn't help come yet? What's keeping them from finding the plane?

Beth shivered as she glanced around. In an effort to hold in heat, Beth wrapped her strong arm around her chest and moved toward the fire. As she walked, she heard drops of snow sizzle on the coals around the flames.

Blown by a steady wind coming up the canyon, the flames of her fire leaned uphill, dancing in the wind. Her hair blew into her face, and she brushed it away from her eyes and mouth.

Wind. Wind sucked a person's body heat away. Suddenly Beth worried about the condition of her fire. She needed to keep it going strong.

She dragged a large piece of wood over to the fire and tipped it up on one end. Letting go, the chunk dropped onto the center of the fire, spraying sparks all over her jeans. She sprang back, brushing her pants with one hand. *How stupid,* she thought, scolding herself. With Bill gone, she could not afford to be careless—not about anything. In the growing cold and wind, high in the mountains of the northwest, Beth had no one else to depend on.

As she stood beside the fire, the snowfall grew heavier, and Beth felt her hair getting damp. Knowing that she needed to stay warm and dry, she walked back up the small hill to the airplane. Though she had put Allen's yellow down coat on earlier in the day, she could not zip it closed over her injured arm. She remembered that the pilot's jacket covering Bill had a fleece lining, and the heavy denim would block the wind. Bill no longer needed Ken's jacket, but she did.

As she crested the hill, she remembered the supplies she'd left lying outside the fuselage. Unless she moved them, they would be completely soaked by falling snow. She could not afford to lose a single item. After she changed jackets, she would put the supplies back inside.

She repeated the procedure of crawling into the plane, scooting over to where Bill lay in the middle of the fuselage. The inside felt warmer—much warmer—than the wind outside. She noted this and decided that she would spend the night inside the downed plane. Both safer and warmer, the plane itself would insulate Beth from the cold wet ground. For a moment, she wished she could move the fire from the depression below the crash site. How much nicer it would be to sleep near a hot fire.

Trying not to look at Bill's face, she tugged the coat off his body and dragged it back toward the side door. Seeing him again brought back all her painful emotions. Knowing she could not bear to look at him every time she came in the plane, she rolled her feet toward Bill's body and pushed him gently off to the side—against the wall behind the pilot. Then she covered his face with the torn remnants of the pilot's shirt. Unfortunately, even though out of sight, Bill was not out of mind.

Beth sighed. She had to hurry if she wanted to keep her supplies dry. In the time it took to climb back outside and drape Ken's coat over her shoulder, the wind had picked up, and the snow had begun to stick to the ground. Beth shoved her left arm down the sleeve and fastened the collar and the hip button of the coat. Though the jacket hung open around her chest, it felt much warmer than Allen's coat. Clutching the front closed with one hand, Beth tried to keep out the wind.

Beside the cargo area, Beth began throwing unusable supplies into the tail section of the plane, her ribs groaning with the effort. She placed the more valuable items close to the cargo door, within easy reach. Though hardly organized, at least everything would stay dry.

She grabbed two of the sleeping bags and walked around the tail. At the passenger door she stuffed them between the top of the seats and the ceiling of the plane. Whatever else happened, Beth planned to sleep tonight. Warm and dry.

Back at the cargo door, she again came upon the case of freeze-dried food. As she slid it toward the door, a hunger pain squeezed the inside of her stomach until she nearly doubled over.

Why wait? Certainly I have enough food to eat now. She tore open one of the inner cartons and selected a packet of beef stew. Bringing it to her mouth with one hand, she held it with her teeth, about to tear the foil package open.

Wait! I have water. And I have a fire. Can I cook it somehow? She looked frantically through the mess strewn about her feet but saw nothing she could use to heat water. She leaned inside the tail section, moving boxes, scanning the supplies. Nothing.

She found only plastic, nothing that would stand the heat of a fire. Giving up, Beth removed one of the water bottles from the case and popped the lid. Tearing open the food packet with her mouth, she balanced the container carefully on the ground between two boxes. Then Beth poured water from the bottle into the foil enve-lope, mixing the contents with her index finger. Kneeling beside the package, Beth used three fingers of her good hand to scoop up clumps of food, tipping her head back and dropping dollops onto her tongue. Without chewing, she swallowed eagerly, feeling hun-ger own her body. Beth quickly consumed the entire portion. When she finished, she tore the package, pulled the foil lining flat, and licked the inside. Sitting down on the edge of the cargo hold, she grabbed her water bottle, tipped it back, and drained it.

Doyle made his way down the hill to his campsite, thinking as he walked. After all, he reasoned, he had at least one distinct advan-tage over the woman stranded in the meadow. He had his health; she was badly injured—or at least she appeared to be. Doyle knew the land around the mountain with the same familiarity most women knew their own kitchens. She was most certainly lost. It seemed highly unlikely that an injured woman could cause Doyle trouble, at least not all by herself.

Still, Doyle knew that he would have to keep an eye on her. He wanted to be certain that she stayed at the crash site and that her rescuers stayed there as well. A moment of guilt flashed over him, but he quickly rejected it. After all, it wasn't his fault that she'd come up here on the mountain. He hadn't invited her. He didn't drop the plane into the upper meadow.

The injured woman wasn't his responsibility, and he refused to lose sleep over her.

But even as he pushed her from his mind, he found his curiosity growing, and his thoughts returned again and again to the victim at the crash site. Why had she come? Had others survived? If so, where were they? Had they wandered away from the meadow? Fol-lowing this line of thinking, Doyle realized that others might be watching him at this very moment. The thought made him shiver.

Doyle decided to make a long trek around the meadow, leading his possible pursuers on a long chase through wild territory before doubling back to his campsite of the previous night. Though the trip exhausted him, he climbed steep hills through heavy under-brush, forcing himself to keep up a steady pace. By the time he arrived at the campsite, Doyle felt quite certain that no one had tracked him. He would have heard someone in these woods. Gilligan would have signaled the nearness of a stranger. No, Doyle was alone.

Sitting on the cold ground near his fire pit, Doyle pulled out a piece of jerky. As he chewed, he considered the changing weather. He did not want the woman from the meadow to spot his fire. Nor did he want any search party to see his smoke from the air—though that possibility seemed remote at this late hour in the day—especially under increasing wind and heavy clouds.

The weather continued to deteriorate, and to Doyle's experienced eye, the possibility of snow seemed almost certain. Even though it would require additional time and energy, Doyle decided to build a Dakota fire hole—making his smoke invisible from any noticeable distance. *Let the wind blow,* he thought. His fire would be unaffected by wind or falling snow.

Doyle removed the small collapsible shovel from his pack. Kicking the dirt around his campsite, Doyle searched until he found a small patch of soft ground about three feet from a nearby bush. Unlike last night, this time he chose a spot closer to the rock wall behind the campsite. Doyle bent over and began to dig. Soon his back objected to the bending, and he dropped down on his good knee, stretching his bad leg out beside him as he dug.

When he had a large hole, he moved over three feet, where a small bush hugged the ground with low leafy branches. There, below the branches, Doyle dug a small tunnel, slanting it down and toward his fire pit. This digging proved more difficult as Doyle hacked away at the roots of the bush. Eventually, the second hole reached the lower side wall of his fire pit, and Doyle sat back to rest his aching hands and back.

He moved back to the fire pit and posed over it with his shovel. With a single punch, he opened the side tunnel to the fire pit, creating a slanting chimney for his underground fire. With this task finished, he rolled over onto his back to rest.

Looking up at the sky, Doyle saw that the wind had picked up, and sunlight had nearly gone for the day. The clouds continued to drop and thicken; a change in the weather seemed certain. With the expertise resulting from years of experience, Doyle soon had gathered enough wood to have a healthy fire crackling in the base of his larger pit. This he covered with a makeshift grill and began heating water for his dinner. As if instructed, the smoke left the fire pit by way of the secondary tunnel, where it exited beneath the nearby bush. The bush then dissipated the smoke to near invisibility before it rose into the late afternoon light. Doyle watched as the smoke wafted to nothingness near the bush and smiled a proud little smile. *No one'll ever see this fire,* he thought. *This is my territory, and I'm invincible here.*

Beth hoped that eating the beef stew would ease her hunger. To her surprise, it did not. Still, she refused to allow herself another package of food. Instead, she stowed all of her precious supplies in the cargo hold.

As she finished, an intense fatigue washed over her. She looked up at the sky, recognizing the late hour in the fading daylight. Snow had soaked her hair, and Beth felt very cold. The fire needed tending, she knew, and she set out to stoke it.

Beth brushed the snow from a large rock very close to the fire and sat down. Staring into the flames, Beth held her hand up, garnering warmth from the coals. In spite of her injured thigh, she drew up her knees, hugging them with her good arm. For the first time since the accident, Beth allowed herself to consider her predicament.

Before this plane crash, the possibility of physical danger had never occurred to her. She'd flown nearly fifty trips for Davis and Graham, never once considering the possibility of an accident. In her personal life, she'd experienced the normal worries of every mother—viruses and fevers. But Beth had never thought about her own mortality—never considered that she might not live to see her children grow up.

Now, with Bill's death and the deteriorating weather, a new and frightening possibility—that she might not be rescued in time—began to dance around the edge of her consciousness. Her circumstance became the source of a new and nameless fear that she refused to fully entertain. Yet the fear would not leave her alone.

This storm, with wind and falling snow, might mark the beginning of the winter snow season on Mount Rainier. Beth knew from disappointing past experience that snow and wind grounded small planes from flying around the mountain. How often had her own trips been cancelled by weather conditions just like this? She knew that three conditions—wind, snow, and fog—frequently delayed the search-and-rescue missions reported in Washington newspapers. The weather had to be part of the reason they had not yet found her. Otherwise by now she would be home, sitting with Allen and the kids, drinking hot chocolate and reading stories.

As long as the snow fell, Beth would be left on the mountain alone. She shuddered and shifted on her seat. In the fall, with winter on the way, it might be weeks before a break in the weather would allow the search to continue. Would the rescue team give up before then? Did they already believe she had not survived?

Beth had food and clean water—though a limited supply. She could safely stay here at the crash site and wait for a break in the weather—if she could stay warm enough. If she could not keep warm, she would not live to see the rescue planes.

Beth piled fresh wood on her fire, taking great care to protect herself from the sparks and wind-driven smoke. Though the fire would burn for some time without attention, she knew that she must wake during the night and put more wood over the coals. If by chance someone happened by, the smoke and light of the fire might direct rescuers to her location. She could not afford to let the fire ever go out.

Beth went back to the plane and picked up a water bottle from the cargo door. Then, with a final look around the crash site, she crawled inside. Wishing again that she had remembered her watch, she wondered about the time. *Perhaps Bill has a watch,* she thought. She crawled over to his body and reached for his right wrist. To her great delight, her fingers touched a megawatch, one with numerous functions and buttons, held onto his wrist by a broad plastic band.

With her one good hand, Beth fumbled with the buckle, accidentally pushing a button that cast an eerie green glow over the watch face and reflected off the ceiling of the plane. The light startled her, and she dropped the watch in her surprise.

Feeling along the ceiling, she touched the band, snatched up the watch and stuffed it into her vest pocket. At that moment, Beth felt like a thief—like the despicable people who haunt accident sites, stealing everything an innocent victim might possess. *Bill would want me to have anything that might help me survive,* she rationalized. Always a generous man, Bill's generosity continued—even in his death.

Nineteen

BY THE TIME ALLEN WALKED into the search-and-rescue hangar, he knew from the faces of the teenagers who greeted him that they'd already heard about the stand-down. The girls had swollen eyelids, and his big courageous boys batted their lids as they held back tears. Allen felt their worry and wished he might somehow ease their fears.

In the time he'd been in the air, other members of the Maple Hills Church had joined them as well. Several of the Elder Board, some of the choir, and even the Sunday school superintendant had come. Each wore expressions of worry and concern. Their presence gave Allen comfort, and this feeling surprised him. After many hugs and a few tears, Allen went over to pour himself some coffee.

Richard greeted him as he reached the food table. "So how'd it go?" he asked quietly, leaning one hip against the table.

"We heard it," Allen said.

"What?"

"The signal. The EL-whatever thing. We heard it." Allen held the spigot of the coffeepot in the open position, letting hot liquid slowly fill his Styrofoam cup. "Pot must be nearly empty."

"They didn't tell us that," Richard said. "I don't understand. Why are they calling the search off if they've found the signal? The least they can do is call in the ground crew. Maybe they have enough information to find the crash site."

Allen nodded and brought the cup to his lips. His hand shook as he held it. "I saw the place, Dad," Allen said. "It's rugged, dangerous country. Steep slopes. Rock cliffs. The signal came and went almost instantly. We didn't see anything." He took a drink and grimaced as the liquid burned his tongue and the roof of his mouth. "The weather was bad. Real bad." Allen shook his head as the tears threatened to come again. "We had trouble getting the plane down. The wind is fierce. The rain makes it impossible to see. We can't ask anyone to risk their lives in that weather."

"You're right," Richard agreed, putting one hand on Allen's shoulder. "At least we're closer. We'll find her," he said. "Is Jack inside yet?"

"I stayed while he finished his ground check, and then he taxied over to the gas pump. Last I saw, he was putting gas in the right wing."

Richard nodded and said, "I think I'll go out and talk to him."

"Take your coat." Allen managed a weak smile.

Allen carried his coffee over to his designated waiting area and sat down. Though he'd done nothing but sit in an airplane, he felt tired and weak. A feeling of utter defeat crept along the edges of his thoughts, but he beat it back. *We'll find her,* he told himself. *It's only a matter of time.* His mind replayed the last signal they'd heard. If only he hadn't had motion sickness. His vomiting had distracted the pilot. Now, Allen felt sick with regret. If only he could have been more help to Jack and the crew.

Paula Douglas approached, her hands deep in the side pockets of her green flight suit. "How you doing?" she asked. "Can I get you anything?"

"You mean other than my wife?"

She smiled, her eyes kind and understanding, and sat down beside him. "I heard you picked up a signal."

"I think so. Though Jack says the signal could be bouncing around in the canyons." Allen set his coffee cup on his knee, turning it as he considered what had happened. "Jack also said that the sender might be damaged. That could be why the signal is weak."

Again she nodded. "This weather system could blow through fairly quickly." She looked at her watch. "We have another hour before dark."

Just as she finished her sentence, the sounds of fresh grief escaped from the group of teens clumped against the far wall. "They're having a hard time," she said, gesturing to the kids.

"They're young," Allen said. "And they loved her."

"Love her," Paula corrected. "She's not gone yet. It looks to me like that whole group could use something to do." She glanced over at the ever-growing cluster of church members sitting in their own corner. "I'm wondering. How would you feel about getting them involved?"

Allen glanced up, confused. "What can they do?"

"Well," she answered, "we have this whole crowd to feed." She gestured toward the official and unofficial search personnel. "I'd hate to have anyone unavailable because they had to leave to go find something to eat. Would you mind if I sent some of your group to the store? We have a barbecue grill, and I could have them cook for the search team."

"I think that would be a great idea." Allen smiled. "You make a list, and I'll get them organized."

———

Thirty minutes later, Allen and Richard had glowing coals burning in the base of an old oil barrel that had been sawn lengthwise and hung in a homemade frame. They'd dragged the heavy contraption out from under the eaves and placed it on a small patio between the main office building and the search hangar. Designed for this purpose, a small freestanding cover shielded the barbecue from falling rain.

Allen turned up his collar, and Richard pulled the hood of his coat up over his military haircut. Cold wind and blowing rain kept both men moving, hugging the area around the fire. They spread the coals evenly along the base of the barrel. Then together they lifted the grill and set it over the top. "You can start those hamburger patties now," Allen said to the oldest of the boys.

"You got it." The teenager opened a long tube of frozen beef patties and began slapping them in neat rows onto the grill. Next to him, another church member carefully laid hamburger buns along the outside of the fire. She had chosen to heat the bread herself, arguing that every burger is better on toasted buns. Allen smiled as he looked around. The congregation came to life with the project. On another table that had been dragged out from the hangar, women had begun to arrange containers of salads and pre-cut fruit. Next to these, teenage girls opened and set out packages of desserts. They had chosen cookies and cupcakes—foods already portioned—as if by instinct they knew to keep the food line moving.

He felt a certain pride in his church family. Paula Douglas knew what she was talking about. They *did* need something to do. *Most people can work together if the goal is worthy,* he thought. *Perhaps that's what we need at Maple Hills. A more worthy goal.* Allen looked up to find Richard opening a stack of paper plates. It seemed the last of the preparations was complete.

The door to the hangar opened, and the wind caught it, slamming it against the metal wall. Paula, wearing her flight jacket, wrestled with the door, dragging it back and leaning into it until it shut. "Looks like everything is about ready," she said, glancing over the tables. "Shall I tell them to come and get it?"

"Sure," Allen answered. "Go ahead." Then a thought struck him. "Wait, let me."

She raised her eyebrows. "Okay. Whatever you like."

"Folks, come inside for a minute," Allen said. The Maple Hills group looked up, surprised. "Everybody." He waved them toward the hangar. "Please. Just for a minute."

Allen followed Paula back into the hangar. This time, *he* ended up wrestling with the door and the wind. Inside, Paula stuck her index and pinky fingers into the edges of her lips to produce the most piercing whistle he'd ever heard from anyone. The room fell instantly silent. She held one hand toward Allen.

"I'm just here to announce dinner," Allen said, feeling suddenly shy and a little nervous. "But I hoped that you wouldn't mind if I prayed for you before we all eat together."

While Allen folded his hands and waited quietly, he saw nervous glances exchanged between members of the search team. Some of the crew flashed bright smiles toward him. When the crowd settled, Allen began.

"Father, I just want to thank you for the men and women in this room." Allen heard his voice break, and he stopped to clear his throat. "Thank you for their courage and their dedication. I believe that you have trained and prepared them for this moment in time. And I ask your supernatural blessing on every one of them today, Lord. Give them everything they need for this job. Be with them as they work. Guide their every thought and action. Protect them in the air and on the ground. Use them, Lord, to find Beth, and Bill, and the pilot.

"And for the food you've provided, we give thanks. We thank you for the kind hearts of the church family who've prepared it for us. And, Lord, no matter what happens here, we are yours. Yours," Allen whispered again. He coughed and added, "amen."

The group stood silent, unmoving. Perhaps a family member had never prayed for the rescue crew before. "Well, you'd better get out and eat before our youth group does," Allen said, grinning. "Or I guarantee there won't be anything left."

––––––––––

It began to snow just as Doyle finished his evening meal. This he expected. Snow would cover his tracks through the mountain meadow. Snow would keep searchers off the mountain. He smiled up into the huge falling flakes, delighted with the accuracy of his own weather forecast.

Doyle waited patiently until after dark to return to the meadow. For many years, he had tracked through these mountains long after sunset. The black mountain night did not encumber him. Rather than hinder, the night's blackness would aid his intentions. He planned to get as close to the plane as he could, to find out as much as possible about the woman. To see if there were other survivors or victims besides the man hanging upside down from the pilot's seat.

If the plane were a trap, Doyle would know soon enough. By sneaking to the site under the cover of darkness, Doyle would find out exactly who she was and why she was here. The snow would completely cover his tracks. She would never know he had come.

From the edge of the meadow, Doyle saw her fire dancing brilliantly in the black mountain air. He could not see the woman, though, even at this early evening hour, and he wondered where she had gone. Content to wait, he sat on the edge of the meadow, watching, waiting, and listening. Even from this distance the fire looked inviting. She had built a bonfire of sorts—as though she expected a pilot to fly over her campsite after dark. *The fool*, Doyle thought. *Wasting fuel on a fire no one'll ever see.*

Doyle crept slowly away from the cover of the trees. Keeping his eye on the plane, Doyle avoided looking directly at the fire itself.

His night vision depended on keeping his eyes from the bright light. He moved forward silently, stealthily, always watching the plane, listening for movement, mentally reviewing the events of the afternoon.

Earlier, he had watched her build the fire. Watched as she coaxed it into a bonfire. He'd observed her return to the inside of the plane.

When after a long while she still did not emerge, he felt confused and wondered if she'd fallen asleep. It was then that Doyle knew he would need to get closer in order to find out what had happened.

Now, Doyle thought. *I might as well figure it out now.* As Doyle crept toward the plane, he decided that he would begin by putting out the fire. If she were alive and happened to look outside, the fire would make him clearly visible to her. He could not risk being an easy target for the woman. He would simply snuff out her fire.

Creeping toward the flames, Doyle kept one eye on the plane. Then carefully, piece by piece, he kicked the wood away from the flames. He knew with absolute certainty that as snow fell on the wood, cooling it, the fire would quickly burn itself out. There was no need to cover the wood with dirt or douse it with water. When he finished, only a small center of hot coals lay surrounded by the widely separated ends of heavy logs.

Doyle brushed his hand over a flat rock that lay very near the fire. Collecting a handful of snow, he dropped the wet slush on the very center of the coals. In obedience, the hot center of the fire sizzled and cooled. Steam rose from the remains of the bonfire, and the strong wind gusting up the canyon quickly blew it away. Doyle turned up the collar of his coat. Quickly the night around the plane grew black.

Doyle dropped to the ground and closed his eyes. By staring at the center of the fire, he had completely disrupted his night vision. With time, he would regain his ability to see; knowing this, he held his eyes tightly shut.

Long moments later, his attention focused on the hill above him, Doyle opened his eyes. Slowly, he began creeping toward the plane. Just as he crested the rise, the little plane shuddered, and Doyle froze, certain that the side door would open and the woman would emerge. He crouched low, remaining perfectly still.

Glancing around in the blackness, Doyle became frantic. Where would he go? Where could he hide? With no options, he dropped his head and hugged the ground, waiting for the sound of the passenger door.

It did not come.

The plane shuddered again, and a ghostly howl blew through the trees in the meadow. The wind. Doyle brought his head up. It was only the wind catching the tail section of the plane, causing it to rock along the ground. Moving forward again, he kept his eye focused on the door of the plane.

Closer still, Doyle began a slow circle around the fuselage, moving toward the cargo door, where he had first spotted the woman leaning against the aircraft. Only this afternoon, he'd watched her bring out box after box of supplies from the cargo area.

With the wind howling outside, rattling and shaking the plane, he began to wonder what had happened to her. *How could anyone sleep through this storm? She couldn't still be alive.* He drew closer, creeping low as he approached the front of the plane. He put his face to the window and looked inside. The man he had seen earlier was still hanging there, obviously dead. He didn't see anyone else. No movement.

If the injuries had killed the woman, Doyle reasoned, then certainly the plane could not be a trap. And the dead man confirmed it. Doyle felt a twinge of regret. *I'm no animal,* Doyle thought. *No matter what everyone else thinks. I don't like to see any woman die.*

Doyle began to think of all the supplies he had seen outside the plane that afternoon. *If she is dead, then all that stuff is just salvage. First come, first served. That's the law of the jungle,* Doyle reasoned.

He crept toward the tail section and came around the back of the plane. Even in the dark moonless night, Doyle saw immediately that the supplies had been moved. At some point, the woman had put everything away.

At first he felt a wave of disappointment move over him. It would have been so easy to pick through her provisions on the ground. But Doyle shook off his frustrations. He could still recover the supplies. He could do it now and get away long before rescuers came to find her body. He would leave no trace.

The snow fell more thickly now, and the wind pushed hard at him from behind the plane, whistling up the canyon. Doyle had complete confidence that the sound, the awful howling of the wind, covered his presence. In fact, Doyle felt fairly certain he could sing "The Star Spangled Banner" out here, and even if she were alive, she would not hear him.

Step by silent step, Doyle crept closer and closer. Until at last he reached out and touched the rear cargo door of the battered airplane. Ever so gently, he turned the latch, pulled the door away from the plane, and waited.

Hearing no movement inside, no response to his presence, Doyle bent over the opening and looked. She had haphazardly thrown some things deep inside the fuselage, while other items were stacked neatly near the cargo door. Doyle stood in the black night inspecting the containers, guessing which boxes held what. Doyle did not have time for a careful search. That would come later, when daylight made selection easier. Instead, he reached in to grab the first box his hand fell upon.

Less than an hour later, carrying everything he could hold, Doyle moved away from the crash site. Before stealing into the woods, Doyle made one last stop. At the pile where she kept her wood, he felt in the darkness for her ax. After all, if she were dead, she would not need the ax now.

Thief, a voice inside Doyle's head accused him as he walked through the night to his camp.

He shrugged the message aside. "She's dead," he argued into the wind. "You can't call it stealing if she's already dead." *After all,* he thought, *this stuff is just laying here in the meadow for anyone to use. I can't be blamed for pickin' up what someone else just leaves around.*

Over the years, Doyle had argued with himself so much that he hardly noticed it anymore. Ax in hand, he made his way back to his campsite where Gilligan lay waiting, tied to a tree near the fire. With a pot from his pack, Doyle heated water and celebrated his retrieval with a hot snack of freeze-dried beef stew. This he shared with Gilligan. Then with the water in his canteen, Doyle toasted the arrival of the woman in the meadow.

Twenty

ALLEN ENJOYED WATCHING his church family interact with the various members of the ground crew and flight personnel at Thun Field. He noticed that they seemed to blossom as they served. They took initiative, each filling a specific role. One made a tray of drinks, walking around to offer refills to those still eating. Another made the barbecue his personal responsibility. Two of the teenagers kept the food on the table organized, removing empty food containers and replacing them with newly opened packages. It seemed remarkable that this group of people operating like a well-oiled machine belonged to the same planning committee he'd met with just last night. In spite of the horrible circumstance that brought them there, Allen smiled.

"Pretty amazing church you have there, Pastor." Paula Douglas stood at Allen's elbow watching the kids work at the food table.

"I know." He chuckled. "If you'd told me last week that they would work together like this, I'd have thought you were joking." He shook his head in wonder. "I wish I could take credit."

"Maybe you've done more than you know," she said. "We have lots of families at our searches. But we've never been treated like this before." She held a plastic punch glass up for Allen's inspection. "Like royalty," she concluded, making a mock toast.

Allen nodded and turned to face her. "What have you heard about the weather?"

She glanced away, growing serious. "We've called off the search for tonight. But the whole crew will reassemble first thing in the morning."

Allen took a deep breath, blinking hard. "I think I knew that."

"But by morning, the weather might have changed completely. We'll have daylight on our side. And who knows?" She shrugged. "We may locate the ELT first thing in the morning and be at the crash site by noon."

Allen smiled weakly. "I need to know, Paula," he said quietly. "How long can one of those transmitters keep signaling?"

"Depends."

"On what?"

"Truthfully, the battery won't last forever. Depending on when the plane went down," she stopped, put one hand in her pocket, glanced away, and then turned back to Allen, "well, the battery could run out in as little as twenty-four hours. Some of them can keep going for up to three days."

"After that?"

"Well," she hesitated, "after that, we have to just go out there and find the plane."

"Thanks, Paula." Allen said. "Thanks for being honest."

"Don't give up hope," she said.

"I haven't," he answered. "As long as I can still pray, I won't give up hope."

Her smile told him that she'd heard that line before.

————

After a few hours of deep sleep, Beth woke to the sound of wind outside the plane. It howled up the canyon and whooshed through the thick branches of the ancient trees below the meadow. The little plane rocked gently as the wind buffeted it from the outside. As she lay there in the dark, Beth worried about her fire. *The wind will make the fire burn quickly,* she thought. *I ought to go out and put on more wood.*

Beth hated to go back out in the miserable weather. If the air were as forbidding as the wind sounded, she would be too cold to fall asleep again for the rest of the night.

Reluctantly, Beth crawled to the rear door and pushed it open. Outside the wind blew snow into her face and pierced the front of her thick jacket. In the absolute blackness of the mountain night, her feet slipped on wet ground, and she nearly fell. As she tried to catch her balance, brushing her fingers along the ground, she realized that the snow had begun to stick in thick, wet layers.

She stood slowly, blinking in the darkness, unable to see the fire. Not a single ember remained to lead her through the night. Taking another step, she stumbled again and caught herself. The blackness disoriented her, and for a moment Beth thought the fire must be burning somewhere—she had simply misplaced it.

Carefully, Beth backed up to the door of the airplane, and using the direction of the wind as a guide, she guessed the fire to be off to her right at a forty-five degree angle. She turned in that direction and took a timid step forward into the horrifying darkness. Blowing snow pricked her skin, making her eyes water and her nose run. Not more than four steps away, she stopped to brush her dripping nose with her hand. As she did, her feet slipped again—only this time she could not catch herself. She tumbled down the snowy slope until her knee struck a small branch. When her legs stopped moving, her chest pitched forward, and she began to slide down the incline headfirst. Frantically, Beth clutched at the ground with her left hand, digging through wet snow, grabbing at the ground cover underneath, trying to stop her slide. At last, somewhere in the blackness, she skidded to a stop.

In the midst of the howling, blowing snow, Beth began to cry. Why did it have to snow? Why did she have to fall down a slippery slope? Of all the ways to die, what divine justice had inspired this fall? She tried to choke down the rising hysteria she felt, brushing the snow off her face and throat. The fall reawakened the pain in her right elbow, and she rolled onto her back, wrapping the injured elbow protectively with her left hand. The searing pain made it difficult to breath. With rapid jagged breaths, she tried to calm herself. *I haven't died. This isn't the end.*

Beth blinked and looked around, trying desperately to see the fire pit in the darkness. Certain it could not be far, Beth felt the ground nearby. It was covered in an icy blanket, and she could not see a thing around her. What if she had slipped into the hot coals? What if she had been badly burned in her fall?

Going outside in this weather without a flashlight had been a foolish decision. With great care, Beth turned around and crawled back up the hill on both knees, clutching at the ground to pull herself forward. If she continued along this uphill path, Beth felt certain she would eventually return to the plane. She could restart the fire in the morning; after all, she still had matches and paper.

But she would not repeat this terrible mistake of going out in the wintry blackness again—no matter how long she waited for rescue.

Beth finally reached the plane and crawled, trembling, into the fuselage, pulling the door shut behind her. The cold wind and wet snow left her hands numb, and her breath came out in hoarse panting sounds as she shivered with cold. Once inside, her hand began to sting. She had skidded against her left palm, and suspected—though she couldn't see it in the darkness—that she had taken some skin off her hand. Her jeans had gotten wet in the fall, and she knew that she needed to take them off. Shivering, she crept toward the sleeping bags.

Earlier in the night, Beth had laid open one bag and put the other—zippered closed—on top. Now, desperate for warmth, she fumbled in the dark, trying to find the zipper of the open bag. Eventually, Beth remembered Bill's watch and pulled it from her vest pocket, poking each of the buttons until she found the one that illuminated the eerie green light.

Using the watch light, one hand, and her teeth, Beth found the zipper and closed it. Then she stuffed one sleeping bag inside the other. Though her heavy cocoon would keep her as immobile as a mummy, she knew she would have more insulation from the freezing air outside. But Beth did not climb in, not yet. She still needed to take off her wet clothes.

The fingers of her left hand struggled with the knot holding the bandage on her thigh. After fumbling with it, she tore it off, throwing it to one side. Next, she removed her wet jeans and slipped off her shoes, rubbing her cold feet with her left hand. Thanks to her well-worn hiking boots, her feet had gotten cold but not wet. With time, they would recover. For a moment she paused, so thankful for her wool socks that she nearly cried. In all her life, she had never been so thankful for such a simple pleasure as rag wool socks.

Beth rolled onto her side, curled up, and dropped her feet into the inner sleeping bag, sliding all the way to the bottom. As her teeth chattered, Beth held her body tight against the cold that seemed to have followed her inside the plane. She remembered the passenger door and the damage that kept it from shutting completely. *No wonder the inside has grown cold,* she thought. *Tomorrow, I must do something about that door.*

Eventually, after long moments, the cold seemed to abate

somewhat. Still, the wind continued to whistle through the struts outside. From inside the double sleeping bag, she began to grow more comfortable. The chattering of her teeth slowed, and the numbness in her feet and hands eased slightly.

But Beth could not sleep. The weather had taken such a terrible turn for the worse that she could not stop the worry trails running wild through her mind. As long as things continued like this, no one would be able to look for the little plane. *How long can I wait for help? What if they don't come? How long can I survive on this mountain all by myself?*

Beth began to pray, whispering her fear into the cold dark air around her. Still she could not relax. "Father," she said into the night, "I know you are here with me. But I feel so alone. And I'm afraid. I just want to go home. Please keep me through this storm." As she said it, Beth knew that she referred to something much bigger and more frightening than the weather.

Allen arrived home with Richard just after nine o'clock in the evening. Harumi greeted them at the door, anxious for any news of her daughter and the missing plane.

Unfortunately, Allen had nothing new to report. "The weather seems to hold the upper hand. Until we can fly, we can't look for the ELT. We need that to find her, Mom."

"How long will the signal last?" she asked, tears glistening in her dark eyes.

"Not much longer," Richard answered. "Maybe we should sit down a minute."

Harumi chose the end of the couch, sitting forward on the seat, palms down on her knees, blinking back tears. Gently, Richard wrapped his arms around her shoulders, leaning his cheek against her hair.

"Oh no, I can't . . ." Harumi cried, shaking her head. "Not Lizzie too."

"No, dear," Richard spoke softly, as if to comfort a small child. He kissed her head, rubbing her shoulder as he did. "It isn't the same. Beth will be fine. You'll see."

Allen put his elbow on the arm of his chair and let his cheek rest in his hand. He could not keep his own tears at bay watching the tender display between husband and wife. Would Beth be fine?

While Harumi listened to Richard give her more details about the search, her tears rolled down her cheeks unchecked. Though she made no noise, she could not stem the relentless flow of tears.

Tonight, Allen did not feel very confident about the future. As their conversation wound down, Richard stood. "We need to be getting home. You need your rest, Allen. We'll all just keep praying."

Richard helped Harumi up and moved her toward the entry hall. "You're tired, honey," he said. "Things will look better in the morning." He took her coat from the closet and draped it over her shoulders. She brushed the tears from her face and seemed to put away her emotions. A mask covered her expression.

"I will stay with the children again tomorrow," she announced in an even tone. "I'll be fine. You need me to be fine." She accepted Allen's warm hug, squeezing him back.

"I know, Mom," Allen said with tenderness. "Thank you so much."

As Richard's car pulled into the street, Allen wondered if *he* would ever again be fine. How could he sleep under warm covers in a heated house while Beth waited up on that mountain somewhere in the middle of a storm? The thought made him cry again. Helplessness drove him back to the little couch in the living room.

Allen dropped to his knees and began pleading with God for Beth's life. "Keep her safe, Lord," he begged. "Keep her warm. Give her shelter from this horrible storm. Comfort her. . . ."

As Allen gave himself over to the fervency he felt rising from inside his soul, he did not hear the doorknob turn or the hall door open. He did not hear the soft steps of his older daughter as she crossed the living room. Only when she touched his shoulder and spoke did he realize that she was there.

"Daddy?" she said. "Daddy, my stomach hurts."

He turned to see her tiny face looking directly into his own. "Bekka, I didn't hear you come in," he said, wiping his face with one hand and then scooping her into a warm hug.

"Daddy, why are you crying?" she asked, her expression full of surprise.

"I was praying," he said, as if that explained everything. "Don't worry about it." He got off of his knees and turned to sit on the couch. "Now tell me about your tummy."

"It hurts," she said in a sleepy voice. "It woke me up."

"Did you take your medicine tonight?"

"No. Grams couldn't find it."

Allen picked her up and put her on his knee. "Well, where does Mommy keep it?"

"In the medicine cabinet."

"Would you like to help me look?" She nodded gravely and slipped off of his knee. She offered him one hand, rubbing sleepy eyes with the other.

In the kitchen, Allen pulled out the step stool and reached into the cabinet above the microwave. After Noah was born, Beth had moved all their medications into this childproof location, designating it as the medicine cabinet. Allen took everything from the cupboard, one item at a time. But he could not find the prescription for acid stomach that their pediatrician had prescribed for Bekka. "Where would it be?" he asked her again.

She shrugged. "Mommy always takes care of it."

Allen wondered if perhaps Beth had left the bottle out for some reason and began to scour the counters.

"Daddy, it hurts," Bekka whimpered.

"I know," he said, growing more desperate. As he turned around to look again, he found a note. *Pick up Bekka's refill.* Written in Beth's precise printing, it hung by a paper clip to the calendar on the refrigerator.

Beth had planned to pick up the medicine at the pharmacy—perhaps on her way home from the airport. That explained why he couldn't find the container of pills anywhere. She must have called it in and thrown away the bottle. For a moment Allen felt completely overwhelmed. What should he do? He did not even know which pharmacy filled Bekka's prescriptions. And what could he do in the middle of the night?

Beth had always taken care of these details so efficiently that Allen never even paid attention. And now, long after most pharmacies had closed for the day, Allen found himself trying to cope with something she took care of without effort. He fought down a moment of panic. *Lord,* he prayed, *can you see how lost I am without her?*

Twenty-One

DESPERATE, ALLEN WONDERED WHO he could call, who would know what to do about a stomachache at this late hour. *Beth would know,* he thought. Even if she forgot to pick up the medicine, she would know what to do.

"Honey," he began, "what does Mommy do when you have one of your tummy aches?"

"She gives me a pill," Bekka answered.

Bekka, who rarely expressed her emotions, frequently suffered from an acid stomach. No amount of parental comfort seemed to change this. Bekka's stomach served as an accurate thermometer of her emotions.

Allen let a long sigh escape unchecked. "I mean," he said pointedly, "if you don't have a pill, what do you do?"

"Sometimes I take one of those chewy things."

Allen tried to imagine what she had in mind. "Do you mean an antacid?"

She nodded and walked toward the medicine cabinet, pointing.

He reached up and found a box of antacid tablets. Punching an antacid from the foil wrapper, he said, "There you go."

"And then we rock together," Bekka answered, chewing. White paste began to show at the corners of her mouth.

"She rocks?"

"In the rocking chair."

"Hmm," he nodded. "And do you think I can rock as well as Mommy?" Allen couldn't suppress a smile. Bekka looked very doubtful. Allen wondered how many times Beth had performed this same ritual while he slumbered, completely unaware, in the master bedroom. "Let's go rock," he said, leading her by the hand through the dining room.

Settled in the big oak chair, Bekka sat with both legs across his lap, her head snuggled down against his chest. "She sings too."

"Mommy sings?"

Bekka tucked her thumb through the space between the buttons of his shirt and tickled him with her fingers. "Can you sing?" She looked up for the answer.

"I can try," Allen smiled. The two of them rocked, and Allen sang a weak chorus of "Jesus Loves Me." Just as Allen began to think about putting Bekka back to bed, he heard a noise and looked up to see the hall door open again. An even smaller replica of Beth stood against the door in a white cotton nightgown. This childlike vision of his wife struck Allen painfully.

"I miss Mommy," Abbey whined as she moved across the room to the chair. "And I want up," she said.

To Allen's complete surprise, Bekka seemed content to share her father's lap with her little sister, and the three of them began to rock, both girls snuggling into his chest. "I miss Mommy too," he whispered, kissing the top of each dark head. "I miss Mommy too."

The next morning, Beth woke up feeling cold and stiff inside the double sleeping bag. She'd managed only short catnaps throughout the rest of the night. The cold air made it hard to relax, and in the early morning light, Beth yearned more than anything for a hot bath and a warm bed. Though exhausted and aching, at least she'd made it through another night.

Beth yawned and began to stretch, her body freezing in mid-motion as the pain in her chest reminded her of her broken ribs. At nearly the same time she doubled over and grabbed her leg with her hand. A new and frightening pain in her thigh made her eyes water. She closed her eyes and took a deep breath. When the pain eased, she tried to gently straighten her knees. There, again. What was that?

The ache in her leg had amplified overnight and changed into a burning sensation. She would examine her leg when she dressed. For now, she felt too cold to expose her bare skin to the chilly morning air.

Beth opened her eyes and gazed around the inside of the plane. Something seemed different this morning. The light inside seemed brighter somehow. She looked at the windows and discovered ice covering the inside of the windshield. She listened for the wind and recognized it in the rush of air around the fuselage. Was it coming from a different direction? She could not be certain.

Feeling very thirsty, she reached out to grab the water bottle she had placed near her sleeping bag. As she brought it back to her mouth, she discovered that the water inside had partially frozen. She knocked the plastic against the ceiling of the plane. Reluctantly, the water broke into chunks of ice and a small amount of water. At least it had not frozen solidly. She pulled up the top with her teeth and sucked cold water into her mouth.

Beth lay very still inside the bag, knowing what had happened, yet wishing, hoping, she was wrong. The weather had not improved. She rolled over and reached for her jeans. As she picked them up, she realized that the wet fabric had not dried during the night as she had hoped. Instead, her pants had frozen.

The idea of wearing frozen jeans did not appeal to her, but she had no other choice. Once she had a fire going, she could stand next to it until her pants dried, she assured herself. Eventually, she would feel warm and comfortable again. In fact, the thought of hot denim sounded like a slice of heaven.

Beth crawled out of the bag and rolled onto her back. Her chest didn't hurt as much this morning, she noticed, feeling encouraged. Gently, she probed her right arm, from her wrist to her elbow, and discovered that the puffiness had not gone down. Her right hand seemed even more blue this morning—though her chubby fingers had not swelled further. Still, she could not straighten them.

Beth snatched up her jeans. As she bent her knee to raise her foot into the pant leg, another pain seized her. She doubled over in the cramped quarters of the plane to examine her injury. On both edges of the cut, along the entire length of her thigh, a red streak had developed. She touched it gently and realized that the skin along her thigh had grown hot. As she poked, she felt an intense burning along the whole incision. Beth knew enough to recognize the cardinal signs of infection. Heat. Swelling. Pain.

Bacteria had invaded the wound.

She reached for the cloth bandage Bill had cut from the pilot's shirt and wrapped the wound again carefully. Perhaps she would find some kind of antibiotic ointment in the emergency kit. Surely her body could beat this little invasion. She tied a knot in the bandage and forced worry from her mind.

The fire. I must see to the fire. Beth pulled on the frozen pants, cringing as iced denim hit her skin and goose bumps covered both legs. She shivered. *In this weather, only a fire will help them find me,* she thought. She pulled on her hiking boots, and in her hurry, left the laces untied. Crawling out the door, she dropped onto the ground and reached down to tie the laces. But before she touched her shoes, the changes in the scenery took her breath away.

During the night, nearly five inches of fresh snow had covered the ground. It lay stacked neatly along the underside of the wing and over the horizontal tail section of the plane. She turned around to see it balanced over the curving body of the fuselage. Above her, heavy low clouds continued to drop snow at a frightening angle, blown by a cruel and unrelenting wind.

This was not the weather she had hoped for. The night before, the wind had blown in fitful gusts. Today, it blew a steady gale from the same direction as yesterday—blowing up the little canyon from down below.

With the cold, stiff fingers of her only useful hand, Beth could not adequately tie her own shoes. Instead, she pulled the laces tight and stuffed them under the tongue of the boot. Standing next to the plane, even in the morning light, she could not see her fire. Only the small pile of wood she had stacked in the depression below the plane remained to signal its original location.

Looking around, Beth's heart sank. No one would come looking for her in this weather. And she could not blame them. No one could fly—or should fly—in this. No one would rescue her today. Hitting the side of the fuselage with her left fist, Beth fleetingly expressed her frustration. Then she sighed, a long heavy sigh, swallowing her disappointment like a dose of castor oil.

She eased down the depression toward the fire pit, choosing her path carefully, unwilling to repeat last night's fall. With every step, the contraction of muscles under her thigh caused pain, and before she got to the bottom, she had nearly bitten through her lower lip.

She kept moving for a single purpose—to get the fire started. She needed to be ready in case there was a break in the weather. Who knew when her rescuers would fly over the mountain again, looking for signs of her little plane?

At the bottom of the depression, she located the remains of the fire and began brushing snow from the wood—touching the snow lightly, careful not to burn herself on the hot coals. When she had removed enough snow, she made a most surprising discovery.

The coals at the base of the fire were not hot—they were not even warm. Her fire had been out for a long time. Long enough to cool completely. She continued to clear the snow away, stopping periodically to warm her hand in the pocket of her heavy coat. Eventually Beth uncovered the charcoal from the night before. The fire had burned completely away in the middle—leaving unburned wood in a strange circle around the center of the fire.

Gingerly Beth gathered the wood together, placing the old coal in the center of the fire pit. She picked up the wood, constructing a tepee of half-burned fuel over the coals of the day before. Just as she brought her container of matches from her jacket pocket, she realized that she had not laid tinder or paper to kindle the flames.

She would have to go back to the plane to get some.

The thought made her sigh with exhaustion. She had wasted a trip from the plane, and now she must repeat the slow and painful trip back up the snowy hill. She started up, grabbing the brush through the snow, pulling on branches to help her up the hill. Once more she circled the back of the plane, heading for the cargo door.

As she pulled open the handle, she spied something barely hidden beneath the snow. She bent over, wondering what she might have left outside, and uncovered a foil food package. Had she dropped it? She thought back, trying to remember her meal of the night before. She had been hungry, she remembered, fiercely so. Had she dropped a second package while pulling the first out of the carton?

Perplexed by her discovery, she picked up the foil envelope and tucked it into her jacket pocket. She would have to eat breakfast, so she might as well take everything she needed back down to the fire in one trip.

Inside the cargo section, she rummaged through the supplies looking for loose paper to start the fire. Beth tore the rest of the plastic off her water bottles and dropped them into a half empty box. Then she snatched the cardboard tray that had held the water. This cardboard, along with more paper, would quickly get the fire going again.

Tucking it all under her arm, she turned to shut the door and remembered the medical supply kit. Perhaps she could put some antibiotic ointment on her thigh. She went through the supplies, looking for the white plastic emergency kit. Finding it, she tucked it under her elbow, then decided at the last minute to take another package of food down to the fire.

As she dragged out the box of freeze-dried meals, she noticed that it felt lighter than it had yesterday. She pulled it close to the door, where she could see more clearly, and pried open the lid. Inside, she found one of the cartons missing.

Strange. What had she done with the other container? She remembered the first time she opened it. Inside there had been two cartons of ten foil envelopes each. This morning only one carton with eight envelopes remained. The unopened box was missing. What could have happened to it?

She glanced at the supplies strewn about inside the plane. Had she moved the other carton and forgotten about it? Beth could not shake a new feeling of uneasiness. Baffled, she wondered. *These last two days have been crazy. Am I losing touch with reality? Why can't I remember where I put the second box of food?*

Beth shook her head, forcing herself to think clearly. In spite of her effort, she could think of no reasonable explanation. Putting the question out of her mind, she focused on her primary objective. She had to get a fire going. Tucking another meal envelope into the back pocket of her jeans, she tossed the box back into the cargo area.

When Doyle woke up to a new day, the new snow startled him.

Though he had expected winter to arrive soon, this sudden change in the weather carried the frightening surprise of an airburst. Even considering the late fall season, the nighttime temperature had dropped far below normal.

The arrival of cold weather always left his hip and knee with an unrelenting ache, which no amount of flexing or motion could ease. As of this morning, the warmth of Indian summer had become only a memory to Doyle, which he blamed entirely on the arrival of the woman in the upper meadow. *She brought this awful change in the weather,* he thought bitterly. *If she hadn't come, I'd be layin' in that meadow right now, soakin' up the warmth of fall.*

As Doyle restarted the fire in his pit, the wind howled through the woods nearby. Though his position protected him from the wind's chilling intensity, Doyle could not avoid the falling snow. He pulled a military poncho from his pack and slid it over his head, pulling his long gray ponytail from inside and dropping it over the back. He did the same with his beard, shaking it loose over the front of the poncho. Then he heated water and made a small breakfast of coffee, biscuits, and jerky.

In spite of a satisfying breakfast, Doyle could not shake his concern about the airplane in the meadow above him. This snowstorm certainly precluded a search by any fixed-wing aircraft, he realized. But for how long? How much time did he have to remove any salvageable items from the crash site before crews came to remove the bodies of the woman and any other victims?

He could not afford to let this opportunity escape.

Doyle put the leftover food in the lap of his poncho and called Gilligan. Trotting obediently out from under the shelter of a nearby silver fir, Gilligan lay down in the snow beside his master. Patiently, the dog waited for Doyle to hand-feed him, rewarding each handful with a generous lick of his master's hand.

Still, Doyle did not pet the dog.

Twenty-Two

NEARLY TWENTY MINUTES LATER, in spite of gusting wind and falling snow, Beth had her fire burning. As the flames danced high, she chose a flat rock on the windward side of the fire and sat down.

She took only a moment to expose her thigh and slather the red wound with antibiotic ointment from the meager emergency kit. Having no other bandages, she rewrapped her leg with the torn strips from Ken's shirt before pulling her jeans back up. She knew these bandages held an entire army of bacteria, but Beth had no choice. It would have to do.

There on the rock, cold wind penetrated her many layers of clothes, stabbing her back. It burned her neck and her ears. Her hair, carried forward by the wind, continually whipped into her eyes and mouth. Beth stayed on the rock as she ate a lumpy breakfast of cold freeze-dried stew mixed with water. This she followed with a chaser of bottled water.

She tried to consider her situation objectively. Just a thousand feet lower on the mountain, the weather might be very different. In the Northwest, even a slight change in elevation could make an enormous difference in weather conditions. Beth imagined a lower elevation where nothing more than light rain fell through cool breezy air. She might not feel so miserable if she weren't so high up in the foothills. She shivered and tucked her face behind the collar of her jacket, trying to get out of the wind.

From her seat on the rock, Beth stared up at the wreck. She

observed the torn metal and broken glass, marveling again at the shell that had once been an airplane. Having taken only one physics class in college, Beth had no idea what kind of force could crack open the shell of a plane and fold back the heavy propellers like that.

She saw electrical wires hanging uselessly from the opening between the wing and the fuselage. Only a miracle let her live through such horrific damage. But now she began to wonder about the purpose of such a miracle. *What's the point, God?* she wondered. *Why survive the crash only to die of exposure up here on the mountain?* The deteriorating weather made that possibility seem frighteningly real. She pushed the hair out of her face and stared again into the flames.

She considered that possibility for a long time, and then another terrifying thought occurred to her. She looked around the meadow at the snow-covered trees and white surroundings. If she were looking down at this meadow from an airplane, the white underbelly of the fuselage would blend perfectly into the backdrop of newly fallen snow. In all of creation, God had never designed a more successful camouflage than the one now hiding her broken plane. With a sickening dread, Beth realized that in this snow, no one would ever spot the crash site from above. No matter how low the altitude or how slow the speed, the crash site had become essentially invisible from the air.

Realizing that rescuers would not see the plane from the air made her signal fire critically important, and Beth decided to get up and collect more wood. In spite of the wind and snow, in spite of Bill's death, in spite of her injuries, in spite of her own deep sadness, Beth had to keep the fire burning. The image of Allen holding Noah in his arms as he reached for the kitchen phone flashed before her. She had to make it home—for Noah, for the girls, and for Allen.

Beth limped to the woodpile where she had stored the ax. The fuel supply had grown perilously low, with only a few large pieces and a small pile of foot-long branches. Though exhausted and cold, Beth knew she needed to cut more wood. She would not let discouragement win. Kneeling awkwardly, cautious of her wounds and her sore ribs, she ran her hand under the pile along the dry ground where she had hidden the ax.

With wiggling fingers, her left hand crept along the ground, feeling nothing. Beth could not locate the ax handle. Surprised, she leaned forward, stretching until her chest complained, reaching as far under the wood as she could. Nothing.

Confused, Beth began taking the woodpile apart piece by piece, shaking the snow off the wood. Still, she found no ax. Underneath, only the naked green of woodland brush covered the ground. Bewildered, Beth stood completely still, the wind swirling around her. She watched the snow begin to stick to the exposed ground before her. What had she done? Where had she left the ax?

She retraced her steps around the fire, kicking at the snow with her boots, looking for signs of the ax handle. How could she have lost something so valuable? Frustrated beyond any emotion she had felt so far, Beth wanted to kick herself. *Where did I put it? How could I have been so careless?*

She dropped another piece of wood on the fire and crawled back up the depression to the crash site. Walking carefully around the plane, she searched the ground for the ax. Perhaps she had dropped it there last night. Perhaps in her eagerness to check on Bill she had misplaced it. But the ax was not to be found.

Now even angrier with herself, Beth walked to the perimeter of the meadow, where trees grew in short thick groves. Her ax hadn't walked away; eventually she would find it. Until then, she would gather wood with her bare hands.

Because she had only one arm to use, Beth gathered large pieces one branch at a time. Some she kicked off of the trunks of fallen dead trees. Others she sat on, bouncing harder and harder until a piece broke loose. More than once, she lost her balance and fell into the snow, leaving wet patches of snow clinging to her jeans. The motion left her arm aching, the same deep unnameable ache that brought tears to her eyes. But Beth refused to give in to her pain. Piece by piece, she re-created her woodpile.

It did feel good to be moving and working. The cold didn't seem to penetrate as deeply while she dragged branches across the meadow to the fire. She made several trips before she suddenly ran out of energy. Exhausted and trembling, she decided to take a moment to sit beside the fire. The snow had let up some, and she spent several minutes praying for a break in the weather. *I need to go home, Lord. Please let me go home. I can't do this Daniel Boone thing.* She opened her eyes and brushed away new tears.

Her first glance at the fire irritated her. The constant wind made the flames burn hot and fast, using fuel unevenly. The side toward the wind had burned to ashes before the leeward side even began to burn. With a stick, Beth reached forward to stir the wood. She poked and pushed, trying to rearrange the wood without having to use her hands. As she did, a large pop startled her, and she jumped as sparks flew out from the fire. As Beth scuttled out of the way, she dropped down onto her left elbow. She had narrowly escaped being hit in the face with burning embers.

She crawled back to her rock and sat again, panting heavily, the ache in her arm and shoulder reaching a new high. Frightened by the sparks, she vowed to be more careful around the fire. This combination of wind and flames proved dangerous, and her weakened state left her vulnerable to mistakes. Here in the woods, such errors could be deadly.

She threw her stick into the fire and sat motionless for a moment, mesmerized by dancing flames. As she closed her eyes, letting the heat warm her face, a strange odor caught her attention. She glanced around to see what would cause such a foul smell. A marble-sized coal had landed on the front of her vest where it lay unprotected by the denim jacket. She glanced down just in time to see the errant spark glow red on her chest.

Startled, she stood abruptly, brushing it away from her clothes and hurling it back into the fire pit. The hot wood burned her left hand as she brushed it away.

"Ouch." Beth carefully examined her blistered fingers, bitterly frustrated by the mistake. A small white bubble had already formed on the inside of her middle finger and at the tip of her index. "Great job, Beth," she told herself.

She had started to pick away the melted fragments protruding from the synthetic fleece of her vest when a memory surfaced. In high school, the mother of one of Beth's friends had struck a match only to have her entire blouse explode into flames. The woman had suffered severe burns as she tried to pull off the flaming blouse. By comparison, blistered fingertips didn't seem so horrible. Beth sighed.

Beth pulled away another chunk of burned fleece and dropped it on the ground. The spark had burned through her wool sweater

as well, leaving a perfectly round ashen hole. She pulled her protected right hand away from her chest to better examine the hole,
and in doing so Beth discovered a small burn on the skin of her
injured wrist.

She shrugged off the burn. She couldn't feel it anyway.

Immediately, the significance of this fact startled Beth. She had
not felt the burn! Again she poked the red spot with her left hand.
Under the severe blister, she could feel the deep touch of her fingers pressing down on her skin, but she could not feel the burn
itself.

The realization slapped her. Early on, Beth guessed that she had
fractured her right arm somewhere near the elbow. But the burned
skin signified something else. Something else had to be wrong
inside her arm. She had lost the feeling in the skin. Over time,
either the swelling of soft tissue or the fracture itself had cut off the
blood supply to the nerves in her forearm. Though her fracture
would certainly heal, this kind of damage might be permanent.

The prospect of permanent damage frightened Beth, bringing
tears to her eyes.

If she didn't get help soon, Beth might never use her right hand
again. The shock of it, the blinding fear of this possibility, took her
breath away.

Moments later, Beth made her decision. She would hike out.
After all, she had a map. She would not sit on this rock forever,
keeping a fire while she lost her memory, her possessions, and her
health. She refused to let the nerves in her right hand continue to
deteriorate while she waited for someone else to save her. She
would save herself.

She would not sit beside an invisible plane crash waiting for winter to turn to spring. She had a life to live, children to raise, a husband who needed her. She could walk out. And she would.

She had no more than arrived at this conclusion when she
found herself assailed by doubt. Was she thinking clearly enough to
make this decision? Perhaps her reasoning skills had already left
her. Would she wander in the woods until she died of exposure, far
away from the help she knew would come eventually?

She thought of the ax and remembered with certainty that she
had tucked it under the wood. She had wanted the tool to stay dry,
she remembered. And now she couldn't even find it.

And now the threat of losing her hand pushed her forward, leaving her with no easy choices.

But you don't even know where you are. A map won't do you any good. Another doubt tossed her off course.

But I have an idea, she argued. *I know where we were heading when the plane went down. I can't be more than ten miles upland from Clearwater Township. I've walked that far in one weekend before. From here, anything downhill is going to bring me closer to civilization. Maybe I'll get lucky. At this time of year, I might run into a hunter or a hiker. Someone with a cell phone.*

Beth thought quickly. Mentally, she sorted through the supplies inside the plane, choosing what she would carry out with her. Not too much, she decided. She would make better time with a small load.

Suddenly Beth felt lighter, freer. She would walk out. Simple enough. Down the mountain. Away from the plane. Away from the freezing weather. And she would walk straight into Allen's arms. The thought gave her hope, and she felt a surge of energy for the first time since waking up alone inside the plane this morning. A little tingle of excitement made her feel warm and alive.

She crawled back up the hill to the plane. Rummaging through the cargo area, she found the nylon bag that had stored the sleeping bags. With the drawstring closed, the bag had a long string loop she could drape over her strong shoulder. She pulled the bag shut and practiced. Yes, she would carry supplies in this.

She pulled the container of matches from her back pocket and dropped it into the bag. Then she added all the remaining envelopes of freeze-dried food. Eight packages should hold her. Then she remembered the water bottles and added four. With all this snow, water wouldn't be hard to find.

Beth yanked the two sleeping bags from the inside of the plane and separated them. Using one hand, she rolled the inner bag, brushing snow from it as she rolled. At last, she wrapped the elastic bands around the outside of the bag. She could carry this under one arm as she walked.

Glancing at Bill's watch, she saw that the morning was almost gone. With only five or six hours of daylight left, Beth had to get moving. She crawled to the rear passenger door of the plane and pulled her work crate from the wreckage. Taking her notebook from the crate, she penned a note in an awkward left-handed scrawl.

Day two, she wrote. *Weather deteriorating. Snowing heavily. I have decided to walk out. Will head downhill with map.* She signed the note. *I love you, Allen. Beth.*

Then, worried that rescuers might not find the note, she left the book open and wedged the cardboard cover between the plane's passenger door and the frame. Holding the notebook with one hand, she shoved the door closed with her knee. *There,* she thought, satisfied with her work. *No one could miss that.*

Turning away from the plane, Beth started down the meadow. As she faced the wind directly, it seemed stronger, driving wet flakes of snow into her face. She tucked her head down into the collar of her coat. *It will be better when I get below the trees,* she told herself.

Then, thinking only of home, she walked away from the crash site.

Twenty-Three

THIRTY-SIX HOURS AFTER THE FAA declared the little plane overdue, Beth's father drove Allen back to the search center. This time they brought the keys to Beth and Allen's car, knowing that it must be removed from the Thun Field parking lot. The thought of bringing the car home without Beth seemed like a violation to Allen. The extra car keys felt like a brick banging around in the pocket of his jeans.

On this second day of the search, the number of people waiting in the hangar had not changed. But the atmosphere was markedly different. They didn't share the same light joking or jovial conversation of the first morning. Even the searchers' card games seemed less spirited. The volume lower.

They were somber, quieter, and Allen realized that he had seen this kind of crowd before. They resembled the kind of visitors he'd seen in the homes of the bereaved after a funeral, and the thought threatened to make him angry.

Part of Allen wanted to go around the room cheering them on. "Don't give up! The weather will change. We'll find her!" Instead, he gritted his teeth, poured himself a cup of coffee from the still-chugging urn, and took his usual seat in a hard plastic chair next to his father-in-law.

To some extent the quiet room provided a welcome relief to the house. Everything about their home reminded Allen of Beth. Her presence filled the rooms, the closets, the decorations.

Her gardening shoes waiting at the door to the backyard.

Her ongoing grocery list held by a butterfly magnet on the refrigerator.

The empty pillow next to his own.

At the search center, the absence of these reminders relieved Allen's overtaxed emotions. Here he felt closer to Beth, closer to the people and the action that would bring her safely home.

Allen and Richard watched the last of the crews arrive and check in at the operations desk. Clear disappointment showed on the pilots' faces as they requested and received the latest weather update. *They came to fly,* he thought. *The waiting must frustrate them as much as us.*

With nothing else to do, nearly everyone picked up a doughnut or filled a cup with coffee. One by one, they paused at the table and nodded politely to Allen and Richard before moving back to their chairs. Some smiled. A few murmured encouraging words. One or two introduced themselves. Others sat alone, reading novels. One or two groups huddled together over search maps, discussing their progress. The waiting felt heavier than rain-soaked cedar.

Doyle woke up early the next morning and decided to break camp and climb back to the upper meadow. He planned to strip the plane. But first he would find a hiding place in the trees surrounding the meadow, where he could stow the things he had scavenged from the crash site.

With any luck at all, Doyle hoped to find lots of things he could use. He hoped to remove enough sheet metal to fix a persistent roof leak he'd battled with through two winters. Insulation from the firewall would keep the wind from penetrating his cabin wall below the front window. As he walked uphill, the possibilities danced through Doyle's head like a child's Christmas wish list. He might be able to salvage the plane's rear window and add a skylight to his dark cabin. Perhaps they carried a medical kit. And if he were very lucky, the dead pilot might wear a size ten shoe.

But he had to hurry. He must finish stripping the plane before the search team arrived. He didn't have time to make trips back and forth from the cabin. However, if he hid his treasures, he would finish in plenty of time, no matter how suddenly the weather cleared.

This morning the pain in both his hip and knee left Doyle limping. Because of the pain, Doyle started off cautiously, slowly. Newly fallen snow, blown by a fierce southwesterly wind, covered the ground unevenly. Doyle had always worn army boots with flat soles and slick bottoms. These did not manage the uneven ground well. Doyle swore as he slipped frequently, each stumble jarring his injured joints and increasing his misery.

The difficult hike made his pack unstable as well. It slid off to one side with each misstep, making him pause often to reposition the weight on his shoulders and adjust the straps. *It's her fault I'm up here in this weather,* he thought. *Her fault.* And then, instead of cursing the weather, or the path, or his boots, Doyle began to curse the dead woman in the meadow. *If only she hadn't come. If only she'd stayed where she belonged.*

The walk up the mountain took a great deal longer on this snowy morning. Pausing frequently to catch his breath, Doyle sought protection from the wind by standing under the trees. With every uphill step, Doyle's anger and bitterness grew. The familiar ache in his knee had grown into a monstrous pain, and his chest hurt as well.

It seemed as though Doyle could not breathe deeply enough to satisfy his body's need for air. Though the breathing itself did not hurt, the pain in his left shoulder would not go away. The sudden winter temperatures had caused his unrelenting ache and breathlessness, he reasoned.

Frustrated, Doyle paused and looked for a place to sit down. Gilligan, as usual, stopped running to return and check on his master. He sat before him, tipped his head, and seemed to ask why they were stopping.

"Cuz I can't go like I used to, ol' boy," Doyle said, his voice tired. He sat down in the snow, ignoring the cold ground as he panted, struggling for air. When the clamping in his chest subsided, he told the dog, "I won't last much longer out here."

Maybe soon, he thought, *the memories, the pain, all the misery will finally come to an end.* And in the midst of his bitterness and anger toward the woman, Doyle felt the slightest tinge of relief.

When he could breathe normally again, Doyle resumed his trek. The slope and the snow forced him to focus on his steps. Today he made no effort to watch for signs of others. Instead, he wanted only to get to the woods near the meadow. He needed to rest. This kind of trekking got harder every time he did it.

At last, Doyle crept through the woods at the upper end of the meadow. He chuckled when he first spotted the plane. Now covered with snow, it had become virtually invisible. He wouldn't have to cover the plane with tree branches as he had originally planned. Winter had covered it for him.

In the woods, the falling snow was more sparse. Doyle chose a place away from the plane behind a small grove of misshapen silver firs. He would not build a fire; he could not afford to leave evidence of having been there. The thick trees standing between Doyle and the prevailing wind would provide adequate shelter.

From this location, Doyle could not see the wreck itself. He removed his pack and tied the dog to a small bush. Then he dropped to the ground and crept forward until he found the perfect observation spot. Resting his elbows on a small bump, he brought the binoculars to his eyes. In the flat midday light, Doyle knew his lenses would not be seen. He scanned the meadow.

A fire!

Someone had built another fire. The woman must not have died during the night, as Doyle had believed. A sudden rush of guilt swept over him. While Doyle had plundered the supplies, the woman lay injured and helpless inside the plane. He never meant to hurt the woman. The more he thought about her up there in the plane alone, the more his thoughts and feelings got tangled up—like fishing line off a broken reel.

After all, she was not his responsibility. He'd never invited her up here.

Yet only an animal would leave a woman to die.

He raised his binoculars and looked over the site again. He could not see the small dark-haired woman anywhere. Why not? Had she gone back inside the plane? He crept back to his place by the silver firs and pulled a piece of jerky out of his pack. Chewing thoughtfully, he wondered about her. Where had she gone?

He tried to think clearly. Not only had she managed to live through the bitterly cold night, she had enough stamina left to build a fire—a good fire by the looks of it. And she'd managed to do it without her trusty ax—the ax he had stolen.

In spite of his bitterness, Doyle had to admire her. The woman had spunk.

He decided to circle the meadow again. Perhaps he could get a better view of the situation from another angle. As he moved, he rationalized, *This woman doesn't need my help. She can survive up here for as long as it takes for someone to find her.*

Leaving the pack and the dog behind, he started the same wide slow circle he had made the day before. As he came around the other side of the plane, Doyle noticed that the cargo door was wide open. Still, he had not seen the woman.

Something felt different about the crash site this morning. But Doyle could not quite identify the source of his uneasiness. He looked up at the sky, checking the weather again. The clouds had not changed. No sign of blue flickered among them. Snow fell into the meadow with the thickness of sifted flour. Why hadn't he seen her?

Doyle decided to risk giving the plane a closer daylight inspection.

He continued slowly around the meadow until he came to a place where the woods protruded in a narrow peninsula into the meadow. Creeping stealthily from bush to tree, Doyle approached the plane. At last, keeping one eye on the plane, he dropped to his chest and crawled along the snow-covered ground, confident his poncho would keep him dry. Slowly, cautiously, Doyle approached.

Scanning the ground before him, Doyle's gaze caught something so startling that he stopped moving entirely. Before giving all his attention to the discovery, Doyle glanced up again to check for the woman. All clear.

Focusing on the ground again, he saw a single set of tracks made by a small treaded boot in the untouched snow. Doyle rose up, carefully eyeing the path of footprints as they pointed away from the plane. Completely forgetting his concerns of being spotted, he moved onto his hands and knees. For as far as he could see, heading down the meadow and away from the crash site, a single line of footprints made a path leading away from the plane.

Doyle knew that the woman had frequently left the plane and walked into the trees. He'd seen her gather wood. But this set of tracks did not follow the usual pattern. This time she had not walked into the woods closest to the fire, but away from it. Where had she gone?

Perplexed, Doyle crept toward the cargo door, which now hung partially open above him. When he reached the tail of the plane, Doyle squatted. He spent a few moments carefully observing the ground. A mass of fresh prints—each with the same sole pattern—clustered around the cargo door. Inside the tail section, boxes lay opened, and materials of all kinds lay strewn across the ceiling of the plane. Without moving, Doyle listened carefully. He heard nothing but the sound of the wind whistling through the trees and the gentle rocking of the airplane.

He bent over and looked forward from the cargo area. From this viewpoint, he couldn't see clearly into the passenger area. Doyle knew that the pilot had not survived. But had there been others with the woman? If so, where had the other passengers gone?

Doyle slunk around the tail of the plane and silently approached the rear passenger door. He put his ear to the side of the plane and listened. No sound came from inside. Glancing around, he reached out and turned the door handle. Pulling gently, he opened the door, scowling as the first screech came from the damaged hinge.

Doyle leapt out of the way, hiding behind the door. Carefully, though with more boldness, Doyle reached out and pulled again. As he did, a small notebook fell to the ground. He bent down to pluck it out of the snow, knowing instantly that she had left a note. He held it face up, squinting as he tried to read the words. Snow had soaked the paper, the ink running in dark streaks down the page. Unable to decipher it, Doyle threw the book aside and crawled into the plane.

The hulk that had blocked his view turned out to be a body. He pulled the remnants of a yellow cotton shirt from the face of an older man. Doyle went through his pockets, hoping for a new pocketknife. Instead, he found something even more valuable—a Leatherman tool attached to the key ring in his shirt pocket. Doyle slipped it into his own coat. He checked the man's wrist. A white strip on his tanned forearm betrayed the position of a wristwatch, now missing.

Oh well, Doyle thought. *I don't need to tell time.*

Though the man's body bore no obvious signs of trauma, Doyle knew that internal injuries often left no trace. He checked the man's shoes before continuing his search. He moved toward the pilot he had first observed through his binoculars. Checking his pockets and the area around his seat, Doyle found only keys and a credit card, which he left behind. He tried on the man's baseball cap. Delighted with the fit, he chose to keep it. Then he checked the soles of his shoes. Too small. Doyle backed out of the fuselage.

Doyle surmised that the crash had killed the pilot instantly. He had never been removed from his seat belt. The first man—the hulk in the passenger area—had somehow gotten out of whatever seat he had occupied during the flight. He lived, Doyle figured, at least for a time. Perhaps his death explained the eeriness of the crash site this morning. Or perhaps it explained more than that.

Whatever the exact order of events, Doyle knew one thing with certainty.

The woman was gone.

Twenty-Four

BETH HAD NOT GONE FAR before she realized the gravity of her decision. Her hike would not follow a smooth raked trail like those in a national forest. She would not traverse the paved byway of a county bike path. Instead, Beth realized, she must make her own trail. Walking into the wind, through waist-high thickets and tall grass covered with deep wet snow, she trudged downhill.

In some places, the presence of rocky berms made the ground cover higher than her head. These impenetrable sections of the meadow forced her to skirt large islands of thorny bushes in search of an easier way. Snow made the ground slippery, and the simple act of staying on her feet took intense concentration. Soon her knees ached with the effort of keeping her balance, her ribs ached with the effort of standing erect. Her thigh, engorged with the swelling blood supply of a painful infection, throbbed. Lowering her body down steep drops increased her pain to excruciating levels. Still, Beth put one foot in front of the other, determined to go on.

Having only one good arm, Beth found it increasingly difficult to stay upright. Whenever she slipped, her left arm would fly up and away from her chest. Her right arm, which seemed to forget her injured elbow, tried to help too, jerking roughly inside her vest. These abrupt movements brought tears to her eyes. *I must go on,* she told herself sternly. *I can't give up.* Another slip, another misstep, and the pain in her elbow made her hug herself with her good arm, biting her lip to keep from crying out.

Inadequate for the great task ahead of her, Beth felt weak. Exhaustion made it difficult to focus on the terrain below her feet. The wind stung her face and burned her nose. She had not traveled a full hour before she decided to stop and rest. She dropped her sleeping bag and pulled her pack from her shoulder, fishing out a water bottle. Even in the cold air, she panted, and a trickle of sweat made its way down the center of her shoulder blades. She pulled up the top and drank long swallows of cold liquid. She relished the refreshment of water, drinking greedily.

Beth sat down on her sleeping bag, thinking, but beyond caring, that doing so would soak the bag. Before she sat down, Beth had not felt the full impact of the cold, even though wading through the snow had drenched her jeans all the way up to her knees, and the wet fabric flopped against her legs. But when she stopped moving, frigid air enveloped her like a blanket of ice.

Shivering, she missed her signal fire. She remembered that she'd stoked the fire before she left the crash site and then walked away from its blazing warmth. Doubt lingered on her mind. Should she have stayed? She took another swig of water, wiping her lips with her jacket sleeve. One look at the blue fingers of her right hand confirmed her desperate need for medical help. She could not have stayed another hour.

No. Whether good or bad, she'd made her choice. Whatever energy she'd expended by walking this far would be doubled or even tripled by turning back. She must continue down the mountain.

She touched her right forearm, testing the sensitivity of her skin, wondering if the nerve damage had gotten worse. Gratefully, she realized that she could still feel the touch of her own left hand. Lightly, she scraped along the back of her right hand with the fingernail of her left index finger. Watching the motion, she saw the tiny white line left on the skin of her hand. But she could not feel the touch. She had no sensation of the scratch of nail against skin. Her hand seemed to be anesthetized—as heavy and leaden as her mouth after a dental filling. But had it gotten worse? She could not tell.

One thing she knew for sure. If she did not get help soon, she might lose the use of her hand. She couldn't go back to the meadow.

No. She must go on.

Allen waited at the search center for nearly two hours before a grim-faced Harry Armstrong approached.

"Good morning, Allen, Richard," he said, nodding at both men. He pulled a chair out in front of them and spun it backward, wrapping his knees around it. "I gave Paula the morning off," he began, sitting with his forearms resting on the chair back. "I thought you'd like to know what we have so far." Allen nodded. "From your last flight, we have the approximate coordinates for a crash site. Perhaps we have nothing more than an unexplained ELT, maybe something bouncing off of canyon walls—though I doubt that. Right now, I have commercial traffic listening for the ELT."

"Have you heard the signal again today?" Richard asked.

"Not yet," Harry answered. "And we may not. It may be that the impact damaged the transmitter, or . . ." He paused and took a deep breath. "Well, the battery could run down soon. Still, we'll listen." He toyed with the end of his beard. "I'm considering sending in a ground crew. They might be able to get close enough to hear the signal somewhere nearby. They're on alert, preparing to go in."

"When will you decide?" Allen asked.

"I think, judging by the Doppler radar and the wind speed, that the worst of this system will pass in the next hour or so. Of course there are two or three more disturbances parked off the coast, waiting to take its place. We'd be so much better off if we didn't have this arctic blast sitting just north of the mountain. But we can't control that. When this system goes by, I'll reevaluate the weather and make a decision. Whatever we do, our crew will be prepared to spend the night."

Richard and Allen exchanged glances. "You don't think you can find anything before dark?" Allen asked.

Harry smiled, "I doubt it. Though who knows." He shrugged. "We could get lucky. I'll let you know as soon as I decide."

"I want to go in with the ground crew."

Allen's request seemed to startle Harry. "I don't think so. You don't have any idea what you might find up there. If they do find the plane, it won't be a pretty sight. You don't want that to be your last memory of her." Harry looked at Allen, his eyes intense. "Our crew has trained to work together. You'd only be in the way."

"I promise you I won't interfere. But I have to be there. I have to see it with my own eyes."

"They might not find anything."

"But I might find Beth. If she's still alive up there, she needs me." Allen tried to calm the sense of near hysteria he felt. In order to get permission, he had to convince Harry that he would be an asset to the ground crew. "I might be able to help the crew positively identify . . ." Allen's voice cracked and he glanced down. "And if she was killed, I can't live the rest of my life without knowing what happened—what she faced. What it was like for her."

"Okay," Harry said, his voice solemn. "I'll consider it. But only because you are young and in good shape." He coughed and glanced away. "I'll let you know."

"Thank you," Richard said. "Thank you for working to find my daughter."

Allen saw tears in Beth's father's eyes.

Harry Armstrong nodded, "I know it sounds trite, but it *is* what we're here for."

That the woman in the meadow left the crach site surprised Doyle. How had he missed the fact that she had survived the night? He'd come back to the crash site believing that she was dead. Instead, he found her not only alive and well, but wandering off into the mountains alone.

Why would she do that? Only a fool would consider striking out alone in this weather. This development forced Doyle to rethink his plan.

Carefully, he made his way down the nearby depression to the fire pit. He chose a broad flat rock and brushed the snow away. Sitting down, he dropped his chin onto one hand and stared into the fire.

She had built up the fire before she took off, but left no wood stacked nearby. Perhaps she had gone out to locate more wood. If so, why had she chosen the direction she had? No, Doyle decided. This woman had chosen to leave. She must have planned to hike down the mountain for help. She must have guessed that no help would come after her in this weather.

From the looks of it, it seemed to Doyle that she had headed toward Clearwater. A wise destination, he thought. In the woods near Clearwater, she would find skiers' cabins, campers, and snow-mobilers. Among these stood the cabins of other loners. Someone down there would surely be fool enough to take her in, he thought. That is, if she made it that far.

Mentally, Doyle pictured the rugged terrain lying between the meadow and the tiny unincorporated town nearly fifteen miles below. *A smart choice, but a miserable and dangerous trip.* Along the way, she would have to ford a fast-running stream, climb through rocky ravines, avoid unexpected drop-offs, and unless she were very care-ful, she might even run into a cliff or two. Most women would never make it.

This new situation frustrated Doyle. By choosing to hike out alone, she would undoubtedly manage somehow to die out there on his mountain, forcing rescuers to do an even more extensive search of his territory. He began to resent her presence even more. He hadn't asked her to come. He had no intention of caring for some lost woman. He shouldn't have to be the one to help her. But by leaving the plane, she had become his responsibility. She had wandered into his territory, and he had to see her through to the other side in order to protect himself from being discovered.

Doyle held his hands up to the warmth of the fire. What kind of crazy woman would come up here in the first place? Sitting there in the heat of her waning fire, Doyle made his decision. He would follow her. Perhaps she *would* make it out on her own, and he could be certain of her safety without ever having contact with the woman. A small flame of hope began to rise in his heart. Yes, just like the elk hunter, Doyle would follow this woman at a distance, watching over her without her ever suspecting a thing.

But first, he would raid the airplane.

Reluctantly, Beth stood up. Stiffness had already set in, even after only a brief rest. *I must keep going,* she encouraged herself.

Glancing up at the sky, she wondered about the time. How long had she been walking? She checked Bill's wristwatch. It was already quarter after one. This late in the fall, limited daylight would restrict the distance she could cover before nightfall. She needed to keep moving if she hoped to get below the snow level. How far down, she wondered, would the snow turn to rain?

She tucked her sleeping bag under her left elbow and picked up the strings of the storage bag with the fingers of her left hand. Since she had nearly emptied her water bottle, Beth decided to carry it in her good hand as she walked. With slow steps, Beth headed down the meadow again, moving toward the stand of trees lining the lower end.

Facing this direction, the wind blowing up the canyon hit her head-on, biting her face. Gusts of freezing air forced her to lean forward, tuck her head down, and gasp for air. For a moment Beth wondered why she found it so hard to breathe facing the wind. With her head down, Beth had trouble looking ahead as she walked. More than once, she stumbled and narrowly avoided a bad fall.

Perhaps when she reached the trees, she would not have to fight the wind. She could only hope. She trudged on. Without warning, the thorny branch of a snow-covered bush reached out and clutched the rough fabric of Ken Bohannan's jacket, pulling open the front. Frustrated, Beth stepped sideways, twisting as she did so in an effort to yank the coat loose. Pain coming from the wound in her left thigh stabbed her, and Beth lost her balance. Her right foot slid away, and in an instant Beth felt her body start over the edge of a steep hill on her right. Though she tried to pull left, she could not stop the fall.

As she tumbled, Beth made a conscious effort to hold on to the water bottle. Falling hard, Beth rolled faster and faster. As her body plummeted down the hill, Beth tried desperately to grab at the ground with her left arm to stop the fall. Bumping along the hill, she struck her shoulder and elbow repeatedly, screaming in fresh agony.

At last, Beth slammed into the trunk of a small tree and stopped rolling. As she waited for the pain to subside, she lay very still. She lifted her face and brushed the snow from her forehead. From her position on her stomach, Beth saw that she had fallen down a steep, though soft, ravine. Trembling, she moved into a sitting position, hugging her knees and waiting for her breathing to return to normal.

Eventually she got up, brushing herself off, and began searching for the bag that had been thrown from her shoulder during the fall. Looking down, Beth gasped. She had fallen to the very edge of a nearly vertical cliff, punctuated along the way by rocky outcroppings. If the little tree had not stopped her fall, she would have gone sailing out into the air over the trees, only to be battered on the rocks below. Beth breathed a prayer of thanks.

Then she saw them. In the force of her first roll, Beth had launched her pack into the air. It had gone over the edge, along with her sleeping bag. Both lay far below, near the middle of the cliff. Still trembling from pain and fear, Beth sat down and began to cry. Why couldn't anything go right for her? Why did she seem doomed to so many unexplainable mistakes? She gave in to sobbing, weeping in an anguish born of loneliness and fear. She had lost everything in the fall and had barely managed to avoid going over the cliff herself.

I shouldn't have left the plane, she thought. *I've made a horrible mistake. I'll never get out of here alive.*

Stop it, the stronger part of Beth coached. *Crying will not retrieve your things. They're gone. Let them go. Besides, if you keep moving, you may not need them. You may find someone just below the tree line.* But even her most severe coaching could not stem her tears.

Slowly, Beth stood, feeling a little dizzy as she began brushing snow from her clothes. "Help me, Lord," she begged. "I have to get down this mountain. I have to get home." Every part of her body seemed to hurt. The fall had managed to multiply her discomfort. She rotated her head, tucking her chin to her shoulder on either side, hoping to ease the pain in her neck.

Opening her jacket, she pulled up the collar of her vest. Beth wiped her face dry and turned to face the hill behind her. Hemmed in by the cliff, she could not proceed down the mountain from this position. She had no other choice but to climb back up to the meadow.

The hill looked daunting from this position, and Beth wondered how she could ever make it back. She didn't have the strength or stamina to scramble straight up. She decided to work back and forth across the hill, zigzagging her way to the top. It would take more energy, and she would have to be very careful, but she could do it.

She started up and across the hill. When she came to the place where she planned to switch back, Beth used the toe of her right boot to dig into the edge of the hill, making a small step. Then, slowly and with great care, she turned to face the hill. Here the hill was so steep that only three feet separated Beth's nose from the snow-covered ground in front of her. Keeping her toes together and letting her heels hang out over the incline, Beth inched her way around until she changed direction and started up the hill again.

Two zigzags up, near where she had started her tumble over the hill, a shiny reflection caught Beth's eye. She bent over and touched the snow. Her bottle! While her other things had been hurled over the cliff by the force of the fall, a small clump of grass had stopped her rolling water bottle.

She picked it up and stuffed it inside her vest. In spite of the situation, Beth smiled. With the bottle, she could find and carry water. With water, she could survive.

Long moments later, shaking and exhausted from the effort of the climb, Beth emerged from the edge of the hill. Her pounding heart and trembling legs forced her to sit and rest. She lay down on her left side and closed her eyes, willing her whole body to relax.

After a few moments, a wave of hunger passed over her, and she realized that she no longer had any food. Part of her suddenly panicked. How could she walk so far without food? But Beth refused to give in to the fear.

No problem, she told herself. *I'll be down the mountain in less than forty-eight hours. Hunger is always worse at the beginning.* Beth rolled onto her back and let the snow fall on her face.

Twenty-Five

HAVING NO IDEA HOW LONG the plane might remain unattended, Doyle decided to raid it immediately. At some point, the presence of search crews would keep him from the meadow. Doyle walked up the small depression directly to the cargo door.

One by one, he brought boxes out of the cargo hold. Taking his time, he opened each container and pulled out the contents, examining everything carefully. Doyle had no use for the technical items, the vials, or telemetry supplies. Having hidden in the mountains these past thirty years, he could not identify most of the strange black boxes with their dials, knobs, and readouts.

As snow continued to fall, Doyle worried less and less about covering his own presence. Boldly he walked the shortest distance between the plane and his campsite, accumulating goods slowly, choosing the best first, leaving less valuable items for later trips.

Doyle chose the emergency kit but passed over both cameras. He had no use for pictures. He didn't need to remember where he'd been or what he'd seen. Doyle didn't have to remember, because he'd never left. For what seemed like an eternity, these mountains had been his only home.

Doyle delighted in the little fishing kit and in the bandages and medicines that had been so carefully packed with it. He found a gray plastic crate in the passenger compartment and dumped the contents out so he could use it to carry the smaller items.

Going through the contents of the crate, he found a small

purse, a leather-covered Bible the size of a paperback book, and reams of paper covered in scientific gibberish. Curious, he opened the purse and went through it. In the wallet, he found a driver's license with a tiny picture of the same slant-eyed, black-haired woman he'd spotted resting outside the plane. From her birth date, he calculated that she had just passed her thirty-first birthday. Her height and weight resembled those of most junior high students. *Cheng.* Her last name was Cheng.

He searched through her wallet and found eight dollars in cash, a single credit card, and two pictures. In one photo, two girls, both elementary-school aged, sat together in a rattan chair. A plump baby boy sat grinning between them. In another, a professional-looking man sat smiling in a navy jacket and burgundy tie. He, too, looked Asian, and while Doyle gazed at his face, he felt his anger ignite toward the man in the picture. Another one, just like her. In addition to the wallet, he found tissues, keys, and hand lotion. These things Doyle ignored as he tucked the purse into the bottom of the crate.

Since he had already searched the dead men, Doyle moved directly to the cockpit of the plane. Using the tools in his new Leatherman, he spent a long time curled under the dashboard of the small plane, carefully removing one of the four radios. To protect it from the falling snow, he covered it with the cloth from the dead man's face and carried it to his stash. Though the radio might never work again, Doyle looked forward to tinkering with it. Such a project would keep him busy during the long dark winter. If he could repair it and find a battery, Doyle might be able to listen in on the various agencies present in the federal forest. In spite of the snow and cold, he smiled. With a working radio, Doyle might actually be able to stay one step ahead of them.

When he had taken all of the most important items, including two sleeping bags that had been stuffed into holes in the damaged fuselage, Doyle stopped for a moment's rest near the woman's campfire. So far, he guessed that he had spent nearly two hours taking things from the crash site. With only a few hours of daylight left, Doyle felt torn. Part of him wanted to trail the woman. Another part wanted to get his stash safely moved to the cabin, where it would not be discovered by the prying eyes of a rescue crew descending on the mountain meadow.

After considering the situation, Doyle decided that his new possessions deserved at least some attention. He went to his stash and covered it all with an open sleeping bag. Then he used his new ax to cut branches of meadow foliage. These he draped carefully over his new treasures. Though the preparations took time, Doyle felt better knowing his things would be safe and dry when he returned.

With everything hidden, he wouldn't have to worry about what might happen at the upper meadow. Falling snow would soon cover his tracks, completely hiding his presence there. He could now focus on following the woman.

Having left two hours ahead of him, she might be difficult to catch. Doyle decided to drop down off the meadow, circle behind her and cross over her trail somewhere in the woods. Her injuries would slow her down, and she would not make good time. Furthermore, because she would make no effort to cover her trail, he should still be able to find her tracks, even with the falling snow.

Hopefully, she wouldn't get herself killed before he caught up with her.

As the morning turned into afternoon, Richard and Allen waited helplessly while the storm outside intensified. It seemed to them that the weather system was not going to pass over. Instead, it had parked overhead, where it had been joined and magnified by the storm behind it.

Richard had called Harumi several times over the course of the morning. She reported on things at home; he kept her up to date on the progress of the search.

Allen continued to keep his own parents informed about the progress—or lack of it—of the search. But even these calls had become taxing as he told them over and over that he knew nothing more. They wanted to come to Seattle. Allen convinced them to wait for more definite news.

The moments slid by like honey on a cold day. Though Allen had his Bible along, he found himself unable to concentrate. He tried to read Psalms one line at a time, stopping to meditate and focus on the words as he read them. Even this seemed useless. His mind stayed fixed only on the storm outside and the mountain in the distance. Allen worried about Beth, wondering what had happened and wishing he could do something, anything, to help.

He saw tension on the glum expressions of the rescue crew as they glanced out the hangar window at the rain running over the glass. Eventually they began to filter out of the building. Allen watched as they checked out at the mission desk, giving their cell phone numbers to the record keeper there. They had joined in bands of three or four to go out for a good meal, he suspected, traveling in the cars of members who lived close enough to drive.

Fortunately, the kids from the youth group had not come in today. They would not survive this cruel waiting without entertainment. As much as he loved them, Allen had nothing left to give to the kids.

Harumi reported that the youth group planned to meet in the basement of the old church to pray for Beth after school that afternoon.

Richard nearly cried when he relayed the message to Allen. "We need the prayer," he said. "Only God can help us find her."

Once again, the cold enveloped Beth. Before she felt completely rested, shivering began in her teeth and continued until she shuddered from head to toe. Knowing that she had to keep moving, Beth rolled over and stood up.

As soon as she faced the wind, she knew by the fierce bite of snow on her face that it had picked up. She knew the effect of wind on mammals—that it sucked away body heat, putting them at high risk for hypothermia. Still shivering, she checked her right hand again, wondering how badly the cold might damage an already compromised nervous system. She needed to get out of the wind and find shelter quickly.

Beth started down the hill. Though she tried to be careful, in her hurry to get out of the wind, she stumbled frequently. As she neared the lower tree line, the ground began to slope away at a steep angle, forcing Beth to work harder to maintain her balance. She grew hungrier with every step, feeling more weak than she had since the crash itself. She cursed herself for not having had the good sense to put her pack over her shoulder. If she had, she would not have lost her food, and she would have fresh water to drink whenever she needed it.

Adding to her difficulty, the ground below the snow had changed. Rather than thick underbrush, Beth now stepped across a wide bed of loose rocks. These tipped as she stepped, and the strain on her ankles reminded her of the discomfort of wearing ice skates.

She had not thought of skates in a long time. Beth had only worn skates when she had visited her grandparents in Colfax as a young girl. As children, she and her sister, Christine, loved to skate at Grandpa's house. Every winter during their Christmas vacation, they'd skated on the pond near his farm. These cold weather joys were new and exciting to girls raised on the milder side of Washington.

Christine had always loved the snow. She loved skating and sledding. The new sled had been her idea, a Christmas gift she'd begged for, beginning in September. Both girls had squealed with delight when they'd discovered it under the tree. Christine took the first ride.

Beth stopped walking. She hadn't thought of Christine in months. Forcibly shaking herself, she thought, *I can't think about her now. My folks can't bear to lose another daughter. I must survive, if for no one else but Mom and Dad.*

At last Beth came to the lower edge of the meadow where small, widely spaced trees began to appear in clumps. The ground grew less rocky, more solid and not as treacherous. For a moment, Beth stopped to look at the view. Perfectly shaped trees, with thick trunks and widely spaced limbs, dotted the landscape. Though the wind blew fiercely, the trees somehow managed to retain their snow-covered cloaks.

In spite of aching muscles and growing fatigue, the sight of so many trees, so beautifully shaped and covered by thick snow, nearly took her breath away. Beth knew that under different circumstances the scene would have looked like the cover on a Christmas card by Currier and Ives. Today, it felt like the next act in a nightmare that refused to end.

Discouraged, Beth struggled as she willed one foot in front of the other. Though still dry, her feet felt icy cold and numb—like tree stumps. Her eyes watered constantly in the wind, making her nose run. As she wiped it dry with the coarse sleeve of Ken's coat, the skin above her lip grew raw. No matter how gently she touched it, the combination of wind and abrasion made her exposed skin burn.

Beth needed a rest, but only if she could get out of the brunt of the cruel weather. She turned her back to the wind and stopped to take stock of her surroundings. She began to notice a new and subtle change in the weather.

Down here below the meadow, a heavy fog crept low along the ground, hugging the thinly limbed trees. In puffy wisps, white clouds clung to the cliff above her, blending deadly granite with the soft white of snow. Now hidden in a shroud of dense whiteness—above, below, and hanging in the air—the mountain possessed a new and deadly camouflage.

Fog. No one would launch a rescue effort in wind *and* snow *and* fog. She had been right to leave, she realized. If only she could get down below the snow level and find some kind of shelter.

On her right, as she faced up the hill, Beth noticed a group of trees standing very near the base of a rocky cliff. *If I could just get over there,* she thought, *the trees would block the wind and I could rest.*

Beth trudged through deepening snow toward the trees. She ducked around behind them and instantly felt relief from the gale blowing up the mountain. Beth pushed several lower branches aside and stepped into the empty space between the trees. Inside the natural shelter very little snow covered the ground. It felt almost cozy compared to the trail. After brushing the ground to make a clear spot to lie down, Beth curled up on her side to rest.

She congratulated herself for finding the shelter and considered staying for the night. Just then, in the relative quiet of her tree-lined sanctuary, she heard a new noise—the sound of trickling water—and the sound made an intense thirst rise in her throat. She moved the branches aside, trying to identify the source of the sound. There, not fifteen feet away, a small trickle of water cascaded over bare rocks and flowed into a natural ditch.

Beth fished her water bottle out of her vest, anxious to fill it. As she stood up, a wayward branch slapped her in the face, and she cried out as she quickly turned away. The prickly branch had snapped her eye, scratching her face. "For heaven's sake," she said, rubbing her face with her hand. "What else can go wrong?"

The sight of flowing water encouraged her. It meant that the ground temperature hovered very near freezing—but not below. In the atmosphere from which the snow fell, the temperature had to be below thirty-two degrees, but not here—not at ground level. Having liquid water meant that Beth would not have to eat snow. She would not have to risk the dangerous drop in body temperature associated with letting snow melt inside her stomach. She had water, and God himself had thawed it for her.

Beth almost smiled. If she had water, she could continue walking until dark. Now that she had found shelter once, she believed she could do it again.

She walked over to the hill and held her bottle under the flowing water. Slowly the container filled, and Beth waited eagerly, impatient for a long drink. She downed one full bottle and then filled it again. This she would carry with her. Then she went back to her shelter under the trees and rested.

The cold soon drove Beth back onto the trail. Shivering violently, she knew she could not stay any longer, no matter how badly her back ached or how tired her legs were. She made her way across the drifted snow back to her previous path. As she walked, she kept her face down, protected from the wind. Her footprints were barely visible now—hidden by the newly blown snow—only the deep trench her legs made gave any hint as to the route she had taken.

Beth trudged on.

Her hunger eased as she walked, and for this she felt grateful. But her exhaustion grew steadily worse. As she walked, her legs felt heavier and heavier, and for brief moments, she stood completely still, allowing her eyes to drift closed. Occasional gusts of wind blew snow over her hair and face and down the collar of her coat, forcing her to turn away, holding the coat closed with one hand.

As she continued downhill, a steep cliff grew on her left, and the ground cover thickened, growing higher and more menacing. In places, Beth stepped inside the brush, following what seemed to be an animal trail—something like a tunnel through the vegetation.

Under normal conditions, Beth would have identified what kind of animals made the trail—determined whether it was deer or elk or bear. Today she did not care. As long as the tunnels continued downhill, Beth would follow them. Low branches forced her to duck, using her left arm to push aside the stiff stems falling down into her face and hair. Inside the tunnels, Beth found herself protected from the wind. She felt warmer and walking took less energy.

Then, unexpectedly, the vegetation ended.

Surprised, Beth took a few tentative steps forward, wondering about the sudden change. As she moved outside the tunnel, a biting gust of wind slapped her face. With her next step, the brush under her foot suddenly gave way, and Beth found herself falling.

Twenty-Six

IT TOOK LONGER THAN DOYLE expected to cover his stash and pack his supplies. By the time he finished, his knee ached and his stomach growled. He sat down by the woman's fire and enjoyed a meal of freeze-dried chicken and noodles.

Anxious to get back on the trail, Doyle knew he could not waste time in front of the fire. He wanted to keep track of the woman, to know what mischief she might be getting into while he ate her food. He hoped she had not gotten too far ahead of him.

Reluctantly, Doyle stood, slung his pack over his shoulder, and whistled for Gilligan. He and the dog started out again, traveling away from the upper meadow and dropping rapidly off the plateau. A quarter mile down the trail, they started climbing uphill, moving along a line that Doyle expected would intercept the woman's path.

The wind on this side of the meadow blew more gently than at the crash site. Still, the uphill trail and deepening snow brought the familiar dull ache to Doyle's shoulder. He found himself stopping often to catch his breath, waiting for the cramping to ease before moving on. Gilligan sat patiently waiting through these frequent stops, with his head cocked to one side until Doyle gave the signal to move on.

Doyle traveled across the hill, gaining altitude quickly but paying for his effort with exhaustion and unrelenting discomfort in his bad knee. By the next morning, he knew, this discomfort would blossom into full-fledged swelling. Still, it could not be helped—unless he could find a walking stick.

Doyle left the trail, searching among the trees and along the ground for a long branch. After some time, he found one, and using his new Leatherman tool, cleared it of dead branches. Holding the stick in his downhill hand, Doyle pushed himself up the hill. *Not bad,* he thought, as the stick took some of the pressure off his knee.

At the crest of the hill, the wind hit Doyle with surprising power. Quickly, he dropped his head and ducked behind a tree, seeking protection from the icy gale. He had emerged just below the tree line of the upper meadow—exactly as he had intended. From here, he could easily catch up with the woman and track her off the mountain. Doyle smiled, proud of his own cleverness, as he took a moment to rest away from the wind.

Doyle drank from his canteen, the water still warm from the campfire. As hot liquid began to warm his body, he rested. Eventually, his shoulder began to feel normal again, and Doyle looked up in time to see Gilligan run out into the weather. Doyle watched the black-and-tan dog drop his long nose to the snow and begin to sniff enthusiastically for some unseen prey. Could the dog be trailing the woman?

Doyle stood slowly, eager to move on. *This sure would be easy,* he thought, *if Gilligan could find the broad for me.*

Like Alice in Wonderland, Beth's fall seemed to go on forever. When she hit bottom, her weakened legs folded underneath her, pitching her forward onto her chest. One outstretched arm managed to break her fall, and when Beth opened her eyes, she could not believe what she saw. Wooden spikes, embedded in the ground, stood just in front of her forehead.

Beth had narrowly escaped being impaled by sharpened stakes.

She dropped her head onto her elbow and rolled over on her left side. Her right arm screamed from the impact, and her heart pounded as her body released the terror of yet another fall. She lay quietly, her eyes closed, waiting for her heart to stop racing and the pain to let up.

When the thudding in her chest eased, she opened her eyes again and sat up. Looking around, she saw the fir branches that had fallen to the bottom with her. Below these branches, spongy wet earth lined the pit. The earthen walls, more than twice Beth's height, appeared perfectly vertical. Beth could see no notches or steps or roots—nothing that might help her climb out.

Trying to stay calm, Beth assessed her injuries. The skin of her left palm, now covered with mud, bled mildly from a loose flap of skin at the base of her thumb. Her landing had covered her chest with muck, which by itself didn't bother her. Beth didn't mind dirt on Ken's jacket.

But mud covered the front of her jeans as well. Not a good way to care for a flesh wound, she thought. She tried, with no success, to brush her thighs clean.

Beth scooted toward the downhill side of the pit and sat with her back against the wall. Now exposed to the weather, snow had begun sticking to the base of the hole and to the branches she had brought in with her. Stunned, Beth took in her surroundings.

Who would build something like this? In her years with Davis and Graham, Beth had seen many hunting traps. But most hunters used spring traps. Evil-looking things with jagged teeth and long spikes holding the trap to the ground. Those things tore into the flesh of a cougar's leg. Beth had found dead animals so desperate to get free that they had chewed through their own limbs in order to gain their freedom. In the end, they'd lost their life.

No. This hole was not like any trap she'd seen on a mountain before. She shivered, as much from fear as from the cold. Obviously, whoever had built the pit didn't intend the victim to live through the experience—no matter what kind of victim the builder had in mind. The thought made her shudder. Somehow, perhaps because she was so petite, Beth had not been impaled. Her body had fallen short of the sharpened spikes.

Impaled. The word triggered a memory. Had she seen this trap in a movie? A photograph? Yes. Something in her memory registered traps like this one. Where had she seen them?

She had to get out, and she had to do it soon. Beth did not want to spend the night in this unprotected shelter. Knowing there was very little daylight left, she had to figure out how to get out of this place. She rolled over and stood up. Carefully, she walked around the perimeter of the hole, gazing up at the vertical walls that held her captive.

The base of the hole had been constructed just large enough to prevent someone from wedging himself between opposite walls. The vertical sides had been smoothed so that no handholds existed on the way up.

Undaunted, Beth decided to climb out anyway. She bent over and removed one hiking boot. Then, choosing the shortest of the four walls, she carved a handhold above her head with the toe of the boot. When she finished this notch, she began kicking a second notch at the height of her knee.

She could climb out—if she was patient enough—using only her boots to create notches along the walls of the pit. Even with only one arm, she could do it. The process would be slow and difficult, but she could get out. She felt certain of it. She had climbed a man-made rock at a local sporting goods store once. Of course, she'd worn a harness and climbing shoes then. And she had used both hands. Still, how hard could it be to climb twelve feet?

Beth made two toeholds and climbed eighteen inches. With another handhold, she put the shoelace of her hiking boot into her mouth and took a step up. The effort of clinging to wet earth made her muscles tremble. If only she had eaten today, she thought, this would be easier. But she would not give in. She moved up another step.

Her hair hung in her face, but she did not have an extra hand to brush it away. As she held her weight on her feet and reached for the next hold, she felt the earth crumbling below her right foot. She swayed in midair, placing most of her weight on the toes of her left foot. She paused, breathing slowly, deliberately, willing the fear to go away. *Stay calm,* she told herself.

Resting on her left foot, she lifted her right foot to kick out a new toehold. Punching carefully, the earth gave way and a new notch slowly formed. But before she could step up, the ground below her left foot gave way, and Beth tumbled roughly onto the floor of the pit, dropping onto her seat.

Beth lay back, exhausted, and breathing hard. The soil forming the walls of the pit would not hold her weight as she climbed. Perhaps later, in another spot, she would succeed.

Now Beth found herself exactly where she had been in the beginning. Angry, she sat down again with her back to the wall, her arm hugging her chest. Every part of her body hurt, and a new, nearly overpowering wave of hunger left her weak and dizzy. She felt thirsty too, and she thought of the bottle of water she had filled from the stream near the trees. Had she lost it in the fall?

She crawled away from the side of the pit and, moving the branches aside, felt along the ground until she discovered the water bottle. Covered with mud, the bottle was still full. She wiped it on the side of her jacket, removed the cap, and drank. With only one bottle, Beth planned to ration her portions.

She chose to rest in the most protected corner of the pit. After she regained her strength, she would try to climb out again. Leaning her head against the dirt wall, Beth closed her eyes and tried to picture Noah's smiling round face and lovely brown eyes. He had so many first events left to live through. The first day of kindergarten. Learning to ride his own two-wheeler. As she imagined her baby, Beth felt her resolve come back. She refused to let this one horrible event keep him from having his mother at his side on these important occasions. She would not miss his first music program, his first soccer game. Noah needed his mother, and Beth resolved that she would make it home for her baby.

This train of thought led her to picture him as he might be right now, sitting in his crib, sucking his thumb, and wailing for his mommy. She heard him cry and watched the tears roll down his chubby cheeks. Suddenly Beth felt herself growing very angry.

This pit would not keep her from her son.

Dennis Doyle followed Gilligan through the trees below the meadow. He could not be far behind the woman. Even in the heavily falling snow, he could clearly see her tracks. He felt the wind against his face, stinging his eyes and biting his nose. Her injuries, combined with the wind and snow, must have slowed her progress. That explained his catching up with her so quickly. Gilligan barked and began to make a wide circle along their course.

"Smell somethin'?" Doyle asked. He watched Gilligan suddenly take a wide detour, bounding off the trail. Now wildly excited, the dog leapt through the snow toward the hill on Doyle's left, where several clumps of trees grew. "Gilligan! Come!" he shouted, slapping his thigh. The dog turned back and sat down, whining softly. Then ignoring Doyle, the dog ran toward the hill again.

"Miserable hound," Doyle muttered. "Why can't we just follow the trail? She went that way," he said, jerking his thumb down the mountain. Gilligan, completely uninterested in Doyle's analysis of the situation, found a hidden entry into the sheltered space between the trees and disappeared inside.

When Gilligan did not reappear, Doyle moved closer. Then pulling the branches aside, he bent over and peered into the darkness. The dog was lying down, his nose on his paws, grinning up at Doyle. "Come, Gilligan!" Doyle shouted. The dog did not move. "All right then, be that way. I'm goin' on without ya." As Doyle turned away, something hanging from the lowest branch caught his eye. Strands of glossy black hair clung to the branch, like tinsel on a Christmas tree. He reached for it and brought it to his face, examining it carefully.

She had been there.

As Doyle stood, movement under the tree caught his eye. He turned to find Gilligan snooping in small circles around the space, his nose low to the ground. "Gilligan!" The dog ran out from under the tree, barking as he headed back down the mountain.

Doyle followed, cursing the dog. "Why couldn't someone have left a bag of cats to die instead of dogs?"

Returning to the place where they had left the trail, Doyle started down the hill. She had to be very near, and for a moment Doyle raised his face to the wind. Like the old days, perhaps he could smell her too. In the cold wind, he felt only the bite of frozen air stinging his eyes and nose.

Glancing up, Doyle saw that daylight was fading. He would need to camp out again, he knew, and should begin looking for a new place soon. He had camped on this part of the mountain so frequently that he knew it as well as his own cabin. He had trapped it often over the years. . . .

A new and frightening thought struck him, and he swore bitterly.

What if she fell into one of his pit traps? Years ago, when he was much younger, Doyle had dug four pits between here and the western boundary of his territory. Though he'd never had anyone fall into the pits, Doyle had never bothered to fill them in. The pits had become a kind of passive perimeter security. He didn't believe that he needed them. Still, he couldn't quite bring himself to get rid of them either.

He remembered how carefully he'd chosen their locations, how carefully he'd anticipated where a stranger might enter or exit his perimeter. Shaking his head, he thought, *She would be just dumb enough to manage to fall into one of them pits.*

What would he do if the woman had fallen into one of the traps? This new terror set Doyle to patting the pockets of his coat in search of his liquor flask. If ever Doyle needed a drink, he needed one now. In fact, if he could, he would empty the flask.

But he had not brought any liquor along. Doyle started walking as quickly as his tired legs would carry him, following the trough of disturbed snow the woman's short legs had left behind. She had to be cold and wet and very nearly exhausted. Perhaps she had sought shelter already. Perhaps, even as he followed her, she slept comfortably out of the wind in a sleeping bag she'd absconded from the airplane.

Why hadn't she stayed by the plane? Why did that woman have to cause so much trouble?

The dog ran out beyond Doyle, disappearing around the next bend. Doyle knew that the dog sensed her presence and had gone on ahead to find her. They had to be close. He wanted to stop the dog, muzzle him, and put him on a leash. He didn't want Gilligan to warn her of his presence on the mountain.

Thinking that he might make up time, Doyle picked up his pace. He took longer strides—ones that used less energy while speeding his progress—a technique he'd learned long ago. Following the dog into a bramble tunnel, Doyle began to make better time. Here, the bushes protected the ground from snow and wind. But as the tunnel got smaller, Doyle had to duck down, avoiding the branches that reached out to grab him as he passed. Still he hurried after the dog.

Just as he approached the end of the bramble tunnel, a vine caught the toe of Doyle's left boot, pitching him forward. He fell onto the ground, both arms spread out in front of him in an attempt to protect himself.

Swearing, he pushed himself up and rested on his hands and knees. From his position so close to open space, Doyle decided it would be easier to crawl to the edge of the tunnel and stand up outside. As he crawled, he heard the dog barking in excitement. *Stupid dog*, he thought. *I'm gonna have to get ridda that thing.*

He inched forward, determined to catch and tie up his rebellious dog. At the edge of the cover, Doyle lifted his head to yell at Gilligan. But just as the dog's name formed on his lips, he saw her.

From his position, still hugging the ground and hidden behind bushes, Doyle could only see the top of her head. Sleek black hair, unmoving. Though the nearest wall of the pit obscured her face, Doyle knew. The woman had fallen into his trap.

Twenty-Seven

BETH MADE TWO MORE ATTEMPTS to climb the walls of her tomb. The second time she tumbled from four feet up the wall, rolling onto her strong shoulder and narrowly avoiding seriously hurting herself. In the process, Beth grew weaker. When she stood, a new dizziness overcame her that made further climbing impossible.

A new and painful thirst began to occupy her every thought. Beth suspected that she had begun to dehydrate, and though she knew water would end her dehydration, Beth did not want to drink all her water at once.

Though snow had begun to accumulate on the open floor of the pit, Beth knew better than to eat snow to hydrate herself. While that would slow down her dehydration, it would suck the warmth from her body. She would not eat snow—not yet. Almost as much as a drink of water, she yearned for a toothbrush to scrape the foul taste from her mouth.

Beth sat down in the most protected corner of the pit. Even here, where the wind did not reach her, the air temperature continued to drop as the afternoon light faded. She watched her breath as she exhaled, wondering how long she would stay warm enough to see little clouds of breath rise above her face and disappear in the cold mountain air.

She chastised herself for entertaining such depressing thoughts. She should be fighting, thinking of a way out of this hole. But she knew she could not get out on her own. Beth sighed. *Maybe I should accept it,* she thought. *I don't have a chance.*

Again she thought of Christine, wondering if her sister had been this aware when she died. Would Christine welcome Beth into heaven? Beth blinked back tears, suddenly saddened by memories she had not considered in many years.

Hunger had finally abandoned her. But thirst continued to clamor around in her consciousness, captivating her thoughts. Her lips felt dry and swollen, and the tissue in her mouth papery. She had never been so thirsty. Though she tried to hold off, Beth had no choice. Her body needed water desperately. She drank all of the water in her bottle. Still her body demanded more.

Using her feet and one hand, she scooted away from the wall toward the middle of the pit, where branches covered the stakes she had narrowly missed as she fell. Deepening layers of snow concealed the needles of the fir branches, and Beth used her left hand to scoop wet snow into her palm. Eagerly, desperately, she dropped handful after handful into her mouth, compressing it quickly and sucking the water from the snow. On her tongue, each bit of snow melted instantly into a tiny teaspoon of cold water.

Beth felt an intense, urgent frustration. She continued to scoop up and swallow more snow until her efforts exposed a large patch of green fir branches. In her eagerness, she did not taste the pitch from the needles. To her the snow tasted wet and wonderful, and she could not get enough.

At last she leaned back to rest, trembling from the effort. She took deep, calming breaths as she willed herself to recover. Already the cold liquid had chilled her, and she scooted back into the protected corner of the pit, away from the falling snow. Leaning back, she straightened her legs and closed her eyes. *I'll rest,* she thought, *and then I'll try to climb the wall again.*

She began to pray, though this time not for herself. Instead, she began to pray for her family and for Allen. She prayed for her mother. Though she would not admit that her own hope had begun to evaporate, she could not help but notice it coming through the words of her own prayers. She heard herself ask God to sustain them in their loss.

Huddled in the corner of the pit, Beth drifted off to sleep. Even as she felt it happening, she knew how dangerous it was to sleep in the cold. But, she could not help it. Though she shivered, she did not care as an overwhelming fatigue came upon her, pressing her into the ground, making her thoughts sluggish and her body feel heavy and slow.

Without the slightest hesitation, Doyle dropped onto his stomach, covering his head with one hand. He buried his face in the dirt and froze. Minutes passed while he waited for the sound of gunfire, for the buzzing of ammunition as it passed near his ears, for the smell of powder and the anguished screams of the injured.

Silently, Doyle brought his right hand down to the small of his back and inched his fingers along the top of his pants until he felt the cold metal of his gun. He drew it out and brought it back to the ground near his face. He waited, his body as fully cocked as the trigger, knowing that he could use deadly force, even against a woman. They had taught him that much.

Instead, Doyle heard only the dog barking.

Doyle slid backward, his stomach pressing against the dirt- and snow-dusted tunnel floor. He did not look up again, would not expose himself to the enemy. The soldier inside him did not feel the dampness creep through his clothing, or the cold air around him, or the painful complaining of his old knee. Doyle had only one concern. He wanted to back out undetected.

Once out of sight, Doyle brought himself into a crouched position and turned away, stepping carefully through the debris covering the trail. He would not allow her to know he had been so near, would not let her hear his movements. Doyle felt confident in his ability to remain undetected. After all, he had been carefully trained for exactly this kind of work.

Doyle emerged from the other end of the tunnel, breathing hard. The familiar ache, the one just below his left collarbone, had reappeared. He stepped out into the clearing and, bending low, hustled across the open area to a clump of snow-covered bushes. Hiding behind them, Doyle dropped onto his good knee and waited for the pain in his chest to ease up. It always improved when he stopped moving.

Doyle wondered if he had been followed. He kept both eyes focused on the entrance to the bramble, his gun in his hands, waiting for a figure to appear in front of the dark hole. By the time he could breathe easily again, Doyle convinced himself that no one would emerge. Dropping onto his backside, he forced himself to relax as he considered his options.

The fact that she had fallen into the trap complicated things. If she had not already died there, she would soon, of starvation or exposure or both. But then what? How long would this early-season storm last? When would rescuers come looking for the little plane? Certainly they would try to find her body.

If they found her body here, they would soon find him. At all costs, he had to avoid detection. The only way he could avoid discovery would be to move her body. Would he have enough time? Could he move her without the search team suspecting his presence on the mountain?

Whatever he did, he had to move her quickly. He had to carry her body back up to the crash site. After all, she was a tiny woman—not much bigger than a bale of hay. He could leave her near the plane, where no one would ever ask another question. If he moved quickly enough, the falling snow would cover his tracks. Rescuers would never figure out that she had been moved. They would believe that she had gone outside and died of exposure.

This plan would work provided that she had not landed on his stakes. The thought made Doyle shudder. If rescuers found her body bleeding and broken from the stakes, his time in the cabin would be over. He would be wanted for murder, not assault like last time. And he would have no place left to run. They would confine him in a prison somewhere, forever trapped with his haunting memories. No. He could never survive in a cell.

Dennis Doyle would never go down the mountain alive.

Doyle sat in the snow, thinking about the terrain and how far uphill he would have to carry her body. Just considering it made Doyle tired. He reached up with his right hand and rubbed the hollow place below his collarbone. He could almost feel the heat and the nagging discomfort that would rise to its habitual position if he tried to haul her body that far.

No, he decided, he would not carry her all the way back. Instead, he would drag her body up the hill only far enough to be found. They would think she had tried to walk out. Yes, that would work. He would leave her body somewhere close enough to the plane to find—yet far enough away to explain death by exposure.

Mentally, Doyle began constructing a stretcher from the tarp in his pack. Using his own rope and two long branches, he pictured making a kind of travois. It might work—dragging her up the hill.

Doyle gazed up at the sky, blinking back the snowflakes that landed in his eyes, as he tried to gauge how much daylight remained. Did he have enough time to move her body? Or should he camp now and return to the pit in the morning? Once the rescuers found her, they would go away and leave him alone on the mountain. At least her loved ones would have the comfort of finding her body.

Not everyone who grieved was that fortunate.

———

Beth woke briefly to the sound of barking. It startled her, in spite of the fact that it seemed to come from somewhere far away. Though she tried desperately, she could not force the curtain of sleep from her mind. A heavy shield of fatigue pinned her to the ground. She tried to force herself awake, mentally shaking herself. But sleep wrapped Beth like a comfortable quilt, and she willingly surrendered.

But Beth's body did not feel comfortable. She opened her eyes for the briefest moment, and before they drifted closed, she wondered why she had chosen to sleep sitting up. *Silly*, she thought. She let her back slide down the wall behind her and rolled over onto her left shoulder.

Something hurt there, and she rolled onto her back. Cold. So cold. Why couldn't she get warm? Beth reached out as if to pull up a blanket but found nothing. She rolled again, curling into a ball, and felt her body, heavy and wooden, drift back to sleep. Comfortable, restful, wonderful sleep.

A funny animal smell drifted up to her nose, and Beth turned her head, trying to get away from it. What was that smell? She shifted, still trying to avoid it. But the smell followed her. So close. Beth felt a feather tickle her nose, and though it bothered her, she could not push it away. She turned her face again.

Then, quite suddenly, Beth began to grow warm, as though someone had wrapped her body in fur. She wondered for a moment if she had died. But even then, she did not care. Beth gave in to sleep, snuggling down under the warm blanket that someone had been kind enough to throw over her.

"Thank you," she murmured from the depths of a beautiful dream.

——————

When he finished building the stretcher, Doyle carried it back to the pit. This time as he approached he made no effort to creep silently toward the pit. A dead woman would not hear anything.

He stepped out of the bramble tunnel and walked to the edge of the trap. With his first glance inside, he swore. Gilligan's big hairy body lay over the woman, covering most of her trunk and the upper portion of her legs. The dog, who heard Doyle arrive, raised his head and cocked his ears but didn't move or bark his usual greeting. Instead, he lowered his face to his paws.

"Get outta there," Doyle said, gesturing the dog away with one arm. Gilligan did not move. "I said, get up!"

The dog stood, three of four feet still on her body, the fourth on the ground near her face. He looked at Doyle, tipped up his face, and whined. Then Gilligan lay down again, covering her body with his own.

"Okay," Doyle said, "if you won't come out, you can rot in there." He threw down his pack and dropped the two sticks of the stretcher near the edge of the pit. Pulling a coil of soft rope from his shoulder, Doyle walked over to a nearby tree. He tied the rope to the base of the tree and stepped back toward the hole, unrolling the rope as he did. When he reached the trap's edge, he dropped the coil inside. Though the dog watched his master's every move, he would not leave the woman.

"Turncoat," Doyle said, though this time with irritation rather than anger. Sitting at the edge of the pit, he grabbed the rope and rolled over, lowering himself hand over hand down into the emptiness below.

It would not be easy to remove her body from the hole. But he thought he could do it if he tied the rope under her armpits and fashioned a harness of sorts. He would use the tree as a pulley.

He dropped the last four feet onto the ground, feeling a solid twang in his bad knee. He swore to himself. It was her fault his knee hurt. If it weren't for her, he would be sitting in front of his own stove right now, warm and comfortable.

He moved to the corner where her body lay. Her eyes were closed and her elbow was curled underneath her head, with the stupid dog lying on top of her. Doyle gestured to the dog. "Off," he said. Gilligan did not move.

Doyle grabbed the fur at the dog's neck and dragged the whimpering mutt off of the body. Bending over her, he took a close look at her face. Though he did not wish it to happen, he began to think again of the other girl. A terrible anger hit him like a bullet, and as he stood, he kicked the wall of the pit, splattering dirt over the body.

Why had she come? Why hadn't she stayed in her hooch where she belonged? If she hadn't come, she wouldn't have died outside in the cold. She should have stayed home with her dink children. But she hadn't, and now he had to drag her out of this pit. He turned back to reach for his rope. When he faced her again, the dog had resumed his position, lying over her chest.

Doyle's anger boiled, and he yelled as he booted Gilligan in the hindquarters, driving him off her body. The dog yelped and growled but did not challenge Doyle further. Doyle squatted near her shoulders and tucked the rope under her neck. Without lifting her trunk, he slid the rope down until it slipped behind her shoulders and into the hollow that was her waist. He tied a knot, leaving a long free end, and began to run the rope back up and over her chest. He intended to make another knot on her upper back, but he couldn't reach it without turning her over.

Standing very close to her, Doyle bent down and began to lift her shoulders from the floor of the pit. Just as his hand pulled on her upper arm, her eyes fluttered open, and her face grimaced in an expression of intense pain. She moaned as she looked for the source of her agony.

When her eyes focused on Doyle, her expression changed, and he saw confusion in her wide eyes and raised eyebrows. Her eyes traveled from him to the walls of the pit, to the dog, and back to his face before closing again.

Doyle swore a long angry oath and dropped her onto the ground. He turned away still swearing. Why on earth wouldn't this stubborn woman just die?

Now, Doyle realized, he had a brand-new problem. One he had

not planned on. He couldn't just drag her back up the hill and leave her. Alive, though just barely, she'd seen his face. No matter what happened now, she would tell the others about him.

What on earth was he supposed to do with her?

Twenty-Eight

THE WEATHER DID NOT IMPROVE. At the county airport, where searchers had set up headquarters, blowing rain pelted puddles on the tarmac and splattered against the windows of the hangar, running down in endless rivulets toward the window ledge. Whenever someone opened the hangar door, the wind plucked it away, slamming it hard against the wall. The weather seemed determined to keep them from finding Beth and her plane.

For what seemed like an eternity, the afternoon and evening hours passed while Allen and Richard sat grim-faced among the search-and-rescue team members, waiting for a weather break so that a ground search could begin. Mount Rainier had turned herself into a torrent of fierce wind, plummeting temperatures, and swirling snow. For some reason only a meteorologist could explain, a rush of arctic air had crashed into a series of moisture-laden weather fronts approaching the mountain from the south.

The collision between the weather systems over the mountain made access impossible. Though a ground crew could brave the mountain weather, even helicopters could not approach the upper meadow where they had heard the ELT. And without air access, there was no access; the meadow was too far from the nearest road to get in by truck.

The adults from Allen's church continued to stay with him at the hangar. It seemed to Allen that the members of his congregation had chosen lots, different groups coming in shifts to sit with him in the echoing hangar at Thun Field. Their presence, their kind expressions, even their gentle touches provided a measure of comfort. As he waited, Allen found that he needed all the encouragement he could get.

Allen spent this time fighting. He fought with his fear. He fought with God over the weather. He wrestled with faith issues. Why had this happened? What possible good could come from something so terrible? Why would God choose to leave three children without their mother? Why would God take his best friend? Suddenly these were no longer sermon topics—they were life. And Allen found that for all of his training, all of his education, he had no real answers.

He wrestled with his own imagination. What had happened to Beth? If she had already died, had she suffered? How had she spent her final moments? If she had survived the crash, how could she possibly survive the cruel turn of weather that now stranded her on the mountain?

As he wrestled, he did not want to talk. He did not want conversation to drag him from the horrible, but compelling, course of his own thoughts. He could no longer answer simple questions. He did not know if he was hungry, or if he had slept, or if the children were doing well. Instead, when someone spoke, he stared back, blinking and confused, trying desperately to recall the question, until at last Richard began to answer for him.

At first Allen tried to be brave. But as the search team continued to be grounded, his bravery collapsed into shock. And from shock he seemed to withdraw all together.

He had lost his appetite. He could not eat or drink. He even gave up coffee. What did it matter that he stay alert, awake? In fact, Allen began to long for the wonderful escape of sleep. Beth had always been more than his wife, more than his partner. She was his soul mate. Without her, he felt like a mannequin—visible, but dead. Solid, but hollow inside. Positioned, but without strength.

They had no options.

"Allen," a man's voice spoke. "I need to head back to Bellevue."

Allen felt a hand placed softly on his shoulder. Jarred from his thoughts, he turned to see the face of a close friend looking anxiously into his own. "Sure," Allen said. "I understand." But he did not. He did not know how long Larry had been with him, or what time of day it was, or for that matter, even what day it was.

"My secretary paged me," Larry said. "The board of elders has set up a prayer meeting for early tomorrow morning. The whole congregation is going to gather for prayer."

Allen could only nod. Prayer. As if he hadn't prayed endlessly from the moment he realized Beth was missing. "Yes. That would be good."

"We don't expect you to come. I know how hard this is for you, Allen."

Allen nodded again, though he knew it was a lie. His friend could not know. He could not know what it felt like to live with this horrible uncertainty. To wait while the weather determined the fate of the one you loved. He could not know.

"Do you want me to bring you anything?"

Allen shook his head. Richard, always nearby, stood as Larry slipped one arm into the sleeve of his overcoat. Then Richard and Larry shook hands, and something about their movement cued Allen. He stood and extended his own hand.

"The ladies are helping Harumi with the girls. I think you'll have enough chicken casseroles to last you the rest of your life."

Allen recognized the humor and smiled weakly. "Thank you," he said, wishing for the briefest moment that he could say something more. He did appreciate it, their being with him, their many acts of kindness. But from the center of his own emotional vortex, he could not bring the right words to mind.

As Richard walked Allen's friend to the hangar door, Allen sank back to his chair, weak with relief.

Once again the woman's eyes opened, and her gaze fixed upon him. "Thank God, you've come to help me."

Doyle did not answer. Instead, he backed away, moving to where the rope ran up the wall of the pit. Calling the dog, Doyle bent over and lifted Gilligan by his belly. Scrambling, the dog pulled himself up as Doyle shoved his furry rump from behind until the dog escaped from the pit. The dog turned immediately to bark over the edge.

Then he returned to the woman and finished knotting the harness that he had started. The dazed woman didn't protest. Grabbing the rope that was hanging into the pit and pushing against the wall with his feet, Doyle lifted himself hand over hand up the embankment. At the top, he picked up the rope and took the slack out of it, wrapping it once around his own hips. He called down to her, "If you can walk to the wall it'll go easier."

She looked down at the rope with a startled expression on her features and seemed for the first time to recognize the harness he had fashioned around her. He waited while she rolled onto her hands and knees and tried to stand. Doyle saw her eyes roll sideways as something—perhaps dizziness—came over her. She stumbled and fell.

Doyle yanked hard, quickly putting pressure on the rope. She lost consciousness before she ever hit the ground. "Great," he muttered. "Now I get to drag her out."

Her weight surprised him. She did not appear to be much heavier than a hundred pounds, but she felt much heavier. As he dragged her up, Doyle felt the old familiar pain burning in his shoulder as sweat beaded his forehead. Slowly, he dragged her out and dropped her over the edge of the pit like a roll of carpet. Then he bent over her and removed the harness. For the first time, he examined the wound above her eye, where her hair lay matted to the skin in dried crusty blood. Good. It was clean.

He reached down and pulled on the front of her jacket, anxious to examine the injured arm. He'd noticed it when he first saw her leaning against the back of the plane. He touched the black, swollen fingers of her right hand. *She broke somethin' somewhere*, he thought, *and managed to stuff the arm inside her vest, probably trying to keep it from moving*. In the process she had compromised the circulation. The woman would be lucky to use the arm again.

Still, she looked better than others he'd seen.

He rolled her onto her back, slipping his fingers into the tear in her jeans. The rip extended from her hip to the knee of her jeans. His fingers touched the bandage covering the flesh, instantly registering the heat radiating from her skin. *Infected*. She had managed to let the thing get infected. He swore again and reached up to scratch his beard while he thought.

Perhaps it wasn't too late. Perhaps he could return her to the upper field. With any luck at all, she would die before anyone found her. He cursed again. Luck? Why would he even think about luck?

Doyle's luck had run out in 1968. He'd been operating on borrowed time ever since. Besides, as tough as he liked to sound, Doyle knew that he could not do it. He could not refuse to help her. Though he might wish her dead, wish she had never come, he could not watch her die. Not now.

No. Whatever happened now, he had to help.

He dragged the makeshift litter over to where she lay and rolled her onto the tarp stretched between the two poles. She moaned as he moved her, and as he lifted her feet onto the stretcher, her face contorting into a grimace of pain. He suspected that she needed water and decided to try to give her some. He retrieved his canteen and lifted her by the back of her neck, bringing her mouth to the lip of the can. He tipped the canteen, letting a dribble of water run down over her mouth. Almost by instinct her thin lips parted and she swallowed.

Well, that's a start, he thought.

———

Beth opened her eyes and saw a face bending over her in the dim light. Though she felt too sick to care, a single thought flitted across her consciousness. *Hairy.*

Her body ached and she felt heavy. Heavier than she had ever been in her life. So tired. So sleepy. She wanted to sleep more than anything else she'd ever wanted in her whole life.

Through her fog came the realization that she had been moved. The air here was warm, and she smelled burning wood. She was lying on something dry and soft—in a lumpy sort of way. And the comfort of this new place conspired to make her even more sleepy.

But this heavy hairy man seemed determined to keep her awake. She sensed his nearness and felt him begin to unzip the zipper on her fleece vest. She tensed, wanting to protect her arm from the motion. She tried to roll away from him, but the freedom he had given her elbow and hand brought a new and agonizing pain to her arm. Beth cried out, holding her right hand with her left. She began to cry as he pulled the vest away from her arm. "Please," she pleaded. "Don't touch it. It's broken. I know it's broken."

He did not answer. Instead, he ran his fingers along her arm, beginning at her wrist and moving toward the elbow. Then starting from her shoulder he moved down, touching and prodding.

Now, quite awake, she objected again, "Please, don't touch it." Her words had no effect. He continued his ruthless exploration of her arm, moving down to the elbow. The rough skin of his fingers caught in her sweater as he felt Beth's arm. Through her tears, she tried to move away from him, to get him to stop. "I want to see a doctor. Don't touch it until I can get to a doctor." When her left shoulder bumped into the rough wooden planks of a wall, she could move no farther. "Stop it," she said, trying to sound authoritative. "I'll hurt you."

His hands stopped moving at her elbow, and his prodding fingers became focused. She felt his fingers slide along the bones below her elbow joint. When his fingers touched the fracture, Beth cried out in anguish. She looked up into his face and saw a smile in his clear blue eyes. Then, without warning, he straightened her elbow, and a new intense stabbing pain made Beth scream.

Before she could pull away, he gave her elbow a rapid tug combined with a peculiar twist. Beth saw white light flash through her vision, and she screamed again. She had never felt this kind of pain, ever. Not once in her life had anything ever hurt like this. Now wide awake, Beth wished for the sweet relief of unconsciousness. But she did not pass out.

She continued to cry while he fastened a long narrow piece of wood to her right arm. Holding her elbow straight, he began wrapping the arm and the wood together with a strip of torn fabric.

Beth knew that he had set her fracture, sensed that he had experience with this sort of thing. Still, he had hurt her, and she could not stem the tears that continued to roll down her face. With her good hand, she pulled up the collar of her vest, wiping the tears away. The aching in her elbow did not ease, and she squirmed with pain, clenching her teeth together, panting as she blinked through tears.

When he finished, he lifted the arm by the wooden splint and placed it up high on a rolled pillow of sorts that he had tucked near her waist.

"Please," Beth said. "There's been a plane crash. Two men have died. I need to call my family." His face did not change. He said nothing in response.

Instead, Beth watched as he offered her a small brown medicine bottle.

"For pain," he said, the smell of alcohol on his breath.

"What is it?" she asked.

"Just drink."

The pain in her elbow had not subsided at all since he wrapped it, and Beth did not know how long she could stand it without some kind of help. She realized how dangerous it was to accept his gift—without knowing what was inside the brown bottle. Still, he had just set her arm. . . .

"Just a single swallow," he said.

She drank and instantly regretted her decision. The fluid had a peculiar stinging flavor, and she wondered if she had just tasted her own death. Before long, the room swirled, and Beth's fear increased.

What if he had poisoned her? She had no more than formed this thought when she felt her body begin to float. As the screaming in her elbow eased, she sank into the first real relief she'd felt since the plane went down.

———

When Beth next woke, she remembered her pain. Remembered the medicine. But she had no idea how much time had passed. Her arm ached more now—though not the intense, unbearable pain she'd experienced before. Instead, she felt a constant dull throbbing from her arm—as though someone had pumped the arm full of air, like an old inner tube.

In this half-conscious state, Beth became aware of him moving above her and of the soft surface on which she lay. She did not feel cold any longer; in fact, something nearby was very hot, and she felt heat in the air and on her face.

The man seemed very near. She could smell him—a rough, unbathed scent. She sensed his nearness as he moved. She felt him touching her leg, moving it, and it surprised her that the leg did not hurt when he touched it.

She heard a tear, a ripping sound, and then felt heat touch her leg. She opened her eyes and saw him bending over her, a piece of denim in his hands. "Don't," she said, hearing her own weak objection. "My jeans."

The bulky man did not answer. She felt his hands on her leg and heard the sound of water. Then she felt him touch her again, and this time it hurt very much. Beth cried out, trying to pull away. But she was too weak, too sick to object. Instead, she cried as he worked. In her pain she became very alert, even with her eyes closed.

He had something, a cloth perhaps, and it felt to her that he had begun to peel away the skin above her right knee. The sensation, an intense burning, brought tears to her eyes, and before she could do anything about them, they escaped down her cheeks.

Beth smelled something new, something horrible. A foul odor came from somewhere near her leg. She could not raise her head to see what he had done. She did not know if the wound smelled so bad—or if he had put something on her skin. Perhaps he had made some concoction to fight the infection.

Too late, she thought, relaxing into the rhythmic motion of his touch. *Too late for this. It's already infected. Too late.*

His ministrations—if one could call them that—seemed to go on forever. Beth thought he would never stop. She felt him tug at the loose flap of skin, and as she tried to pull away, Beth felt the man hold her leg firmly, his palm pushing hard against her ankle. Eventually he stopped, and Beth felt a heavy warm weight placed over the wound. She knew it was wet; she felt liquid running down the sides of her leg. Then she felt a blanket being drawn over her and smelled the peculiar smell of wet wool. He had finished his work, she realized.

"My family," she said again, before submitting to the fatigue that enveloped her.

Twenty-Nine

LATER, THOUGH SHE DID NOT KNOW how much later, Beth woke again. She had rolled over in her sleep and now faced the wall beside the bed, her stiff, splinted arm forming a ramp down to the mattress. She saw a window on the wall above her, a large single-pane opening, and Beth recognized that darkness had fallen.

She could not see a thing outside the window—there were no clues to give her any hint as to her new location. At her feet she saw a single flame, dancing weakly in the glass confines of a lantern. Her thigh burned, and she squirmed in discomfort. She heard nothing, and the room felt empty. Beth wondered if the man was still nearby.

Trying not to draw attention to herself, she took a moment to observe the place. She was in a cabin—the kind of one-room building a hunter might have used somewhere in the woods. By arching her back and tipping her head, she could see the wall at the head of her bed. The room had a single door.

She was lying on a single bed. In the dim light, she saw a badly stained and lumpy mattress covered in navy-and-white ticking. With her good hand, she reached up to feel the pillow underneath her head. As lumpy as the mattress, the pillow had no case.

She straightened her knee and flexed her thigh muscle, knowing then that the dripping wet thing he'd placed there had dried and now clung to her skin. She resisted the urge to touch the wound, though she wanted to know how much worse the infection had become. Once again, she turned her attention to her surroundings.

The wooden walls next to her bed showed marks where the timber had been rough cut. Neither stained nor painted, they had the furry look of very old cedar shingles. Beth wondered if the man had cut the wood himself. Had he built the place?

And where was he now? With effort, she rolled onto her back, lifting the board supporting her right arm with her good hand and placing it back on the pillow near her hips. She turned her head and saw him sitting near a wood stove, his chair tipped back on its rear legs, his denim-covered legs stretched out on a table that was just big enough for his legs, a pitcher and a cup, and a kerosene lamp. He concentrated intently on something he held in his lap.

Something wet touched her ankle, and a soft whine drew her attention. A black dog with tan spots stared back at her from the end of the bed. The dog moved forward and nuzzled her fingers as they dangled in the air—as if demanding to be petted. Compassionate brown eyes smiled up at her as the dog crept forward and tried to lick her face. Unwilling to accept such affection, Beth turned her face away.

No pictures hung anywhere in the single room. In fact, from her position on the bed, she could not see a single memento of any kind. No photos, no books. The room appeared as barren as a room in a convent. And in its barrenness, the room asked more questions than it answered.

She turned toward the man, staring as she watched him work. From his chair, he glanced up, met her eyes, and turned back to his work. "Thirsty," she said, recognizing the pasty taste of dehydration in her mouth.

He turned again to look at her, a scowl crossing his features. His eyebrows drew down and together, and his face seemed to freeze in an angry expression as he dropped the chair onto its front legs and stood. She noticed as he took his first steps that he limped. Then walking more steadily, he reached out to lift a grimy plastic pitcher and tin cup from the table. He carried these over to the bed.

As she observed him, Beth felt her curiosity grow. Shoulder-length hair, an even mix of gray and brown, covered his round head and mingled without definition with his chest-length beard. Both his beard and hair waved in the frizzy wild way of natural curl. The color reminded her of steel wool fresh from the package. Though he avoided eye contact, Beth saw that he had clear pale blue eyes and a colorless mole that clung to one cheek just above the beginning of his beard.

Watching him walk toward her, it surprised Beth that she felt no fear. After all, he had rescued her, had brought her to this place and set her arm. He had done something to her leg. This strange hairy man filled her with curiosity. Where had he brought her? When would he take her home?

Without speaking, he offered the cup to her, and awkwardly Beth tried to sit up, wanting the water too badly to risk spilling a single drop. He leaned down to support her back as she reached across her body with her good hand, accepting the cup. She brought it quickly to her lips. Instead of satisfying her, the cold water made her want more. She handed the cup back, saying only, "Please?"

He nodded and poured again.

Eventually satisfied, she thanked him and lay back down on the bed. She hoped that he would speak to her. Instead, he frowned and moved back to his chair. Sitting again, he lifted one leg with his hand, and stretching it out on the table, he settled the knee carefully. She saw that as he did this, a fleeting expression of discomfort crossed his features. Then, apparently comfortable, he reached for a tool and a small block of wood from the table. He leaned back and began cutting on the wood.

His work so occupied him that he seemed to forget she even existed. His face expressed utter concentration as he bent over the small tool, his gaze never moving from the tool or from the wood he was working on. Beth watched for a while, her curiosity absorbed by the strange old man.

But she felt tired, so weak in fact, that even as she watched, her body demanded rest. She had a fever; she felt it burning in her body, aching in her joints. She knew instinctively that the fever came from the infected wound in her leg and it had begun to attack her entire body. Her joints complained, and her skin burned with the flush of fever. In spite of the medication, Beth could not get comfortable, and she squirmed as she tried to ease the aching in her leg, her arm, her ribs, her back, and her joints. Even her head hurt. Eventually, utterly exhausted, Beth gave in to sleep.

When she woke again, her clothes dripped with perspiration. A new chill rattled her body. She pulled the wool blanket higher, trying to tuck it up over her shoulders and around her chin. Her headache was worse, and the aching in her joints had grown more severe.

Darkness filled the cabin, though she could tell that a fire continued to burn in the stove. She felt the heat coming from it, heard the sound of air being pulled into its belly by the burning wood. Looking in that direction, she recognized the eerie glow of fire coming through the seams of the potbelly's front door.

She heard heavy snoring and knew that the man had fallen asleep, though she did not know where. In her observation of the room, she had not seen another bed. Other than the single chair, the table, and the bed, she remembered no other furniture. She lay shivering, aching, and listened to his snoring blend with the sound of the wind whistling through the trees around the cabin.

Suddenly an intense feeling of homesickness washed over her, and Beth felt tears spring to her eyes. She did not want to be sick here. She did not want to hide here in this strange, silent man's cabin. She wanted to go home. Beth wanted to hold her son, to hug her girls. She wanted to rest in her own clean sheets, under her own comforter, with Allen snuggled beside her. If only she could touch Allen, bury her face in his shoulder, smell his warm familiar smell, and hold him. If only she could tell him how much she loved him.

Responding to her imagination, Beth felt her fingers close—as if by their own will they could touch and hold Allen. As they did, Beth felt her right elbow object. She grimaced and her hand relaxed instantly—but not before Beth realized that the fingers of her right hand had closed for the first time since the accident.

She reached out with her left hand, trying to touch the back of her injured hand. When the two hands touched, Beth recognized the beginning of a miracle. Both hands felt the touch. Both hands. Both hands!

She scratched the skin of her right hand with the nail of her left index finger. To be certain, she repeated the motion. Beth smiled. She felt it! She felt the scratch against her injured hand. She giggled softly in the dark; then remembering the sleeping man, smothered her delight.

In setting her arm, the old man must have relieved the pressure on the nerves of her elbow. What he did had been horribly painful—cruel, in fact—still, his abuse had brought health to her hand. She smiled again and thanked the Lord for the healing, and before she even considered what she was saying, for the man who had brought her here.

Beth tried to ease herself back to sleep. In her excitement, she had grown warmer. But she wanted water. This new thirst commanded her attention, sticking her mouth closed. She tried to lick her lips, but her tongue felt as dry as a paper grocery bag.

She began thinking about the water in the pitcher. Had he left it there? Did it still rest in the middle of the table near the stove? She tried to remember the water in his hand. Had the container been full? Did she dare get up and help herself to water?

Beth tried to put the idea out of her mind. But her imagination refused to cooperate. She could almost feel the cool water on her lips, sliding over her tongue and going down her parched throat. She imagined it, cool and refreshing, easing the heat that burned the skin on her face. She could feel it on her teeth, taste it. She wanted water.

She opened her eyes in the darkness, willing them to get used to the black room. Could she get to the table without stumbling and waking him up? She pictured the room as she had last seen it. She imagined the chair and estimated the number of steps from her bed to the table. If she stepped away from the stove as she moved, she felt absolutely certain that she would not stumble over his chair in the dark. She might be able to reach the table and return to the bed without waking the man.

The glow from the stove would protect her from inadvertently touching the hot metal. She did not need to add another burn to her long list of injuries. As she considered the layout of the room once more, she decided she could do it. She could help herself to water, and the old hermit would never even know.

Beth reached over her body with her good arm and lifted the board holding her elbow. She lowered the splint onto the bed beside the mound where it had rested and dropped the pillow on the other side of her hip. Then, in one swift motion, she sat up, holding the splint as she did.

The springs below the mattress creaked as a sudden dizziness set the room spinning, nearly dropping her onto her back. Taking deep breaths, she swung her legs off the side of the bed and lowered her head over her knees. Blinking, Beth sat motionless, waiting for it to pass.

She brought her head up slowly and looked around the room, trying to see through the blackness around her. She saw only unrecognizable shadows and wished that she had paid more attention earlier to the exact shape and placement of objects in the room.

Eventually her lightheadedness eased, and Beth scooted forward until she was perched on the very edge of the bed. The bed creaked with every motion, and Beth held her breath, willing the bed frame to be silent.

Ever so slowly, she eased herself onto her feet and raised her body from the bed. Then, in a half-standing position, Beth waited for a new wave of dizziness to pass. She bent forward, reaching for the bed, holding it with one hand, her head down, swaying slightly. Nausea rolled in her stomach, and for a moment, she wished she hadn't gotten up.

Her movement caught the attention of the dog, and he whined softly in the dark.

Good thing the cabin isn't on fire, she thought. *At this pace I'd never get myself out of here.* She smiled in the dark. When she felt better, she straightened up and turned to face the stove.

Like a blind woman, Beth used her strong arm to hold her splinted arm up as she took a single step forward. She had not realized until this moment that she still had her hiking boots on. At least she wouldn't stub her toe as she walked. One step. She shifted her weight and stood still, listening for the man. Still sleeping, his snoring continued—deep and regular. She heard the sound of the dog's paws in the dark.

The water drew her forward, and she eased her weight onto one foot as she slid her other foot forward. Cautious step after cautious step, Beth moved toward the table, her arms out in front, twisting her trunk as she swept the air for obstacles. The old man snored.

She had to be very near the water now. Almost there. She lowered her hands to the level of her hips and stretched out, hoping to catch the edge of the table. She took another step, and her foot hit something soft. She pulled back and froze.

She heard his voice, a sudden abrupt shout, and instantly he was up. He tackled her at the waist, dropping her to the floor in a heap. Her head slammed back onto the wooden floor, and she reached up to protect herself—though clearly too late. His body was on hers now, holding her, reaching for her throat.

Completely shocked, Beth had no chance against him. She twisted out of his grasp, but the man stayed with her, tackling her again, this time from a crouch, like a linebacker for a football team. Beth dropped without resistance.

All thirst forgotten, Beth struggled to get away from him. She felt his bulk slam down on top of her, smelled his unwashed body, and felt his thick hands grabbing her hair, pulling her head toward him. She screamed, loud and piercing, but this had no effect. It came to her suddenly that here in this isolated place, no one would hear her scream. No one would ever know about her struggle.

Terrified, she tried to roll again, yanking her hair from his grasp as she did. She felt her hair slip out of his clumsy grip, but she did not move fast enough. She rolled onto her broken arm and felt an immediate siren of pain in her elbow and broken ribs. With her left shoulder facing the ceiling, she struggled to get away. But he reached across her face, his fingers again clutching her neck.

Clearly he intended to choke her to death. She felt his fingers close. Though Beth struggled against him with all her might, she knew she could not win. Weak, fevered, and broken, Beth knew with certainty that this man would succeed in killing her.

Thirty

HE HAD TO KILL HER. *Had to kill the woman who now threat-ened his life. Kill or be killed. This was the most important law Doyle had ever learned. More important than gravity. Kill or be killed. He would kill her, or she would certainly kill him.*

He struggled with the single-mindedness of one about to die. Just as he finally reached her, finally closed his fingers around her skinny corded neck, a searing pain hit him in his forearm, and he lost his grip. The pain hit him again, and he rolled away, blinking against the darkness.

The motion, the hard wooden floor, the pain, all of it brought him back. *A dream,* he thought. He had been dreaming. Panting, he stood. Doyle knew instantly where he was and what had happened. Again. He had done it again. Doyle swore.

He needed light. Knowing every inch of the little cabin, he reached the table and pulled the kerosene lantern toward him, lift-ing the glass cover. He struck a wooden match and touched the flame to the wick, turning the handle, to brighten the darkness.

With a sharp exhale, he blew out the match and dropped it on the floor near the stove. By the time he picked up the lantern cover, Doyle's hands shook so hard that he had difficulty setting the glass on the brass frame. He closed his fist so that she would not see his trembling hands and turned to face the woman.

She had not moved. Still staring at him, she sat holding her neck with her good hand. Her eyes were wide with fear, moist with emotion. Just like the other woman. He had done it again. Nothing would ever change for him. No matter how long he stayed away, he would always be the same. Doyle uttered a curse. Though he had left civilization in order to keep it from happening again, here he was. When would this agony end?

She did not speak. She kept her eyes riveted on him as she scooted away, sliding along the floor toward the farthest wall of the cabin, one hand still holding her throat. He saw redness there, and the beginning of bruises forming where his fingertips had crushed her neck.

"I won't hurt you," he said, though he knew she did not believe him. *Why should she?* he thought. He had never been able to keep that promise—not since he'd come back to the States, anyway. He always ended up hurting someone.

She did not answer. With wide eyes, she leaned against the far wall and began to massage the skin and muscles of her neck. He heard her sniffle and saw her lift her hand to wipe the tears dripping off her cheeks. Though she tried to control her emotions, he could smell her fear. He swore again. He should never have brought her here. Should have left her there on the mountain. Never mind that she would have died.

She was trouble, this woman. Trouble. And he had made the huge mistake of bringing trouble to his home. Glancing away, he put his hands on his hips and swore again.

Hearing the dog whine, Doyle watched as Gilligan padded across the floor and placed himself protectively between the man and the woman. Doyle rubbed the bite marks on his forearm. His own dog had bit him, trying to protect the woman from the maniac he'd become.

Gilligan moved again, his gentle footsteps padding quietly around her, and he lay down on the floor, placing his muzzle on her lap. Looking up into her face, the dog whined, raised his eyebrows in a pleading way, and edged his nose under her good hand. The dog squirmed until she noticed him.

The woman looked down, and in spite of her fear, she smiled. She touched the dog's nose, gently rubbing the short black fur with her thumb. Then she brought her hand up and scratched behind the dog's ears.

"Look, Dink," he said. "I didn't mean to scare you. I don't have visitors."

She stared up at Doyle, and he could see by her raised shoulders, by the tension of her posture, that fear still gripped her. Clearly, she did not trust him. Still, she nodded—the slightest hint of a nod, as if she understood.

But Doyle knew that she did not understand. No one would ever understand. Why should they? Even professionals didn't understand. He watched her take a deep breath, though it did nothing to stop her trembling. Still she did not move.

"You scared me," he said. Even as he said it, he wondered why he felt obliged to explain himself to this stranger. "Why'd you get up, anyway?"

She blinked back tears as she glanced down and continued petting the dog. "I wanted water. I was thirsty."

He glanced at the pitcher sitting on the table and saw that it was empty. "Go back to bed," he said, instantly regretting his gruff tone. He had used his command voice. "I'll get more water." He picked up the pitcher and started for the door.

She did not move. Her hand froze on the dog, and he saw her glance from him to the door beside her. As she sat directly between Doyle and the door, he knew he would have to pass very close to her feet in order to go outside and get water from the spring. He recognized the fear that rose again to her face.

The thought of watching her withdraw, trying to slide away as he passed by, made Doyle sick. "Look," he said, pointing to the door near her feet. "I have to go out for more water. You go to bed. I'll bring it inside." He took several steps away from her.

Keeping her gaze fixed on him, she rolled slowly onto one hip. The dog sat up, watching. Without taking her eyes off Doyle, Beth stood and backed toward the edge of the bed, where she sat down. Her haunted, cautious motion told him more than words ever would. Still, she said nothing.

Doyle felt a deep sadness wash over him. *I've gotta get out of here.* Without another glance, he stepped toward the door. Opening it, he went out into the swirling, blowing snow.

The air temperature felt no colder than the temperature of his soul.

As soon as the door closed behind him, Beth gave in to her fear. Her trembling became violent, and tears came to her eyes. She covered her face with one hand and bent low over her lap, crying. In her fear, she began praying—asking for help. Beth wanted out. She could not survive with this crazy mountain man.

What kind of man would wake in the middle of the night and try to choke her to death? What craziness possessed him? Beth couldn't begin to guess. On the other hand, she did not care. She only wanted out. Away from him.

Still sitting on the side of the bed, she concentrated on calming herself. He had not killed her. Not yet. Still, he was very dangerous. She would not give the man another opportunity. She would stay with him only until she felt well enough to escape. Then in the middle of the night she would run away and find her way down the mountain by herself.

He had delivered her from her injuries. And she would deliver herself from him. Carefully, Beth lowered herself back onto the bed and pulled up the green wool blanket. The blanket did not stop her trembling. She rolled onto her right side, putting her back against the wall, sticking her injured arm out in front of her. It hurt to lie down this way, but after what had just happened, she wanted her back to the wall. In this position, Beth felt less vulnerable.

Still shivering, though now from fear rather than fever, Beth took deep breaths. She brought to mind pictures of her children sleeping peacefully in their beds at home. They needed her to keep her wits, to live through this long nightmare. Beth had to stay calm and alert. She closed her eyes and concentrated on the sound of air coming in and out of her lungs.

Long moments later, the door opened and he came in. She heard him cross the room to the table, where he picked up the tin cup. "Here," he said as he came toward her, shoving the cup at her. "Drink." His gruff voice gave not the slightest hint of kindness or remorse.

She sat up and accepted the cup, drinking it dry. Handing it back, she did not say a word. She noticed that he avoided eye contact.

"More?" he asked.

She nodded and drained the cup a second time, still without words.

"Don't get up again," he warned her, taking the cup back to the table.

"I won't," she said, shivering. "I'm sorry." She could think of nothing else to say. His fierce features did not invite conversation. But Beth did not want to talk to this crazy man anyway. She lay down again. Lying on her side, Beth watched him move around the room. As she did, she felt something inside her change. Though he still looked angry—very angry—Beth suddenly did not believe that he was really crazy.

Standing beside the table, he turned down the lantern wick, and darkness filled the cabin. She heard him move back onto the floor and settle down. For a long time, she listened in the darkness. He did not go back to sleep. His snoring did not resume. Neither of them moved. Beth lay perfectly still and listened to the old man breathe.

Just as Beth began to feel herself grow sleepy, she felt the bed creak. Startled by the noise, she jumped. Then she felt the successive steps of the dog as it walked up next to her on the bed. She felt its wet tongue lick her cheek. She turned her face away, and the dog settled down beside her and sighed.

Feeling the motion of the dog's chest and the warmth of its fur, Beth at last gave in to exhaustion. Her last thought was of a psalm. "I wake again, because the Lord sustains me." Tonight, in this dark cabin, with the cold wind outside and a frightening old man inside, the psalm had new meaning.

———

When Beth woke, the cabin had grown very cold. She lay still for a moment, hugging the wool blanket, wondering what exactly seemed different this morning. The stillness of the cabin frightened her a little.

She rolled over and discovered that he had gone.

She shoved the sleeping dog off the bed and crawled out, standing slowly. Again, she felt dizzy. Her headache remained, and her thigh felt engorged and stiff. He had completely removed the leg of her jeans, exposing the wound to his doctoring. The poultice he'd put on had fallen off during the night. As she bent to examine her leg, the room began to swirl around her. Beth dropped back onto the edge of the mattress.

Bending her knee pulled the skin around her wound, letting little trickles of fluid escape and run down her leg. The infection had not improved.

However, her hand felt better this morning, less swollen. The dark bruising had begun to change into an ugly greenish yellow. She tried moving her fingers and found that though the motion made her elbow ache, the fingers wiggled freely. Her sensation seemed to be improving as well. Her ribs still ached, but the pain seemed minor compared to her arm. Overall, the night in the cabin had been good for Beth.

She breathed a prayer of thanks as she walked over to check the antique stove. Inside she found the meager remains of last night's fire. She stood up and looked around the room for wood. A full box rested against the far cabin wall, and Beth chose several pieces.

Working carefully, blowing on the coals as she did, Beth managed to get the fire going again. Satisfied, she closed the stove and turned to pull up a chair. Only then did she discover a bowl of hot cereal, now congealed, and a clean—though dented—spoon waiting on the small table.

The man had left her breakfast. But where had he gone? When would he return? Beth had never met anyone more puzzling.

Beth stuck her finger in the cereal and discovered that it had cooled to match the cabin temperature. She picked up the chipped enamel bowl and set it on top of the stove next to an old teakettle. She lifted the kettle and discovered warm water inside.

As the stove began to give off heat, Beth filled her tin cup with water and sat sipping in front of the stove as she waited for her breakfast to warm. It occurred to Beth that she needed to use an outhouse. Certainly the man had something like that up here in the mountains. She tested the cereal again and added a bit of warm water to the bowl.

She went over to the bed and wrapped the blanket around her waist, tucking the ends into her jeans. Then, at the cabin door, she removed her coat from a nail on the wall. She dropped her good arm into a sleeve and wrapped the coat over her shoulders. Reaching for the door, she lifted the latch and pulled. Though the door moved slightly into the room, it did not open.

She tried again, only this time she pushed on the door. Still it did not give way. She turned sideways, shoving her good shoulder into the door. Nothing.

Beth eased herself into the corner beside the door and tried to see through the crack afforded by the door's slight motion. She let her gaze travel down the light visible along the edge of the door until she spied the problem. A metal bar crossing the opening very near the latch. Beth recognized the bar as part of a bar-and-hasp lock. The lock on the outside had provided just enough motion in the door for her to recognize the truth. The man had locked her inside.

Anger surged through her, and for a moment she felt she would explode with it. How dare he? How dare he even consider holding her captive here? Her heart beat faster, and she slammed the door with her left hand. She had been through too much, had survived too many obstacles, to let this complete maniac keep her from her family. *Who does he think he is, anyway?* she wondered.

She kicked the door again before any semblance of calm came back to her. *I'm beginning to behave like my own kids. I guess I didn't need to go to the bathroom that badly anyway.* She took off the coat and went back to the chair, determined to eat her cereal and drink the water. She would do everything she could to stay strong. She would eat and drink, rest and care for herself. And then, when the opportunity came, she would walk out alone.

Beth ate and sat for a long time before the fire, staring at the kerosene lamp, which the man kept going during the day. She could see out now, through the filthy window over the bed. She saw snow, still coming down heavily, covering the limbs of the trees outside. A loud *whump* sounded on the roof, and Beth jumped. *What was that?*

She went over to the window and looked out. She saw nothing disturbed—nothing that would explain the noise. Then on a nearby tree, a clump of snow dropped from the lowest limb. That had to be the noise, she reasoned. Snow falling on the cabin roof.

She could hear the wind still blowing in the tops of trees in the distance, though the trees outside the window did not move. Something protected this cabin from the prevailing wind. In her mind, Beth pictured a map and tried to imagine where the cabin might be located. But in her condition this much thinking only made her tired, and she went back to sit in the chair by the stove.

After drinking more water, she decided to take a look around, to find out what she could about this bizarre man who had taken her captive. When he returned, she might not have another opportunity. Anything she discovered might help her stay alive.

The room had one cabinet. A kind of sideboard—not unlike the rough workbenches found in a garage—stood against the wall opposite the bed. She walked over to it and opened the left upper cabinet. Here, she found dishes, all mismatched and in various states of disrepair. These were not the kind of dishes sold in a secondhand store. These looked like something stolen from someone's garbage. Still, the cupboard was clean, the dishes neatly stacked.

In the next cupboard, she found food. The man had flour, sugar, beans, a few other staples, a mixing bowl, and even a baking dish. She noticed several stacks of flat brown tins that she did not recognize and picked one up. They had darker lettering across the top, but no other labels. They seemed to be military food of some kind. She put the tin back on the shelf and closed the door.

In the lower left cabinet, Beth found clothes. The man had one other pair of pants, a heavy jacket, and two shirts. In addition, he had one pair of green wool socks and a black sweater. Obviously, he was no slave to fashion.

In the next cabinet, she found a small wooden box. Inside this cigar-sized box she found a set of tools, all shiny clean and meticulously arranged by size. She recognized them as carving tools—the kind of tools a wood craftsman might use. She lifted one, holding it up to the lamp to examine it more carefully. A long narrow blade, no wider than a pencil lead, was attached to a small handle by a dappled metal collar. Even the tool seemed handmade, beautiful in its perfection. The sharp blade flashed in the light.

She replaced the tool, closed the box, and set it back on the shelf. As she did, she discovered another box beside it. This one, about the size of a jewelry box, shone with a finely polished finish. Each corner featured tongue-and-groove joints, so perfectly smooth that as she ran her fingers over the edge, she could not feel where one piece of wood ended and another began. The top, which rested on a lip formed by the sides, had been covered with the delicate carving of dogwood blossoms.

On each of the four corners, a supporting leg had been carved in one piece with the bottom of the box. She held it to her nose, breathing in the sweet aroma of cedar. Beth had never seen a more beautiful box.

She carried it to the table and put it down so that she could open it with her good hand. What she found inside surprised her. Medals, all tied together with a twist tie, had been dumped in the bottom of the box. Among these, she found patches—the kind of patches she'd seen on military uniforms—though she didn't know what branch of the service these represented. Stripes, ribbons, and smaller unrecognizable pieces lay among the medals, thread still hanging from where they had been removed from a uniform. She spied a larger patch, a single white rectangle with black letters. *DOYLE* was printed on the patch. She picked it up and ran her fingers along the letters.

Was that his name?

She put the patch back in the box and lifted the medals out, walking toward the bed, where she could examine them in the light of the window.

Seized with curiosity, she wondered whose they were and how they had been won. She turned them over, inspecting each one, looking for signs of their origin.

The medals so captivated Beth that she did not hear the cabin door open, did not know that he had returned—that is, not until she heard his voice shouting, "What're you doing with my things?"

Thirty-One

SHE BACKED AWAY AS HE CROSSED the cabin with long angry strides. "What are you doing with these?" he said, snatching the medals from her fingers. His expression seething, he dangled them in front of her, the medals rattling. "What gives you permission to go through my things?" Then, with a cold stare, he dropped the jingling bundle into his pants pocket.

As Beth backed away from the bed, her heart beat a timpani in her chest, and she could not stop her own trembling. What was wrong with this nut? Why did he have to hide this sad collection of stuff? How should she respond to someone who could at one moment set a broken limb and then without warning turn deadly? How should she handle a man like that?

Then Beth remembered the locked door. She thought of him holding her against her will and felt her own anger ignite. "What do you mean—what am I doing?" she asked, pointing to the cabin door. "You locked me in here like a prisoner."

Her words slapped him; his face contorted, and he glanced away. "I didn't lock you in to keep you from leavin'," he said, spitting out the words. "I locked the door to keep you from killin' yourself." The lines in his forehead deepened, his muscles grew more tense, and anger seemed to ooze from his pores.

"Right," Beth said, her fear completely replaced by anger. "I'll just bet you did." She backed up, leaned against the counter, and crossed her arms. "What exactly could kill me out there? It seems that *you* are the most dangerous creature on this mountain."

Her comment hit the mark, and he turned away. "You can leave whenever you want," he said. "I didn't invite you. I only brought you here cuz you were gonna die out there on your own. You've already shown how capable you are in the wilderness. Go ahead. Leave. It'd be a relief." He moved to the stove and picked up a piece of wood. Busying himself with the fire, he dismissed her.

"Look." She took a deep breath. "I was doing just fine until I fell into a pit—dug by some crazy person. I can't be blamed for that!" As she spoke, a picture of the nylon bag resting on the rocks below the cliff flitted across her mind. She shook her head and began again. "I'm grateful for what you've done. My arm is already better," she said, holding the board out and closing her fist for him to see. "I can feel my fingers again. And the bruising is going away."

Why argue with him? She lowered her arm, and her argument fell away at the same moment. She shrugged. "I just needed to use an outhouse or something."

He turned back to face her. "There's an outhouse on the left side of the porch. Behind the woodpile."

Completely baffled by the man, Beth watched him for a moment. *This guy could use a course with Miss Manners,* she thought, still irritated. *In fact, he could use an entire year with her.*

Beth refused to expose her bare right leg to blowing snow. So she snatched up the wool blanket from the chair and wrapped it around her hips once again, securing it in the waistband of her jeans. Leaving the old man sitting by the fire, Beth quietly lifted the door latch and slipped out onto the porch.

The cold outside air slapped her, biting her throat as she breathed. Snow continued to fall onto the wooden porch and completely covered the step. Beth looked down at footprints leading away from the house. More than two feet of snow had already fallen here. *How long have I been here?* Thinking back, she could not remember anything about her arrival at the cabin. She had no idea how long it had been since she left her car at the airport.

What about Allen? How long has he worried about me?

From the porch, she spotted the path the man had taken up the hill from the cabin. Deep footprints trenched up the hill, the snow undisturbed on either side. Not far off the porch, a tarp made a new indentation in the snow. Apparently, he had moved something only this morning, and for a moment, Beth felt curious. What had he been doing? Was that the reason he had left her for so long?

On the other hand, what did she care? He'd locked her inside. She felt a shudder of revulsion and put the thought out of her mind.

Directly in front of the cabin, the white of snow and thick fog blended so perfectly that it completely obscured the line where earth gave way to air. Whiteness stretched out endlessly before her, making the view both magical and frightening at the same time.

In the swirling fog, she saw pale green cones appearing and disappearing in the mist and wind before her. These she identified as the tops of old trees—though she could not be certain of how she knew this. They seemed to hang at eye level just out of reach, not far from the front of the cabin.

The mountain man was right. Her chances of surviving alone in the wilderness weren't good.

Just steps away from the door, a steep cliff dropped suddenly enough to make treetops appear right before her eyes. If she had gone out without him, Beth might have stumbled over the edge, falling into the abyss below her.

She shivered again and readjusted the blanket, pulling it up around her shoulders.

Stepping off the porch, she walked around the cabin to her left, looking through the swirling whiteness for the woodpile the man described. She spotted it about twenty feet from the house. A high stack, taller than a man—each piece exactly the same length—partially hidden under a tattered blue tarp.

Beth went around the pile, turning toward the hill behind the cabin. After one or two steps, she noticed that very little snow covered the ground. She looked up to see the trunks of two enormous trees whose long broad branches made a natural roof over both the cabin and the clearing around the woodpile. This location couldn't be more perfectly protected from the wind and weather.

Beth found the little outhouse and used it, eager to get back inside. On the way, she heard the sound of water falling. Curious, she walked toward the sound until she discovered a wooden sluice inserted in the hill behind the cabin, and water dripping freely into an oak barrel. She put her hands in the cold water and washed her face, taking care to massage her forehead gently.

Beth leaned forward, dipping her entire face into the ice-cold water, still working to loosen the blood from her hair. Eventually, cold air and frigid water chilled her until she gave up and headed inside. Still, she felt better, cleaner, and somewhat refreshed.

———————

When the woman came back inside, Doyle noticed that her face and hair were wet. She shivered from the cold. "What'd you do out there? Take a bath in the water barrel?" he asked.

"I just washed my face," she answered, brushing wet hair away from her forehead.

He sighed and stood up, limping slightly as he reached the sideboard. Silently, he cursed his bad knee, angry for the impression of weakness it must give. He opened the bottom middle cupboard and pulled out a single towel, the only one he owned. For an instant he regretted that it had a hole in it and that both long edges were frayed. Then he scolded himself. After all, he hadn't invited her to be his guest.

He held the towel toward her. "You should've asked me," he said. "I would've heated water." She took the towel between the fingers and thumb of her left hand, reluctantly, almost as if she believed that the cloth was contaminated.

He lifted the large cast-iron pot from the counter.

Before she could respond, he carried the pot out the cabin door into the cold mountain air. He filled the pot from the barrel and lugged it inside. By the time he closed the door behind him, the pot had grown enormously heavy, and his arms felt leaden. The little ache below his collarbone had returned. He lifted the pot onto the back of the stove. The pain in his shoulder caught him as he lifted, and he winced, dropping the pot as he did. It fell with a flat-bottomed clang onto the metal surface.

She sat before the fire, her face in her hands. When she looked up, he noticed that her eyes glistened, and a look of intense sadness seeped from her dark, almond-shaped eyes. "What's the matter?" he asked, wishing that he didn't bark when he spoke, that he could make his voice sound reassuring instead of gruff. He rubbed the ache under his collarbone.

"Nothing."

She was lying, of course. He recognized it easily. Women often lied, he knew, and she was no exception. What did he expect?

"I wanna look at your thigh," he said, and this, too, came out as an order. "How does it feel?"

"It hurts," she answered, stretching out her knee. At least she sometimes told the truth.

"It should," he said. "It's got a bad infection."

"Here, let me see." He pulled out a large chunk of firewood and set her heel on it, straightening her knee as he did. Then, in one quick motion, he tore the fabric bandage from her wound. She cried out—a quick, urgent sound. At least she didn't cry like a child. Blood and fluid began to trickle from the hot infected wound. He noticed that fibers clung to the tissue.

He bent over her, using his thumbs to prod the swollen flesh. He pinched the flesh together in places along her thigh, causing a green fluid to ooze from her scabbed skin. Small indentations remained where his thumbs pushed. "This has to drain."

She looked down at him, blinking fresh tears. He couldn't tell if they were from the injury or some other pain. "I'll have to clean it again," he said. "But first, you need to wash."

He saw clearly the surprise on her face.

He pointed to the stove. "When the water is warm enough, you can take a spit bath. I have things to do outside," he said. With two fingers, he kneaded the spot below his shoulder, wishing that this strange ache would go away. *I must've hurt it chopping wood*, he thought. *It'll go away. After all, the wood is finished for the winter.*

He moved back to the cupboard, pulling out his extra clothes—a pair of pants and a clean shirt. "When you're clean," he began, tossing them onto the table, "you can wear these."

She looked confused, almost baffled, by his words. Still, she said nothing.

"Put on the shirt," he explained as though speaking to a child, "and then wrap yourself in the blanket. When you're ready," he said, pointing to her thigh, "I'll work on that. I'll dress it again, and then you can put on the pants. Any questions?" he asked.

She shook her head.

Why wouldn't the woman speak? Most women never stopped talking. Why was this one different? Frustrated, he shook his head, and went back outside. Early this morning Doyle had dragged most of the things from the plane back to the cabin. He wanted to stow them quickly, before anyone discovered them. He would put things away while she bathed and changed clothes.

Years ago Doyle had dug a small underground storage area directly behind his cabin. He had designed and built a cover, fitting it securely with a latch and padlock. Bit by bit, he carried things from the tarp to the storage area, carefully climbing down the three-step ladder, putting things away, and then returning to the tarp. He had just picked up the radio and turned back toward the cabin when he saw her standing at the edge of the porch, wrapped in the blanket from the hips down, staring at him.

Her cheeks gleamed, shining clean, even from a distance. In one hand, she held the handle of the black pot, steam rising around her hand. Surprise changed to anger as she recognized the radio in his hands.

She stepped down from the porch and set the pot on the snow, then pushed it over to empty the warm soapy water.

Ignoring her, he continued carrying the last load back to the storage area. He felt her eyes watch him as he crossed in front of the woodpile, going near the house to the storage area. Just as he climbed down the little ladder, he heard the front door close.

When he went back inside, he found her in front of the stove. Doyle poured fresh water from the pitcher into the kettle and put it back on the stove. "Put your foot up," he ordered. Never taking her eyes from his face, she placed her heel over the log.

Doyle began kneading the flesh again, forcing the wound to drain. Then, when the water had heated, he scrubbed the wound with the rag. She blinked away tears. His scrubbing hurt her.

"Must you take off all three layers of skin?"

"I've gotta get it clean," he answered, scrubbing harder.

"Stop it," she said, pulling away. "Don't. You don't have to kill me."

"I'm not gonna kill you."

A long moment passed while she stared at his face. Then she ran her fingers along the skin, trembling fingers that never quite touched her own flesh. She placed her heel back on the log and nodded. He dipped the rag in the kettle, rinsing it carefully.

"I saw the stuff you stole from the plane," she said, her eyes on his face. "It doesn't belong to you. Why did you take it?"

"I didn't steal it. I found it. Finders keepers."

"That's good." She gave a mocking laugh. "That's the same kind of childish reasoning my girls give me."

He avoided her eyes. What right did she have to talk to him about morals? What did she know anyway? He'd learned more about morals in one year than most people do in a lifetime. He threw the rag in the kettle and went over to the cabinet. With his back to her, he pulled several glass jars from the upper shelves, mixing a concoction he hoped would help her body battle the infection. He heard her sniff. "What are you crying about now?" he asked, bringing a pasty mixture back to the stove.

"My girls," she said. "You'd never understand, but I miss my girls," she answered, whispering, wiping her dripping nose with the back of her hand as she blinked away tears.

She had managed to hurt more with her words than his scrubbing ever could. "For your information, I do have a family." He knelt down again beside her foot, ready to apply the homemade paste with a clean fabric bandage. He did not quite know what to do with this kind of feminine emotion, but before he could explain further, she continued.

"You have a family?"

"Hard to believe?"

"No. I mean, yes . . ." She seemed to struggle for words, and then giving up, she shrugged. "What I meant is, if you had a family, why would you live up here in the mountains by yourself?"

He did not respond. What did she know about what a man would or would not do? This woman from her sheltered, safe life—she had no idea what would drive someone away from the people he loved.

"I'm sorry. I didn't mean to be rude," she said, brushing hair from her face. She squirmed in discomfort as he rubbed her thigh.

"Hold still," he barked.

"I'm sorry," she said, her voice full of sadness. Her tears began again. "I'm just tired. I've been gone so long. All I want is to go home. And I don't know who you are or why I'm here." She snorted and wiped her dripping nose with the sleeve of his only spare shirt. "I don't feel good. I have a fever, I think."

"Look," he said, "just shut up, will ya?"

Hurt flitted across her features. She nodded.

"I didn't invite you. I don't want you around any more than you wanna be here."

She blinked at his sudden change in tone. "So take me home," she said, her voice quiet and even. "Take me now."

Thirty-Two

IN HIS HURRY TO REACH THE HANGAR, Allen nearly fell out of his car, leaving the keys in the ignition. He noticed, but did not care, that he had forgotten to lock the doors. At least he'd turned off the engine. *Who cares if the car is stolen*, he thought as he pulled open the hangar door.

In the trip from his home to Thun Field, Allen had done nothing but pray. Truthfully, Allen's prayers would be more accurately classified as begging. Three days had passed since the afternoon Beth's plane went down. Three days of wondering whether or not she was still alive. Since then, though, time had passed more slowly than ever before in his life. Allen could truly not remember any single detail about those days. They existed in his memory as an excruciatingly painful longing, an emptiness like nothing he had ever experienced.

Still, after all this time, Allen dared to hope, dared to believe, that she had survived. Even more, he dared to trust that prayer would bring her home. Allen had not completely ignored the facts. After all, he had officiated at his fair share of funerals. Up until the last minute, every believer has hope for his loved one. Allen was no different from those he had served over the years.

Still, rather than focus on the logic of his experience, Allen chose only to trust in the goodness of God.

For now, he would pray. He would deal with whatever happened later.

His glasses fogged as soon as he walked inside. He took them off, wiping them on his shirt as he scanned the room for Harry.

"Allen," Duane Eastburn, his close friend, put a hand on his shoulder, "we should talk about the speed limit sometime." Duane had followed Allen from Bellevue in his green Honda Prelude. He didn't plan to stay the whole day, and Allen refused to leave the hangar until they turned out the lights. "Maybe you should have let me drive."

Allen smiled. "Sorry." Turning his attention back to the people in the hangar, he shrugged. "I just didn't want to miss anything this morning."

The room seemed hauntingly empty. Since Allen had left the hangar the previous evening, even more search-and-rescue aircrew had gone home. Though he knew that these men and women had families who needed them, and other jobs—real jobs—to maintain, Allen hated to see them go. He understood that every passing hour reduced their chances of finding anyone alive. Allen wanted to find Beth alive.

They would be back, the mission coordinator had explained, as soon as the weather cleared. But the weather had not changed. And they were definitely not back.

Allen spotted Harry Armstrong standing behind a small group of men at the communications table. Walking toward them, he noticed their intense, focused expressions as they pointed to areas of a map spread out on the table in front of them.

Harry looked up and smiled. Stepping around the group, he moved toward Allen, extending his hand. "Allen, you certainly made good time," he said. Allen exchanged a guilty glance with Duane. "Would you like some coffee?"

Allen nodded, and the three men moved to the snack table. "Where is your father-in-law this morning?"

"He's coming in a little later."

Harry smiled again. "I understand."

"You said you thought something might be happening this morning?" Allen asked, cutting through the polite talk.

"I think we have a development," Harry said, handing Allen a Styrofoam cup. "Because of the weather and the length of time we've been kept off of the mountain, the Air Force is willing to lend us a helicopter. This morning, I decided to try to drop a search team. I can get them close, and they can hike down to the meadow you spotted on your flight with Jack."

"Wonderful," Duane said, slapping Allen on the shoulder. "That's wonderful news."

Allen could not hold back the smile he felt spread across his face. It was such a relief to smile. "Oh, thank God," he breathed, closing his eyes. "When can they go?"

"If the weather cooperates," Harry said, pouring himself a cup of coffee, "we have a group of searchers getting ready to go in this afternoon—I'm targeting a takeoff from here at about one fifteen."

The relief Allen felt made him almost dizzy. At last something was happening.

———

"I can't do that," Dennis Doyle said, shaking his head. This woman had nerve. Why should she expect him to drop everything and escort her down the mountain? He felt no obligation to her.

"Why not? Why can't you take me down? We can't be far from Clearwater."

"You don't know what you're askin'. The terrain is too difficult. This mountain isn't like a park. You won't find trails or handrails—no carved steps on the way down."

"Look, I'm a woman, not a wimp. I can make it."

"I said no. I won't take you."

She dropped herself on the mountain; she could get herself off of it. He eased the homemade drain into the skin flap along the wound and began wrapping her thigh in clean cotton strips. When he finished, he stood up, washing his hands in the pot beside her ankle.

"I think you should get some rest," he said. "I don't think you slept too good last night."

He saw a scowl cross her features. "I don't feel very good," she agreed. "But can't we let someone know that we're here? If you can't take me down, maybe someone can come in to get me."

"I don't have a phone. No way to contact anyone." He lifted the cast-iron pot by the handle. "You should feel sick," he continued. "You have a fever. You should've had stitches and surgery about three days ago." He set the cauldron on the table and lifted the water pitcher. Pouring a full cup, he held it out to her. "You should be pushing fluids. Your body can't fight an infection without water."

She took the cup, careful not to touch his hands as she did. She drank the water and wiped her lips with her sleeve. He tossed a slice of beef jerky into her lap.

"Try to eat something. And I'd leave the pants off if I were you," he said. "We can keep a better eye on the infection that way." He picked up the pot and walked toward the cabin door. "I'm gonna do some work outside. You should try to nap while I'm gone." He pulled a heavy green jacket from the hook by the door and lifted the latch with the same hand. "Stay outa my stuff," he said pointedly. "I can't scare you too bad from outside."

Beth stood up, pausing to let her dizziness pass before carrying the extra pants over to the bed. Her thigh felt so swollen that bending her knee hurt. No matter how much she disliked this man, he was right. She could feel fever burning in her joints, aching in the small of her back. She felt weak—weaker than she had been since the crash itself. She wanted to sleep, even more than she wanted to go home.

But first, no matter what he'd told her, she would put on the pants. She didn't need the old man looking at her leg anyway. She sat down on the side of the bed and used her good arm to slide the pants over her ankles and up to her knees. Then, lifting her injured leg onto the mattress and lying down, she pulled them over her hips. *So tired,* she thought as she lowered her head to the smelly pillow. *Too tired,* she thought as she pulled up the blanket and let sleep overtake her.

Outside, Doyle buttoned his coat as he paced behind the woodpile. He tucked his hands deep into his pockets as he considered the woman inside. He hadn't meant to hurt her. Didn't mean to frighten her. It's just that he never said anything right. Every time he tried to explain himself things came out wrong. He didn't mean to keep her captive. He just knew that in her condition, with the weather so bad, she could never make it down the mountain alive.

He took a canteen to the sluice and filled it.

She didn't understand. She never would. After all, to her he was just a crazy mountain man, a hermit, unwilling to help her get home safely. *So what,* Doyle thought. *What does it matter what she thinks, anyway?* He'd been misunderstood before. In fact, it felt comfortable to be in the same old place again. Labeled. Misunderstood. Why should he care about this woman knowing the truth about him?

Doyle needed a break. He whistled for the dog and waited several long moments before he remembered that his own dog would not leave the woman's side. *Betrayed again,* Doyle thought bitterly as he lifted the cover to the storage area. *I just need some time away, to be alone for a while. People always make me feel this way. I just can't be around people.*

Doyle decided to go down to the storage area and spend some time looking through the things he'd recovered from the crash. He needed to sort through them and put them away so they would be protected from cold and moisture.

He went down the wooden steps and lit a lantern. Picking up the packet of items he had taken from the blue crate, he laid them out on the floor. He had clearly found her purse—if that was what it should be called. This one looked like an envelope made of brown leather hanging from a very long narrow strap. He remembered the pictures inside—of pigtailed girls and a grinning baby.

"A mongrel," he muttered, shaking his head. "An Asian mongrel." As he set it aside, Doyle remembered her words. *"I miss my girls,"* she'd said. *"You wouldn't understand."*

What did she know? He thought about how many years it had been since he had last seen his own family. What about his parents? Had they changed? Grown old? Would they even recognize him now?

Had Sandra remarried after he left? And the boy? What had happened to the boy? Doyle pictured his son stumbling across worn carpet, pushing a popping toy ahead of him. At nearly thirty years old, where was Michael now? What had Sandra told him about his father? What did the boy believe about the man who had abandoned him for a life alone in the mountains?

Doyle shook himself from his thoughts. It did no good to think of these things. He didn't care anyway. He tucked the purse inside his jacket and picked up her worn leather Bible. Perhaps if he brought these to her, she wouldn't be so afraid of him. She would see that he was not really dangerous. She might finally realize that he had no ill intentions toward her.

Yes. He would take her things inside. Doyle stepped up out of the storage area and glanced at the sky. The whiteness above him seemed brighter somehow, though snow continued to fall, and Doyle found himself squinting.

Perhaps the weather had begun to ease off. A search crew would come for her soon. What would he do when they came, he wondered. Doyle stopped for a moment, not far from the cabin porch, to take a drink from his canteen. He had just replaced the lid when a sound caught his attention, and he froze.

From some distance away, Doyle recognized the unmistakable *whumpa-whumpa* of helicopter rotors.

Instantly, explosions around him forced him onto his hands and knees, crawling for cover. He reached the trees and dropped into a trench. Doyle smelled powder and mildew and felt the unbearable heat and humidity of the jungle. The chopper was close, and soon the enemy would have the bird in their sights. From under the cover of trees, he saw her, limping toward the chopper, waving both hands, trying to get their attention.

He ran after her, skidding and slipping through the snow as he made his way uphill. He kept his head down, trying to avoid being picked off by snipers. The sound of bees whizzed by his head. Ammunition! His heart beat fast, and perspiration ran down the sides of his face and the center of his back.

He had almost reached the crest of the hill when he heard her words over the sound of rotor blades, "Wait, I'm here. Here! Come down!"

"No!" Doyle screamed as he tackled her at the waist, sending them both flying. She fought like a wild animal, rolling and biting, screaming at the chopper while the fight continued. "It'll go down," Doyle shouted. "The enemy has it. It's going down."

Without seeing them, the chopper crested the hill and disappeared. As suddenly as it began, their struggle ended. Doyle looked down into the terrorized eyes of a woman. Packed snow clung to her hair, and her cheeks flamed red in the cold.

And she was crying.

Thirty-Three

"HOW SOON WILL WE HEAR from the chopper?" Allen asked.

Before answering, Harry stroked his white beard thoughtfully. "I think the chopper should be at the landing zone within the next ten minutes. We'll hear from the pilot after he drops off the ground crew." He and Allen leaned over the topographical map spread out on the communications table.

"Show me where exactly you'll be putting them down."

Harry turned the map to get a better view. "As nearly as we can tell," he said, running his pencil lightly along the paper, "somewhere in this long finger of space right here is the meadow where you heard the ELT." He pointed with the eraser. "But I'm dropping them in here." He tapped the map again and then brought his hand back to his mustache.

"How far is that from the meadow?"

"As the crow flies, it's only about a mile." Harry looked up at Allen. "But it's rough terrain. This is a steep tree-covered hill"—he brushed the map—"almost a cliff, really. It lies between the landing zone here," he pointed, "and the meadow. I want the crew to work their way down this hill, listening for the signal, searching for the plane."

"You think the plane flew into the hill?"

"It's possible." He nodded. "Actually, it happens all the time. These meadows get smaller and narrower at the uphill end, and then suddenly they disappear into the rocks. Sometimes, the narrow end is hidden in fog, or because the air is thin, pilots don't get as much lift as they expect in time to pull out." He shook his head. "But the reason I want them here is that the crew will be uphill from anything in the meadow. If the unit is still sending a signal, they might be able to hear it from there."

Allen felt tears well up in his eyes. He didn't want to picture Beth flying into a mountain, but he couldn't stop his imagination. In the theatre of his mind, a tiny plane flew in slow motion into a vertical wall, collapsing like an accordion as it did. As chunks of the flaming airplane fell through the air, Allen closed his eyes and shook his head, forcing the image away.

"Anyway," Harry tried to sound more upbeat, "by having the crew search that hill all the way down to the meadow, we'll know for certain that the plane isn't there. They should make it down just in time to set up camp."

"They'll spend the night?"

"Absolutely." Harry dropped his chin onto one hand. "They have all the supplies they need. They'll be warm and dry, and until dark we can keep in touch with High Bird."

Spend the night. Another night without knowing. Another night without Beth. Harry said it flippantly. To him, this was just another search and rescue. He could never understand how this waiting felt. Waiting without knowing. Hoping without reason. Allen felt the energy escape from him, as quickly as air from a punctured balloon. He looked down at the map, trying to focus on it— in a vain effort to hide his tears.

————

Doyle carried the woman back down to the cabin. Her tears had grown to hysteria, a wild sorrow beyond his ability to cope. She shivered violently as she cried. *Probably from having her face stuffed in a snowdrift,* he thought. By the time he reached the porch, his shoulder ached with a fierce intensity.

It had happened again. Without knowing, without even a hint of it coming to warn him, he had fallen back into his past. Like a parachuter dropping from the belly of a plane, Doyle had dropped back into his living nightmare.

He placed her on the bed, and she rolled away from him, still sobbing, curling herself into a ball with her splinted arm stuck awkwardly out in front of her. He'd seen children do that. He rubbed his shoulder, took a deep breath, and dragged the bed over to the stove, leaving just enough room to open the stove door. She needed to warm up, and quickly.

As soon as the bed stopped moving, Gilligan jumped up onto the mattress and snuggled down beside the woman. He whined, crept closer, and dropped his muzzle onto his paws.

Doyle covered her with a blanket, tucking it in around both the woman and the dog. Then he filled the woodbox and opened the air vent, letting the fire inside the stove build to a raging inferno.

He took the towel from the table where she'd left it and began to dry her hair, pulling chunks of snow from it with his fingers. Without acknowledging him, she cried, a haunting, hopeless moan—unlike anything he had heard before.

But her crying did not make Doyle feel sorry for her. Instead, as he watched and listened, something grew between them. And he felt a peculiar sense of envy. She had the ability to express sorrow in a way that he could not. If only he could cry like that. If only he could let go of all the ways that he had been hurt.

He pulled a chair very close to the bed and watched, aware of a bizarre wonder growing inside him. He did not try to stop her or comfort her. In a flash of understanding that came from somewhere outside himself, he knew that she cried for much more than the loss of a helicopter. Hers was a greater loss. A profound loss. And in this loss, no one could comfort her. Doyle sat watching, waiting quietly for her sorrow to pass.

She moved from hysteria to wailing, and from wailing to sobs. These trickled down to sniffs and tears. When at last the crying stopped, she lay very still. From her deep and even breathing, Doyle knew she had fallen asleep. *She might be hungry when she wakes up*, he thought. He moved to the stove and began to make hot cereal.

As he filled the water pot and placed it on the stove, Doyle considered his situation. So far he had made many mistakes. Having a woman in his cabin put him at a particular disadvantage. Of course, now that she had been here, she would tell the authorities about his presence. That signaled the end of his life in this particular cabin. Though the cabin wasn't much by any normal standards, it had been his home for twenty-some years. He had managed to survive here—as much as he had managed to survive anywhere. And now, when she got back to civilization, she would tell, and he would have to leave.

But he had made other mistakes as well. He should never have allowed himself to fall asleep while she was there. The nightmares had always been a problem. Doyle knew how dangerous he could become if something woke him from a sound sleep. He should have stayed awake. Should have done something—anything—to keep that from happening.

The thing with the chopper—that bothered him too. From years of experience, he knew he could never predict the episodes. If only she had stayed in the cabin. She must have heard the chopper and come out to try to make herself visible. He should have gone away and left her at the cabin to fend for herself. She would have stayed warm and dry, and when the weather cleared, she would have managed to get down the mountain on her own. At least she wouldn't have seen him go crazy like that.

She would be safer alone.

Doyle sat down beside the bed. He didn't want to hurt this woman. But like always, like everything he'd ever done in his life, this, too, had gone wrong. Every part of it had gone completely wrong. He felt the old familiar shame wash over him. How had he turned into this madman? What had happened to the boy he had once been?

Doyle determined to keep watch, to stay awake and let her sleep peacefully. As long as he stayed awake, he would not hurt her again.

———

When Beth woke, her head ached—a thundering, throbbing ache that made her wince when she opened her eyes. She felt hot. Sweat stuck Doyle's shirt to her back and arms, and the fabric itched. She wished she could take off all her clothes.

Instead, she threw off the blanket. The pounding in her head hurt more than any headache she had ever felt. She licked her swollen, dry lips and felt a profound thirst overtake her. She tried again to open her eyes, but even the dim light in the cabin hurt. She covered her eyes with her good hand.

She felt him there, very near. Without opening her eyes, she knew that he watched her.

"How you doing?" His voice sounded harsh, still angry.

"My head aches."

"Water?"

"Please," she said, trying to sit up.

"Don't." He leaned over the bed and slipped his hand under the back of her head. He supported her as she drank.

She lay down. "Thanks."

"Your fever's up."

She did not answer. What could she say? What could anyone say to this man, this crazy old man, who tried to kill her one minute and offered her water the next? She nodded and reached up to brush away the sweaty hair stuck to her forehead.

"I . . ." he stopped and cleared his throat. The single word hung in the air a long time. "I'm sorry about that."

Though she did not want to think about it, tears burned behind her eyelids. She blinked, and they rolled down the sides of her face onto her pillow. "Why?" she whispered. "Why did you do that?"

"I can't explain it."

"Try. You owe me that much."

"Sometimes it happens. I just go back in time."

In spite of her aching head, she opened her eyes and looked at him. "Go back?"

He glanced away. "Yeah. I told you it doesn't make any sense. I hear something—anything—and I just go back in time. I can't stop it. I don't even know when it's about to happen. I just find myself somewhere else."

She nodded and closed her eyes. He *was* crazy; that proved it. Part of her wanted to scream at him, to tell him how much getting the attention of the helicopter meant to her. She might be home resting in her own bed right now. The thought brought new tears, and she shook it away. Tears would not get her home. "So where did you *go* today?"

"Look, you wouldn't understand—even if I tried to explain." He stood.

She knew he was standing, even with her eyes closed, because she heard the chair scrape back, heard him take a few limping steps away from her.

"I made some food," he said. "You should eat." She heard him limp back to the chair, pull it out, and sit down.

She opened her eyes again and shook her head. "I'm not hungry." He sat close by.

"Doesn't matter. If you don't eat, your body will burn your muscles for food. If you don't eat, you'll never get off this mountain."

Everything about this man confused her. First he tried to kill her. Then he apologized. He left her food and cleaned her wounds and then tried to tackle her when she signaled the rescue helicopter. Beth watched as he placed the bowl of hot cereal on the bed beside her. He stood and walked around the bed, taking off his coat as he did. She heard a thump and looked to find her purse on the floor beside his boots.

"Oh, I forgot. I found a couple things for you," he said. He bent over to pick up the purse, handing it to her. "I went back to the plane. Found these." He reached inside his jacket and found the Bible hidden deep in a chest pocket. "This is yours too," he said, dropping it onto the bed beside her.

She accepted the purse, resisting the urge to check inside, and dropped it beside her hip. Had he taken anything? "Thank you," she said.

He rolled his jacket into a ball and stuffed it under her pillow, helping her to sit up a little more. "Try to eat."

She took a small spoonful of cereal. It tasted warm and sweet, and Beth found she did not miss the milk and sugar she would have put on it in her own kitchen. "It's good," she said. "Better than I make at home."

He nodded, taking his seat again. It seemed to Beth that he had decided to stare at her for the rest of their time together. "I looked inside," he said, nodding toward her purse. "I saw your family."

At these words she smiled. "You are an amazing person," she said with the slightest shake of her head. "I don't understand anything about you."

Hurt flitted across his gaze, and he glanced away.

"Really, I mean, you've been so good to me. You set my arm and clean my leg. And then you turn around and try to choke me to death. This morning you left me breakfast, and this afternoon you tackled me to keep me from going home." She held the bowl out to him. "I'd think you'd want me out of here."

He accepted the bowl and turned to slide it onto the table. "I told you I didn't invite you. But now that you're here, I don't have many choices." He folded his hands in his lap. "You should sleep."

"I can't sleep. My head hurts."

"Okay. Whatever suits you. We should check your dressings."

"Tell me why you live up here. I want to know. You're a capable guy. You know your way around the mountain. Why do you stay up here alone?"

Bending over her leg, he glanced at her, and she read a look of warning in his expression. "I like it here." He placed his palm on her thigh. "It's hot. Can you take 'em off?" He gestured to the pants. "I need to see."

She blushed, embarrassed, and reached down under the blanket to expose one thigh. Slowly, carefully, he began peeling away the fabric covering her wound.

"How long have you lived up here?"

"A long time." He lifted her knee gently and eased the bandage out from under her. Unwrapping slowly, he came to the fabric drain.

"Where did you grow up? What did you do before you lived up here?"

"What is this?" he asked angrily. "An interrogation? I'm only supposed to give my name, rank, and serial number."

She sat quietly for a moment as he worked. "You've been in the military then," she said. "That explains a lot. The military clothes, the boots, the food containers in your cupboard." She paused. "And the medals," she said, understanding dawning like a winter sunrise. "Of course, the medals. Your name is Doyle." She'd hit the mark; his expression told her so. "I'm right, aren't I?"

"You wouldn't know that if you hadn't gone through my stuff," he said. "So my name is Doyle, Dennis Doyle, and I've been in the military. What's it to you?"

"Both my grandparents were in the military too," she answered. "My father's father flew during the Korean War. And my grandfather on my mother's side fought in World War II." She paused, remembering her Hawaiian grandfather's pride in his European war service. "You must have been in Vietnam." The surprise on his face could not be mistaken. She had hit the mark again.

"What makes you think that?"

"You called me a dink," she answered. "I'm half Japanese. My mother was born in Hawaii to American citizens." She scooted up the bed and let her head rest on the pillow behind her, closing her eyes. "I grew up in Seattle. We didn't have a lot of prejudice, but I knew all the put-downs. You thought I was Vietnamese," she said. "Only a vet would use that word."

Without answering, he continued to unwrap the bandage on her thigh. When he got to the bottom layer, he pulled the fabric drain he had placed there just that morning. She felt the tug and opened her eyes to watch. Beth held her breath as the fabric tore away from her partially clotted wound. It hurt, but not as much as it should. This had to be a bad sign.

The drain came out tinged with blood and covered with wide areas of pale green fluid. She closed her eyes and leaned back against the pillow, listening to her heart pound in rhythm with the pain inside her skull. The infection had not even slowed down. No wonder she felt so crummy.

If they didn't get control over the infection soon, she wouldn't have to worry about getting off the mountain.

Thirty-Four

DOYLE WATCHED HER SHOULDERS SLUMP as he pulled out the homemade drain. She blew air through pursed lips, blinking back tears. "It's not so bad," he said. "I saw lots worse in the Nam." He turned to the table, where a fresh drain and more of his homemade salve waited.

"It's bad," she said, draping her head back over the pillow and closing her eyes. "I'm no nurse, but I know an infection when I see one."

Doyle didn't know what to say. She was right. The wound had developed a serious infection. But the condition of her skin didn't bother him as much as the expression on her face. She had given up.

Deftly, he finished dressing the wound, rewrapping her leg in a clean bandage. He dropped the old fabric into the kettle and put it on the stove to boil. Adding soap to the pot, he covered it. By the time he turned back, she had fallen asleep.

Though he could not explain why, it bothered him to see the fight go out of her. She who had been so full of spunk, so eager to find her way home, seemed to have given up hope. He could tell that she didn't believe she would make it.

Trying to ignore the knot growing in his stomach, he sat down in the chair beside the bed and picked up his carving tools. With strong hands and a sharp knife, he outlined the shape of a mountain in the wood. As he carved a view of Reflection Lake, he wondered why he'd grown to care about her. How had this stranger wormed her way into his heart?

Dropping the carving into his lap, Doyle stopped to think. A panorama of young faces paraded in front of his eyes. Boys. All of them no more than boys. How many had he seen die? How many, in their last hours, had given up the fight? Hardly older than the boys who served under him, Doyle hated watching them die. Hated being responsible for something he could not control. Hated the meaningless deaths he'd been forced to participate in.

No. He would not do it again.

Making his decision, Doyle slammed the wooden block on the table. He would not let the woman die. No matter how much trouble she was, he would make certain that she lived to get down the mountain. Maybe, if he was clever enough, he could help her down without being discovered himself. After all, she didn't really know where she was. She would never find her way to bring anyone back to the cabin. Maybe, even if she got home, he would be safe.

But he would worry about that later. For now, he would see to it that the woman lived.

———

At quarter to five in the afternoon, Allen sat alone in the search-and-rescue center. He'd given up on coffee and now nursed a bottle of purified water. The room had grown surprisingly quiet, partly because of the weather, partly because of the hour, and partly because of dinner. Most of the crew had gone to eat.

The mission coordinator sat in his seat, still poring over the search map, comparing it to the call-in reports he'd gotten from people in the area. Thanks to the news media, he'd received plenty of reports about small planes over the mountain. He'd shown the messages to Allen, all twenty-six of them. With careful evaluation they hoped to find a pattern matching the sightings and the path of Beth's plane.

Next to him, a full-faced, close-shaven communications officer sat reading a novel by Stephen King. The big black telephone had rung all through the afternoon, and each time, Allen had jumped and then waited impatiently for the man to pass along the message. But for the last ninety minutes, the phone had not rung. Allen found the silence even more frustrating than the slow-moving communications officer.

Allen took another drink, swishing water around his mouth and teeth before swallowing. He hadn't eaten since breakfast. Maybe he should go get a bite to eat himself. He tried to picture the restaurants along the road by the airport and could not remember a single place. Just then the telephone rang again, and as if on cue, Allen jumped.

Instantly, he checked the time on the clock above the restroom door. Answer it, he urged. The communications officer picked up a pen and answered the phone. Allen watched as he scribbled on a Post-it Note. Without any change of expression, he reached over and dropped the pad onto the topographical map.

Harry Armstrong picked it up, frowned slightly, and pushed back his chair. Allen hurried over to the table to meet him. "What did they say?"

"Nothing, really," Harry answered. "They combed the hill above the meadow. The plane isn't there." This news seemed to perplex Harry. His eyebrows maintained their position, screwed together in the center of his forehead. "The ground crew is making camp in the east end of the meadow. In the morning, they'll continue the search."

"You thought they'd find the plane on the hill."

He nodded. "I did. It would have explained why the signal was weak and why it seems to have completely disappeared."

"But the plane isn't there. Isn't that a good thing?"

"Allen, the plane is three days overdue. At this point, nothing about the accident is good."

———

Doyle moved the blanket aside to check her wound for drainage. Though he tried to be gentle, the motion woke her, and her flushed face held a listless expression. It frightened Doyle. "Tell me 'bout your family," he said. "I saw you have kids. And a baby. You must miss the baby."

Closing her eyes, she nodded. "Two girls. Bekka is eight, and Abbey is six." She seemed to drift away for a moment before answering. "And an eleven-month-old baby. Noah."

Keep her talking, Doyle thought as he offered her water. "What about your husband?" He saw the edges of her mouth lift in a smile. Even in the tiny expression he recognized it. *She loves him*, he thought, feeling a flash of envy. *What would it feel like to be loved by your wife?*

"He's a pastor. He serves a small church in Bellevue."

"I grew up in a church," Doyle said and instantly regretted the slip. He had not meant to talk about himself. He didn't want her to know about his life or his past.

"No kidding?" Her eyes fluttered open, but her hand flew up to cover her face from the light. The light bothered her for some reason. Doyle turned to the table and dimmed the lantern.

"I don't look like a church kid, do I?"

"Not in the least."

This woman had no fear of speaking the truth. When she said nothing more, Doyle wished he were better at conversation. With most women, once they got started, you couldn't shut them up. But he couldn't find the key for this one. "How's your headache?"

"About the same."

"I could give you somethin' for pain."

"No." The eyes came open. He saw fear. "Nothing more."

"Your driver's license says your name is Elizabeth."

"Beth."

"Okay. Beth. What were you doin' flying up here around my mountain?"

Her hand moved and her eyes flashed. "It isn't your mountain," she said with great emphasis. He saw her take a deep breath. "I work for an environmental consulting firm. We're doing work for the Elk Ridge ski area."

"What d'ya do?"

She made a face. "I count goats."

"Goats?" He reached down to lift her knee, slipping a new bandage under her thigh.

"Ouch," she said, pulling away. "Where did you learn to do this, anyway?"

"You're the expert. You tell me."

"Look, let's put away our bayonets." She sighed. "I don't feel like fighting."

"Okay," he agreed. "I learned emergency care in the service."

"The service?" She turned her face to him, asking an unspoken question.

"You don't wanna know," he said. He heard the bitterness in his own voice.

"You're right. I don't. I only want to go home."

"What is it at home that you want so bad?"

She opened her eyes and stared at him, looking so surprised that she seemed to have forgotten her own headache. Looking at her brown eyes swimming in tears, he wished he hadn't asked.

"It's family. You couldn't possibly understand."

"You mean 'cause I live up here. Like a hermit. Smelly and sick," he said. "Crazy. That's what you're thinking. You think I'm crazy to live up here alone." This straight-talking woman could irritate a saint. One minute he wanted to save her life, and the next he'd like to end it.

She sighed, clearly frustrated. "I'm sorry. I shouldn't have said that. Actually, at first I did think you were crazy. But the whole thing is starting to make sense to me now."

Her words surprised him so much that his hands stopped moving, still in midair. "What makes sense?"

"The flashbacks. The paranoia. You aren't crazy," she said. "In fact, you're pretty normal from what I've heard."

"What're you talking about?" In all the years since he'd returned to the States, no one had ever told him that he was normal. He'd heard almost every other explanation—but no one had ever chosen the word *normal.*

She opened her eyes and stared at him again. "Are you kidding?"

Deliberately, he pulled the blanket over her legs and turned to face her, speaking slowly and with great seriousness. "I have no idea what you're talking about."

She seemed confused for a moment, but then took a deep breath and plunged forward. "I don't know anything about the war," she said. "When I was in school, we studied American history up through World War II. By the time we started the Vietnam conflict, it was the last week of school. I think we covered the whole thing in about an hour."

He nodded. "I was there. It was no conflict." That students of American history knew nothing of the war did not surprise Doyle in the least. He'd been abandoned by his country from the first hour his chopper landed in the Nam. When he came home, he'd been abandoned by the service. Abandoned by medical personnel. Abandoned by his family. Doyle knew better than to think that anyone would care to remember his sacrifice for the country.

She took a breath and opened her eyes. "In college, one of my psychology classes covered posttraumatic stress in lots of detail. Everything anyone knows about PTSD began with research on Vietnam veterans."

He struggled to follow her words. What did she mean? He thought back to the few times he'd tried to get help. One military doctor had diagnosed Doyle as psychotic. Another had loaded him up with sleeping pills. "P . . . T. . . ?" He could not remember the initials.

"P-T-S-D." She spelled it slowly. "You've never heard of it?"

He shook his head. Part of Doyle wanted to hear what she had to say. But another part refused to believe her words. What if she was like everyone else—a liar? A user. Why should he believe anything this woman had to say? Who was she, anyway? Someone who dropped into his lap from out of nowhere?

"Wow. I guess I don't know quite where to start." She glanced away for a moment, rubbing her forehead with the fingers of her left hand. She paused for so long that Doyle wondered if she had fallen asleep. Then drawing a deep breath, she said, "It stands for posttraumatic stress disorder. And what we know is that anyone who has experienced any kind of trauma—from wartime trauma to sexual abuse, child abuse, rape, or a beating—just about any pain humans experience can leave an emotional scar." She gestured slightly with her good hand. "And the scar leaves symptoms. Like flashbacks, unreasonable reactions to people and situations, hypervigilance, even dangerous explosions of rage—it's all completely normal in people who have been through severe trauma. It even explains being attacked in the middle of the night"—she gave him a pointed glance—"when all you want is a glass of water."

In the silence that followed, Doyle wondered if she could be telling the truth. He thought back to his own experiences in the vet hospital. He remembered the shining face of the psychiatrist he'd been assigned to after returning to the States. So young he barely needed to shave, Doyle's doctor had never served in the military, never even seen combat. While Doyle had been slogging through the mountains of Vietnam, the doc had been sitting in a class somewhere. At the end of their first appointment, the doctor asked Doyle about his relationship with his mother.

"This didn't start with my mother," Doyle shouted. "It started in Vietnam." The doc stared back unblinking. Finally, after a long silence, the doctor offered Doyle a prescription for sedatives. Desperate for dreamless, restful sleep, Doyle tried the drugs. They didn't help. Instead of better sleep, Doyle slipped into a full-time stupor. After two weeks he threw the pills away.

Though his wife begged him to get help, Doyle never went back to a VA hospital. The United States government had lied to him, taken advantage of him, and abused him for the last time. He would give them no further opportunity. He'd only applied for his veterans' benefits ten years ago—and that at the insistence of his contact in the valley.

"So what happened to you in Vietnam?" the woman asked.

He heard kindness in her voice—not scorn. For the briefest moment, he wished he could answer the question. But he knew better. "You need some rest," he answered, wishing he didn't sound so gruff. "Get some sleep."

He sat back in the chair and folded his hands, staring into space. With no further opportunity for conversation, she nestled down into the pillow, putting her left hand under her cheek. As he watched, her body relaxed, and her breathing became deep and even. She even snored—a soft little purr.

He sat staring at her sleeping face. Could she be telling the truth? Could everything that had happened to him be explained by some crazy initials? Doyle stood and paced along the walls of the cabin. Perplexed, yet intrigued, he wanted to know more. Did she have the key? Could she explain what he'd been through? Did he dare trust her? No. He wouldn't—not after all these years.

Thrusting his questions aside, he picked up his carving tools. He would work while she slept. She would never catch him sleeping again. Even if he didn't sleep for the rest of the winter, he would never allow her to wake him from sleep again.

———————

Beth felt a gentle tugging at her shoulder, but she resisted. "Beth"—the tugging continued—"you need to drink somethin'."

She turned away, trying to return to the comfort of sleep. Even before fully waking, she felt her joints aching and sensed the head-ache. She did not want to open her eyes. The tugging became more urgent. "Beth," the voice said. Hands under her armpits lifted her into a semi-sitting position. "You slept through the night. That's good. But you need fluids. Here, I have some broth."

She opened her eyes and saw the faint light of a new dawn min-gling with the illumination of the kerosene lamp. She had lived through another night without Allen. "Okay," her scratchy voice managed to croak.

Her mouth had a horrible taste, and she felt her tongue plas-tered to the roof of her mouth. She tried to help by sitting up, but weakness pinned her to the mattress. She gave up and turned to look at him. He sat on the only chair in the cabin, very near the bed, leaning toward her. In one big hand, palm up, he held the white enamel bowl. In the other, he had a battered spoon filled with a golden liquid. He brought it to her face, urging her gently, "Here, take this."

She sipped. Warm, but not hot, the broth had the rich flavor of meat. But she could not identify the flavor; it wasn't chicken or beef. He had salted it heavily, and the salt tasted good to her. Beth murmured approval. "Thank you," she said, leaning back on the mound behind her, too tired to continue.

"Oh no, you don't. More'n that."

The thought of lifting her head seemed overwhelming, and she closed her eyes. "No," she said, turning her face away. She heard the chair scrape along the wooden floor as he moved closer. An overwhelming heaviness pervaded every part of her body and pinned her down; she was unable to resist. She turned her head to watch him beside her.

"Take more, Beth."

"I can't. I want to sleep." She closed her eyes and snuggled into the pillow

"Okay," his voice brought her out of her haze. "I'll make you a deal, Miss Curiosity." He held a spoon so close that it touched her mouth. Broth dribbled down her chin. "If you'll eat, I'll talk." He forced the spoon between her lips, and she had no choice but to open. Such a supreme effort just to swallow.

Even in the stupor of illness, Beth realized that he had offered her his most valuable bargaining chip. "I give up," she answered.

And with that, Dennis Doyle began to tell her about the boy he had once been. "I grew up in a family of three girls—three sisters and me," he began. "My father was an army lifer. He did World War II and then Korea." Doyle offered another spoonful. "He was a big guy, an athlete, a field man, with big expectations. But he loved us. He did his best to be a good dad. He taught me to work hard and to believe that hard work would take me anywhere I wanted to go."

"Your mom?" Beth spoke without opening her eyes. She couldn't help herself; her curiosity got the better of her.

"Mom was a really gentle woman. She loved her kids, took us to church. Went to all our school programs," he said, offering another spoonful of broth. "I grew up on the edge of a small town, in a *Leave It to Beaver* house, with two parents who loved me." He looked at Beth and laughed suddenly, a derisive laugh.

"What?" Beth asked, wondering what caused him to laugh like that. She drew back and felt her eyebrows draw together.

"You should see your face," he said. "You might as well say it out loud. You thought I had to be the only child of a prostitute and a serial killer. And now you're wonderin' how someone from a normal home could end up like this—a crazy man, livin' like a hermit in the woods. Don't deny it. You might as well have words printed across your forehead."

Beth glanced away, perplexed. She hadn't meant to imply such a thing. "I've never said you were crazy," she objected. "Nuts, maybe. But never crazy."

"Nuts?"

"Needing help does not make you crazy." She stopped to rest between the sentences. "To refuse help makes you nuts."

"I thought we were puttin' our bayonets away."

"Okay," she agreed. "Tell me how it happened. How did a nice kid like you, from a perfectly healthy family, end up living here—like this?"

"That's easy," he began bitterly. "It all started in a little country on the other side of the ocean. I am what I am because of Vietnam."

Thirty-Five

FOR THE FOURTH TIME, Allen and Richard made the early morning drive from Bellevue to Thun Field. Though spending the night in Puyallup would have saved time and energy, Allen could no more stay away from his children than he could abandon the search. He simply made the drive over and over, hoping that each trip would be the last—that this time, searchers would find Beth.

But the first three days after the crash had produced no answers.

At ten minutes after nine on the fourth day, Allen heard the jarring ringing of the communications telephone and watched as the officer lifted the handset. Without moving, Allen watched again as the officer handed the message pad to Harry. Then Harry signaled the public information officer with his index finger. Paula Douglas went to the mission table, and the two talked in low tones. Allen felt himself leaning forward, wishing he could catch their words.

Allen watched as she walked over to the group waiting in the right corner of the hangar. Bill Peterson's family fell silent as they caught sight of her coming toward them. With Paula's every step, Allen felt their rising fear.

Then Allen caught sight of Harry as he stood, sighed visibly, and walked in slow motion across the hangar. As he moved toward Allen and Richard, Harry managed to hide his expression in a void, emotionless mask. In spite of this, Allen knew what message the telephone had finally delivered. He read it in the deliberately empty features of the search coordinator. He anticipated the horrible news he so dreaded. And for a fraction of a second, Allen wondered how long it took Harry to learn how to deliver bad news this way.

"We've found the plane," Harry said, pulling a seat very close to Allen.

Beth's father leaned in close, his face white. "Where?"

"In the meadow, about a quarter of a mile from the place where the ground crew camped last night. They began working their way down the hill about an hour ago."

"What about Beth?" Richard asked, his voice flat.

Allen squeezed his eyes closed, as if by shutting them he could hold back the truth he knew Harry would deliver. In the background, loud cries rose from the family on the other side of the terminal. Allen felt his stomach twist, his heart pounding an urgent, frightened beat. He clutched his knees in an effort to stop his hands from trembling, trying to stay calm, trying to listen.

The search coordinator took a deep breath. "The pilot died— apparently on impact," he said. "We still have to notify his family. They found Mr. Peterson's body in the fuselage."

Allen glanced over at the grown Peterson children, seeing their anguish and knowing his would soon begin.

Richard's urgent voice interrupted, "But what about Beth?"

Harry glanced away, looking at the other family. When he turned back, he did not look sad, as Allen expected, but perplexed. "Her body isn't with the wreckage."

"Not there?"

"Not at the crash site," Harry said. "The pilot was still strapped into his seat. Mr. Peterson was apparently badly injured in the accident and moved from his seat. But right now, it looks like your wife survived the crash." Harry paused to take a deep breath. "The ground crew has finished a preliminary search. They've found a fire pit, and supplies scattered outside of the plane. Even with the continued snowfall, we've identified her tracks—pathways actually, trenches in the snow—into and out of the woods, away from the plane in all directions."

"But where is she now?" Richard's voice finally broke, and Allen, blinking back confused tears, put one hand on his father-in-law's shoulder.

"We don't know," Harry admitted. "That's why I wanted to talk to you. It's a confusing picture up there. We think she may be injured. The plane landed upside down, and there is blood all over the ceiling of the plane. Peterson's body had no obvious signs of injury. No bleeding." He sighed. "It looks to the ground crew like she left the crash site. We don't know why.

"With the weather the way it is, we need to move quickly. I think we may have another system coming in late this afternoon. I've made the call for a bloodhound. But I need a personal item from you in order to track your wife."

Allen felt relief bubble up inside of him, wanting to burst out, to be set free. He almost laughed. "Of course. No problem."

"Now, you need to know that—depending on how long ago she left the plane—we may not be able to track her."

"Why not?" What could be so hard? *Anyone could follow tracks in the snow,* Allen wanted to shout but restrained himself.

"I mean that your wife's scent won't last forever. If she's still alive and out in the woods somewhere, the dog might be able to pick up an air scent."

"An air scent?"

Allen must have looked puzzled, because Harry stopped to explain. "Humans leave a scent on the ground, but they also put a scent out into the air. If the person is still around, the dog can pick up the air scent and go after him. A dog won't wander around aimlessly like a lost person is likely to do. Instead, if he can pick up an air scent, the dog tracks straight to the victim." He fiddled with his beard. "But a ground scent won't last forever. We have to move quickly.

"I have a hound in Issaquah," he continued. "I trust this dog. He's proven. Good. I'd like to have you meet the dog and his handler at your home in Bellevue. The handler's name is Doug Zimmerman." Harry wrote the name and phone number on the back of his business card. "I'll call him and have him meet you at your house. Then, after he gets what he needs, he and the dog will head straight to the airport in Renton." Allen, eager to get going, had already started to put on his coat. Harry continued, "I'll have a chopper meet him there and take him directly to the crash site."

"Can I go up with them?" Allen asked as he fumbled through his keys, looking for the one to his ignition.

"No. I'm certain of that."

"I won't get in the way."

Harry sighed. "That isn't the problem. Your scent will confuse the dog. You live with your wife. Her things will have your scent on them too. The dog tracks best if family members aren't around."

"All right. We'll get whatever Zimmerman needs," Richard said. "We'll be back in a few hours." He snatched his coat from the back of the chair and began moving toward the door. Still walking, he called over his shoulder, "Thanks, Harry."

————

Beth's body hurt everywhere. It seemed to her that even her eyelids hurt—as if she had joints above her eyeballs. Her headache had eased, but it still pounded in rhythm with her heartbeat. Too hot to lie still, too weak to move, and too tired to talk, Beth wanted to have the mattress swallow her whole. She tried to accept Doyle's broth, but the effort of moving her lips to open her mouth seemed far too great a sacrifice.

"I never was a student," the old man continued. "I liked working with my hands. I put a new engine in my first car—all by myself. It ran too." He shook his head, lost in the memory. "That was a nice car." He dropped the spoon into the bowl with a clatter and leaned back in his chair. "I played sports some. Didn't like football much—wasn't very good at it. I had bulk, but no real coordination, no muscle power. Everybody would look at my size and assume I could tackle. But it just wasn't for me. I wasn't fast. Didn't like getting hit. I prob'ly only played five minutes during my whole senior year."

He leaned forward and offered another spoonful of broth. "When I got out of high school in '66, Vietnam was just some disaster on the news. I really didn't know anything about it. Hadn't even looked on a map."

His voice had taken on a certain droning quality to Beth. Though she tried to listen, she found it difficult to concentrate. Why had he decided to tell her this? Why now? After so much silence, why talk now?

"I signed up for community college cuz my mom thought I needed it. But I didn't have any idea what I wanted to do. Didn't know how to study. Heck, I don't even like to read." Here Doyle paused. "Still don't. Anyway, I nearly flunked out the first quarter, and I found myself on probation the second. I mean, what would anyone expect? By then, my dad had decided that I should go in the military."

Though she said nothing, Beth shuddered, thinking about sending Noah off to war.

"Dad thought I'd grow up there. It worked for him. He thought it'd be good for me." Doyle shook his head. "He hoped I'd come back a real man, with discipline and goals—maybe even a career. So I signed up in January and went to boot camp a month later."

"You went straight to Vietnam?"

"No, I took Special Forces training."

"Why would you do that with a war on?"

"I knew I'd end up in the Nam eventually. No matter what I did, I was gonna end up there. I figured if I got more training, I'd put it off—delay it. I guess I hoped the war would end before I got there. At least I knew I'd be better trained when I finally arrived." He grimaced as he shook his head. "Boy, was I dumb."

Through her fod, she wondered about Special Forces, about the movies she'd seen of the powerful, aggressive men who served there. "How'd you get in?"

"Boot camp," Doyle answered. "It toughened me up. I lost weight and worked hard. I wanted in, and if you want something bad enough, you get it." He picked up the bowl and offered her more broth. She accepted a single spoonful, then leaned her head back on the pillow to rest. Eating was hard work.

From this position, looking directly at him in the lamplight, Dennis Doyle didn't seem so threatening. In fact, as he talked, Doyle underwent an almost miraculous transformation in Beth's eyes. He became human. Even as she listened, he'd already changed. His words, once sparse and apathetic, came more easily and with deep passion. Some of this change, she realized was only in her perception of him. She'd thought of him as a recluse, uneducated and plain. When in fact, Dennis Doyle was articulate and thoughtful. She'd had him all wrong; she realized that now.

"When I was a kid," she said, "we talked about Vietnam as though it were a story, like the Knights of the Round Table. I guess I never thought about real people being there. I don't think my teacher did either. I mean, we used words like *conflict* and *skirmish*—

maybe to cover up the real truth." She shook her head. "We certainly didn't talk about it like a war."

"It was more than a skirmish."

"What was it really like?"

"I couldn't begin to tell you."

There it was again. The wall that he put up whenever she tried to talk with him. "Try," Beth urged, pulling the blanket up as she rolled onto her side. Even with this effort she could not find a comfortable position. She wanted to watch him as he spoke. Doyle's face told her as much as his words did.

He seemed to think about her invitation for a moment. Then he set the bowl down and leaned one elbow on the table. He tucked his chin on his hand and stared off into space. "I've never tried to tell anyone," he began. "I didn't think I could."

"Why not?"

"Cuz what we saw there, what we did—it was so far from life in America that no one would ever believe it."

Beth spoke more gently. "What was the hardest thing?"

He shook his head. "I don't know. The bodies, I guess. I left the West Coast on a Thursday afternoon and was dropped into the jungle by chopper two days later. I joined a unit that was moving south. They threw us in a transport truck." He paused, brushing at the corner of his eye with his thumb, followed by a whisk at his nose. "When I jumped out the back, I slipped—nearly fell down. I thought it was mud." He looked directly into her eyes. "When I looked down, I realized I'd stepped on a dead body. It was rotting in the jungle and the skin had begun to slide off." His voice gave way, and he coughed. "Welcome to Vietnam."

Beth saw the anguish in his features and felt a sudden wave of sorrow pass over her. The muscles in his face trembled as he spoke. Whatever he had gone through had hurt him deeply.

Taking a deep breath, he shook himself and continued. "New guys are considered dangerous to their units. I won't repeat what they call 'em. They don't know what they're doing. They're scared and stupid. They can get their whole unit killed. So the old guys work hard to get the new kids used to death."

"How can anyone get used to death?" Beth's horror came out in her voice.

He rubbed one thumbnail with his other thumb, lost in

thought. "But that was only the beginning. You know, you drop in on a chopper and all your options just go up in smoke. It's kill or be killed." He looked directly into Beth's eyes. "In the end, it wasn't a real war. There wasn't a front or an objective. We fought the way we were told to fight. The big guys wanted us to take ground. But the land didn't mean nothin' to the guys in the North. We'd fight for days just to take a hill. Just some little bump on the landscape. And lotsa guys died doing it. Then days later, after we won the hill, we'd go in and find out the Gomers just gave it to us. They'd abandoned it—and you could almost hear 'em laughing as they left it behind."

Beth expected Doyle to be bitter, though the depth of his bitterness surprised her. His words flowed freely, like pus from a draining wound.

"They disappeared into the jungle, laughing. And you lost your best friend trying to take the hill." He shook his head, flashes of anger in his quiet blue eyes. "And maybe someone else's blood was splattered all over your chest. And maybe the whole thing happened cuz your commanding officer made some stupid decision in order to climb his own career ladder."

It seemed to Beth as though Doyle wanted to let go of his story, wanted to unburden himself. His words tumbled out, one over the other, like water over rocks in a streambed. Through the cloud of fever and the unrelenting pain of her injuries, Beth found herself attentive to his story, wanting to understand the torment that had possessed Dennis Doyle.

"We had officers who only wanted to climb the ladder of success. They wanted rank. Didn't care if they put their own men in danger to get it. More than one of 'em died at the hands of their own troops. We had rules to fight by. Stupid rules. Rules made by politicians in D.C. Politicians who had no clue what the war was really about." Doyle stood up, limped a few steps, and turned to face her. She watched as he struggled for composure.

Calmer, he sat again. "The worst was what it did to the inside of a man. There was no safety in the Nam. No front. No battle zone. The enemy didn't wear a uniform. It could be a kid with a grenade strapped to his back or an old lady with explosives in the bottom of a bowl of rice." He shook his head. "They sent civilians in to a group of GIs and then watched body parts float through the air.

The North Vietnamese would kill anyone or anything. If an old man happened to be between you and the VC, they just shot through him." Doyle shook his head and ran his fingers through his hair as if he might wipe away the memories. "Sliced him clean in half.

"You learned to sleep with a rifle. To be ready to kill all the time. For thirteen months, I never really rested. Not once. And you got so tired that you just kept going like some mechanical thing. You just followed your platoon leader into the jungle and tried to stay alive until your DoERS. And you saw things. Horrible things."

Once again, he stood up and went to the counter of the sideboard. She watched as he pulled out a bottle of alcohol, saw his hands shake as he poured a full tin cup of it. From behind, she watched him lift the cup and tip his head back. She heard him swallow. When he'd emptied the cup, he started to pour again, changed his mind, and slammed the bottle onto the counter with a thud. Pushing the bottle away, he leaned over, his head resting on his arms. For a long moment he stood there, breathing deeply, fighting for control.

"You said DoERS," Beth said as gently as she could. "I don't know what that is."

"Date of estimated return stateside. Every man in the Nam had a date. If they lived to the date, they got to go home." Doyle turned again to face her, still leaning against the counter. "Thirteen months and you go home. But the person you were when you left home? No matter what happened, he never came back."

"I'm so sorry," she said. "I had no idea."

Beth saw anger flash in his eyes. "You still have no idea," he said. "You'll never have to know what it feels like to line up another human being in your sights for the first time."

He began walking again, as if the memory could be erased by motion. "I went thinking that the people wanted us to save them from aggressors. But they didn't want us there. They didn't want to be saved," he said. "And who were the aggressors, anyway? In my unit, we killed first and asked questions later." He shook his head. "And then politicians asked us to tell 'em how many we got rid of."

"How old were you when you went over? Eighteen?"

"I turned nineteen just before boot camp."

"So young." At nineteen, Beth had been about to start her second year of college. She hadn't owned a car or had a boyfriend. She'd never even been really sick. How could she have faced the kinds of things Dennis had survived?

"My father hoped that the service would turn me into a man," Doyle said, shaking his head. "I don't know if I became a man or not. But I changed. The real Dennis Doyle never came back. I left him in the Nam." He stopped talking and glanced up to the ceiling, blinking fiercely, pursing his lips together. He drew another deep breath and looked at Beth. "In some ways, the guys who died over there got the better deal. At least their war is finally over."

"I'm sorry, Dennis."

He didn't seem to hear her. "It'll never be over for me. I fight it every day. I'm still a soldier. I wish I weren't. I wish it would leave me alone. . . ." Suddenly, as though he heard his own words and wished he could take them back, Doyle changed the subject. "You're supposed to be eating." He took his seat and picked up the bowl again.

Beth accepted the spoonful of broth, grateful for the emotional break that eating gave them. As she ate, she found herself praying for the man who had taken her in, asking God to guide her in caring for this badly wounded sheep. It seemed so important, having the right words, the right answers for this man. She had no answers, no training. In fact, of all people she felt the least capable to bring comfort to Dennis Doyle. Why would God lead *her* here? Why not someone who had better skills with emotional things?

Looking up at him she asked, "How long have you lived up here?"

"More'n twenty-five years."

"And you've never gone back?"

"Never," he said, his voice wooden. "I won't go back. I don't belong with people."

"But what about supplies? You have groceries. How do you get the things you need—food and"—she gestured at the lamp—"things like kerosene?"

"You never run out of questions, do you? I make boxes. A man in Clearwater buys 'em and brings me supplies."

"Another vet?" she guessed.

He nodded, offering her another spoonful of broth.

So many years all by himself. What would cause a man to leave everything behind in order to live alone? It didn't take a psychologist to realize that Doyle was far more wounded than Beth. Though she'd survived a plane crash, he'd survived a much more traumatic event. How could she help? What could she say?

As she prayed, a part of her marveled at this change in her feelings. Just hours ago, she had been terrified of him. Now, in the place of fear, Beth felt an almost overwhelming compassion.

Where once she'd wanted to help only herself, now she wished that she could find a way to help her captor.

Thirty-Six

WHEN ALLEN AND RICHARD TURNED onto the street in front of Maple Hills Baptist, they spotted a brilliant blue pickup truck parked at the curb in front of the house. Leaning against the tailgate, a tall blond man, wearing jeans and a mountain parka, waited for them. Allen pulled in behind the pickup and hurried to unhook his seat belt.

As Allen shook hands with the man, a dog barked excitedly from a large animal crate in the back of the truck. "Allen Cheng," Allen said. Turning to his father-in-law, "This is my wife's father, Richard Harding."

"Doug Zimmerman." The man smiled as he shook hands.

Richard said, "We called my wife and asked her to take the kids out of the house. We were told that your dog could work best if there was no one else inside."

"That's good. Thanks," Doug said, rubbing his hands together. "Well, shall we get started?"

Allen nodded, and Doug leaned over the bumper to drop the back panel of the truck. "This is Boomer," he said, opening the crate. "Boomer is a five-year-old bloodhound. We've been tracking for about three years now." He unlatched the kennel door, and a huge reddish brown hound lunged out of the crate, licking his master's face enthusiastically. Zimmerman took a leash from his pocket and snapped it onto the dog's collar. With a crisp hand signal the dog sat obediently, and Doug murmured approval as he patted the dog's head.

"Now," he said as the dog jumped from the truck, "I'd like to take Boomer into your wife's bedroom. He works best if he can smell everything there—her pillows, her sheets, her closet, her shoes. Then I need you to tell me where I can find something that she's worn. Something not yet washed, that hasn't been in contact with laundry from other household members. The purer the scent, the better."

"I think I understand," Allen nodded. They walked up the front steps to the door, and Allen took out his key. "I hope we can find something my mother-in-law hasn't already washed," he said. "Beth's mom has been here with the girls for a few days. She's worried, and when she worries, she cleans."

"We'll find something," Richard assured them.

Allen led the way to the back bedroom, where Doug removed a pair of surgical gloves from his pants pocket and put them on. Then, pulling out a clean plastic bag, he and the dog entered the bedroom.

From the hall, Allen saw only part of the way into the bedroom. He and Richard heard Doug speaking soft commands to the dog. "The laundry basket is empty," Doug said, loudly enough for them to hear. Richard smiled and raised his eyebrows.

They heard the closet door open. "Her clothes are in the same closet as yours." The disappointment in Zimmerman's voice was unmistakable, even from the hall. They heard dresser drawers open and close.

Suddenly, Richard said, almost laughing, "I just thought of something. Try under the bed. Harumi hates to crawl around under beds."

From the hall, they saw only the back of Doug's feet as he crawled under the bed. "I see something," he said, stretching to reach it. "A sock!"

He stepped to the doorway, triumphantly holding the sock between his gloved thumb and index finger. "Unless you wear socks this tiny, with embroidery on the cuff, I'd guess that this belongs to your wife."

Allen nearly cried. "It's Beth's. She wears those all the time."

"Then that's all we need." Doug bent over and let the dog smell the sock. "This is it," he said, encouraging the dog. "This is who we're looking for." Then, carefully, he dropped the sock into the plastic bag. "Okay. Next stop, the Renton airport."

Allen walked Zimmerman and the dog out to the truck. Just as he opened the crate, Allen said, "I'd like to go with you."

"It won't work," Doug answered.

"I know. I've heard it. But you have a pure scent. And I promise to stay out of the way. If I stay behind you and Boomer, I won't interfere with the scent. But I can't sit down here any longer. I have to see it myself. I have to go up. If you don't let me go with you, I'll go by myself."

Zimmerman hesitated, one hand on his hip, the other holding the dog leash. Allen read frustration all over his face. "Get your things," he said, shaking his head. "But I swear, if you get in my way, I'll tie you to the plane and leave you there."

When Beth finished her soup, Doyle ordered her to rest again. She didn't need much encouragement. The simple effort of eating, combined with the battle raging in her leg and body, exhausted her. She drifted off to sleep almost as soon as she closed her eyes, but hers was a restless sleep full of disconnected dreams.

She dreamt of her children, of Allen, of being lost. She dreamt of snow and bitter cold. She dreamt of a wooden sled with red metal runners. And she saw a hill. A steep icy hill. And a car. She saw flashing lights and heard the wailing of the ambulance. She saw police officers, and the white cloth over her sister's face. In her sleep Beth heard children crying. And she cried too.

She knew without being told that the car had hit Christine. She knew that the burden of telling her parents would fall on her shoulders. Where were they? Why wouldn't they stop and listen to what she had to say?

"Stop," Beth cried out, sitting up. "Listen to me."

She felt hands on her shoulders, holding her back, and she struggled to free herself. "Dad!" she called.

"Beth," the voice said, "it's a dream."

She opened her eyes, and for a moment, she did not recognize the cabin. She saw a man's face but could not remember why she was there. She reached up to wipe the sleep from her eyelids, her hands still shaking from the vivid dream. And then it came back to her. Feeling the ache in her elbow and the pain in her thigh, she remembered. And then an ache came to her soul. She did not have these dreams at home. Beth wanted to go home. "Sorry," she said. "A bad dream."

"It's the fever," he said with a new kindness in his voice. "I've seen it before." He bent down, putting his tools on the floor beside his chair. "You try to rest and the dreams are so real and so terrify-ing—you think you might as well stay awake."

"It was real."

"No," he touched the bed. "It was just a dream."

"No, really," she said. "It was something that happened when I was a child. Fourteen, actually. I haven't thought of it in so long, I'd forgotten some of the details. But when I saw it all again in my dream, I knew. Just like it happened that night." She closed her eyes against the images.

"What happened?"

She looked at him, his gentle eyes, his body leaning forward just the slightest bit. He seemed to want to hear her story, though she could not guess why.

"My first winter in high school. I don't know why I dreamed of it now, here. It was so long ago."

"Tell me."

"We grew up in North Seattle—near Lake City Way, actually—in a split entry house on a very steep hill. Of course, in Seattle we almost never got snow. And when we did, the whole city closed down. So one night, during an unusual week of snow, my little sister and I snuck out of the house with our sled and met the neighbor kids at the top of the hill in front of our house. Our parents' bed-room faced the backyard—away from the street. We knew they couldn't hear anything. They never even knew we were out." She sighed, shaking her head. "I'd give anything to have gotten in trou-ble before it happened."

"What?" he said. "What happened?"

"We had a little road that intersected with ours just before the end of the street. A group of kids would go up the hill and slide down while one person watched for cars. We'd been taking turns. Normally, not much traffic crossed that intersection. And that night, in the snow, we hadn't seen a car the whole time we'd been outside.

"When it was my turn to watch, a boy came out. A boy I knew

from school. He lived just down the hill—and we talked for a while. And then I heard the screech of brakes and saw a car in the intersection trying to stop and a sled sliding into it. I saw it happen. And I never even moved. Never warned anyone. I just watched."

"The car hit the sled?"

Beth looked at him and nodded. She sensed that she had his full attention, but she did not know why this old hermit would care about her childhood trauma. "My sister was on the sled," Beth said. She could see Christine's face even as she told the story. "She died instantly. Right on the street. Never even made it to the hospital." Beth brushed away a single tear.

"I was the one who was supposed to be watching for cars. We had a system. If the lookout saw a car, she would signal, and the kids on the sleds would turn off into a yard to stop. But I was so busy flirting with this neighbor boy, I didn't see the car until it was too late." She shook her head and let it fall back on the pillow. "I don't even remember the boy's name. Christine died, and I can't even remember his name." She glanced over at the soldier beside her and saw that he had tears glistening in his eyes. "I'm sorry. I didn't mean to be so gruesome. But you asked."

He blinked and leaned forward. "We should check the wound again," he said as he moved the blanket out of the way, tucking it carefully around her healthy leg. He untied the knot holding the bandage in place. "How'd you tell your parents?"

"I didn't have to, really. My dad heard the sirens and came outside."

"What did he say to you?"

Beth's voice got very quiet. "He held me and let me cry. We cried together."

"Of course. It was an accident."

"No. She died because I wasn't watching."

"But you were a kid."

"Even kids have jobs. She died because I got distracted, because we snuck out of the house when we should have been in bed. I was more interested in this boy than I was in my responsibility. I carried that for a long, long time." Beth shook her head as she used one hand to lift her leg so he could reach underneath it. "Actually, I had to get help. And even with help, some things will never be the same. I hate the snow, even now." Beth looked up at Doyle and shrugged. "Sounds screwy, I know. But I just don't want to play in the snow anymore."

He looked at her, and she saw his lips form a stiff straight line. "Help," he said, spitting out the word, as though it were used tobacco.

"What? Don't you believe in help?"

"No." She could not miss the bitterness in his voice. "I don't. For some things, there isn't any real help."

"I don't believe that," she said softly. "I believe that there is help for every problem. For everything, no matter how bad, there is help."

A gruff sound escaped his lips.

"You don't believe me," she challenged him.

"When I got home from the Nam, I nearly killed a man who didn't think like me. I tried to pick fights in bars. I hated everyone. I hated the people who didn't go to war. I hated the people who sent me over there. I couldn't sleep. I couldn't work. I couldn't be around people." Abruptly, he tore the last bit of fabric from her skin, and Beth cried out in pain. He made no apology but continued working. "There wasn't any help for me. In fact, the army decided I was the problem."

Doyle grabbed the pot of water at the back of the wood stove and put it on the floor beside the bed. Then he rinsed his rag and began working at cleaning the pus oozing from her skin. "I went to a VA hospital. My wife told me I had to or she would leave me."

Beth nodded. Clearly, this man had seen and experienced more than she had ever guessed. As she listened, she felt guilty for having judged him, for evaluating the man based on his appearance, his way of life. The past held him with a tenacity she could not begin to imagine. "What did they say?"

"I met with a psychiatrist. He was maybe thirty years old. Hadn't ever been in combat. Hadn't ever even fired a rifle—let alone aimed it at a person. I guess I told you this already. He had no idea what I'd been through." Doyle shook his head as he thought of the tall redheaded kid he'd met with at the clinic.

"Didn't he try to help you?"

Doyle laughed bitterly. "He gave me stuff to make me sleep." Doyle looked directly into Beth's eyes. "And he asked me about my relationship with my mother."

Beth felt her eyes fill with tears. "He didn't tell you that what you were going through was normal?"

"Normal? Trying to kill your wife is normal? I don't think so."

"That isn't what I mean. I mean that what you experienced is normal for anyone who has been through something so terrible. It happens to everyone. The memories. The dreams. The emotions— going everywhere—up and down and back again. It's normal."

"How would you know?"

"I told you that I had to get help. It's true. About eight years after my sister's accident, I met Allen, and we decided to get married. After we chose my engagement ring, I went into the most terrible depression. I cried all the time. I was short-tempered. I couldn't sleep. I had bad dreams. I nearly had to quit my job."

Doyle stopped working, leaving both hands palm down on the bed beside her leg, his eyes focused on Beth's face. She took a deep breath. "I went to a counselor. It was hard for me. In our culture— I mean the Asian culture—we are taught not to show our emotions. But I was falling apart. My mother didn't understand why I needed to talk about it with anyone. My own mother seemed hard and cold. She told me to just accept it. But I had to talk to someone, or I was going to lose everything—including the man I loved."

"So you talked to someone. What difference does talk make?"

Beth took a deep breath. "I think I fell apart because a part of me realized that Christine would never ever meet someone like Allen. She would never fall in love. Never marry. And I knew that was my fault. I couldn't get past it. My whole world shut down in grief. I cried nonstop for nearly two weeks.

"Part of me missed her—missed having a sister to share all the fun of wedding preparations with me. And part of me felt guilty— because after all it was my fault—that she had missed the whole rest of her life. And the whole thing got so tangled up in my mind and emotions that I couldn't keep going." Beth glanced down and noticed that her fingers were working the splint on her right arm nervously. Somewhere deep inside, she felt the importance of the moment. In the course of the conversation, Beth realized that perhaps she had been chosen for this moment with this man.

If she could muster the right words, she might be able to give him the keys to the cage that had held him captive for so long. Her heart beat faster, and her fingers trembled. Dennis Doyle had saved her life, and now she might be able to return the favor.

"I needed forgiveness," she said simply.

Thirty-Seven

"OH NO, YOU DON'T," Doyle objected. "Don't hit me with that junk." He stood so suddenly that his chair tipped over backward, hitting the stove as it fell. What right did this woman have to shove her religious junk down his throat? Just like everyone else—she thought of him as nothing more than a notch on her belt. He felt his throat tighten and anger rise in his chest. "I've done the church thing, grew up in the church, went to Sunday school and youth group. And you know what the church did for me? Nothing. Absolutely nothing."

He read surprise and hurt in her expression. "Dennis, you may know about church. But it didn't take. You're as empty inside as those little boxes you make."

"You shut up!" he shouted. "What do you know about the inside of me?" Her surprised look changed to fear. But what did it matter, anyway? After all he'd been through, why should he worry about her feelings?

Had anyone ever been concerned for him? Had anyone worried about his feelings? Not one single time. Doyle remembered his last experience with church. His mother's face, flushed with embarrassment, appeared before him. "You churchgoers," he spat the words. "You're all the same. You talk about love on the outside, but on the inside you're as mean and hateful as jungle rats."

He stood with both hands on his hips, letting the anger boil and churn inside. He had to move, or he might do something he would regret. He spun on his heel and began pacing, taking quick, limping steps back and forth near the stove. Suddenly, he stopped walking and turned to face her. "When I got home from the Nam, I drove for two days—straight through—just to go to church with my mom. I didn't sleep or bathe. I didn't change clothes. Didn't stop to eat. I just wanted to go home. And I drove in on a Sunday morning, exactly four days after leaving the jungle. I picked her up at home and drove her to church, and guess what?"

The woman shook her head, eyes wide.

Doyle stepped toward her. Leaning forward, he put his face close to hers, pointing his finger at her. "The usher told me I couldn't go in. He said I wasn't dressed for church. And my mother cried." Doyle looked at his hand in time to see it shake and dropped it quickly, tucking it into his pocket. "My mother hadn't seen me in thirteen months, and the usher said we couldn't go in to church because I wasn't dressed uppity enough for their taste."

Looking down at her face, Doyle recognized her expression of horror. *Good,* he thought. *Someone ought to feel horrible about it.*

"I'm so sorry," she whispered, her lips trembling. "They shouldn't have done that. I'm sorry that happened to you."

"Right. I'll just bet you are," he yelled. "You and all your self-righteous, know-it-all Christians. I went to Sunday school. I believed that stuff they taught me back then. I believed it."

His voice broke, but he recovered quickly. "I believed it. Every worthless word of it. And then I flew into the Nam. And I found out there that none of it was true. None of it."

"What? What wasn't true?"

Doyle shook his head and folded his hands across his belly. A sob nearly escaped from his chest, but he caught it in time. He touched the corner of his eye with his thumb.

Where could he start? How could he even begin to tell her what he'd been through? She wouldn't believe it anyway. No one had. Until this day, not a single person had ever really cared about what had happened to him. He turned away, walked to the counter, and took a deep breath. She didn't care either. Not really.

Slowly, composing himself, he turned back to look at her. In spite of her fever, her eager brown eyes followed his every move. She looked perplexed but not angry. Did she really want to hear him? Would she listen? Would anyone really listen?

No. Doyle knew better. He took a deep breath, willing the heaviness in his chest to pass. As the silence grew, Doyle recognized the familiar ache in his shoulder. It jabbed at him from under the outer section of his collarbone, and he felt as though he'd developed a sour stomach. He leaned against the counter and rubbed his shoulder with his hand. He saw that she noticed.

"Something bothering your shoulder?" she asked. In the window behind her, Doyle recognized the full-blown light of midday. Light filled the windowpane behind her, making her face difficult to distinguish against the white background.

"No," he lied. "Never mind. Never mind what I said. It don't mean nothin'." He stepped toward the door and pulled his jacket off the hook. "I'm going out to bring in more wood for the fire. We're out."

While he gathered wood, Beth concentrated on the strange story he'd told her. She prayed as she went over his words in her mind. What kind of church would ban him because of his appearance? And what might have happened to him in Vietnam to cause such a horrible sense of betrayal? *Lord, show me,* she begged.

She leaned back on her pillow and cuddled up under the green wool blanket. Doyle's despair seemed to have filled the cabin with ice, leaving only frost for air. She could feel his anguish in the cold metal surface of the bed frame. She could see it in the dark corners of the cabin. But as much as she concentrated, she could think of nothing to say that might help.

In all of her Sunday school classes, in all of her seminars and church training, Beth had memorized scriptures and learned the correct verbiage. And now she felt betrayed. After working so hard, she discovered that in the face of Doyle's despair, she had memorized answers to questions Doyle did not ask.

What could she possibly offer?

Beth closed her eyes and gave herself over to prayer. This time she did not pray for a rescue. She did not pray for her children or Allen. She did not pray for a break in the weather. This time she prayed for the tormented man who had rescued her from certain death.

Doyle came in later, and the sound of him moving about in the cabin woke Beth from a light sleep. Without a word, he brought water and offered her a biscuit. Still she had no appetite. She tried to eat, knowing that her body needed the food. But she could barely swallow the few crumbs she managed to bite off.

She returned the empty cup to him and pulled the blanket up around her neck. Beth began exercising her thigh, contracting and then relaxing the muscle that straightened her knee. Even this much motion hurt, but Beth believed that it would help pump blood in and out of the leg. Contract, relax. She repeated the motion several times before giving in to complete exhaustion.

Doyle had been right. She would never get down the mountain on her own.

"What's the weather like?" she asked.

"Better," he answered. "The wind is down, and it stopped snowing. Still overcast, though."

"When do you think you could you help me down the hill?"

"I'm not taking you anywhere," he said, the cold tone returning to his voice.

"How am I supposed to get down?"

"You got up here on your own."

He picked up his bottle and tin cup from the counter on the far side of the room. Filling his cup, he pulled his chair to face the stove, setting the bottle on the floor beside him. He drank the first cup in one swig.

"Look," Beth said, trying again, "I didn't mean to end up here. It was an accident. The plane crashed, for heaven's sake. I didn't plan it." She tried to stem the tears that seemed so close to the surface. "I don't know all that happened to turn you into such a mean old man. I'm sorry it happened. But don't take it out on me." Her voice rose and Beth checked it. "Please don't take it out on me."

"You've got a lot of nerve," he said. "You don't have any idea what I've been through. You don't know what it feels like to live on the edge of death for thirteen straight months. To be so scared that you sleep holding your gun. To know that at any moment—night or day—you could be taken out by an enemy you never even see. You don't know what it is to hold a friend while his blood spurts out onto your hands. To know that his heart is still trying to pump—even though his arm is missing. You don't know what it is to be in the middle of a firefight so thick you can't see what you're shooting.

Or to take body parts out of the tracks when you clean up in the morning, and . . ." He filled the cup a second time, took a drink, and stood frozen in his past. Long moments ticked away.

"You don't know what it feels like to have the helicopter that holds your best friend blow up over your head." He leaned forward in the chair and took a shuddering breath. "Or to kill an enemy soldier only to find out that she's the mother of two boys. You can't possibly know."

He leaned forward, dropping his face into his hands. A silence fell on the cabin like the blade of a guillotine. Beth felt his anguish.

Sadness swallowed Beth, and though she tried, she could not hold her tears back. As he waited, head down, she began to weep. She let the tears drip off her chin onto her sweater. She felt her nose run—dripping off her face.

He turned in the chair and faced her directly, his voice becoming monotone. "You don't know what it is to come home and have someone ask if you hurt your leg in Vietnam—and then have them say, 'You deserved it.' You'll never know what it's like to find out that everyone you know has moved on but you. That your girlfriend has dumped you and is dating someone else. That your friends don't want to be with you anymore. That your own parents are afraid of you." He was almost shouting now, and Beth smelled the alcohol on his breath. He turned back to the fire.

"You don't know what it is to go thirty years fighting nightmares that never go away. To live a lifetime wishing for a full night's sleep. Or to have your mind take you back to that place—at any time, whether or not you wanna go—suddenly you are there. You can never know."

Doyle stared at her face, as though her tears startled him. Silent for a long time, he finally turned back to the stove. He seemed to Beth like a bucket finally empty. Having let everything out, he seemed spent.

But as the moments passed, Doyle began again. This time, with more sorrow, he said, "You don't know what it's like to have your father be ashamed of you. Of who you've become. Or to have your mother feel sorry for you. To see it in her eyes every time she looks at you. You don't know what it is to be so alone, so dead inside, that you have to live away from everyone you love."

"You're right," she said. "I don't know. I couldn't possibly know."

"You don't know what that kind of anger does to a person. For years, you hope it's gonna go away. But it doesn't. It stays with you. Even when you finally find someone who says she loves you, the anger comes back and destroys everything. And before you know it, you're so full of rage that you have to leave your own child before you hurt him. You'll never know what that feels like. You'll never know what it feels like to see terror in your wife's eyes and know that she's afraid of you." Doyle took a drink and shook his head. "And you could never know what it's like to go visit the parents of your buddy, hoping to tell them how sorry you are—and then have them throw his medals at your feet. To hear them blame you for his death. And to know that they're right."

His eyebrows drew together, and his tone turned bitter. "And while I was growing up, they told me that God would be with me everywhere I went. I'm telling you, God wasn't in the Nam." Doyle shook his head and used both hands to brush the tears from his eyes. He brought his shirttail up to his nose and blew it hard. Then he laughed, a cold dispassionate laugh. "God wasn't in the Nam," he repeated. "Any God worth his salt woulda stopped it. It shoulda never happened."

With one hand, she brushed her own tears away, but they continued to flow. She could not stem the tide. "I know that anything I say could never undo what has happened to you. I know it." She looked up to find him staring off at the lantern, his clear blue eyes soft and moist. "But I am sorry. It was my nation that put you there. And we didn't take care of you after you came home." She paused and took a deep shuddering breath. "We used you and then abandoned you. God didn't do that, America did. I was part of the nation that did that to you. I just want you to know that I'm sorry. It was wrong. And I'm sorry."

He blinked hard and turned to face her, looking into her eyes for the first time. His face seemed white, as if the telling of it all had exhausted him. He reached up to knead the spot under his shoulder. Shrugging, he said, "Don't mean nothin'."

He reached down for the bottle and refilled his cup, sipping the liquid. "Don't mean nothin' at all."

The silence between them lengthened until Beth, spent from effort and emotion, fell asleep.

————

Beth woke instantly, completely alert. What had she heard? A sound? An aircraft? She closed her eyes, concentrating. There, in the distance, she heard the unmistakable sound of a helicopter passing nearby. It seemed clear to her that the chopper was flying up the mountain, closer, louder. Perhaps it was headed toward the crash site from the valley below. Though Beth could not be certain, it seemed to fly with an objective, in a direct path.

Still listening, Beth sat up and glanced around the cabin in the afternoon light. In the chair, Doyle sat slumped over the table, snoring loudly. She spoke quietly, "Dennis?"

He did not answer.

Could she sneak out and make it back to the plane before the searchers gave up on her? Was this her last chance to get home? Beth swung her feet over the edge of the bed, holding on to the mattress, already prepared for the swirling that accompanied sitting up. Her thigh throbbed as her knee bent over the bed, and Beth winced with the new pain. She leaned on her strong arm, taking deep breaths and then regretting it as her ribs complained.

He's had too much to drink, Beth thought. *He'll never even hear me leave.* Doyle had hung her coat on the wall next to his own, only inches from the door. If Beth could get up and take the coat, she could make it up the hill. She could. With only ten or twelve steps to the door, she knew she had to try.

Pulling his pants over her hiking boots and legs, she twisted the waistband into a knot. She stood, clinging frantically to the edge of the mattress as the room spun around her aching head. Could she get out? Could she get away and make it to the meadow before he knew she'd left? She had to try. For the kids, she had to try.

Limping as she walked, Beth took her first tentative steps toward the door. The floor creaked, and Beth froze, looking back at Doyle. He did not move. She took several more steps, reaching for the coat as she walked. Gilligan raised his head and padded across the cabin. "No," she whispered, holding one finger over her mouth.

Then, holding the coat, she lifted the latch on the cabin door and slipped outside, leaving the dog behind.

Thirty-Eight

OUTSIDE, THE COLD AIR slapped Beth, stinging her face and her nostrils. She slid one arm down the jacket sleeve and buttoned the collar against the wind. Then she put her hand in the pocket and stepped off the porch.

Following Doyle's tracks, Beth started uphill, pushing the snow out of her way like a plow as she walked. Only ten steps later, she stumbled and nearly fell. She stopped, panting with the effort, allowing herself to rest. *Go on, Beth,* she coaxed. *You must make it up the hill. You can't be far from the plane.* She had never felt this weak before.

She continued, taking one step after another, sliding over the surface under her feet. Snow clung to Doyle's wool pants, and they grew heavier with every step, threatening to slide off her hips as she walked. Beth had to hold them up with her good hand. She had not gone four steps this way before her exposed hand objected to the cold air. She thrust it deep into the pocket of Doyle's pants, pulling them up from the inside, stumbling over the drooping pant legs as she climbed.

Exhaustion hit her before she reached the place where Doyle had tackled her only the day before. "Oh, Lord, help me," she pleaded, panting. "I want to go home." She paused to catch her breath. Then, with the cold stiff fingers of her left hand, she rolled up the legs of Doyle's pants.

Stumbling forward, Beth wondered how far she could go in this condition. *It doesn't matter. I have no choice.* She pressed on. Cresting the hill, she came to the place where the trail seemed to end in a stand of small trees. No more footprints. No path. Which direction should she go?

Uphill. She felt the urge to move uphill and followed it. Doubts assailed her again. *What am I doing? At least I was warm and dry in the cabin.* Her thigh ached, and her throat burned with the cold.

Putting her thoughts aside, she trudged up the steep path. The snow deepened, and the wind, now blowing from behind, pushed her up the hill. *Go on,* a voice inside urged. *Keep moving.*

"I can't," she said to the wind and stopped to rest. She didn't dare sit down; Beth knew she wouldn't have the strength to get up again.

Standing alone, she listened to the wind whistling through the trees. Something was missing. The sound of the helicopter had completely disappeared. *Go on,* the voice said again. *Hurry.* She brushed hair from her face and turned up the collar of the coat. Starting off again, her legs felt stiff and heavy, like wooden limbs. Her ribs ached as she tried to get enough air. In spite of the climb, Beth had grown cold, and she shivered as she walked. Still she stumbled on.

She came to a log lying across the path and, in her cold and stupor, wondered what to do, how to get over it. It was too big to step over and too long to go around. She placed one foot on top of the log and used both hands to pull herself up. Though her elbow objected, she climbed up, panting. *This takes too much work. Look at me. I'm a wreck,* she thought.

As Beth shifted her weight to step off the other side, her hiking shoe slipped on the bark, dropping her into wet snow. She dragged herself up and brushed the snow from her face, determined to go on. But her legs would not cooperate. Though they moved forward, they felt like stumps—uncoordinated and unwilling.

Thinking of Noah, she trudged forward, stumbling again. *For Noah,* she thought. One step, another step. Her head pounding and her feet getting heavier, Beth stumbled, falling into the snow. She wanted to go home. Only to go home. She dragged herself forward, trying to bring just one foot up underneath her. She tried. But her body betrayed her.

Doyle woke to the sound of banging wood. His head pounded, and his mouth felt dry. He lifted his face from the table, blinking against the light-filled room. Cold. Had his fire gone out? Getting out of his chair, he saw the cabin door rocking back and forth on its hinge, rapping against the doorframe. Who left the door open? Confused, he glanced around the cabin.

Her bed. She had gone. The woman had gone. Doyle limped to the doorway and grabbed his coat from the hook. Perhaps she had gone to the outhouse. As he stepped onto the porch he put on his coat, looking for signs of the woman. It didn't take a tracker to see where she had gone. Her feet left a deep furrow in new snow all the way to the top of the hill.

Is she heading back to the plane? Or does she think she'll just walk down the mountain alone? What will she tell the authorities about me? Doyle wondered. He swore softly to himself. He should never have taken her in. She'd brought him nothing but bad luck. Winter had already arrived, and Doyle didn't have time to build another shelter. If the authorities came looking for him now, he was in trouble. He had no place else to go. No other place to hide.

He shook his head. She had forced his hand. His decision made, he whistled for Gilligan and started up the trail after her.

———

The helicopter pilot had strapped Allen into the jump seat in the very back of the rescue chopper. From here, Allen could not see the ground below. Instead, he focused only on the backs of the pilot and Zimmerman as they chatted back and forth. The dog, who seemed completely comfortable in the noisy shuddering contraption, slept quietly in his crate across from Allen. Anyone looking at Boomer would think the dog was napping on a fireplace hearth.

They'd given Allen a headset as soon as he climbed into his seat. Through this, he kept track of the conversation between Zimmerman and the pilot. The earphones also served to cut down on the noise from the rotors and the turbine engine. But nothing cut the anxiety he felt as they flew toward the crash site.

"I'm going to dip in from the south," the pilot said.

Allen saw Zimmerman turn to the pilot and nod.

"Wind is still pretty stiff. And once we get into the foothills, the visibility is bad. We'll have to fly low."

Allen closed his eyes, shutting out their conversation, and prayed.

———

Beth rolled over in the snow. Lying on her back, she looked up into the white sky.

Knowing she could not go farther, she felt content to rest. "Father, I tried. I only wanted to go home. I'm sorry," she whispered.

Beth heard a noise and looked down the trail in time to see Doyle climbing over the log. He came toward her with strong steps, a determined look on his face.

"No," she said. "I won't go back." She started to roll away, trying to escape before he reached her. "I want to go home. No. No," she cried, sobbing as she crawled through the elbow-deep snow. Fear made her heart pound in her ears, replacing exhaustion with raw terror. "I won't go back," she said, crying. She tried to get up but stumbled. She hurried forward, clawing at the ground.

Just as he reached out to grab her, Beth felt her world give way to blackness.

———

A jarring up and down motion woke Beth, who felt as though she were being thrown up and down over and over again. She opened her eyes to see Doyle's beard only inches from her face. He carried her—her knees bent over one of his arms, her head against his shoulder. Her splint draped roughly over his forearm. She lifted her splinted hand and placed it on her knee, closing her eyes again.

"No," she said. "I want to go home."

"Shut up."

"Please," she whispered.

"Please shut up." She heard him panting as he walked, carrying her roughly. "This isn't easy."

She tried to struggle, raising her hips and pushing her legs away. But he held her more tightly. "If you'll cooperate, you might actually get home," he said.

She opened her eyes and looked over his shoulder. Doyle carried her uphill—not down the mountain toward his cabin. He was carrying her back to the plane!

"I heard a chopper," she said.

"I know."

With a sigh, she settled down. "Thank you," she whispered, her voice hoarse with cold air. She closed her eyes again, nestling into the rhythm of his steps.

As Doyle trudged uphill, panting and struggling against the deep snow, she heard the sound of air rushing in and out of his lungs. Beth's mind wandered, and time had no meaning. Then, without warning, Doyle gave a fierce cry and stumbled, falling with her into the snow. The pain in her thigh made her cry out, and Beth rolled away, startled. "Hey..." she began. But seeing Doyle, she said nothing more.

He held his shoulder with one hand, clutching, clawing at the arm, rolling and moaning with pain. Snow covered his clothes and clung to his beard. But he didn't seem to care. Then, as suddenly as he had fallen, he stopped moving.

Beth scooted toward him on her knees. "Dennis?" With his eyes closed, his skin gray, Doyle did not respond. "Dennis! What's wrong?" Beth searched his expressionless face, knowing instinctively that something terrible had happened—but what? No answer came but the sound of the wind in the trees above her.

Still kneeling in the snow, she ignored the knifing pain of her wounds. She crept closer, bending over his face to put her ear above his nose. Nothing. No air moved in or out of his lungs.

Her fingers, cold and stiff, trembled as she checked the pulse below his jaw. Nothing.

A heart attack. The thought came to her with absolute certainty. *Of course,* she thought, *why didn't I see it? The way he always rubbed his shoulder when he worked. His heart. He has a bad heart. Oh, Lord, what should I do?*

Sure about her diagnosis, Beth felt a surge of adrenaline. Her own heart pounded in response, and she felt strong and healthy, as if all her injuries had disappeared with this new crisis. She leaned back to consider his position. He'd fallen with his body across the slope, slumped in a fetal position. She needed him on a level place if she wanted to try anything. From her position beside him, she tugged at his coat, but his big body would not move.

Even as she tried to move Doyle, she began recalling the steps of CPR. She remembered the position of the practice dummy she had resuscitated, and in her mind, she heard again the calm, encouraging words of her instructor.

"Stay calm," she said out loud. "Think!" She ran her hand through her hair, pushing it away from her face and tucking it behind her ears. Beth rolled Doyle onto his back so that his torso rested on the flat surface of the snow. As she stood up, she felt the horizon swirl and took a deep breath against her dizziness. "Help me, Lord," she whispered, grabbing his collar with her good hand and pulling hard.

Leaning away from him, she used the full weight of her body to drag him up the hill. Slowly, his trunk inched upward. With his body lying uphill, Beth let go, and Doyle dropped onto the snow. "Now, his legs," she said and took a deep breath. "Hurry, Beth," she said aloud to herself as she stumbled to drag his feet into place. "Hurry!"

When she had him positioned, Beth opened Doyle's jacket and began pressing against his chest with her left hand, throwing herself against his sternum. "One, two, three . . ." she counted as she pumped. *One hand,* she thought, *is one hand enough? Air, I must give him air.* She bent down and tipped his chin back. Looking down at his shaggy face, Beth felt one instant of hesitation—which she forcefully rejected. "He saved you, Beth," she said as she moved his mustache out of her way. With a tiny shudder, she placed her mouth over his and blew air into his lungs.

Ignoring the smell of stale alcohol, she gave another long blow before she began the chest compressions again. *Not enough,* she realized. *I need more force.* She leaned back, thinking wildly. She scooted closer again, this time leaning her right knee against his rib cage, squishing it deeply into the cold snow. Beth held her injured elbow up and away as she lifted her left knee and balanced herself against his body. Then, placing her left hand beside her knee on his chest, she continued her compressions, using the full weight of her small body against his sternum. Knee and hand working together, the effort and her fear made her sweat. Again she counted aloud. "One, two, three . . ."

As she pumped, a sound startled Beth. Not far away, she heard the unmistakable rumble of an engine. The helicopter! Yes. Now she recognized the sound of rotors breaking the mountain air.

"Help me!" she screamed, bending to give Doyle air again. "Please help me!" she shouted.

As Beth continued her compressions, the sound of the engines increased. *They're leaving*, she thought, incredulous. *Leaving! The helicopter is getting ready to leave.* She felt panic rise in her chest. *They've found our plane and they know I'm not there. And now they won't come to look for me.* "Help me," she screamed again. "I'm here! Please come help me!"

Beth continued the compressions, watching Doyle's expressionless face for a response. *He'll die if I leave him*, she thought. *He doesn't have a chance without help. I can't walk away and let him die.* Beth cried as she bent down to breathe for him, tears of fear and frustration running down her cheeks. *But if I don't get up to the meadow, they'll leave without me.* One breath. Two.

"I want to go home, Lord," she said, brushing the wetness from her cheeks. "I want to go home." As Beth's compressions fell into a rhythm, she heard the engines scream and knew without a doubt that the rescue helicopter had already taken off. She had made her choice. Still pounding on his chest, she realized that she would die here, trying to save Dennis Doyle.

She bent down to breathe for him again. Blowing once, she stopped in midbreath. What? What was that sound? Barking? She leaned back, nearly toppling over in her precarious position. She glanced around but saw nothing. Gilligan had curled up under a tree just a few feet from his master. She blew into Doyle's mouth again, and restarted the compressions.

Yes, she *had* heard something. It was a dog! But not Gilligan. Another dog?

Beth looked up in time to see an enormous bloodhound running down the trail toward her, reddish brown skin flopping from its narrow face. Within feet of her, the dog plopped into the snow and began howling. "Please!" Beth yelled, overcome with joy. "Help me, I'm here!"

She breathed again for Doyle and looked up in time to see a tall blond man come traipsing over the hill, his walkie-talkie squawking. Seeing her, he jogged forward, grinning. "Boy, are we glad to see you," he called, stopping to reward the dog with a treat.

"Please help me," Beth said, still compressing Doyle's chest. She had grown so weak, so tired, that she could barely continue. Slumping forward, she panted. "I think he's had a heart attack."

The man glanced again at Doyle, his clear blue eyes taking in Doyle's face and her position over the body. Gently, he moved Beth from Doyle's chest, pulling out his radio as he began the compressions she could no longer manage.

Beth dropped back onto the snow, straightening her legs before her as she did. Her thigh screamed, and her shoulder ached. Though her ordeal was over, she cried. Her rescuers had arrived, but too late for Doyle. Everything had come too late for Doyle. Weeping, she thought of the man who had saved her life. Too late, she thought. Beth hugged her good knee, letting go of all the tension and emotion of the last few days in the raking sobs that followed.

It was in the midst of uncontrollable sobbing that Beth felt strong arms wrap her shoulders. Exhausted and sick but grateful for human touch, she leaned into the warm embrace. As she wept, the strong arms held her, rocking gently and smoothing her hair. Beth relaxed into the caress.

"I'm here, Beth," a voice said. "It's over now."

And in the voice and the scent, the unmistakable odor of Polo, Beth knew. Allen. Allen had found her. She spoke his name, still crying.

And he leaned down to comfort her with kisses.

As the helicopter ascended above them, Beth felt Allen lean over her stretcher, his body protecting her face from blowing snow. "Whew," he said, straightening up and brushing snow from her hair. "You okay, Beth? Really okay?" His eyes brimmed with tears.

She nodded, and they both looked up in time to see Doyle's helicopter change direction above them. They watched as it cleared the trees on the southeast side of the meadow and disappeared.

Taking her hand in his own, his gloved hands rubbed her fingers gently. "I can't believe how good it feels to touch you. I just didn't know." He brushed her cheeks with his fingers. "I prayed. I've never prayed so hard. Still, I didn't dare hope that I would have you back again. I'm so grateful."

She reached up to caress his face, rubbing his cheek with her thumb. "I know, Allen. I don't understand any of it. But I'm here.

I'm here." Nothing had ever felt so wonderful as his face did to her hands in that moment.

Beth shivered, and Allen tucked her hand back inside the wool emergency blanket. "You need to stay warm."

"Hmm . . ." she said, nodding. "How long until they come for me?"

Allen checked his watch. "Another fifteen minutes and the next helicopter will be here." He kissed her fingers. "First stop, the hospital."

"Oh, clean sheets," Beth said with unmistakable longing.

"And showers and food," Allen laughed. "And doctors. You'll feel like a princess when you get there. The kids and your parents will be so happy to see you." Allen tousled her hair with his hand. "I still can't believe you're alive," he whispered.

"I feel like a princess now," she smiled. "By the way, do princesses do dishes?"

Epilogue

Three weeks later

As ALLEN PULLED THEIR CAR onto the driveway of Star Lake Veterans' Hospital, Beth took a deep, calming breath. "Nervous?" he asked her.

"A little," she answered. "I can't help it. Being here reminds me of everything we've been through. I don't really know what to expect." She sighed and silence filled the car. Beth looked out the window at the leafless trees standing along the narrow, winding driveway. She heard only the sound of car tires moving slowly on wet pavement, and her mind wandered far away to the cabin in the mountains, where she remembered the sounds of gusting wind and snow falling in clumps onto the roof. In spite of the warm car, she shivered.

Allen reached across the seat and held her hand. "I know. Sometimes I still feel the fear. I find myself worrying about you— even when you're just in the next room." He glanced over to smile at her.

"I still have dreams," Beth said, turning again to gaze out the window.

"Bad ones?"

She nodded. "Scary sometimes." Beyond the big oak trees, a golf course boasted the deep green of perfectly maintained and manicured lawns. "It's beautiful down here," she said. "I had no idea."

"There's the lake," Allen said, pointing through the windshield to his left. In a small wooden pram, a man rowed just offshore. "I've heard about it. But I've never been here before. I hear the fishing is good."

They passed through an unmanned security gate and came to a circular cluster of aging, identical white buildings connected by winding sidewalks. Black streaks fell like tears from the casements of the square windows on both floors of the identical structures. Beautiful grounds could not hide the grim reality of bar-covered windows and aging construction.

Groups of people wandered along the paths. Some wore the telltale scrubs of medical staff. Others seemed to be visitors. "Where should we park?" Beth wondered aloud.

"Mom, which building is Mr. Doyle in?" Bekka asked.

"Building thirteen," Allen answered.

Beth glanced over her seat at Abbey, who leaned forward, peering intently out the side window as she sucked her thumb. She had chosen her best Sunday dress, with black patent leather shoes and lacy ankle socks. "Your thumb, Abbey," Beth said.

"That one is number four," Bekka volunteered, pointing.

"Thanks." Allen smiled at her in the rearview mirror.

"At least the grounds are beautiful." Beth squeezed Allen's hand. "I'm glad he's in such a peaceful setting." As Allen pulled cautiously around a double-parked delivery truck, Beth tried to ignore the flutter of anxiety in her stomach. Bringing the whole family to visit had been her idea. Still, she didn't know how she felt about seeing Doyle again. How would he react?

Though she'd visited him in the hospital when they'd first come off the mountain, she hadn't seen him since he'd moved to the veterans' hospital. During that visit, exhaustion had completely stolen his personality. He'd been too tired to speak. Too tired to do anything more than thank her for coming. What would he be like now? Had he changed? Would he be angry with her all over again? After so many years of living like he had, could a man like Doyle ever really change?

"There's the one," Allen said, pointing out Beth's window. Like all the others, building thirteen, a two-story structure made of white cement block, stood about twenty feet from the main sidewalk. Standing in the grass, a dark wooden placard announced the number. Allen began searching for a place to park. Two buildings later, he spotted a sign indicating a visitors' parking lot, where he stopped and turned off the ignition. Pulling out the keys, he turned to face Beth. "Are you really ready for this?" he asked.

"As ready as I'll ever be," she answered, unhooking her seat belt. Bekka had already opened the side door.

"I get to hold the leash," Bekka said, jumping onto the sidewalk.

"Okay. If you promise to keep it tight. Don't let him get away from you." Allen leaned in to encourage the dog from the car. "Come on, Gilligan, old boy."

They helped Abbey from her seat. In one hand, Abbey held her gift basket with the solemnity of a flower girl on the way to the altar, her thumb hanging again from her mouth. "No thumb," Beth reminded her gently.

Allen unfastened the belt holding Noah in his car seat and lifted the baby into his arms. Beth watched Allen settle Noah onto his hip with a sinking feeling. The hardest part of breaking her elbow was not being able to lift or carry Noah by herself. Beth looked forward to resuming her full responsibilities as a mother. For now, she contented herself by patting his diapered behind and leaning up to kiss his cheek. He held his arms out for her. "Only three more weeks, Noah," Beth said, rubbing her thumb over his dimpled baby hand. "Then Mommy can hold you."

Beth's doctors had repaired her shattered elbow with pins and plates and grafted new skin onto her thigh. After about six weeks, they told her, she'd be as good as new.

But only on the outside. The inside of Beth would never be quite the same. She shivered in spite of the mild temperature and pulled her coat closer to fasten the top button.

Allen offered his right hand to Beth. She felt him give her a gentle squeeze. "Shall we go?"

The girls had gone on ahead. Their skipping gave way to a full running dash, each intent on being the first to climb the four concrete stairs leading to the wooden entry of building thirteen. Gilligan seemed as eager as the girls to reach the doorway.

Beth smiled as she observed the differences between her two girls—Bekka in overalls and tennis shoes, Abbey in all her finery. Both ran with the zeal of Olympic sprinters. She closed her eyes and gave thanks again for the gift of life, and most especially for the gift of mothering. So many times on the mountain, her greatest fear had been that she would not be able to see the girls and Noah to adulthood. Of all of the regrets she had faced on the mountain, this one had frightened her most. How it hurt to consider leaving that job unfinished.

Allen stopped walking, pulling her back. "You okay?"

"Yes. I was just thinking about the kids." She smiled, trying to reassure her worried husband. "About how glad I am to see them grow up." Allen probably thought she'd gone crazy. She'd cried a lot in the past three weeks.

He pulled her close and kissed her gently. "I understand. I feel the same way about you."

"I'm pretty lucky, aren't I?"

"Absolutely." He grinned. "You have me."

She laughed, and they resumed their walk. By the time Beth and Allen reached the stairs, the girls held both doors open for them. "Thank you, ladies," Beth said with mock solemnity.

Inside, the building showed its age. Dark linoleum floors met cheerless white walls decorated by exposed but painted pipes. Security screens and thick bars covered the few windows in the entry. Couched in the warm air that greeted them, Beth smelled the unmistakable scent of antiseptics.

At the opening in a Plexiglas window, they asked a bored looking receptionist for Dennis Doyle. "He's in room 227," she said in a monotone. "Down the hall to the stairs and up to the right." Beth's little entourage started away from the desk. "Wait," she said, her voice rising as she stood up. "No dogs are allowed upstairs. You'll have to see him in the solarium. I'll have the nurse bring him down." She picked up the phone and pointed. "Last door on the right."

Beth glanced at Allen and shrugged. "I called ahead to ask about bringing Gilligan," she whispered.

"You know how bureaucracies can be." He smiled and turned to lead the way down the hall. "The rules often depend on who answers the phone."

At the stairs, Allen pointed to his right and said, "Should be in here."

They came to a burgundy door standing partially open. Beth leaned in and found a large empty room decorated with low vinyl couches and large potted plants. Their footsteps echoed on the red tile floor. "Let's sit down," she said. "Over here by the window." Abbey sat beside her mother with the basket on her lap. Bekka and the dog explored the room.

"Mom," Bekka said, her voice rising. "I think Gilligan needs to go outside."

"I'll take him." Allen held his hand out for the leash.

"I can do it myself," Bekka said, her voice indignant.

"Sure. Just come right back inside as soon as he finishes," Allen agreed.

A few moments later, a nurse walked through the doorway, escorting a slightly worn Dennis Doyle. He stood, his hands in his pockets, his expression closed. The nurse excused himself.

Beth stood and moved toward him. "Hello, Dennis," she said, offering her left hand. "How are you doing?"

He accepted her hand, squeezing it gently. "Better," he said gruffly. He touched his mustache and cleared his throat. Wearing sweatpants and a T-shirt, he seemed uncomfortable. For a moment, Beth wondered if they should have come.

"Dennis, I brought my family to meet you," she began, gesturing to Allen. "This is my husband, Allen Cheng."

"Hello, Dennis." Allen stepped forward and reached out to shake his hand.

"And that's our baby, Noah," Beth continued. As Allen turned the baby to face Doyle, Noah grinned, as if on cue, patting his daddy on the lapel of his jacket. Allen laughed. "This is our youngest daughter, Abbey."

For the briefest moment, Dennis Doyle almost smiled. "Sit down," he said. "All of you." He gestured to the chairs. "It was nice of you to come. I don't get many visitors."

As they settled into the vinyl seats, Beth asked, "How is your heart?"

"They say my ticker will be just fine," Doyle answered. "I have to watch my diet though." He clasped his hands in the space between his knees.

Though his heart would recover, Beth couldn't help but wonder about the condition of his soul. What progress had he made with the demons that had haunted him these past thirty years? After all, it had only been three weeks. What could anyone expect in such a short time?

"So," Allen said as he leaned forward, "how do you like Chuck?"

Doyle smiled. As she saw it, Beth realized this was the first genuine smile she had ever seen fill the man's face.

"Chuck is great," he said. "He talks straight, and he knows what I've been through. I've never met anyone like him."

Beth glanced at Allen just in time to see a self-satisfied expression flit across his face. She'd have to live with that for a while.

"He should," Allen said. "He's been through it too, though I think he was in Vietnam a couple of years before you were. Did he tell you that he had to kick a drug habit himself?" Doyle nodded, and Allen continued. "I met Chuck at a pastors' seminar. He told his story to more than a hundred strangers—all of it—and I've never seen an audience so captivated. When Beth told me about you, I knew you needed to meet Chuck."

Doyle nodded again, and as he reached up to scratch his nose, Beth noticed his hands. Mountain dirt no longer stained the folds of his skin. Cut and clean, the nails and cuticles had been neatly trimmed. Though his hair and beard remained long, they shone with washing and brushing. At least part of Dennis Doyle had changed.

"Mom, can we give him the stuff?" Abbey asked, pulling on Beth's arm.

Beth nodded.

"Mr. Doyle, we brought you some presents," Abbey said, placing the basket in his lap. She smiled and lifted the tissue from the top, as if to show him how to find the treasures inside.

He did not seem to know what to do. Glancing from Abbey to Allen and then to Beth, he simply said, "Thank you."

"So open it!"

He seemed aware of Abbey's eagerness and obligingly lifted the tissue. Inside, he pulled out the first of the two cards the girls had made, unfolding it gently.

Thank you for helping Mommy, the first card read, with a picture of a stick woman lying in bed with an enormous cast over her arm. He smiled at the picture and looked at Abbey. "Did you draw this?" he asked.

She nodded. "All by myself," she said with pride.

He smiled. "Very nice," he said softly.

On the second card, Bekka had made a careful drawing of Doyle's cabin, including the many details she'd taken from conversations with her mother. Underneath the drawing, Bekka had copied a verse from the New Testament: *Whatever you did for one of the least of these brothers of mine, you did for me.*

His hands trembled slightly as he held the card. "Thank you," he said to Abbey.

"That one's from my sister," she said, dismissing the praise with a shrug.

Doyle found other gifts inside as well. The girls had included a package of homemade sugar cookies, and Allen had chosen a new set of carving tools nestled in a small velvet-lined wooden box. He'd also bought a selection of tiny clasps and hinges from the local hardware store. "Beth told me about the beautiful boxes you make," he said. "I thought you might enjoy having something here to work with."

Doyle found the large-print New Testament that Beth had included at the bottom of the basket. When he had examined everything, Doyle said again, "Thank you for the gifts. I didn't expect anything."

As he spoke, the sound of paws came echoing across the tile floor, and he looked up just as Gilligan leapt onto his lap. "Gilligan! Where'd you come from?"

Bekka tried for a moment to pull the dog off the old man. Then, unable to make any progress, she gave up and dropped her end of the leash. "We've taken care of him for you," she said, flopping into the seat beside her father.

"This is our oldest," Allen volunteered by way of explanation. "Bekka, this is Mr. Doyle, the man who helped Mommy on the mountain."

Bekka crossed her arms, nodding as she did.

"And you've been taking care of Gilligan for me?" Doyle seemed amazed.

"Sure. You took care of Mom. We take care of Gilligan."

He reached up and patted the dog's head, a look of glad reunion on his smiling face. "Well, ol' boy, I wondered what happened to you." When he looked at Beth, she saw tears in his eyes. "Thank you. I didn't expect you to do this."

"But you saved my mom's life," Bekka said, surprised.

"Oh, I don't know about that," Doyle said. "I think maybe your mom saved mine." He glanced again at Beth, and the expression on his face was so earnest, so sincere, that she felt her face grow warm with embarrassment.

Allen noticed. "How long will you stay here?" he asked.

"My heart doctor says I'm fine. I had a stent put in, and it looks good," he answered. "But the alcohol treatment lasts nine more weeks, and I want to stay in the vet group as long as I can. I've applied for a position in a halfway house."

"What does that mean?" Beth asked.

"It means I can stay on campus after I finish my alcohol treatment." Dennis smiled. "I have to work to pay for the rent. But I know I need the extra time here."

Beth could not contain her joy, and she giggled out loud. "Good for you, Dennis," she said. "I'm so happy for you."

"My son is too."

"Your son?"

"I've talked to him twice since I've been here," Doyle answered, his eyes twinkling. "He wasn't hard to find. My social worker helped me. He's coming up to visit."

Allen patted Doyle's shoulder. "That's wonderful news."

Beth and Allen stayed to talk with Dennis only a few minutes more. Though he had come a long way, anyone could see fatigue in his face. After all, he'd suffered a full-blown heart attack only three weeks before. He still needed rest.

"We should be going," Beth began, finally standing. "We don't want to wear you out completely."

"It isn't tiring," Doyle said, though his slumping shoulders and sagging expression told a different story. "Before you go, I have a gift for you, Beth."

"Dennis," she objected, "you don't need to give me anything."

"But I do," he said. He pushed himself forward in the chair and stood with difficulty. Leaning sideways, he pulled something from the pocket of his sweatpants and reached for her hand. Placing the object inside, he closed her fingers around it. "For you," he said simply.

Opening her palm, Beth looked down. What could he possibly want to give her, she wondered. Inside, she found the little bundle of medals, still tied with the same wire tie. She gasped. "I can't take these, Dennis. They're yours. You earned them."

"No, Beth. Only some are mine—given for bravery in the face of grave danger. I think you deserve 'em as much as I ever did." He smiled. "You had the courage to survive. To tell me the truth. To find your way home. Besides," he rubbed his finger across his full mustache, "since I've come down here, I think I want to let go of the past—I don't want to hang on to things anymore." He pointed to the medals. "Some of those medals belonged to an old friend. Guilt made me keep them. I used to cling to it. Wallow in it. But I've decided to let go." He stroked his mustache again, smiling. "Do you remember what you said? You said that I'm as empty as those little boxes I make." He shook his head. "You were right, Beth. But not anymore. I'm not empty anymore."

"Thank you, Dennis," Beth said, pulling the big man into her gentle one-armed embrace. "I will keep these for you and take courage from them. Always."

As they said their good-byes, promising to return soon, Beth could not help but marvel. She'd come to the veterans' hospital wondering if Dennis Doyle could ever change. She'd wondered about the damage to his heart. In her wildest dreams, she would never have imagined the healing wrought by the heavenly heart doctor. Though Doyle still faced a long recovery, he had started down the right path.

As Beth and Allen walked down the hall, hand in hand, Beth giggled.

"What? What was that about?" Allen glanced toward her.

"I just remembered something that always makes me laugh," she said, shaking her head. "The New Testament says somewhere that common people were surprised that Jesus did all things well." Beth stopped walking and looked up at Allen. "You know, honey, even after all these years, sometimes He still surprises me."

Acknowledgments

The idea for this project came during a midnight ambulance run in downtown Chicago in December of 1999. One of our Midwest Band Clinic students had an allergic reaction, and we spent the night with her in the emergency room. Our ambulance crew included a Vietnam veteran, whose offhand comment about Washington started my creative wheels spinning.

"Oh yeah, Washington State," he said. "You guys have a lot of veterans hiding in the woods out there."

I could feel my eyebrows rise. *Really?*

Actively ministering to these men, fellow Vietnam veterans Mike Harris, Jim McElreath, Bob Silverea, and Allen Cutter added their perspective. Research pulled me forward. I owe great thanks for the invaluable advice of Delores Kuenning (author of *Life After Vietnam*) and Chuck Dean (author of *Nam Vet: Making Peace With Your Past*). Chuck deserves kudos for answering my every single email as well as reading early drafts of the manuscript. If I didn't get Doyle right, it's my own fault!

When it came time to understand the world of search and rescue, I owe enormous thanks to Karl Moore of the Washington State Department of Transportation. With his help, I attended a search-and-rescue training and flew with Lt. Col. Bill Kennedy of the Paine Field Civil Air Patrol. Thanks, Bill. You were great! The CAP and WASAR crews answered my every question with patience and finesse. Their dedication, cooperation, and commitment save lives all year long. On behalf of all Washington citizens, I thank you!

I also owe thanks to Bill Steel of Crystal Mountain Ski Area, who helped me understand the complexity of ski expansion in a sensitive forest area. Thanks also to John Ives and Steve Hull of Jones and Stokes. These men actively work with land management and forestry issues and helped me to step into the shoes of a wildlife biologist. They answered endless questions with accuracy and grace.

I owe a great debt to my friends Jeannie St. John Taylor, Naomi Hunt, and Susan Duplissey. Jeannie's coaching helps all my work come to life. Thanks, Jeannie! All three read early versions of this work and helped me to see it more objectively. And to Ray Taylor, whose experiences in Vietnam have been included, my sincere thanks as well. Of course, nothing is possible without the many folks at Bethany House, who keep me going. Thanks, Ann.

In recent times, we've been made very aware of the heroism of the men and women who risk their lives on our behalf. Soldiers. Firefighters. Police. Search-and-rescue crews. These men and women labor day in and day out, most often behind the scenes, without our thanks, keeping us safe. From the bottom of my heart, I want to personally say thank you! Your heroism gives me courage. Your faithfulness gives me rest.

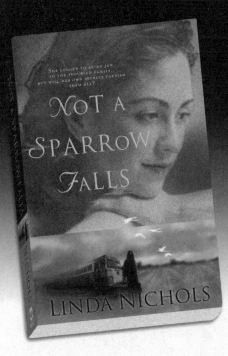

ONE ACT OF FAITH CAN CHANGE A LIFE

Caught between a past that won't let her go and a desire to keep a troubled girl from making the same mistakes she did, Bridie Washburn learns that God uses the willing, not the perfect.

Readers Love *Not a Sparrow Falls*

"I'd definitely recommend this story. It reminded me that we need to remember to hold our loved ones in prayer and be sensitive to God's prompting—even when we feel inadequate."
—Linda H., Colorado

"This book has love, forgiveness, anticipation, wonder, and smiles. It's always a wonder to read and be reminded that no sin is bigger than the cross."
—Nancy E., Iowa

"This book shines the light of hope and victory!"
—Dawn J., California

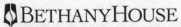